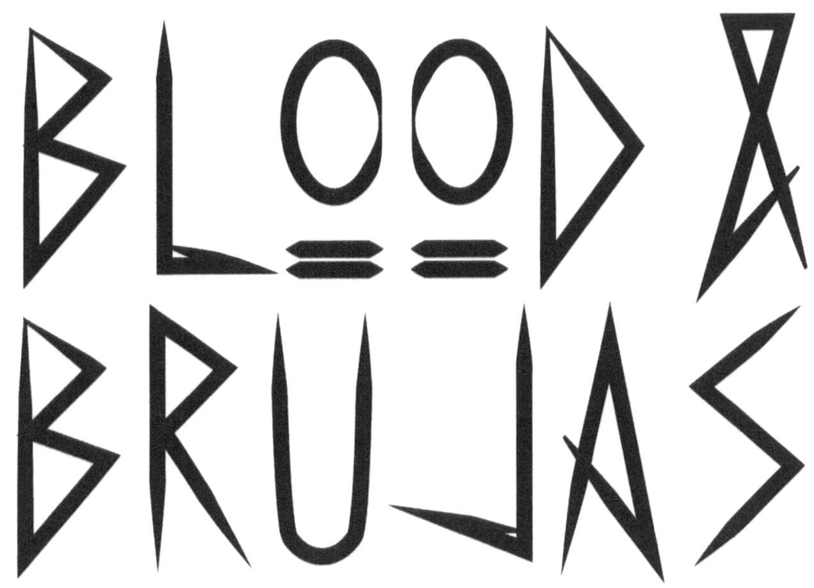

BLOOD & BRUJAS

AN ELEMENTS OF ITERIA NOVEL

FATE OF THE ACNA BOOK ONE

MIKAYLA D. HORNEDO

Published by GXLD Page

Editing: EJL Editing & Crab Editing

Author's Note

Please visit my website mikayladhornedo.com/blood-brujas for an up to date list of content warnings.

Thank you so much for picking up this story! This is the first book in the Elements of Iteria series, and I am so beyond excited. There will be many books in this world overall, but this series focuses on Dayanara. She is a morally grey bisexual witch who has been so much fun to write. She is feisty, she is violent, and while she may be quick to react at times, I promise she's a work in progress! A reminder that this is a why choose, so she will have multiple love interests throughout the story. We've got a bit of a slow burn situation going on here, so buckle in and enjoy the ride :)

Listen to playlist on Spotify –

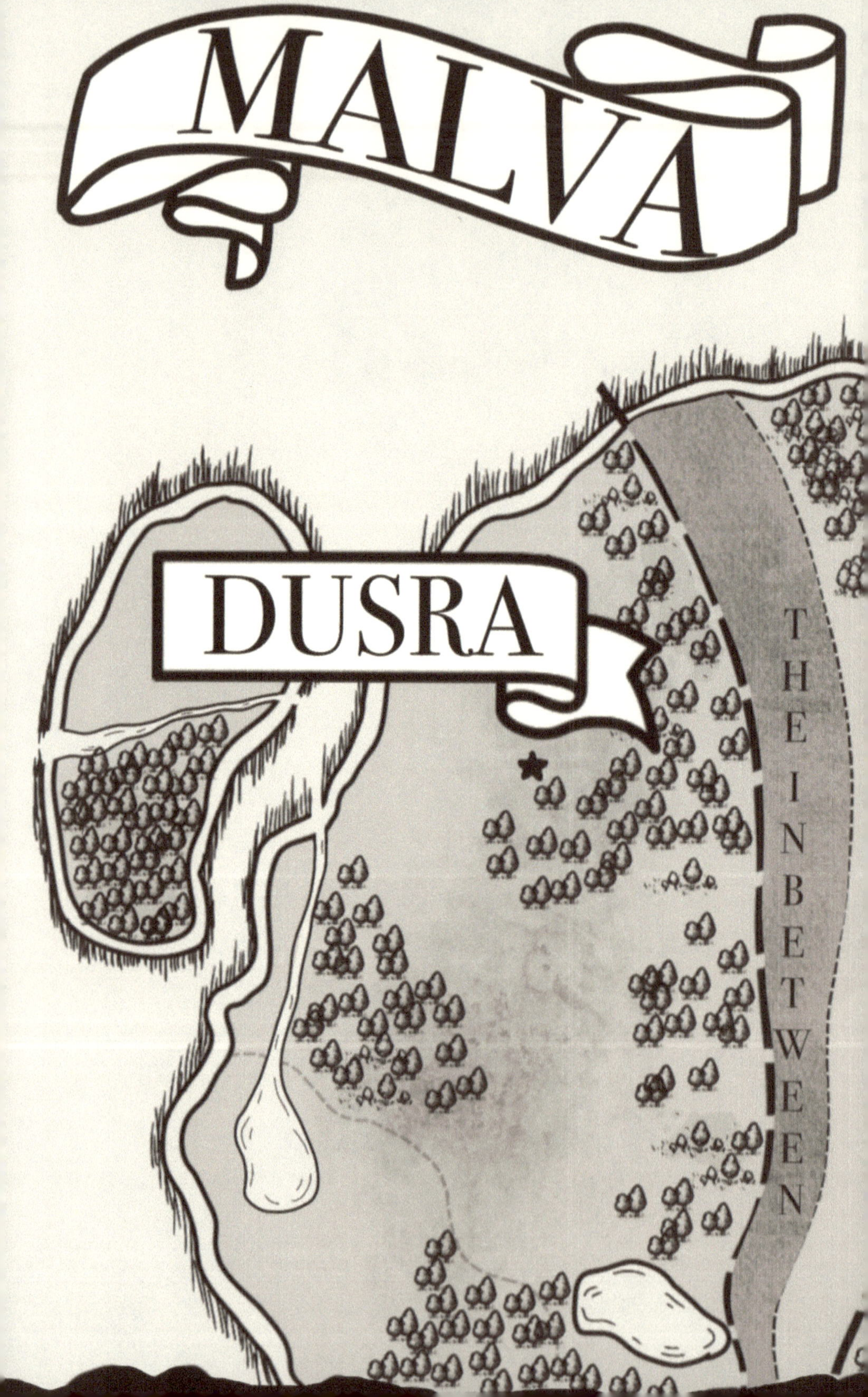

MALVA
DUSRA
THE IN BETWEEN

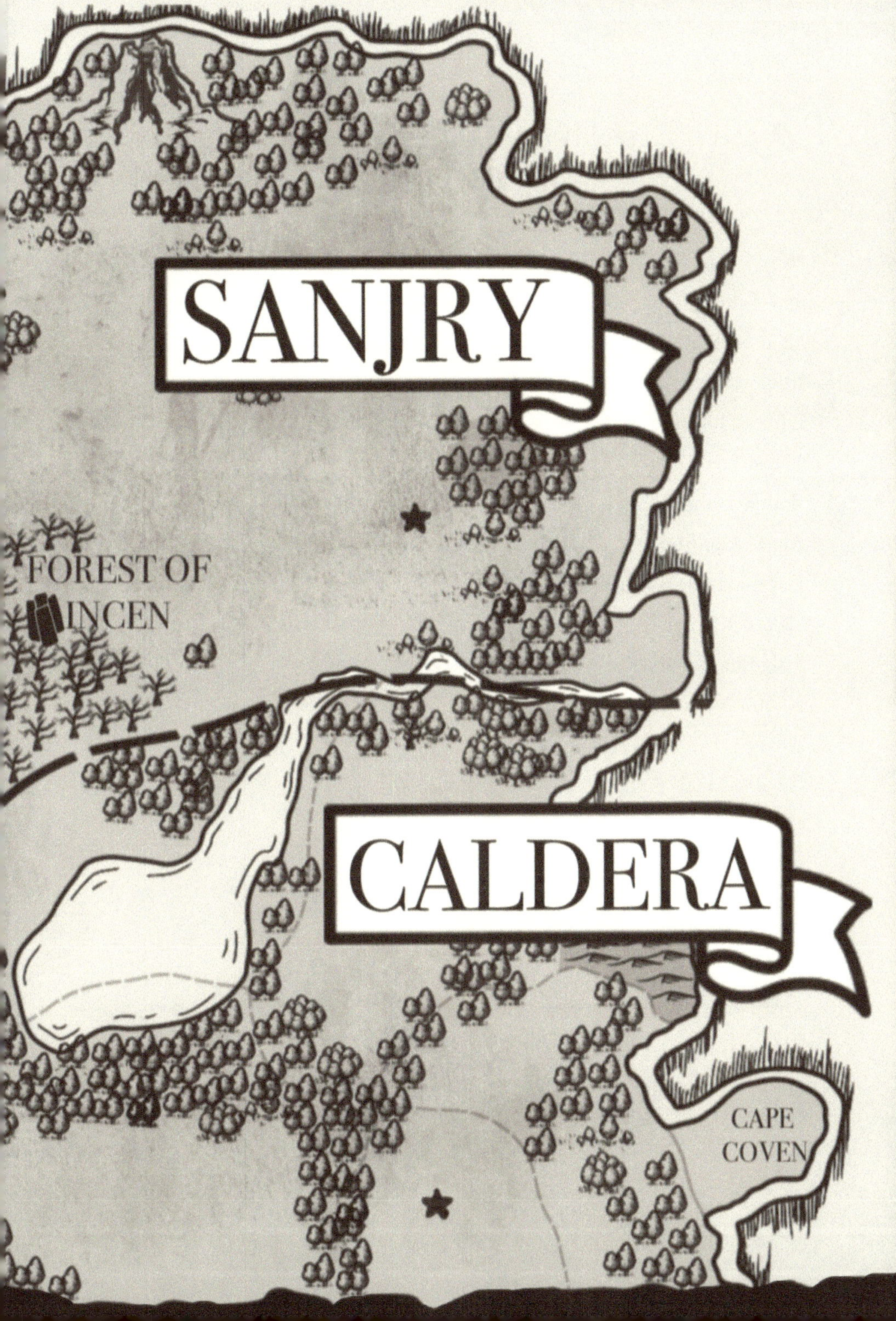

SANJRY
CALDERA
FOREST OF INCEN
CAPE COVEN

Pronunciation Guide

Sanjry- Sahn-jree

    Caldera- Kahl-dehr-a

    Iteria- Eh-tear-e-uh

    Dusra- Doo-srah

    Malva- Mahl-va

    Bonda- Bohn-duh

    Acna- Ahk-nuh

    Dayanara- Dai-uh-naa-ruh

    Kaizer- Kai-zur

    Sanguijuela- Sahn-gee-hweh-la

    Naom- Nay-ohm

    Zalvoh- Zahl-voh

    Coleb- Co-leb

    Cama- Cahm-ah

Full world of Iteria-

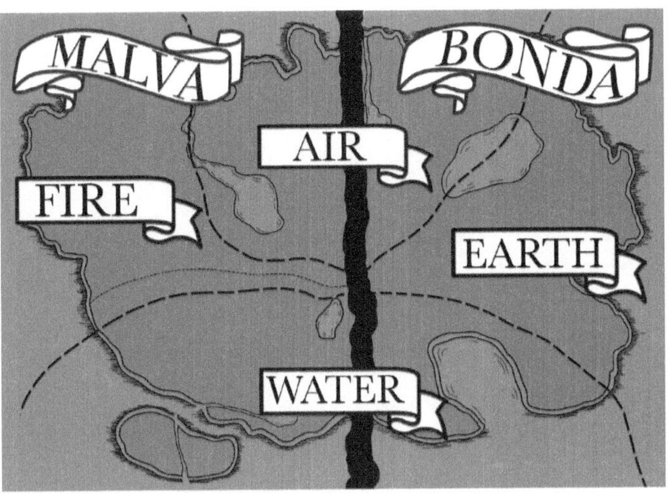

Dedicated to all the readers who never fit into this world's mold. Keep pushing the boundaries. Keep making them uncomfortable. Keep being you.

"At the end of the day, we can *endure much more* than we think we can."

— Frida Kahlo

Chapter One

Dayanara

The coppery tang of blood filled my mouth as I sliced through the soldiers with a precision obtained from my years of battling. The Sanjryans had been trying to take over our kingdom for centuries. Unfortunately for us, they were much closer to achieving that than they ever had been before. A heavily armored soldier stepped toward me, and I rolled my eyes. I didn't know how they functioned in all that metal. Our suits were made of a material just as impenetrable but allowed me a much better range of motion. Not to mention I looked ridiculously hot in it.

I smirked as the large vampire charged me. Most of the Sanjryan army didn't have much magic, but judging by the burn marks on his forearms, he was a strong fire wielder. My assumption was confirmed as fire leaped from his sword toward where I stood. I stole the oxygen from the fire with a quick flick of my wrist and blocked his blow with my left sword.

"Come on, you can do better than that, little guy," I muttered with a smile.

"You'll regret that, witch," he responded.

Anger boiled behind his eyes, and he came at me with all his strength, not even attempting to use his magic this time. The sword got closer to my shoulder than I wanted, and I hissed as it grazed my suit. With a burst of air magic, I flipped over his head, my blades already crossed and ready as I landed on his shoulders.

"I regret nothing," I whispered in his ear before slicing my blade through the flesh of his throat, severing his spine, and removing his head completely in one swift move.

His body began to tip forward, and I quickly jumped down to the ground, landing in front of another soldier. His face was tight with anger, but I could see the flicker of fear in his eyes as I moved toward him. I bathed in that feeling. The emotion of fear from a man who didn't expect that tightness in his stomach or the flow of his blood to speed up when peering down at me.

"Now's your time to say a prayer if you're into that kind of thing," I said as I let loose a rope of air and wrapped it around his body. He tensed with wide eyes as I pulled him toward me with my blade already out, skewering him right in the heart.

"Didn't even put up a fight. You're no fun," I muttered as the life left his eyes, and I pulled my blade from his body.

He thudded to the ground, and I felt a presence moving toward my back. I whirled around with my swords, slashing into whoever dared to approach me from behind like a coward.

"Shit, Daya," Catalina yelped as she dodged my blades.

"You know better than to approach me from behind, Cat," I said, as I gave her a sidelong glance.

Catalina was new to our army. We were the same age and grew up together, but she was untested when it came to battle. She was more than skilled with a weapon. Her mother made sure of it, but she had hoped to avoid the position she was in now. Her mother was one of our greatest generals, and her dying wish was for Cat to fill her shoes. She'd been newly promoted to general, and despite her lack of experience, she was actually doing an excellent job.

"You out of bruja magic?" Cat asked.

I sighed. "Yeah, all I've got is air left."

I ran through my bruja magic pretty quickly and needed blood to fill my reserves back up. Air magic, the magic of my region, was fine enough, but it wasn't nearly as deadly as the magic of my order. My bruja magic was hotter than the flames of Sanjry, pure essence that extended from me akin to lightning from a storm cloud.

"I was just coming to say the other side of the battle needs you. You pretty much took care of everyone over here by yourself," she said as she studied the carnage surrounding where I stood.

I shrugged and followed her to the other side of the battle, but before we made it, the ground beneath me rumbled, and I looked over at Cat with my brows pinched.

"Do you feel that?" I asked.

"Feel what—" She stopped her movement. "What is that?"

The hairs on the back of my neck stood on end, everything about my surroundings screaming to figure out what was wrong.

"I don't—"

I was cut off as a vast cloud of black smoke burst from the middle of the battle. It rippled and moved so fast I could barely track it as people on both sides of the fight went up in ash the moment it touched them. An invisible force pushed me off my feet, throwing Cat and me across the land. I landed on my back atop large stones, my head snapped back, and everything went dark.

The first thing I noticed was low mumbling, and then the pain hit me. Everything hurt, but the pain radiating from the back of my head was above all. I kept still, allowing myself a few extra moments to pull myself together. Everything felt foggy. I couldn't make out exactly what was being said, and when I peeked my eyes open, everything was one big blur. I closed my eyes again and tried to focus on listening to the voices.

I took a deep breath, and pain lanced through my chest, causing a grunt to emit from me that I couldn't keep down. The mumbling stopped, and I felt two figures move to either side of me. I tried to keep still, but someone pushed down on my chest and I heaved forward with a groan, as my eyes opened on reflex. I still could only make out large shapes and colors, unable to identify who was with me.

"She's up," a male voice said.

"Do it," a female voice responded.

The following words from the male were muffled, *agreement, protection, union,* and *hurt,* but I couldn't make out the words in between.

"Want...be...better, right?" I heard the female voice say.

"Yes," I muttered, my voice hoarse with the dryness of my throat.

A large hand gripped mine as the male voice said, "You agree?"

Agree to what? To let them heal me? Make me feel better?

"I...agree," I rasped.

Intense magic pulsed between where our hands touched; it trickled up my hand, into my arm, and pushed into my head, making me dizzy again.

"It is done...army...stop," the female voice said before my world went dark once again.

I woke up, but I wasn't in any pain this time. Actually, I was oddly comfortable. Running my fingers over the soft material beneath me, I tried to see if I could sense anyone in the room using my witch hearing. I heard no heartbeats and opened my eyes to find myself in a well-decorated bed chamber, laid out on a large poster bed covered in bloodred velvet blankets. I didn't recognize the room and sat up to investigate further.

It must have been one of the guest rooms in the palace; I had never stayed in any of them since I had my own chamber. But why would my mother not put me in my own room? My bare feet hit the cold stone floor, sending a shiver up my body. The movement made my head spin and I rubbed my eyes until the sensation waned enough for me to move. I wore only a lightweight white shift, the flames of the candle illuminating my naked figure beneath it.

I walked across the room to the bathing chamber and peeked my head into the closet, but it was completely empty. The images reflected in the mirrors stunned me as I moved back into the bathroom. They lined every wall in the bathroom, making me slightly disoriented by how many versions of myself surrounded me.

I didn't know how long I'd been unconscious, but I appeared to have missed a few meals. My face was slightly hollowed, but I had no dark smudges under my eyes. My purple eyes shone bright, like I'd gotten more sleep than needed. My air magic flowed around me, sending my purple waves into a tizzy before they settled back down past my shoulders. The Amapola line, the line of witches blessed by Naom, all had jewel-colored hair and eyes, marking us as the strongest among our fellow brujas. Today the purple was dull, though, so I probably hadn't had any blood since passing out. I snapped my fingers, willing my witch magic to the surface, and I couldn't even conjure a spark.

Fuck.

I turned my head, and my breath left my chest. In the reflection, behind me, above the bed, was a flaming tree. *The Sanjryan sigil.*

I ran back into the room, the realization this wasn't my palace coming fully into focus. The floor was slightly darker than ours, the lack of any gold, the red velvet blankets. It was completely obvious now. There was only one door and no windows, definitely not the openness of my home. My chest started to rise and fall rapidly, and I smacked myself in the face.

Get your fucking shit together, Dayanara.

I tiptoed to the door and tried to turn the knob, but the door was locked from the outside.

"Fuck," I muttered, running my gaze up the door to see how much force I would need to knock it clean off the hinges. Right before I barreled through it, I heard a faint heartbeat approaching and pressed my ear to the door; footsteps were coming in my direction.

I need a weapon.

This room was completely empty, and the footsteps were too close for me to keep searching. I glanced around, trying to see if there was anything for me to use in the last few seconds. There was a ceramic vase, and I quickly smashed it, using my magic to soften the fall of the pieces and avoid the clatter that was sure to come. I grabbed the biggest, sharpest sliver of the vase, stood beside the entrance, and situated myself so that when the door opened, I'd be behind it. I quickly threw up a wall of air a few feet from the door so that whoever came through would run into the invisible force. I let my nails extend to their longest length for good measure, they could do a bit of damage themselves.

A key was pushed into the keyhole, and the lock clicked as the door swung open in front of me. The heavy footsteps led me to believe it was a large individual. Probably a man.

They walked into the room and ran smack into my air wall. I slammed the door shut and in one swift move I came up behind the man. With the shard of ceramic in my right hand, I pressed it to his neck and used my left arm to push into his back so his chest was forced into the wall of air.

"Who are you?" I hissed.

The man tensed as I held my makeshift weapon firm and grunted, "Kaizer Curran."

I vanished the air wall and moved around him with the shard pointed at his throat as I studied him. The man was tall with blemish-free tan skin. His thick white hair fell to his shoulders in waves, his blue gaze boring into my soul. He leaned on his hands at the end of the bed, smirking as if I should have been expecting his presence.

"Rey Falso," I muttered, my mouth pursed in disgust.

We referred to him as the Rey Falso, False King, because he overthrew the royals that sat on the throne before him, taking it for himself and calling himself king. I'd never had the pleasure of fighting against him in battle. By his design or not, I had no idea. His staple white hair was a clear indication of his identity.

"Ah, you witches do love that name, don't you." He chuckled. "Please, as I said, call me Kaizer, Daya."

"I don't understand why it's necessary to call you anything. Why am I here?"

He shifted closer, and I raised the weapon again, so he stopped. "You don't remember?"

"Obviously not, asshole," I responded.

He chuckled again. "The agreement when you were injured, the reason you have that tattoo on the inside of your wrist." He pointed toward my arm.

I turned my arm over and lifted the sleeve of the shift; an iridescent flaming tree sat stamped onto my wrist in one of the spots not already covered by tattoos. My fist tightened around the ceramic, shattering it and sending the pieces to the floor.

"You fucking branded me?" I yelled before shifting toward him and slashing at his neck with my nails.

My nails grazed his skin, just as close as I had the shard, but they remained there on the surface instead of ripping out his throat as I wanted. My hand shook as I tried to take control of whatever the fuck was happening and snapped my gaze up to Kaizer's eyes.

"You can't hurt me, part of the deal," he muttered as he grabbed my wrist and took a step away. "I see why your mother suggested that now."

My lip pulled back. "My mother was part of this?"

"Oh yes, she was very eager to cease the war. Offered you up to me herself. I didn't even ask," he replied, and my blood boiled as I squeezed my fists again so tight my nails drew the substance from my palms.

Kaizer's eyes snapped to my palms as the blood pooled in my hand.

"Fucking vampires," I muttered as I wiped the blood on my shift.

Vampires drank blood from mortals, unlike the brujas, who only drank from animals and out of a cup at that. They called us uncivil, but that always seemed more uncivil than anything the witches got up to—mostly.

"Have you ever tried it? Blood from a person?" he asked.

"No, and I have no desire," I snapped. "Where is my mother?"

Kaizer leaned against the bed rail. "She's around here somewhere. I can have her sent to your room when I leave."

"What is this arrangement that I apparently agreed to while half-conscious?"

He looked away quickly before bringing his gaze back to mine. "You are to be my wife. We will join our kingdoms and end the war."

"And?" I pushed.

"And you will not be able to hurt me unless we release each other from the agreement the magic has bound the both of us with," he said flatly.

He lifted his arm, offering me his wrist. I didn't take it, but looked down where a pair of iridescent wings were branded into his skin. Caldera's sigil, the wings of Naom, the Goddess of Air and Essence and the brujas creator.

"Can you hurt me?" I asked.

"No, the agreement is that neither of us could hurt the other," he responded.

I ran my tongue over the front of my teeth. "Is that it?"

Kaizer's jaw ticked. "You can't...leave. Not without us both agreeing to it."

"What the fuck does that mean?"

"Your mother was worried that you'd portal away, so part of the agreement is that you can't leave the capital."

My rage was rearing to the point I could barely fucking think. "Well, I'm not marrying you. You can let me out of the agreement."

"I can't, Daya. The well-being of both of our kingdoms relies on this union. If we break it, one of us will be ended."

"Stop calling me that," I growled.

His eyebrow ticked up. "Your mother said your name is Daya?"

"My name is Dayanara. Only the close members of my clan call me Daya," I scoffed.

"Fine, Dayanara, although once we are married, I'd say I would be a close member of your clan, no?"

I groaned and walked toward the bathing chamber as he chuckled to himself. The reflections of all the candles bathed me with light, and I glanced down, remembering the thin see-through shift I was wearing.

"Fuck," I muttered, peering over my shoulder at Kaizer.

He dragged his gaze over my body, every dip of my silhouette on full display for him.

"You'll do." He smirked as he walked toward the door. "I'll send your mother," he finished without looking back.

I heard the key slide back into the lock and ran over to the door, banging on it. "Don't fucking lock me in here!"

"Sorry, Daya, I can't let you escape," Kaizer yelled from the other side, his voice getting further away by the second.

"It's Dayanara, asshole!" I screamed into the wood.

I stormed back into the center of the room and flipped the mattress over with my air magic. A tornado formed around me, tossing blankets and pillows around the room before I sat on the floor and extinguished my magic.

I needed to get a hold of myself. There had to be something better I could use for a weapon in here.

I scoured every drawer, every shelf in the closet, but there was absolutely nothing in this room. It had been a few hours since I woke up, and my stomach was so empty that I swore my navel was touching my spine. Footsteps and the rattle of keys approached, and I moved into the center of the room, readying for a fight. Tendrils of air wrapped around my arms as the door was pushed open. I slung them forward, and my mother blocked them with her own shield of air.

"So dramatic," she muttered, waving me off with one hand, holding a tray full of food in the other.

"I don't know about you, Mother, but I woke up in a bit of a foul mood."

She had the audacity to chuckle, and my jaw tightened to the point my teeth throbbed.

"Saving your people from extinction has you upset, does it?"

"Extinction? Last I remember, we were winning the battle. I took out a whole section of their army myself," I responded.

"Do you know what knocked you unconscious? Had you out for nearly two weeks?" she asked.

The moments before I hit my head started to come back to me, the large black cloud that eviscerated both armies.

"What was that?" I asked.

She huffed before stepping over a pillow on the floor and setting the tray down on the table along the wall. "A magic the Rey Falso should not have. I don't know how he did it, but he has access to an ancient magic that hasn't been seen in thousands of years."

"So you just sold me off like cattle because you're afraid of some old magic?" I asked.

"Watch your tone, girl. Don't forget your place. I am *the Acna*—you do as I say regardless of how you feel about it. One day, you will hold that title, but today is not that day."

The only part about my clan I despised. The blind loyalty to the Acna. *'Our mother.'* The head of our people. We were all sworn to protect her and do as she said without argument. As my own mother, she had even more influence over me. I stomped over to the desk and shoved as much of the food into my mouth as possible. I groaned as I chewed down what appeared to be chicken; at this point, it could have been rat meat, and I wouldn't even have cared. I tossed the cup of water down my throat and sighed as my stomach pulled tight as a drum. My mother watched me with her lip pulled back, and I straightened my posture as I wiped the crumbs from my mouth.

"Your wedding will take place in two months. The remainder of our clan will be here for the wedding," she explained as she ran her fingers over the silk of her dress.

It was unnerving sometimes, how much I favored her. As if I had no father at all, and she cloned herself with some spell. Outside of her dark green hair and eyes, we were damn near identical. Only separated by the century and a half between us. She stared me down with those emerald eyes, the flame of the candle illuminating her bronze skin.

"You will do this. You will not give Kaizer any trouble. I don't care what he does. Short of killing you, you will do this for our clan," she said, face hard as stone.

She was serious. I'd learned the hard way how serious my mother was. When she threatened you, it was a promise, and I had the scars to show for it.

"Yes, Acna." I barely got out through tight teeth. "How many of us remain?"

"Soldiers? About thirty thousand, outside of the soldiers, we didn't lose many. Thanks to the battle being on their grounds," she responded as she looked up at the flaming tree sigil above my bed.

That was nearly half what we started with; I needed to figure out what magic the False King used.

I nodded. "I don't understand why you didn't wait until I woke up. You know I had no idea what I agreed to, right?"

She barked a laugh. "Of course I did. I avoided the whining and complaining. You would have done exactly as you were told either way. This was easier for me."

"Easier for you," I repeated with my head tilted.

She glared at me, a whoosh of air circling around the room. "Good night, Dayanara."

"Wait!" I shouted, "don't lock the door."

"You will be locked in until you can be trusted. I can't say for sure that you won't try to escape right now. Even with the threat of my punishment," she responded as she slammed the door behind her and turned the lock.

"FUCK!" I bellowed.

My magic was flowing out of me, sputtering slightly. A chalice of blood I hadn't touched yet sat on the desk, and I chugged it until my insides tingled with my magic reserves filling back up. I snapped my fingers, and just as Kaizer said, I couldn't conjure a fucking portal out of the capital. Blood dripped down my chin and I licked it clean. It was goat's blood—my favorite. Maybe this was my mother's way of saying she was sorry. She was a cold woman, but every so often, it seemed like she could care for me as a mother does a daughter.

The thought brought me to the scars lining my back, and I ran my finger over one of them that wrapped around my shoulder. I couldn't even tell you why I received half of them. Killing without permission, disobeying an order during a battle, challenging my mother's opinion. The list goes on, and I was sure I was forgetting something. They didn't necessarily deter me from disobeying her—she was right about that. I survived it countless times. I'd survive it again. My life would be utterly dull if I didn't go against what she said occasionally. I was loyal to my kingdom, which she sat at the head of. But after a few decades of doing her bidding, I decided I needed to take some control of my life at the few chances I had the opportunity. But this time...this time, it felt way too big to disobey. This was a command from the Acna, not just my mother.

The Goddess of Air and Essence blessed my line thousands of years ago by creating the first Acna, a witch with power above everyone else. Every Acna had a special gift. They ranged over the generations, but there was no doubting the power in my line's blood. The survival of our clan relied on me. Unfortunately, that came along with being the daughter of the Acna. In Caldera, my kingdom, we didn't label ourselves as king, queen, or princess like they did in the rest of Malva. There was the Acna, and that was it. While I was her daughter, it only meant I would become the next Acna, and I was expected to do everything in my power to succeed in the line. Just short of killing myself, as my mother pointed out. I was her only daughter; if I were to die, she'd have to start from scratch and lure some poor soul into procreating with her.

I wasn't sure how she met my father or even what happened to him. Although one could assume she killed him, the brujas didn't keep men around for too much. We used them to create brujitas—witchlings—and then let them go. Whether that be by ending their lives or scaring them so bad they never wanted to return, even for their children. But it was mainly killing them.

Now, I was supposed to *marry* a man and *not* kill him. I would be expected to run a kingdom with him if I understood the agreement correctly. I'd used plenty of men in my time for my own pleasure, plenty of women too, but never did I think in my one hundred and fifty three years that I would be *permanently* tied to one. Although, I could probably seduce him out of the agreement and kill him after. It wouldn't be hard to take them down from the inside with him gone.

Something to think about.

Chapter Two

The doorknob rattling woke me from my sleep, and I sat up quickly, upset at myself for letting my guard down. A petite woman with light brown curly hair entered the room and flicked on the gas switch that powered the lights, forcing me to blink until I was adjusted to the brightness.

"Good morning, Dayanara. I am Zuri, your handmaiden. You've been summoned," she said, laying a dress on the bed.

I didn't realize people were going to have free rein of my room, and I had to stop myself from snapping at her for waking me up. I looked down at the dress she laid down beside me. The garment was beautiful by Sanjry's standards, but I couldn't easily defend myself in long-flowing silk.

"Where are my leathers?" I asked as I sat up and ran my hands through my tousled hair.

Her mouth pulled down and a disappointing look came over her. "I've been ordered to give you this by King Kaizer; I'm sorry, I don't know about any leathers."

I sighed and stood. "I'll allow it, but I'll be taking it up with my *betrothed* when I get the pleasure of his presence."

Zuri smiled softly at the hint of disgust in my tone and nodded as she stepped behind me and untied the knots in my shift. "Have you had a bath today?"

"No, I just woke up as you came in," I responded.

"Well, that won't do. I'll run you a bath. It won't take long, and we'll have to keep your hair dry, but you should get clean."

"I have air magic. I can dry myself," I said as I let it whoosh through my hair. "Am I being served up for something I need to be clean for, Zuri?"

She just laughed at me like we were sharing some sort of inside joke, and I tilted my head in confusion. Zuri scurried over to the bathing chamber and filled the bath, the smell of eucalyptus oil drawing me toward it.

"Thought you could use some eucalyptus to relax you," she said as she ran her hand through the water. "It's ready."

I dropped my shift and stepped into the tub. I had no idea how long it had been since my last bath, and I was suddenly aware of that fact as the grime separated from my body. The fumes from the oils wafted in the air, and my shoulders drooped with the relaxing scent. Zuri kneeled by the tub, going to grab my arm, and I yanked it back.

"I can wash myself," I snapped.

"Oh, I'm sorry, it's just that I've been told most nobles prefer their servants to wash them," she responded, shrinking back.

I looked her up and down. We weren't necessarily immortal, but we lived so long it was often hard to pinpoint how old people were. She appeared relatively young.

"Where were you before becoming my handmaiden?" I asked.

"I worked in the kitchen but was a handmaiden to another noble family a while ago. It wasn't in the capital, though, so I think things are different this time around," she replied.

I ran the soap over the vines and flowers tattooed on my right arm, and then over the dagger that changed my fate on my left forearm. The girl stood near the tub, waiting for me to ask her for something. I cleared the soap from my body and looked over at her.

"A towel," I muttered.

I didn't necessarily need it, but her quietly watching me bathe was starting to get a little weird.

"Yes, here you are," she said, pulling a towel from behind the tub.

I wrapped the towel around my body and dried off as quickly as possible so I could leave the confinement of this bathroom with Zuri.

Zuri pointed to a vanity in the closet. "Over here, Your Majesty."

I shrank back from the title, but mumbled, "Dayanara is fine."

"Won't be for too much longer." She laughed as she pulled out some items from the vanity.

I caught a whiff of an odd smell, but Zuri dumped some lotion into her hand, and the smell of eucalyptus reached me, getting rid of whatever I had scented prior.

"How stressed do I look?" I asked.

"Do you really want me to answer that?" she replied, and I rolled my eyes as she grabbed my arms and rubbed the lotion into my skin.

"What exactly have I been summoned for?" I asked.

"I'm not sure. They just told me to bring you to the red room as soon as possible," Zuri mumbled as she spread lipstick onto my lips so I couldn't reply.

She pulled my waves back into a low bun, allowing some to frame my face. I initially thought she was petite, but I had a feeling that she was stronger than she let on as I watched her arms flex with the movements. I looked back at the mirror finding my eyes now lined in kohl, accentuating their rich purple color. The lipstick she smeared on was a dark wine red that I would have chosen for myself, surprisingly.

I looked damned good.

Even if I wasn't happy about the dress, or being summoned for that matter, I was glad to feel like myself again. Zuri lifted the black silk dress off the bed and held it open for me to step into. The dress was too tight through my thighs, and the neckline was so high it grazed my neck. I tried to take a step, and my movements were far too restrained for my liking.

"What the fuck is this?" I asked Zuri, trying to move without feeling like my bones were melded together.

"It's a popular fashion here, your highness," Zuri reassured.

I spotted a pair of scissors among some sewing supplies Zuri brought in and grabbed them. I sliced a slit up both legs and was immediately gifted a much better range of movement. I cut the neckline down the middle and tucked the corners into my boobs, creating a deep, pointed neckline that had me breathing better already.

Zuri's eyes went wide and her mouth fell slightly ajar. "He won't like this," she whispered.

"Good, I didn't like the dress he gave me," I responded with a shrug.

She sighed and gathered her things into a satchel before guiding me toward the door. She turned the knob, and I let out a deep exhale as we moved into the hallway. The room I was in was starting to feel more like a prison cell, especially with the lack of windows. We walked down a corridor lined with rooms and turned right at the end of the hallway. I logged all of our movements for if I could escape, or if I figured out how to get Kaizer to release me from the bargain.

A dull orange light gleamed from around the corner, and my heart skipped with the knowledge there had to be some windows coming up. We turned the corner, and the next hallway was made entirely of glass; the floor, the walls, and the ceiling were all completely see-through. I looked out into the distance, the darker shade of the orange sky telling me it was still pretty early. Although here in Malva, the sky was never too bright. No matter if it was day or night, the dullness of the atmosphere allowed the residents sensitive to light to function during the day. Not like in Bonda on the other side of our world, where the sun shined brightly during the day and went to rest during the night.

Bonda sounded like a dreadful place to live.

We were in the capital of Sanjry, Cojmi. I had never been here before, but the infamous flaming tree sculptures outside the palace gave it away. The walls around the palace shot far above the trees, so I couldn't see out into the city, but the grounds were kept in impeccable shape, not a branch out of place. I spotted a beautiful courtyard, but the sound of a bell ringing and a pillar of flames bursting into the sky caught my attention and I turned to Zuri.

"What's that?" I questioned.

"It's the temple of the Embers. The acolytes meet at this time every day," she explained simply before the glass hallway ended, and I was once again surrounded by dark stone.

I sighed louder than I meant to, and Zuri looked over her shoulder with a polite smile.

"We're almost there," she mumbled, picking up her pace.

I tried my best to match her speed, but the shoes she gave me were chunky and uncomfortable. I couldn't do anything with scissors to help them, unfortunately. We rounded one last corner, and a set of red double doors sat in front of us. She pulled a string by the door, and a ringing sound emitted from inside the room.

I homed in on the room and could hear three heartbeats. One was getting closer, and the door was pulled open. I walked inside and glanced back at Zuri as she bowed at the waist and hurried away. Sighing heavily, I continued into the room, through a sitting area, and into an office. The Rey Falso sat behind a desk and my mother in an oversized chair across from him.

"Daya—" He started and stopped as he peered up from his desk at me. "What happened to your dress?"

If my mother was from this kingdom and had the magic of fire rather than air, I was sure she'd have steam seeping from her skull. I'd be getting punished for this; I didn't think to ask if I was being summoned by her too. *Oh well.*

"It didn't fit, so I had to make some adjustments," I said dismissively as I walked around the room and surveyed for any threats.

I noticed a few daggers placed throughout the space, so the king would always be within arm's reach of a weapon. I logged their locations in my memory and looked back over my shoulder at him, his mouth still open with shock.

"You summoned?" I asked seductively.

If I was going to get him to let me out of this arrangement, I'd need to lay it on a little thicker than I usually would. Fortunately for me, flirting came far too easy; it had been a problem for the few partners I had in my years. Partners was a stretch. It was a problem for the people I spent an extended amount of time with.

I hadn't done commitment since Ximena, and I had no plans for it anytime soon, thanks to how that ended.

I looked down at whatever he had in his hand and back up at his eyes, holding them for a second before smiling and sitting in the chair beside my mother.

Kaizer cleared his throat. "Yes, our wedding will be in about two months. I don't plan on holding you in that room, so if you can convince us you're not a flight risk, I'd like to move you into the queen's chambers."

I shifted my gaze over at my mother, waiting for her to add the thoughts I was sure she had.

"There will be consequences should you break this trust, Dayanara," she muttered, and my heart jumped at the fact she was agreeing with him.

Consequences I could handle; I just needed to have my own space, preferably less empty and sad than the room I was currently in.

"I think a room without a lock would make me much less likely to try to fly away," I responded, flashing him my straight white teeth.

His chest rose and stilled momentarily before it fell again, and he nodded. "Very well, I will have Zuri move your things into the queen's chambers. One other thing. Your clan is getting…" He stopped and looked at my mother. "Restless. It would be good for you to address them and inform them of our agreement."

I scoffed. "You haven't told the clan what you agreed to, Mother?"

"No, as you are the one who agreed, I figured that responsibility should lie with you," she responded with a smirk that didn't reach her eyes.

"The arrangement I agreed to? That doesn't ring any bells. Care to help me out, Kaizer?"

His head bobbed between my mother and me, the question of if he should engage in his eyes.

Kaizer handed me a piece of paper instead of responding. "I have written something up for you."

My mother stood and snatched the paper from my hands, reading what he wrote and handing it back to me. "That will do. I have an engagement to get to. I will meet you in your new chambers before you give the speech tonight," she said as she gracefully glided out of the room, and the door slammed behind her.

I reviewed the carefully crafted speech and chuckled. "You left out that I was delirious and basically unconscious."

Kaizer's mouth straightened into a line. "Your mother was rather eager. She said you'd be fine with it."

"I'm sure she did," I muttered. "My clan won't like this. We aren't too fond of you, but it's not a terrible attempt."

I leaned over and laid the paper down on the desk to flash him the sight of my full tits.

"My kingdom isn't too fond of yours either, but we would have continued this fight for centuries to come if we didn't come to an agreement. Neither side is going to enjoy this, but they'll come to understand it's for the best."

I tilted my head, surveying him. "You aren't what I expected," I said a little too honestly.

I quickly snapped my seductive mask back up and smiled at him gently.

He sat back and crossed his arms over his chest with a smirk. "What were you expecting?"

"I don't know, you just look so normal and put together. I wasn't expecting you to be well-polished and clean for some reason. I was expecting a large, dirty man. Maybe with a scar down his face?" I joked.

He was attractive, not nearly rugged enough for my type. His white, shoulder-length hair was so well groomed that not a single strand was out of place. Each wave moved in the same exact pattern, all ending bluntly at the top of his shoulders. His tan skin was smooth with no signs of facial hair. I usually preferred some slight stubble on a man, if not a full beard. His blue eyes were piercing but soft, making him look so...pretty. To be honest, if he was a woman, I might have already been trying to make a move on him, but as a man, it just didn't do anything for me.

I wonder if he has a sister?

All the same, I was on a mission to seduce him, so I continued my long gazes, holding my long, pointed nail between my teeth.

"You aren't exactly what I expected, either," he said, pinning me down with his piercing gaze.

"No?" I asked and leaned forward in encouragement for him to continue.

"Your beauty is talked about in all of Malva, no doubt, but seeing it in person is a whole other thing." He laced his fingers together. "Especially the hair."

I twirled one of my purple locks around my finger. "You could certainly do worse for a bride."

His eyes stilled on my lips and dipped down to the neckline I created with Zuri's scissors. "I'll have a seamstress sent to your quarters, so you don't have to cut up any more gowns," he said with his gaze snapping back to his desk.

I crossed my arms and faked a pout. "You don't like it?"

Alright, reel it in, madam seductress.

"The problem of me liking it isn't in question. However, the problem of the rest of my court respecting you while dressed in such a way is in question."

I scoffed. "Such prudes you are here."

He threw his hands in the air. "I didn't say it was right. It is just how things have been since I—" He stopped momentarily, searching for the correct word. "Became king."

"That's one way to put it," I mumbled.

"What is it your kingdom knows of my history?" he asked, his tone lowering an octave.

"Honestly?"

"Would you give me anything other than honesty, Dayanara?"

I laughed. "We were told you came in, killed the existing royals, set the crown on your own head, and claimed yourself as king. It is why we refer to you as the Rey Falso, the False King." He stared at me, not responding. "Although looking at you now, I'm not sure I can believe that's true. You don't look nearly as viscous as they made you sound."

"What you heard is not entirely wrong, but not exactly the truth either. I did kill them all, but only because they were pointing us in the direction of doom. They didn't hear what the people of Sanjry wanted; they got angry and pushed me to overthrow the royals. We did try to talk to them, but they didn't listen," he explained, his shoulders tight. "I was a distant relative, so not quite as false as you all make it sound."

I pondered that. "Interesting. Still not the normal succession of your line, I assume. But yes, maybe not quite as *falso*."

He shrugged. "They are the ones who started the war in hopes to take your land. I inherited it, my advisers felt we could win, and I listened, but this was never my preferred scenario."

"Interesting," I mumbled.

Kaizer cleared his throat. "Any questions about the wedding?"

I sat forward. "Can I question the wedding itself? We seem to get along well enough. Can we not just draw up a formal agreement between our kingdoms?"

"I'm afraid our union is the only thing strong enough to put a stop to the animosity between our people."

It's not as if I was waiting for some love match, or my Verdaji. I barely believed in the concept of Verdaji—your one true mate picked by the goddesses of our world—as I'd never seen it myself. It seemed like a fairy tale people told themselves, or maybe it was a thing in the old days, but as the Creators had left us, I didn't think that magic remained. A map of our world sat behind Kaizer on a shelf, and my eyebrow shot up with an idea.

"Will this not cause an issue with Dusra? Surely us joining our kingdoms will look like a threat to their king?"

I should have thought about that earlier; it was a much stronger argument. Kaizer's fists tightened at the mention of the third kingdom in Malva, Dusra. If we thought lowly of Sanjry, they felt even more poorly of Dusra. Kaizer had not tried to conquer the third kingdom, as the war between their people was so devastating hundreds of years ago the mere mention of them caused the Sanjryans distress.

We didn't care much about the other kingdoms in Malva. We were perfectly content in our section of the world. We never saw the reason for people fighting over the land when we all had so much of it. We defended our land, but we were never the ones igniting any wars merely for more of it.

"Dusra will be paying us a visit in a couple weeks to discuss just that. I do not intend to push my borders into his land, and I plan to clarify that. *We* will need to make that clear," he said.

Dusra closed their borders off completely after they won, and nobody had seen a Dusran since. I wasn't sure if they even knew about the war happening here, but they never offered any aid to either of our sides. I was fairly surprised Kaizer was able to even get in contact with the kingdom to ask them to visit.

"Will you write a script for me to follow?" I asked, picking up the parchment he wrote out for me to address my people.

"We will have to see how we are faring when the time is upon us," he responded with a polite smile, the anger from the conversation about Dusra melting away.

I stood up and waved the paper in the air. "Well, I'm off to practice my lines," I said as I walked toward the exit. I swished my hips with each step and looked back over my shoulder at him before leaving the room. His eyes were on my ass, as expected. My curves were just another weapon at my disposal, and I had plenty of them. I smiled as I left the room with a wave over my shoulder. The moment I was out of his eye line, my body relaxed, and I removed the fake smile from my face.

He was eating up everything I served him, so I only hoped I could keep up the facade and get out of this wedding all together. I wasn't sure what the next step was yet, but I wasn't going to be bound to that vampire king for the rest of my life, that was for sure.

CHAPTER THREE

The queen's chambers were, well, made for a queen. The fact they were up to even my own standards was impressive, as the rest of the palace wasn't exactly in my taste. The floors were bright white marble, with veins of dark gray running through them that glittered in the light. It was more like a small apartment, with a sitting room, bed chamber, bathing chamber, closet, and even an extra room for Zuri to stay close by.

The four-poster bed had sheer linens draped over its frame, softening the sharp edges. A dark red comforter dressed the bed with pillows in varying shades of gray and black. The flaming tree sigil was behind the bed, unfortunately, but I didn't care because the whole right side of the bed chamber was windows. Floor-to-ceiling windows with draperies covering them, but I pulled the drapes back to see out, allowing me to feel much less trapped. The garden I spotted earlier sat just outside my window, a level down with a terrace off the last panel of windows on the right.

"That's the Queen's Garden," Zuri said as she put the last of my things into the chest of drawers. "So it is yours; we can go visit after you talk to your people if you like."

"Yes, I'd like that," I said, picking up the speech Kaizer had written for me. "Where are you from, originally?"

"From a small village, nothing as fancy as this place," she responded.

"If you were a subject of my kingdom, how would you feel about this?" I asked.

She bit her lip and looked away from me, and I was about to tell her to forget it, but she opened her mouth to answer. "I would believe whatever you believed. Should you go up there and sound like you hate the idea, speaking someone else's words, I may be a little worried," she replied.

"Thank you for the honesty, Zuri."

I read over the speech again, and she was right. These were not my words, and my clan would surely know it. The desk was stocked with stationery, so I pulled out a new piece of parchment and wrote my own speech.

I trailed my finger over the dry ink as Zuri finished with my hair. I asked her to take out the bun and let my waves free. A few braids starting at my crown pulled the hair from my eyes, and they met at the back of my head in a purposeful knot. I looked into my reflection with a smile, and Zuri stood behind me with a smile just as big, surely proud of her work.

I hadn't studied her too hard this morning, only noticing how young she appeared to be. Her brown skin glowed in the light, and her caramel brown hair was pulled back in intricate braids much like the ones she put into my hair, with some of her curls loose in the back. Her eyes were dark, but as she turned her head to the side to set down the comb, the light hit them in a way I hadn't seen before. Where they initially appeared to be black, they were actually a deep gray.

It was a color I didn't think I'd seen before, but they suited her in a wholly unique way, she was gorgeous. I squinted to get a better look, but she turned around to get my cloak, as it was chillier here than back home in Caldera. It was almost always warm there; our homes and palaces were all open, allowing the breeze to move into our homes freely. That was a big reason I felt so claustrophobic here. I wasn't used to not being connected to the outdoors, not having fresh air, and the scent of the earth surrounding me.

Zuri wrapped my black cloak around me and patted my shoulders. "You ready?"

"As ready as I can be," I muttered as she guided us out of the room to meet my clan.

We walked through a maze of hallways, all ones I had yet to see. The sound of our heels clicking against the stone floor threatened to drive me mad, as it was the only thing I heard as we made our way to the gathering hall. The lack of people was peculiar, as I was used to a much busier palace than this. The place was massive and well-kept, I had no idea where everyone who made that happen was.

I pushed through the doors to the hall, and my most trusted brujas sat inside, our coven coterie. I had introduced a few younger witches to the coterie, convincing my mother that the old women she was used to weren't quite as in touch with the younger generations. One of those young witches was Catalina, my childhood friend who was with me when I was knocked unconscious during the battle. I nodded at her with a slight smirk, all the emotion I deigned to show in front of this group. My mother shunned any other emotion outside of ice-cold bitchiness, and so did the older crowd here.

A few were missing, likely killed by the blast. Caldera was made up of four sanctions outside of the capital, and the heads of each were here, waiting to see what I had to say about our new predicament. The evidence that my mother arranged the room was apparent as she sat down at the head of the group in a chair much more significant than the rest. I sat beside her, and the rest of the room took their seats before us, bowing their heads in reverence. My mother cleared her throat, the only sign she'd give them that she expected their full attention. All eyes snapped in her direction as she said our words, the words we began each formal meeting with.

"May the Acna rule long, may the brujas remain loyal."

We sat silent momentarily, my mother always leveraging the power of silence. The fear it brought in the unknown, the anticipation of what was to come.

"Dayanara will address your concerns," she said, her head turning to me.

I'd been in front of this group, groups even bigger, all my life, I was no stranger to speaking publicly. However, this time I did have some nerves. I didn't know how my clan would look at me; I myself disagreed with what was happening. But at this moment, there wasn't any going back. I couldn't guarantee that we would get out of this, and I wouldn't give them any hope until I knew if I could break the agreement with Kaizer without damning us.

My fingers gripped my speech, the parchment wrinkling and crinkling slightly. I took a breath and stood before them, setting the speech down on my chair. My mother's eyes burned into my soul as she realized I wouldn't be using the words she approved in Kaizer's office. I didn't tell her I re-wrote the speech, so she would have been surprised either way.

"My mother—" I started, and she cut me off, clearing her throat.

"I'm sorry, *I,*" I dragged out the emphasis of the word. "Have agreed to marry the Rey Falso to save our clan. It is time that we put an end to the animosity between our people. I know we have no quarrels with fighting, with battle. Even so, it is time that we stopped the war and allowed our kingdom to thrive outside of defending our land. I will rule beside him. We are not losing our voice. The clan will remain strong, the brujas will not suffer," I exclaimed, drawing my gaze across the room, maintaining eye contact with each sanction head.

Rosa, the oldest and crankiest of the group, scoffed. "You expect us to believe that? Sanjry has always been distrustful; I've been alive for many centuries, I've seen it. Now this king who isn't even true to their royal bloodline wants us to believe he won't turn back on his word? You should kill him while you have the chance," she said, and the rest of the group nodded their agreement.

Well fuck, I agreed with the ancient bitch. My mother did nothing to help. She only watched the discourse unfold in front of her with a cold smirk on her face.

Catalina stood as the mumblings of the group grew louder. "Did you all forget what happened? The magic the king used in battle?"

Rosa stood beside her. "I know exactly how powerful it is, how evil it can be. We can't link ourselves to this kingdom," she said with a wave of her old crooked finger.

"What's done is done," I boomed, regaining control of the conversation. "The king and I have a formal agreement." I lifted my wrist for them to see the tattoo. "I will do what I must to ensure the safety and livelihood of our clan. Right now, this is what is happening."

Fuck.

All the witches quirked up at that, the implication that there would be another option.

"Right now? Do you expect the plan to change?" one of the younger witches, Elena, asked, her auburn eyebrows raised.

She sat at the head of her sanction, the place her mother sat prior to the most recent battle.

"Like I said, I will always have our clan in mind before all. Should an issue arise with their king, I will handle it accordingly. You'd all do well to follow your orders," I responded with my shoulders back and chin high.

Elena looked over at Yesenia, another sanction lead, and nodded with a knowing smirk gracing her lips.

"We know you will only do what is best for the clan, Daya," Catalina responded proudly.

"Will you be crowned Acna while you are crowned queen?" Adriana, a middle-aged witch, asked.

I looked over my shoulder at my mother, unsure how to answer the question as we hadn't discussed it fully yet. I should have known the clan would ask this and cursed myself for not thinking about it earlier. My mother stood, and I sat back down in my seat.

"I will advise her, but she will be crowned as the Acna, yes," she said, pinning the group down with her most frigid stare, daring them to question her.

Rosa was the only one who showed any kind of disgust; as she was older than my mother, she lacked a filter or the ability to fake a smile.

"Any further questions?" my mother asked the group.

Catalina stood, too new to the coterie to understand it wasn't an actual invitation.

"What will become of our current positions? Am I still a general?" she asked.

"That will be up to the new king and queen. I'm sure she will be wise enough to keep most of you in the positions you are in," she responded, and the threat in her words didn't go unnoticed by me.

My mother waved her hand as she sat back in the large chair. "You're all dismissed."

I started to leave the room, and she stopped me with a shield of air. "Not you," she said through tight teeth.

Here we go.

I turned around to find her holding the parchment in her hand. She crinkled it up and sent a spark of witch magic that had it disintegrating before me in a cloud of green.

"That was not what we discussed," she said as she prowled in my direction.

The green strands free of her bun shifted with each movement, her emerald eyes burning a hole right through me.

"They weren't my words; I thought it would feel disingenuous. The clan aren't idiots. They know when they're being handled," I responded with my hands behind my back, a position I knew my mother preferred.

"Are you saying I don't know what is best for my clan?" she asked.

"No—" My words were cut off as her hand slapped me across my face with her full witch strength.

I stood still as a statue, knowing if I made any sort of movement, it would provoke her more. Every one of my muscles was tense, my every instinct screaming to protect myself, to fight. She brought her hand back across the other side of my face and marched away from me, sitting in the chair she used as a throne.

"I should be thankful you didn't say anything to *directly* contradict me." She scoffed. "We need them to be fully on board with this, or it won't work. Saying you'll do anything to protect our clan is great, but you said it as if you'd kill the king if it came to that. We can't have any seeds of hope sewn for that future," she finished as she picked lint off her dress.

I said nothing and remained still with my hands behind my back like the soldier I was. She eyed me, and the defiance written across my face had her mumbling curses.

"Goddess sake, speak, Dayanara."

"I don't understand why you're so dead set on this. Why wouldn't you want me to kill him? To take over their kingdom?"

"That magic he used, if he or his kingdom still have access to it, it could mean the end of us. We kill him, and his army wipes us from existence using that magic. I don't know what it is, so I don't know how to stop him from using it. Forming this alliance, joining our kingdoms stops them from ever wielding it against us again." She actually looked unsettled for a moment before she straightened. "This is bigger than either of us, child, just follow orders."

There had to be another way, one that didn't leave me miserable and tied to a city I didn't want to be in. I took a step toward her, and she somehow accomplished to look down her nose at me while I stood above her.

"Why are you giving up your status this easily?" I asked.

"I've been the Acna for half a millennium," she said plainly.

"Exactly my point," I responded.

She arched an eyebrow. "Would you rather kill me for it?"

"No," I answered quickly, not allowing any room for her to believe otherwise.

"You should be grateful I'm giving it to you so easily. The circumstances are outside of our usual traditions. I can't stay the Acna and truly join our kingdoms. Though I trust you'll take my advice above all else," she said, her voice dripping with poison.

Well then, you fucking marry him.

I nodded. "Of course, Acna."

She stood, I had her by a few inches, being taller than average, but she tended to make me feel small. The only soul in the world that could achieve it.

"Did Kaizer tell you about Dusra coming?" I asked.

"On a first name basis, now, are we? You work quick." Her lip pulled back. "Yes, I am aware of the meeting."

I pondered how to ask my question without her assuming I was second-guessing her again. "I worry that their king will see us joining kingdoms as a threat."

"Well, that is the purpose of the meeting, Dayanara," she replied flatly.

I sighed. "You don't have the same worry?"

She scoffed. "Sanjry is so terrified of that kingdom they wouldn't dare cross their borders."

"We have never had a poor relationship with them, but I could see how they might think we could push Sanjry to conquer with our joined forces," I replied.

"Hush, child, you don't know what you're talking about," she responded as she stalked toward the door.

"Will you talk to me like this when I'm the Acna?" I quipped, the words slipping out too fast for me to stop them. She tensed and looked over her shoulder, her lip pulling back from her teeth. No words left her mouth, but the promise of punishment was there. That was worse. I'd rather us go back and forth, let her slap me or throw me across the room. This face told me my punishment would come when I didn't expect it and would be much more painful. Disrespect was something she didn't take kindly to, above all else. She left the room, the frigid air that always loomed around her going with her.

I slumped back down in the chair and ran my finger over the scar on my shoulder. I'd have a few more by tomorrow.

Chapter Four

Zuri ran my bath water, using double the eucalyptus again, and I was still on edge. I dismissed Zuri to her chamber once I dried off, not wanting her to see this side of my clan yet. My mother did this on purpose, made me as anxious as possible before she dealt her punishment. I personally thought she'd gotten lazy in the last few decades with her preference of the whip against my back. It was one of the few things that truly hurt me and stopped me from doing what I wanted for a few days, so that was probably why. But she used to be fairly inventive with her punishments, not all of them were as brash as a lashing. She'd broken me at a young age, pulled every ounce of fear from me by making me face everything head on. I'd been drowned to the brink of death, thrown off cliffs and only being saved at the last moment by a portal, she'd starved me of blood and left me in a room without my magic for days. That didn't even cover the amount of emotional damage she'd done over the years.

She belittled me, made me feel like I didn't matter worth shit. She always reminded me of my place beneath her, and never let me think I could ever rise above it until *she* was ready to give up her title. As someone she relied on heavily to do her more violent work, it never quite made sense to me. I always knew I was to rule our kingdom one day, and she'd prepared me for that in some aspects, but the prompt shift to move me into that position so suddenly was odd. The magic the king had scared her, and that woman wasn't scared by much. She moved through the world as if she was untouchable, and this scenario made me slightly cautious.

I heard slow footsteps approaching my suite and tensed as they reached my door. They paused momentarily, and I released a breath as they continued walking away. Grabbing my nightgown from a drawer, I ran my fingers over the smooth silk and the delicate lace that lined it. It was a beautiful shade of red, dark enough that it was almost purple. I didn't recognize it, it must have been something supplied by Kaizer's people. Before I could slip it on, a puff of green smoke appeared behind me. I let out a scream as firm hands gripped my shoulders, and I was pulled into a transport portal.

"Fuck," I grumbled as the air was punched out of my lungs by the intensity of my mother's magic. She never made this part easy; I could make a transport portal and not feel a pinch of pain. But my mother preferred to make it as unpleasant as possible. My knees hit the hard stone, and I groaned as the impact reverberated through my bones. I caught myself with my hands before my face hit the ground and flipped my head up, my hair falling in front of my eyes. My mother already found a room prime for torture.

I could smell soil, see no windows, hear no other people around. The gray bricks lining the walls were large and offset, like they didn't care about the appearance of this room. Chains and cuffs were linked to the walls, with absolutely nothing else in the space. The door creaked open, and my mother walked in with two of the witches who always helped her deal out her punishments. I never bothered to learn their names, but they knew me well enough. I never saw them during meetings or gatherings, like they only lived to torture.

My mother blew a cloud of green into my face, temporarily cutting off my access to my magic. She was the only remaining witch who knew how to make the magic suppressant. There was a particular crystal needed for it called seraphinite that no one could find anymore, and the spell itself was intricate, only existing in our family grimoire. But because her Acna gift allowed her to perform complicated spells without crystals, she could do it in an instant.

I didn't even fight it this time, as it only added to the number of lashes she'd give me. Her henchwomen grabbed both of my wrists and clicked the cuffs on them, pulling the chains through the metal loops on the wall until my arms were stretched tight above my head. My knees lifted, hovering just above the ground as I swayed until the momentum of being raised ceased.

"I won't waste the breath of telling you why you're here. You're fully aware," my mother muttered.

That sounded like a waste of breath to me, Mother.

Her heels clicked against the stone, and she ran her sharp nails across the stone wall, creating a screech that had the hairs on my still naked body standing on end. My only warning was the snap of the whip as she swung it through the air. The braided wires sliced through my skin on the other shoulder this time, a space I hadn't yet been scarred. My back arched, and my body tightened with the pain. The muscles in my arms strained as they tried to help me pull from the chains and fight back, but I was completely immobilized. The second snap of the whip had me blinking in and out of consciousness, I was scarcely aware of another presence moving into the room, but by the third, I was knocked out cold.

Every muscle in my body groaned as my mother's assistants tossed me onto the bed before disappearing in a cloud of green smoke again. She always brought me back to consciousness by the end of it to make sure I experienced all the pain. Warm blood dripped down my bare legs as I tried to right myself enough to stand and get clean. The evidence of my mother's anger was clear; every move felt like millions of daggers dragging down my back, setting my body aflame with the purest of pain. I got to the end of the bed and held onto the frame for a second as I tried to work up the courage to take my first unassisted step.

Woman up, you fucking ballsack.

I took the step and immediately cursed my inner self for thinking it was a good idea. My leg buckled, and I went crashing down to the ground. My hands reached out to grab back onto the bed frame but missed and I pulled the fabric draped over the bed down with me. I threw a blast of air down to soften the fall, but it didn't work due to my magic being immobilized, and the metal rods holding the curtains crashed beside my body.

"Fuck," I muttered as I still fell harder than I wanted to.

Zuri came running out of her bed chamber connected to my sitting room.

"Don't worry about it," I tried to say confidently before she found me, but my voice was so hoarse I didn't think any of the words were clear enough to understand.

"What the hell, Dayanara," she yelped as she ran over to assist me.

I tensed quickly, trying to roll away from her. The Sanjryans were known for their bloodlust, and I had enough blood on me to send an army of them into a tizzy. My roll was ceased almost immediately as the wounds on my back screamed from the pressure.

"What happened?" she asked frantically, running her gaze up and down my wounded body. "Let me warn Kaizer," she exclaimed, and made to run away.

I grabbed her arm with all the power I had left and pulled her back toward me. "No, just help me clean up," I groaned.

Her wide dark eyes fell on me, her forehead crinkled with confusion. I met her gaze, and whatever she found in my eyes had her reluctantly agreeing. Zuri ran to the bathroom and brought back a bowl of water and a stark white towel. She set the bowl on the nightstand and grabbed my arm to help me up. Her fingers gripped my bicep as she slowly guided me to the bed, and helped me lay flat on my stomach. The red of the comforter was already a shade so close to blood that you could barely see as it dripped from my body onto the soft material.

"What happened?" Zuri asked, pressing the towel down to one of the wounds closest to the top of my ass.

I hissed as she applied pressure and tried to clean the wound. "Punishment for my inability to keep my mouth shut," I got out through tight teeth.

I turned my head in her direction as she dipped the towel into the water, and I watched as the clear liquid shifted into a dark red in an instant, the white of the towel already non-existent.

"Your mother?" she asked.

"Mhm," I replied as she got to the gash on my shoulder and I had to squeeze the blanket beneath me to keep from screaming. The first lash was always the deepest for my mother, and this one was sure to scar.

"I've heard of the brutality in your clan but wasn't sure it would apply to you," she replied, her gaze softening.

I avoided the pitiful look in her eyes. "Just another day."

A warmth trickled over my back, but it didn't feel like blood. It felt like magic. I turned my head back in her direction so fast my back screamed. Healers this skilled were extremely rare, and for one to be a mere handmaiden was practically unheard of. We all had a certain amount of healing power within us, but to heal someone else's brutal wounds, the healing magic you held had to be great. I could see the faint glow reflecting in her dark eyes as she bit her lip with concentration. The pain in my back started to subside, and I took the first truly deep breath since before I was taken to the dungeon.

"You shouldn't have done that." I sat up without pain and pulled the blanket over me. "I'm assuming nobody knows you're a gifted healer?"

Zuri tsked and turned away quickly. "It was a reflex; I couldn't see you in such pain," she replied and ran her hand over her face. "No, they don't know."

I found the nightgown I had grabbed from the drawer still on my bed and pulled it on quickly. I walked over to where Zuri was pacing and grabbed her wrist.

"I won't tell. I'll pretend I'm still in pain. You can put some bandages on me so nobody knows," I replied before I could think about it, unsure as to why I wanted to protect her.

She turned her head, just as confused about my offer as I was. Zuri nodded quickly, running back to her room to grab some bandages. I walked over to the bathroom in my suite with ease. Much like the room I woke up in, there was a wall full of mirrors, and I turned my back to inspect the lacerations. She did an excellent job, the scarring for wounds that deep was inevitable, but all the once open flesh was knit together perfectly.

I leaned my hands against the sink, and my hair fell to my face, still crusted in blood. Secret or not, I was thankful for Zuri's healing magic. I would have been bedridden for another day. Witches healed pretty quickly compared to some of the other orders of our world, but anytime where I couldn't defend myself properly was not a time I enjoyed.

My legs were stronger than before as I walked over to the bath and ran the water for the second time today, throwing in some salts for the ache in my muscles that still remained. Steam rolled off the water's surface, parting as I dipped my body in. I leaned my head against the back of the tub and slid down until my face was under the water. The salts burned slightly as I opened my eyes, but compared to what I had endured, it was nothing. A cloud of red surrounded me, dissipating into the water by the second, and leaving it a murky pink color.

I stayed under the surface, my lungs starting to burn from the lack of oxygen. Bubbles slipped from my nostrils, and I watched them carelessly lift to the surface and disappear. I couldn't stay under much longer, but the control I felt when doing this was motivation enough to push my limits. White splotches appeared in the corner of my vision, and I pushed back through the water, gasping a breath as I hit the air. I ran my fingers through my hair, working out the knots and ensuring no blood remained.

Quick footsteps approached, and I looked into the bed chamber as Zuri found me, her short honey curls bouncing around her head as she jogged into the bathroom with a handful of supplies. I stood from the bath, water pouring off my body and trickling from my hair down my curves. Zuri handed me a towel, and I dried off, using a blast of air magic to dry my hair.

"Okay, I'll just put them in the visible spots," she said as she unraveled the spool of cotton bandages.

I dropped the back of my towel to give her better access, and she carefully placed the bandages on my shoulder and sides. Even though she healed me, her touch was still light and gentle, and she lifted the towel back into place when she was done.

"Look—" She started, and I cut her off quickly, lifting my hand.

"I don't require an explanation; you can tell me on your own time, if you even want to do that," I said, and her shoulders sagged with relief.

We all had our secrets. I had plenty. She stuck her neck out for me and didn't even seem to realize she was doing it at the time.

"Thank you," she whispered.

I nodded and waved my hand, dismissing her back to her room.

She turned to leave, but she looked back before she passed the door frame. "Regardless of what you were being punished for, you didn't deserve that."

There was no pity there this time; I only found rage in her rich dark eyes. Rage and pain. I nodded, and she quickly left the room, the sound of her door slamming behind her reaching me as I returned to my bed and pulled the covers over my body.

I was to be the Acna in a few short months, and I didn't know what my relationship with my mother would look like then. I'd have power. True power, two kingdoms worth of it. A simple command from me could have her strung in the dungeon and left to rot, and she knew that. I wasn't sure what game she was playing, but I would damn sure figure it out.

Chapter Five

My *betrothed* summoned me again, something I was growing irritated with quickly. I had to pretend to be sore for a couple days, but I could move freely now without worrying that my mother caught on to my healing. I only saw her once the following day. She came to my chambers claiming she needed to discuss something with me, but I knew she just wanted to see how much pain I was in. I put on a show, moaned and groaned as I sat up in bed to face her, touching the bandages occasionally to draw attention to them. She left with a smirk I wanted to knock clean off her face, but that only meant she bought into my charades.

Zuri found a gorgeous silk gown that fit me better than the one I vandalized. It was a dark shade of red, Kaizer's colors, but it flowed from the waist down the floor with a mock corset bodice that had my boobs sitting beautifully. The long billowing sleeves flowed behind me as I followed Zuri to wherever the king was waiting for me. I didn't bother to ask where exactly that was; I didn't know where anything was in this castle, so I let her lead the way without question.

The castle could use some art. Everything was so plain and clean here. The walls were bare, only sconces lining them every so often. The archways and columns were a form of art itself, though. Each of them had intricate carvings etched into the stone, they felt like they told a story, but I hadn't had enough time to really look at them yet.

Zuri led us into a small dining hall with just one thin long window near the ceiling. A vast chandelier hung in the middle of the space, the most beautiful thing in the room. It was lined with hundreds of candles, chains, and rows of gems hanging between them, causing small orbs of reflections to dance around the room as the flames flickered.

"Good morning," Kaizer exclaimed, walking through a door on the other side of the room.

We both stood there for a moment, our bodies rigid, as we waited for the other to bow. I kept my chin high and held his stare. After a few moments, Zuri advised that she would meet me back in the room, and the interruption broke our stare down. He held out his arm to the side, gesturing for me to sit down. Kaizer pulled the chair out and waited for me to sit before he scooted it in and took his seat on the other side of the small mahogany table.

"I trust you're hungry," he said as the castle staff poured into the room with their arms full of food.

The smell of pastries and bacon floated over to me as they shifted passed, and my stomach growled. I almost forgot that I was supposed to be wearing my seductive mask and shifted my gaze back over to him.

"Starving," I muttered with a smirk.

I saw his gaze dip briefly down to my breasts as he reached for a bowl of eggs and placed some onto his plate.

"How are you feeling?" he asked.

My body tensed, and I paused with my arm outstretched, wondering if he somehow knew about the beating my mother gave me.

"About the wedding?" he followed up with his brows pinching together.

"Oh," I started and lifted the bowl of bacon to set it beside my plate. "I can see how it would be beneficial."

He chuckled. "Beneficial, yes. Have you had time to think of any questions?"

"What will this look like? Am I ruling my kingdom and you yours?"

"We will rule together; all decisions for either kingdom will need to go through the both of us."

"What about my witches with ranking? I have generals, captains, a coterie formed of the heads of all of our sanctions."

He paused and looked down at his plate for a moment. "I have generals and captains as well. I suppose they can fight it out to see who is most suited?"

"My brujas will be more than happy to prove themselves," I responded.

"As far as the council, we can talk about combining them. Mine is just my adviser and commander of my armies," he said, stabbing some eggs with his fork and bringing them to his mouth.

"How many people live in Sanjry?"

"Upward of one hundred fifty thousand."

I shifted the fork in my hand. "Would we live here?"

"I think my palace is more central to the land if I remember correctly. Yours is closer to the furthest border?" Kaizer asked.

"Yes, it is," I admitted reluctantly.

I didn't want to stay in this stuffy palace, so closed off and disconnected from the rest of the world. I ate my food in silence until the scrape of my fork against the bare plate became too obvious.

"I have some questions for you," Kaizer said, and I looked up at him but his face was unreadable.

"Shoot," I replied with a smile.

"Is it true witches only drink animal blood?"

I nodded. "It is."

"Why?"

"Why do you drink from vampires?" I asked.

He smirked. "Not just vampires, but fair point...Your mother seems." He paused. "Difficult."

"Is the question *why is she such a bitch*?"

He let out a breath of a laugh. "I suppose."

"She's been that way for almost as long as I've been alive," I responded with a shrug.

Kaizer nodded again and folded his hands in front of him. "How old are you?"

"153, you?"

"275," he responded.

He appeared pretty young, but that was above middle age for a vampire, he must have had pretty strong magic. The ones with weaker magic here tended not to live too much longer than that. I held his gaze, inquiring if he had any other questions.

Kaizer leaned forward. "Are you trying to seduce me, or is this just your natural state?"

The question caught me so off guard I didn't have time to hide the surprise on my face. He laughed, the first real laugh I heard from him thus far, and I continued staring at him with my eyebrows raised.

"Just trying to see how much I should read into your behavior," he followed up, and I regained my composure.

"Are you asking to be seduced?" I asked.

"You are a spectacularly beautiful woman; it would be foolish of me not to," he responded with a smirk.

I shrugged, taking a sip of the orange juice set out on the table for me, wondering at what point the tables turned, and I lost control of the situation.

He stood from the table and moved to my side. "I'd like to show you something."

Kaizer offered me his arm, and I looped mine in his, allowing him to guide me out of the room. He was taller than I remembered, his arms lined with more muscle than I had noticed before. We left out of the door that he used to initially enter the room, into a long hallway with a plethora of stairs and one door at the very end of it. I looked around, slightly worried that I didn't know enough of my surroundings to get away should this go downhill.

He untangled his arm and pushed the door open, holding it for me to enter. The architecture of the room was beautiful. Four lines of columns, two plain and two with twisting vines and flowers that ran up the wall all the way to the domed ceiling far above our head, crossing at the middle. The floors were red, nearly black, and glitter flickered in them under the soft orange light of the sky outside. I glanced over to the left of me, where a dais sat high, a decent number of stairs leading up to where two significant thrones rested.

"This is our throne room," Kaizer exclaimed, his arms out wide. "I commissioned the second throne and added it to the dais the day after you agreed to the union."

He gestured toward the throne, and I climbed the velvet stairs, quickly glancing over my shoulder at Kaizer as he followed behind me. His throne was what you would expect from a vampire king, gaudy, black, and all sharp edges. I ran my finger over the arm of it, the cold stone biting at my finger. I shifted my gaze to my throne, and I hated to admit it, but he did a damn good job for someone who didn't know me. My throne matched his in size, but as I got closer, intricate designs were carved into the dark stone. I ran my finger over the flowers and vines twisting around each other and looked up at the columns I saw when I first walked in.

"It's the same design," I whispered.

"Oh, yes. That was a new addition as well," Kaizer said as if it was nothing.

"I'm impressed," I responded, placing my hand on my hip.

"I get the feeling that's not an easy feat."

I scoffed and turned back to look at my throne.

"Sit in it," Kaizer said, and I was still too stunned to argue with the command in his voice.

Lowering into the seat, I rested my arms on the sides; from this position, I could see lines of purple running through the throne in the wells of the etchings. I looked over at him, and he chuckled to himself as he sat down on his own throne.

"I want you to feel at home here. I would be lying if I said I didn't feel bad about forcing you away from Caldera," he said with his gaze up on the glass ceiling.

That snapped me out of whatever odd daze the vampire king had me in.

"As you should," I replied, a little colder than I meant to, and quickly followed up with a slight smirk to hide my distaste.

"A lot is riding on this working. Should the people not like it, they could revolt. They could try to overthrow us," Kaizer said.

"The way you overthrew the previous royalty?" I asked.

Fuck, I need to get myself together.

"Exactly that. The people of Malva respect power, those who have the most naturally rule. Should we look weak or not aligned, it could be a problem."

I nodded because he was right. The creatures that roamed Malva were once primal beasts and some of those primal instincts remained. One of them was to respect the people with the most power and never follow the weak. As if, for some reason, physical strength made you a good leader, it was idiotic but a fact of our circumstances all the same.

"I've been delaying holding court, but I don't want to hold it off much longer. We are supposed to have one tomorrow," Kaizer said, the question in his gaze.

"What can I expect?"

"The nobles and lords of the other cities and towns typically handle minor issues, but once every few months we allow them to come to the capital if they are still unresolved. Problems with their neighbors, with the farmlands, etc. Occasionally, they will come to ask bigger questions, around things like our politics, what our plans are," he explained.

"So I can expect questions about the kingdoms joining," I said.

"I think, for now, we can hold those questions off since it is still new. But yes, those questions will arise over the next two months. I can take the lead on this one; let you get your feet wet if you prefer."

I nodded. "My people are broken out into sanctions, so the heads of each come to us with problems during the small council. It's a bit different. I will speak if spoken to, but I am okay with you leading. This time," I replied, and he smiled.

"Very well. I have some work to do to prepare for tomorrow. I will see you then," he said as he stood and ran his hands over his pants.

He bowed slightly, not a deep bow as expected when addressing royalty, but a sign of respect from one to another.

"Okay," I replied and watched as he walked away, his broad shoulders filling the doorway as the door slammed behind him.

I sat on my throne a little while longer and wondered how my people would react to me sitting up here, helping the Sanjry people.

Chapter Six

Zuri and I had spent a lot more time together since she helped clean my wounds, and I found a comfort with her I typically only found in other witches. We never spoke of what happened again, and I was perfectly fine leaving it alone. I sat in front of the vanity as she finished my hair for court, styling it in a half-up, half-down look that accentuated my face. Most witches wore their hair down, long and free-flowing, but the style represented both kingdoms well.

"I'm thinking we do a bold lip, with just a little shimmer on the lids," Zuri said, grabbing a dark purple lipstick.

I nodded, and she smeared the color on evenly; I smacked my lips and looked into the mirror.

"Perfect," I muttered.

The seamstress came to my chamber last night and dropped off some gowns before taking measurements for future clothing. I asked her to help make another suit and told her where to find witch leather. She advised that she'd never made anything with the material before, so I was a little worried, but I needed something to easily get around the castle soon. I wanted to do some exploring and learn the ins and outs in case I ever needed to escape. It was hard to do that in the bright silks everyone wore here.

Zuri pulled down the gown I was to wear today, a relatively modest, dark red dress. I typically wouldn't be caught dead in such a garment, but as this was the first time I'd be meeting most of Kaizer's kingdom, I agreed. Although this would be the last time, I'd have my bronze skin on display the next time they saw me.

I slid my arms into the tight long sleeves that ended in a point before my knuckles, covering the markings only found on witches. Tattoos on vampires in Sanjry were practically unheard of. Zuri got to work on the million tiny buttons that lined the back as I ran my hands down the sleeves. The neckline was square and high, but as I stepped forward, a rush of air grazed over my leg.

"I added a slit last night. Thought it would be a little more you," she said with a shrug.

I smiled at her, turning my head to the side slightly. "You knew I hated it?"

"I'm not sure if you are aware, but your face shows most of your feelings," she replied as she placed a necklace encrusted in diamonds on my neck. "A gift from the king," she said as she clasped the jewelry together.

I twisted the most prominent diamond pendant in my fingers, the weight of it enough to make me uncomfortable if I wore it for too long.

"It'll do," I said, and Zuri shook her head at me with a chuckle.

I followed her into the bedchamber just as my mother appeared in a puff of smoke, dressed in her signature jade. I really needed to set a magical block on my room so she wouldn't be able to transport in here. She'd be pissed, but I'd rather that than another surprise pop-up from her henchwoman.

"Acna," I muttered as I slid on my shoes.

"You're going to court," she said plainly.

"You're getting information from a good source," I murmured.

"You didn't think to discuss that with me?" she asked.

"You know, Acna, I'm actually not sure what it is I'm supposed to be discussing with you anymore," I responded with my hand on my hip.

"I am still your mother, child. You should discuss anything of importance with me," she said, gliding away toward the sitting area.

"Important to who," I mumbled under my breath. "Did you bring any of my crystals when you dropped me off here?"

The witches had essence flowing through their veins, and had the ability to manipulate it into a weapon of pain, to perform minor spells, or create our portals. If we combined that power with certain crystals, we could do so much more. Things like changing your identity, turning back time to mend something broken, or other significant spells needed the assistance of crystals.

"Why would you need to perform anything of that magnitude?" my mother responded.

I tilted my head. "I'd like to be prepared for anything. I'd say I'm at a disadvantage without them."

She tsked. "I didn't bring any, no."

"Well, I can't exactly purchase crystals here in a kingdom that doesn't even use them," I retorted.

I was sure there had to be some *somewhere*, but vampires had no use of crystals. The only ones I'd seen thus far were set in jewelry, and weren't anything that could be used for spells.

"You don't need them."

I opened my mouth to continue arguing, but Zuri quickly jumped in. "We should get going. You will be late if we delay any longer," Zuri said with a pointed finger toward the clock mounted on the wall.

We exited the room with my mother on my heels, her eyes burning holes in my back.

"Posture," she muttered.

I rolled my eyes and sat up straight, not wanting to hear any other comments she might have had. We turned the corner, and Kaizer stood in front of the door with his hands behind his back. He wore a silver crown atop his head that glittered in the light as he turned to face us, each point ending in a dark jewel. His tunic matched the color of my dress, with black trousers and boots lined with silver stitching.

"Lupe," he said to my mother with a nod of his head.

"Kaizer," she replied, not inclining an inch of her body to him. "I'll see you inside. Don't embarrass me," she whispered before walking away from us and entering the room.

"That woman scares the shit out of me," Zuri muttered behind me before she, too, entered the throne room.

"Are you ready?" Kaizer asked.

I stepped toward the door. "I am."

"One thing before we go in," he said, and I looked back over my shoulder to find him fishing a small box out of his pocket.

My gaze bounced between the box and up into his eyes a few times before he grabbed my hand and twisted me to face him.

"They'll expect you to be wearing the ring," he declared, opening the box to reveal a silver ring with a considerable blood ruby stone set into it.

I raised my eyebrows with my mouth slightly ajar. "A ring and a necklace in one day. I'd say you're trying to seduce me now."

He slid the jewelry onto my ring finger as he chuckled slightly. I held my hand out to inspect it; it looked ancient. Ancient and one-of-a-kind.

"It'll do," I said as I mentally thanked the goddesses that Zuri wasn't here to call me out on my bullshit.

He offered me his arm and pushed open the door to the throne room. The muffled discussions ceased immediately as all the eyes in the room turned to us. I kept my chin high and my mouth pursed, exuding every bit of confidence that lived within me. Patrons were lined up along the walls, and I heard whispers as we passed them.

"Witch."

"Evil."

"Doom."

"Bad luck."

The last came from a man we approached on our way to the dais. I gave him a glare that cut daggers through his soul, and his body tightened as he took a step away from me.

Bastard.

We took our time climbing the stairs, turning to face the crowd, and sitting in the seat simultaneously. Kaizer lifted his hand and shot fire into the sconces lining the walls, the first use of his court's magic I'd seen thus far. This appeared to be a sign that court was commencing as the first in line stepped forward and bowed at the foot of the dais. The fact he only made eye contact with Kaizer as he bowed didn't miss me.

"Your Majesty, I come here today because my neighbor's hunting dogs keep killing my chickens. I've tried to handle it myself to no resolve. My chickens are how I survive; their eggs and meat feed my family. The lord of my town has done nothing to help. This is my last resort."

I looked to the back of the room to find Zuri in the corner. She pointed to her face mouthing the words, "Fix it," and I quickly realized I was scowling at the sniveling man. Chickens. The man was complaining about chickens. He could have killed the dogs himself, but he came here to ask for royal help to protect his *chickens.*

This may be more difficult than I thought.

"We'll send some of our men out there to help resolve the issue. Please see Quinn, and she will help you," Kaizer said, pointing to one of his generals at the other end of the dais.

Quinn was nearly as tall as Kaizer, and by the way her arms strained at her uniform, she also had a decent amount of muscle. She nodded and directed the man to another soldier at the door before returning to her post at the dais.

"Next!" she yelled, and a young woman stepped forward.

She was beautiful, with dark red hair pulled up into an intricate up-do and green eyes framed by dark lashes and freckles. But when she finished her curtsy and looked over at me, her lip pulled back, and her nose scrunched with disgust.

"What brings you to court, Lady Payne?" Kaizer asked, and her gaze softened as she shifted it back over to him through her lashes.

My jaw ticked, and I wasn't even sure why. I didn't like Kaizer or want him as my husband, but something about her blatant disrespect had me ready to rip her throat out.

"I am here because of *her*," she said, not bothering to hide her contempt this time.

"Here to ask for my hand instead, I take it?" I said with a smile, and gasps sounded around the room. The distinct sound of my mother clearing her throat reached me, and I held Lady Payne's stare as she gawked at me.

"Well, go on," Kaizer commanded, sitting forward slightly.

She snapped her gaze back to Kaizer and pointed her finger at me. "She is an outsider. You have an outsider sitting on a throne meant for a Sanjryan. Not *just* an outsider, a *witch*," she said, her voice dripping in venom.

"This was made for me, actually," I replied, and Kaizer shot me a look that screamed, *What happened to letting me lead?*

I rolled my eyes and went back to staring at the nasty woman.

"You should be married to a vampire. A Sanjryan of noble blood, someone who can give you pure children," she followed up, her eyes shooting to the ground for a moment before peering back up at the king.

I chuckled darkly and looked away from her. She didn't care about who I was; she just wanted to be the one sitting beside him. It was clear.

"Athena, you will address my betrothed with the respect she deserves. What's done is done. Unless you have an actual issue I care to resolve, you are dismissed," Kaizer boomed.

She scoffed with her hand to her chest as she burst into tears and ran out of the room. The room broke into noise, gasps, and conversation, growing louder at the king's display of authority.

"Should any of you have similar issues as Lady Payne, you may be dismissed as well. We will address what is to be expected from our union in the coming weeks," Kaizer exclaimed.

The room went deathly silent, a handful of people shifting on their feet and slipping out of the room. Kaizer waved his hand, and Quinn, the general, yelled for the next person to step forward. I sat back on my throne, looking over my shoulder at Kaizer, finding myself a little more attracted to him than before.

Court went on for hours. More neighborly squabbles, issues with the crops, and people inquiring about extensions on their taxes. The taxes seemed heftier here than in Caldera. We only collected enough to ensure the lands and estates continued functioning, but the royals appeared to have pocketed a lot more in Sanjry.

Kaizer offered them an extension, and the families seemed pleased, but from the looks of them, I didn't think it would help much. The last patron left, and we made to exit the throne room with Quinn on our heels. We pushed open the door, and a flash of red hair stormed in my direction. I flicked my wrist, creating a wall of air as I stuck my hand in the slit of my dress and pulled my dagger from the harness on my thigh.

Athena smacked into the air, and I shifted behind her as I held the dagger to her neck and pushed her against the clear force. "You'd be wise not to do that ever again," I whispered in her ear, drawing a drop of blood from her delicate flesh.

"Kaizer!" she yelled.

I stepped back and wiped the blood on the shoulder of her dress. "That's a bit informal, no?"

Chuckling darkly, I released my hold on the air wall so she fell to the ground on her knees. Kaizer looked less than impressed with my antics, but Quinn looked at me with her eyebrows raised and a slight smirk on her face. I shrugged as Kaizer moved to help her off the ground, and I rolled my eyes to stand back and watch this unfold.

"She tried to kill me!" Athena squealed.

"You attacked her. What do you expect?" Kaizer said as he moved away from the wailing woman.

"Kaizer, please. Can we talk?" she looked over her shoulder at me. "Alone, please."

Kaizer opened his mouth, appearing to be fixing to object, but I lifted my hand to stop him. I had no desire to go back and forth with either of them.

"Don't stop on my account," I said and moved over to where they stood.

I ran my finger down Athena's jaw and smirked devilishly. "Return him when you're done."

I walked away, not bothering to look back, and Zuri scurried over to follow me, barely containing her laughter as she reached my side.

"I can't believe you just did that," she said between her breaths, holding in her laugh.

"I can't believe she tried to attack a witch unarmed. She hoped to be queen, did she not?"

Zuri looked back and responded in hush tones, "She has been trying for his hand since I've been here. I believe they had relations, but there were never any whispers of her being queen."

"Interesting," I said. "Did he have a lot of relations?"

"He tries to keep most of that private, but the staff sees everything. He's had a plethora of women in his bed over the years."

"Were they all delicate, petite ladies like Lady Payne?"

"They were. He has a type. That is for sure," Zuri responded.

"A type that is not me," I mumbled, looking down at the abundance of curves that adorned my tall frame.

"None of them come close to matching you, *my queen*," Zuri said, and I rolled my eyes at her use of the title.

"Shut up," I laughed as we made it to the Queen's Garden.

We walked over to the wall of purple bellflowers, my favorites. The flowers were so delicate, but one of the castle staff said they'd been here for years, holding up to all the harsh weather of Sanjry.

I stretched my arms and flexed my muscles. "My witches have all gone back to Caldera. All but my mother, unfortunately. I need to train."

"Why don't you train with the Sanjryan soldiers?" Zuri asked.

"I suppose I could. Their trainings are so open, I don't know if I should show them all what I'm capable of just yet."

"What does that mean?" Zuri questioned.

I felt a growing connection with her since she healed me, but I wasn't sure how honest I should be quite yet.

"We aren't married yet. Things can still go sideways. I don't want them to know everything I can do if they turn on me for some reason," I explained. Not the whole truth, but enough of it.

Zuri shrugged. "Then don't show them everything, but show them you're not to be fucked with."

"Not a bad idea. Where do you train?" I asked, and her eyebrows shot up.

I noticed the muscles that lined her arms the first day I met her, and her reflexes were something impressive as well. I dropped a few things and watched her catch them before they hit the ground.

"I don't have a need to train," she scoffed.

I stared her down, lowering my chin and raising a brow.

"I just want to be able to protect myself, that's all. So I train in my room after you go to sleep," she replied, shifting in the dirt.

Crossing my arms, I continued pinning her with my gaze. "You'll train with me now. I'll train with Kaizer's people, but I'd like you to train with me as well. I'll make sure you have no problems protecting yourself."

"You'd do that for me?" she asked as she smiled widely.

I'd seen her smirk and gently smile before, but her true smile, her genuine smile. It was enough to make the breath catch in my chest. I wasn't offering her anything outrageous, just the chance to make sure she could defend herself from any harm. But she smiled at me like it was the best gift I could give her. I wondered where she'd been, what she'd been through that would make the offer so important to her, but I just nodded.

"Yeah, it's no big deal. If you're going to be with me all the time, you should know how to defend yourself," I answered.

Selfishly, I was glad that she was assigned to being my handmaiden. I was starting to feel utterly alone. Which said a lot, because I'd been alone for a long time.

Chapter Seven

I'd been mentally noting every hall and corridor I'd been in during the day over the last week, but there was still so much of the castle I hadn't been able to see yet. It was truly a compound, a vast, intricate building, and I could almost hear the secrets being whispered to me through the walls. The seamstress dropped off my suit earlier today, and she did an impeccable job for someone who had never worked with witch leather before. It was perfectly molded to every dip and raise of my body, and I'd missed the security of the tight fit. I had her reinforce some of the areas with a thin sheet of malleable steel in the forearms, shins, and above the heart. The leather was damn near impenetrable, but I didn't want to take any chances in a castle full of possible enemies.

Zuri braided my hair down into two thick braids after our training session, and I threw the dark cloak over my shoulders, lifting the hood to hide any more of my identity. I tracked down some boots a few days ago. I was pretty sure they were men's boots, but they fit me, so I didn't really care.

Moving in near silent steps past Zuri's door, I slid out of the entrance to the queen's suite. I slowly shut the door behind me and tiptoed down the long hallway. Kaizer's suite was to the left, but I had no desire to go in that direction yet. I turned right and followed the maze of hallways until I reached the training arena. I had yet to bring up my desire to train with the soldiers, but I decided after a few days I wouldn't ask permission.

But I wanted to know what my surroundings would be, where the weapons were, and even *what* the weapons were. The inside area of the arena was enormous; the far wall was lined with doors that could slide over each other and open up to the outside. On silent feet, I walked over and peeked outside the window to ensure nobody would see me while I was in here snooping. The moon was high, casting silvery light on the mezzanine, and not a soul in sight. Which was expected. Everything around here was in such pristine shape, nothing out of place.

I snuck over to the wall on the other side of the room where they kept the training supplies. There was no shortage of weapons, as the wall was full of hooks with swords, axes, daggers, and any other killing object you could think of hanging from it. They weren't as sharp as they could be, but they certainly could hurt someone if they were wielded with enough strength.

There wasn't too much to look at outside of the wall of weapons as it was just a large empty space. I was tempted to steal one of the blades, but my mother actually brought my weapons to my suite yesterday. We had plenty of issues, but one thing she always did was make sure I could defend myself against anyone who might harm me. Other than her, that was. Even though she didn't bring any of my crystals, I was thankful that I at least had some weapons.

As I couldn't portal out of the stupid fucking capital, I couldn't just go and get them myself. My mother was right; I didn't *need* them, but I wanted to be prepared. Staying close to the wall in case anyone happened to walk by, I carefully tiptoed to the other side of the room. I was doing my best to ensure I didn't make any excessive noise, but the floor beneath my feet groaned slightly and felt odd compared to the rest of the space. I stopped and took a step back, placing my foot down again to see if I was sensing something that wasn't there. I felt the same hollowness that I did before and crouched down to inspect. The floor was marble, so veins of black ran through it, making it hard to see if there was anything odd.

Something had to be there. I couldn't let go of the hunch, so I laid my stomach on the ground and placed my ear on the floor before tapping into my witch hearing. There were no sounds of footsteps or talking, but there was definitely a rush of wind breezing below the floor. I ran my finger across the surface and my finger fell into a slight divot molded into a vein of the marbling; I followed the line until it reached the wall. The very edge of the board the weapons were hanging from sat at the end of the divot, and I ran my finger up the board until I felt a button.

"Fucking jackpot," I whispered as I pushed the button in.

The floor pulled back and exposed a steep staircase leading to a dark area beneath the floor. A slight buzz ran over my skin as I moved closer, the evidence of a detection spell across the open space.

I tsked. "Sneaky, sneaky," I muttered as I worked to get around the spell.

Vampires were capable of casting spells just as anyone else, but witches excelled at it. It didn't come naturally to any other order, and took decades of studying to get anywhere near what we were born capable of. It's why I had access to so much more power. Sure, we all had our elemental magic that coincided with our kingdom, but we could do more.

I broke the detection spell in a moment, and honestly, whoever cast it needed a lesson in spell work. A witchling could have broken this without breaking a sweat. My feet hit the hard ground of the tunnel, and the marble floor above me slid back into its place, leaving no sign that there ever was a secret entrance. I snapped my fingers and cast a purple orb of witch magic above my head, allowing it to float and follow me as I went deeper in.

It appeared to be some sort of tunnel system running along the walls of the palace. I could hear commotion on the other side of the wall, laughs, cheering, and shouting. A small light glowed a few steps down, a hole into whatever room the party was taking place in. I peeked in. The hole was almost too small to see through, but if it was any bigger, it would be a sure giveaway.

A few of the generals I'd seen were drinking and laughing, the most emotion I'd seen from them since my stay at the castle. Quinn laughed as she pulled a woman down into her lap. The woman giggled and whispered something into her ear, causing Quinn to pull her closer and run her fingers down her spine. A quick jerk had Quinn sinking her fangs into the girl's neck, a slight moan coming from her throat as she drank from the woman with force.

"Fucking vampires," I grumbled as I made my way down the hall to see what else I could find.

The spying holes were placed sporadically, and I noticed they weren't in every room. Most of them, but not all of them. I peered into one of the holes to find Kaizer's office, or the red room they called it here. A stack of books sat on his desk. I couldn't make out the titles, but they appeared quite old. An empty glass sat on his desk with a bottle of dark liquor next to it. Kaizer didn't seem like the kind to indulge, but I didn't really know him all that well. He hid behind a stone wall demeanor; always full of polite pleasantries. Always so put together, the perfect image of what a king should be. It was boring. I also had a hunch that it was all a big act, but I had no proof yet. But I recognized it; that bravado that went beyond what was naturally there.

I kept on my journey until I saw another light shone further down the hall, and I tiptoed over as I saw a shadow move across the light. I stilled by the spying hole as I heard Kaizer's voice. I looked down the corridor, counting the turns and rooms leading me to this spot. It was his bedchamber, and he wasn't alone.

Sure, this was an arranged marriage, and we hadn't had any sort of conversation about what that meant for us sexually. Being in a foreign land, supposedly to become the queen of said foreign land, it didn't seem too wise of me to go around making advances either way. As I'd been trying to seduce Kaizer, I didn't want to bring up the question of if this was a monogamous situation. Either way, my heart was racing a bit at the suspense of what I would find.

"Fine," Kaizer exclaimed, a shadow running back across the hole.

I peered in to find him in low-riding linen pants, the lines of muscles running up his back making me bite my lip. I still wasn't all that attracted to him, but damn, the man had muscle groups I didn't even know existed. A giggle caught my attention, and I tried to see where it was coming from, to no avail. Just as I was about to give up, Kaizer walked over to a large chair and sat down, set a journal on the side table, and then held his arms out in an invitation.

Fucking Athena walked toward him in a silk robe, her long straight red hair falling down her back. She slipped her shoulder out of the robe and smirked at him. His face was unreadable, but the grip he had on the arm of the chair said enough. She slid her other shoulder out and pulled the robe down slowly, exposing surprisingly full breasts for someone as petite as she was. Mine were worlds better, but still. She ran her finger over her nipple as it pebbled, and she let out a breathy noise.

"Hurry up," Kaizer growled through tight teeth.

She dropped the robe to the floor, her bony ass sauntering over to him and straddling his hips. He still wore his pants, but she ground against him like he was inside her already. She grabbed his hands and put them on her ass, and he squeezed as he pulled her closer and sank his fangs into her. She let out a scream like she was climaxing, and I watched as his throat bobbed with the mouthfuls of blood he was surely getting from her.

Athena started reaching her hand down, looking like she was making to grab his cock, but she stopped and ran her fingers up her center, rubbing circles over her clit. She continued grinding against him, her fingers pumping in and out of herself until she tensed and screamed again as she brought herself to a real orgasm.

The bitch squirmed, and he held her tighter as he finished drinking from her, licking the blood from his lips as he pulled away. She grabbed his face and kissed him, truly reaching for his cock now. I had no desire to watch them fuck, as I should have stopped watching minutes ago, but I couldn't help myself. Moving down the hall quickly, I tried to figure out how to get out of this secret corridor. I heard the sound of wind again; I hadn't felt the breeze when I came down here, but heard it in this direction.

I followed the sound until I felt the wind on my face, my cloak shifting behind me slightly. A metal grate sat on the wall at the very end of the hall. It was welded shut so no one could get in or out, but lucky for me, I could transport myself to the other side. I needed to make sure I knew how to get out of here should I be too low on witch magic to be able to escape that way in the future. But for now, I had plenty. I didn't want to portal out there if I didn't know *where* out there was so I muttered the spell and allowed my body to dissipate and enter the realm between ours and the spirit world.

The brujas had an intense connection to the spirit world. There were some witches like necromancers who could fully enter the spirit world and contact the dead, but most of us could make it into this realm if we embraced the connection enough. The other orders could train themselves to be connected to it, but it was a gift that came naturally to witches. I took a step through the wall. Nothing was truly solid here, allowing me to move through anything in my way. The physical realm materialized around me as I crouched low in the shrubbery on the other side of the grate.

It was the Queen's garden, the perfect place to end my night of exploration. The terrace outside of my room was directly above me and I figured I might as well get a warm-up in before I crashed training tomorrow. Sinking my fingers into the grooves between the stones, I pulled myself up until I reached a thick vine that ran all the way up the side of the wall. The muscles in my arm stretched as far as they could as I reached out to wrap my fingers around it. A quick tug reassured me that it could hold my weight and I jumped with it in my grasp. My biceps screamed as I hadn't been training nearly enough since this had become my 'home.' I tucked the pain away and continued climbing until I made it to the railing of my terrace.

My feet balanced on the edge, and I ended in a flip onto the terrace. I still had it. I took a fake bow and chuckled as I turned the knob and entered my suite. Sighing, I plopped down on the oversized chair, similar to the one Kaizer and Athena were in. I didn't feel jealousy per se, but I couldn't say I didn't feel it either.

He was to be my husband if I didn't get out of this arrangement. I didn't *exactly* have the desire to fuck him myself, although the physique I saw tonight wasn't a turnoff. I'd always gone about sex as a pretty recreational act. I didn't think there needed to be any sort of emotional connection or relationship to enjoy it. I'd had some of my best orgasms from people I didn't quite expect it from. Either way, it would have been nice to have a heads-up.

Especially against Athena, who would surely be on her most bitchy behavior tomorrow when I was to meet with the 'ladies' of the kingdom. If I stabbed her in her eyeball without warning, that could cause some issues, especially since I wasn't supposed to know about what they did. The option wasn't completely off the table, though.

Chapter Eight

That stupid fucking bell woke me up again. I'd come to find out that it went off three times a day when the acolytes were to come to the temple and pray. I didn't understand why they couldn't just check a clock, and I was ready to track down the bell and destroy the thing. I didn't know where Zuri was this morning, which was the first time since she'd become my handmaiden. She was typically up before me, preparing for the day before she even woke me up. But today, she was nowhere to be found.

Which wasn't exactly a problem. As much as I'd enjoyed her company, and had felt overall lonely since I'd been here, it was nice to be truly alone for a few minutes. There were always people around, ones I didn't really have any desire to talk to. I forgot about how peaceful a morning in solitude could be. We didn't do the frilly royalty thing in Caldera, I didn't have handmaidens or anyone waiting on me hand and foot.

My mother and I had some people who assisted us for particularly special occasions, but other than that, we didn't have any extra hands. I wasn't used to the constant presence. I pulled my suit back on and rolled my eyes as I remembered what I had found when I wore this last night. I'd have to face him at some point today and figured I might as well get it out of the way and piss him off simultaneously. He went to training every morning with his army like clockwork. He didn't seem to like surprises, so my showing up would definitely rub him the wrong way. Me showing up in *this* suit would probably send him over the edge, which I thoroughly planned on. It left absolutely nothing to the imagination, and he liked the women here to be modest and covered.

Fuck it.

My hair was pulled up into a high ponytail, something I found to be considered 'daring' here. Exposing your neck so deliberately was practically a call to vampires that you wanted to be their next snack. I smeared on a lovely sinful shade of red lipstick and smiled in the mirror. The perfect finishing touch.

I made my way down the halls, looking for any of the spying holes I'd found yesterday, but nothing jumped out at me. Either someone used a cloaking spell I didn't feel, or they were so well-placed that they couldn't be seen. I smiled again as I reached the training arena and heard clanging steel. I didn't have to fake an ounce of the bravado I felt as I pushed the doors open and let them slam behind me.

The room went deathly silent as all eyes turned to look at me. My gaze landed on Kaizer, who looked more disheveled than I'd ever seen him. He had his shirt off again, and his hair was pulled up into a messy bun. Sweat dripped down his body, mixing with the blood and dirt already smeared across his skin. Fuck me, he looked good all grimed up and disorderly. I pulled my gaze away from him and smiled at everyone across the room; I saw white-haired movement coming in my direction and ignored it.

"Good morning," I sang, walking over to the wall of weapons and pulling down a sword.

I turned it over in my hand as I pretended to inspect it, and Kaizer made it beside me. I could practically feel the death stare he was giving me without even having to look at him.

I stretched out the sword and pretended to spar with an opponent. "Ah, yes. This will do."

Feigning shock, I lifted my hand to my chest. The room was still silent as they all watched to see how the king would take care of me.

"Oh, hello, fiancé. I've come to train. I'm getting a bit out of shape, wouldn't you say," I said, doing a turn and gesturing to my curves on display.

"As you were!" Kaizer bellowed to his soldiers, his eyes never leaving mine.

His gaze dipped down to my exposed neck for a moment and back up to my eyes.

"Who do I ask about a sparring partner? Is Quinn nearby?" I asked as I side-stepped him and surveyed the room.

Quinn was on the other side of the room, her eyes darting over to us every few seconds while she sparred with another general. A large hand gripped my wrist, pulling me backward, and I could barely contain my smile as I played this game with him. Kaizer pulled me closer, the smell of sweat wafting over to me on the breeze through the open doors. I looked up at him through my lashes and smirked, his gaze traveling down my body and back up to my eyes again.

"This is inappropriate," he muttered.

"What is? My choice of weapon? You're right—I could use a much larger sword. I figured I shouldn't show anyone up on my first day of training, though," I responded.

"That's not what I'm talking about," he growled and squeezed my wrist tighter.

The forcefulness and lack of polish he usually had made my stomach tight for a second before I remembered I was on a mission to piss him off as much as I could. I needed to only take this so far, but unfortunately for me, I didn't always know where that line was.

"Then what are you talking about?" I asked, stepping closer and looking away to expose my neck slightly before looking back at him.

"You shouldn't be here. This is not the place for a queen. And you certainly shouldn't be wearing..." He paused, his eyes on my outfit he was sure to deem scandalous. "*That,*" he said with more than a hint of disapproval.

I raised a brow. "You would have me be weak? Defenseless?"

"We have two armies to protect you. You have me to protect you. You don't need to be a warrior anymore. You will be the queen. There's no need for it," he said, and the stench of sexism he spoke with sent any sort of desire I had for him flying away in the wind.

"Quinn is here. Is she not a woman?" I asked.

"Quinn is...different. She's not the queen," he responded.

"It is part of being a witch, Kaizer. I am a born warrior. Asking me not to train is like asking me not to breathe," I said, more honesty in my statement than I meant to speak with.

He studied me, his mouth tight before he spoke. "Fine," he muttered, "that still leaves the problem of what you're wearing."

"I can't exactly fight in a dress, silly," I said, bopping him on his nose and pulling out of his grip.

"Dayanara," he growled as I stepped backward and lifted my sword.

I pointed my blade toward his weapon. "I suppose I'm sparring with you?"

He chuckled like the comment was a joke, and I joined in on his laughter, but not for the same reason he was laughing.

"There's a reason, you know, that you haven't defeated my kingdom yet. You fought in the last battle. You saw what we're capable of," I said as I lowered into a fighting stance.

"And I'm the king for a reason," he said, taking the bait and charging me.

I smirked and twirled on my feet to avoid his strike. The room got slightly quieter again, people surely noticing that he 'allowed' me to fight. I sliced through the air, aiming for his shoulder, and he blocked the strike with his sword, holding it tight. I let some of my strength show as I pushed down, and his wrist shook slightly with the pressure. I jumped back and twisted around him, making to strike his leg, but he was faster than I expected. He blocked the hit again, countering with a strike of his own toward my chest. Blocking the hit, I redirected it away from me, lunging immediately and bringing my sword across my body in a great arc.

Kaizer jumped out of the way at the very last second, and I took the opportunity of him being caught off guard and stepped toward him, showing a little too much of my power. I swiped at his leg, and his blade bent slightly as he blocked the hit. The sound reverberated off the walls, and the look in Kaizer's eyes said he was getting close to dropping his kingly mask. He charged at me, leveraging his brute strength, but I quickly dissipated and transported directly behind him, placing the point of my sword on his shoulder.

"Yield," I muttered, getting closer to his ear.

He looked back over at me, stuck between awe and pure anger, as he grunted. I'd already embarrassed him enough. I wouldn't make him say the words.

"I'm impressed," Quinn exclaimed as she came over to where we stood. "Although I've seen you fight. You took out a big chunk of our soldiers yourself in the last battle," she finished, flicking her gaze over to Kaizer with a smirk.

Kaizer raised his brow like this was the first time he heard about what I'd done in the battle and looked back at me with wide eyes.

I shrugged. "I know my way around a blade."

"Understatement. Should we have to battle Dusra, I know exactly where I'm putting you," she said, folding her arms across her chest.

"She will not be on the battlefield. Because there will be no battle, we will show them we don't mean any harm." He snapped his gaze to me. "That was enough training for today."

I rolled my eyes and sighed dramatically. "Well, as much as I'd love to spend my time here all day," I said, pretending that I was making the decision to leave. "I'm supposed to meet the *ladies* of Sanjry later today, as they'll be part of my court."

Quinn belted a laugh. "You going like that? Their delicate sensibilities might cause them to pass out with that much ass on display."

Kaizer coughed at his general's crude comment and leveled her with a look. "What? We're all thinking it," she said, throwing her hands in the air.

I laughed and looked down at my body. "No, I'll be donning one of the lovely dresses of Sanjry."

Kaizer looked like he still might burst a vein in his forehead.

"Anything I should know?" I asked him.

"About what?" Kaizer responded.

"About the ladies. The only one I've met thus far is Athena, and she seemed to have a lot to say. Actually, I don't think you ever filled me in on what you two spoke of in private?" I asked, and Quinn slowly backed away from the conversation, pretending to critique someone's strike across the room.

Kaizer started walking toward the door with a gesture for me to follow. I rolled my eyes at his never-ending machismo before following him since I wanted to see how he would squirm about my inquiry around Athena.

"She has...issues," he said as we made it far enough away from the group of people.

"That, I am aware of. What are her issues with me?"

"She thinks a Sanjryan should sit on the queen's throne," he responded. "More specifically her."

I wasn't expecting him to actually admit that, and it caught me off guard slightly as I scrambled for a rebuttal.

"Why would she think she should be queen?"

"We have had..." he trailed off, looking around to search for the word.

"Sex," I filled in for him.

He cleared his throat. "Yes. As she is a lady of noble blood, she thought she could...perform well enough to the point I'd want her to be my queen."

"Has it never been a thought?"

"No," he answered quickly. "Athena doesn't have what it takes to rule; that much was evident to me."

"On my way here, I heard some castle staff whispering about how she told her handmaiden she was in your room last night. That you guys had sex," I lied.

He went still, the blood draining from his face as his throat bobbed.

"If you're fucking her, just let me know; I'd like to be prepared for whatever bullshit she's going to spew when I see her."

His face pulled into disgust at my choice of words, but he shook his head. "I'm not...I'm not *fucking* her," he said, the tone of his voice saying that there was more to his statement, which obviously I knew, but he didn't know that.

"So she wasn't in your room? You didn't have sex?" I asked.

"She was, but I didn't have sex with her. But she did...she allowed me to drink from her. She took her clothes off herself, but I didn't touch her outside of drinking from her."

"What do you mean allowed?"

He looked back into the room again, ensuring nobody else was listening before he took a step closer to me.

His voice dropped an octave as his eyes pinned me down. "When vampires are together, they're supposed to drink from each other. She found out I wasn't drinking from you and offered herself under some of her own conditions...Her being able to get off from it. She said if I allowed it, she wouldn't tell anyone I wasn't drinking from you. If people find out, they could have an issue with it."

I tilted my head and bit my lip before breaking the stare. "They'd think this wasn't a real union?"

"Yes, for you to be queen, they would expect you to follow our traditions," Kaizer replied.

I placed my hand on my hip. "They do understand that I'm a witch? You don't see my people demanding anything from you."

"Vampires are just very set in their ways. Your people move freely, and you find comfort in that freedom. My people find comfort in the known, in the traditions we've had for centuries."

I thought about that for a moment. We didn't have anything like what drinking from each other was to the vampires. We had rituals we partook in when together, but nothing so blatant as sinking your fangs into each other's neck.

"At some point, you will expect that from me?" I asked.

His eyes narrowed again. "We hadn't really talked about it, but yes, I would have expected it at some point."

"I don't know how I feel about that right now. I don't trust Athena, though. She will use that as leverage against us at some point," I responded.

"She gave me her word," he said, his poor, trusting soul shining through.

"I'm telling you, it's going to be a problem. Continue to drink from Athena and let her fuck herself in your lap if you like. But trust me, it will be an issue before everything is said and done," I grumbled before turning and walking away from him.

I felt his presence behind me, but I kept walking, my heavy steps the only sound in the hall until I made it back into my chamber.

"There you are!" Zuri exclaimed as I pushed through the chamber doors, her light curls bouncing as she whipped her head toward me.

"Where were you this morning?" I asked.

She blushed slightly, shifting on her feet. "I fell asleep somewhere else last night and woke up late. When I made it back here, you were already gone. I'm so sorry," she finished looking down at the ground.

I lifted my brows and smirked at her. "You go, Zuri. No need to apologize. A woman has needs."

She looked surprised but laughed and walked toward the bathroom. "Why do you look like that?"

"I went to training. Kaizer was pissed," I laughed as I took my suit off and laid it on the chair near the fireplace.

Her eyes widened with concern for me as she handed over a robe for me to wear. "What did he do?"

"Oh, he just threw a hissy fit about what's appropriate for a queen. He didn't like my outfit much either," I said with a shrug.

"It seems like you were trying to anger him," she muttered as she straightened up.

I trusted her to a certain extent. We'd been training together over the last week. There was a certain vulnerability in the way we trained, not for show like how I sparred with Kaizer earlier. We let each other see our whole selves and didn't hold back a bit. I was more than impressed with her. Even so, that didn't mean I could trust her with the information about the tunnels

"Where are your loyalties?" I asked.

Zuri's eyebrows drew together. "What do you mean?"

"You are my handmaiden, but do you serve the king? Sanjry? Or is it me you're loyal to?" I asked.

She looked away from me, her face tight as she pondered my question. "You, I'm loyal to you," she responded firmly.

"I found secret tunnels last night," I said, and she tilted her head in confusion.

"Tunnels to where?"

"Everywhere in the castle. They ran between the walls of all the rooms. I found Kaizer's room, and he was in there with Athena."

She groaned with distaste. "I hate that fucking woman," she muttered.

"Ditto. Anyway, he was drinking from her, and she was fucking herself while he did it. So yes, I was trying to piss him off a bit."

"Well, shit. Did you ask Kaizer about it?"

"In a way. I lied and said I heard some castle staff talking about it. He said how big of a deal it is that he's not drinking from me and that she promised not to tell anyone if she could get something out of it."

Zuri scoffed. "He thinks she won't use that against him? That woman is pure evil."

"That's what I said! He seems to think she'll keep her word, but I have to see her at this event today with the ladies of the kingdom. I just know she's going to be a bitch."

"I can come with you? I can stand in the back or something but still be there for support," she said as she sat in the chair by the fireplace.

I shook my head. "You can come with me, but you don't need to stand in the back."

"The ladies are very traditional. They don't like the *help* to intermingle with them."

"Well, the ladies can go fuck themselves," I said as I sat across from her.

"Don't shake things up too much before you're married," Zuri laughed.

A groan escaped me and I sat my head back. "I am not made for this. I don't know why my mother thought this was a good idea. There had to be some other way that wouldn't rely on me not pissing off half the kingdom."

"She probably thought it was a better shot than killing off half the population between the kingdoms."

I tilted my head. "Don't be logical right now, Zuri. Whine with me."

"Fine, your mother is stupid. Why would she ever trust her daughter with such an important task," she said, using an incredibly whiny voice.

"Exactly!" I exclaimed as I threw my hands in the air.

I loved my kingdom, would do *pretty much* anything for my coven and my loyal brujas, but...there had to be another way to make sure we survived. A way that didn't have me living in a foreign world with people whose lifestyles were completely opposite to mine. We sat there for a while in comfortable silence, watching the flames dance in the fireplace until it was time for me to get ready.

The dress I was to wear today was dropped off with my suit, the seamstress made it to align with how Kaizer preferred I dressed. The neckline was square, and the sleeves were long, but the part that got me was the layers upon layers of skirts it had. It puffed out at the hips, making me feel like I was the size of a cow. The fabric was beautiful, though. The seamstress let me pick a lilac color that beautifully accentuated my hair and the sleeves were sheer with a sheen that sparkled in the light. I stepped into the dress, and Zuri pulled the corset tight, tying the strings that hung down my back.

"What is it with these corsets? Do people not like breathing here?" I asked.

"I wish I knew. I stay away from them at all costs," she replied as she finished with the bow in the back.

Zuri did quick work of my hair and makeup, and I looked exactly how I imagined the people of Sanjry would want their queen to look. I hated it. It felt sexist in some way, like a man made up some idea of what the perfect woman would look like and spat this image out. I didn't mind a dress necessarily, but I definitely preferred one I could move and breathe in.

"I'm not wearing those shoes," I snapped, pointing to gaudy shoes that were a size too small.

"Wear your boots. The dress has so many layers no one will tell the difference," Zuri suggested before she pinned some of her curls back to make her hair look more formal for the event.

"Fucking brilliant," I whispered.

Chapter Nine

Apparently, I had a whole set of rooms on the other side of the castle dedicated to hosting various events. I wasn't entirely sure what those events would entail, but the rooms were crafted beautifully. Where much of the castle went for the less is more, intimidatingly dark look, these rooms had to be designed by the former queen. They were light and airy; almost every wall in the room had floor-to-ceiling windows, making me feel much more connected to the outside than I had in the rest of the castle. The furniture and decor were in beautiful jewel tones, and a vast painting hung on the wall above the fireplace. It depicted our land thousands of years ago, the old magic of our ancestors dancing around the land in swirls of light and darkness.

The old magic that broke our world in half, the very reason we had the Piedra separating our worlds, letting the darkness thrive here and the light thrive there. As a child, I didn't understand why they got to live in a world of brightness while we were in constant darkness. My mother told me that not all darkness was bad and that the creatures of our world needed the darkness to survive, but that didn't make us all inherently evil. And that the ones on the other side weren't inherently good, for that matter. That was before she turned into the stone-cold bitch of a witch she was now, when she still held a glimmer of joy in her eye.

"Lady Payne has arrived," a guard bellowed from the door.

I turned away from the painting and stood tall, knowing that if there was even a glimmer of unease in me, she'd latch onto it. Athena prowled through the entrance, looking down her nose already with a smirk on her face that said she knew something I didn't.

"Lady Payne," I said, clasping my hands in front of me to avoid using them to claw her eyes out of her skull.

She glided across the room to stand before me. "Dayanara."

The lack of title didn't go unnoticed, but I honestly didn't know what my title was at this point. We didn't exactly do titles in Caldera, and I wasn't sure if there was a name for the future queen here. She ran her finger over her neck, the scar from Kaizer's fangs still pink on her pale skin. She caught me staring and pulled her lips into a feline smile.

"Oh, this," she said, tapping on the wound. "Just a little something I got into last night."

Vampires typically only kept the scars on their necks when they were given to them by their lovers; it only took a moment of healing magic to mend and remove them.

"Moving on from Kaizer so quickly, are you?" I asked.

"I wouldn't say that," she chuckled.

I took a step closer to her, she flinched slightly, and I fed on the flicker of fear in her eye. Zuri shifted closer; I wasn't sure if she was trying to get close enough to stop me or get in on my behavior.

"I don't know who you think you're fucking with, but I doubt you've ever had an adversary quite like me," I said, bringing the pointed tip of my nail to rest on her cheek. She swallowed hard, but the bitch didn't back down.

"He's mine. I have the marks to show for it," she muttered, and I pushed my nail into her flesh hard enough to draw blood.

"I'm aware of the arrangement; he talked to me about it. I'm the one who told him to do it," I lied, "I think you're pathetic, offering your body like that in hopes that he'd want more than just that. If you continue to get in my way, I won't hesitate to kill you. And trust me." I leaned closer to whisper in her ear. "I'd have a fucking blast doing it, so don't test me."

I heard footsteps approaching the door, and Athena pushed some healing magic into her cheek and neck. As the next lady to join us walked in the door, I pretended to kiss both of Athena's cheeks in greeting and took a step back from her. Zuri was behind me; my assumption of her trying to stop me was clearly incorrect. Athena went pale, the seriousness of my threat seeming to sink in finally. I smiled gently at her and moved around her body to greet the woman who just entered the room.

"I am Lady Barrington. It's a pleasure to meet you, Queen Dayanara," she said with a deep curtsy.

Well, I could get used to that.

"The pleasure is mine," I said, gesturing to the table on the other side of the room. "Please help yourself to some refreshments."

Lady Barrington did as I said, and I watched as Athena finally broke from the trance my promise of death put her under with a stomp. She shuffled over to greet the woman, and more people poured through the entrance, taking my attention away from her. I'd be the first and last witch she ever tried to go up against. I didn't lose, and I wouldn't be starting any time soon.

After a few hours of pleasantries, I was genuinely bored out of my mind. The women were starting to gossip about people I didn't know, and I really had no interest in finding out who they were talking about. A blur of motion across the room caught my attention, and I looked up to find Zuri waving her arms at me. She was mouthing words, but I couldn't figure out what she was trying to say; I squinted, and she pointed to her mouth and smiled dramatically.

The sudden realization that my face was fixed into a scowl of disgust as one of the ladies explained how her gardener planted the wrong color flowers at her estate hit me. I softened my features into something a bit queenlier. I really needed to get a hold on my facial expressions for when Zuri wasn't around. I nodded my appreciation to Zuri, again, and she nodded back before going back to talk to the other handmaidens.

A chime from a clock rang, marking the top of the hour and the end of the torture that was trying to entertain these women. I loved women, there was no doubt about that, but I felt it extremely hard to connect with these ladies. They had lived such different lives than the women I'd been surrounded with in Caldera.

"I'm so sorry, but I do have another engagement," I said, standing up and brushing the layers of skirts down.

One thing I wasn't new to was dismissing a group of women.

"It was a pleasure to meet you, Queen Dayanara," Lady Barrington said as she, too, stood, and the others followed. Athena tried to scurry away between two of the other ladies, but I stopped her before she could exit.

"Athena," I exclaimed, and she stopped in her tracks.

She turned around, her mouth pursed and chin high, setting herself back into the bitch mode she seemed to live in. Everyone filtered out of the room except Zuri, and I stepped close to Athena.

"Don't forget what I said. Keep that blood sweet for Kaizer," I muttered, sidestepping her and walking out of the room.

She huffed behind me before running in the opposite direction I went in.

"You're going to hear about that." Zuri laughed. "There is a one hundred percent chance she's running to Kaizer to tell him you tried to kill her."

"I didn't try to kill her," I responded, "I merely threatened it."

"I don't blame you at all. Do you know that she gets a new handmaiden every week because no one can work for her longer than that?"

"That doesn't surprise me," I responded.

I went to turn in the direction of my room, and Zuri grabbed my wrist. "Where are you going?"

"Back to my room to get out of this horrendous costume," I muttered.

"Oh, I forgot to tell you. Kaizer sent word that you are to meet him for lunch," she replied.

"I have no desire to have lunch with him."

"He won't like it if you blatantly disregard him," Zuri muttered, looking around as if he could hear us through the walls.

"I don't care." I turned down the hallway to my chambers. "He only wants to try to make up for this morning."

Zuri hurried to my side, not pressing the matter any further.

"I want to go for a run," I said as we pushed through the doors to my suite of rooms.

Her face pulled into disgust. "For fun?"

"Moving my body helps clear my head. I didn't train long enough, thanks to Kaizer," I responded and Zuri still didn't look convinced. "You don't have to go with me."

"No, I'll go. I can't promise I won't complain, but you shouldn't be out there alone," Zuri responded as she helped undo the ties on my corset.

The first string loosened, and I felt my body relax immediately with the lack of constraint around it. I took a deep sigh of relief and straightened.

"You think I can't handle myself?" I asked.

"I think anyone with half a brain should know that's not the case. Doesn't mean you should be alone, though," she replied.

I shrugged. "You'll have to keep up if you come with me."

Zuri's shoulders sagged for a moment, but she nodded and went to her room to change out of her dress. I pulled mine off my body with quite a bit of effort and heaved the heavy garment onto the bed. My leathers were folded on my chest of drawers from this morning, and I stepped into them, fastening the small buckles that ran up the sides and at the neck.

Zuri came out of the room in her own leathers, but they weren't nearly as nice as mine. She could definitely use a new suit, preferably with the same fabric as mine, that lasted much longer. I picked the pins out of my hair and pulled it up into another high pony to avoid my long waves getting in the way.

"Let's do this." I clapped, excited to get my blood pumping.

Zuri looked less than enthusiastic but followed along all the same. We walked down to my garden and out to the edge of the grounds.

"You lead the way. I don't know where I'm going," I said, stretching my hamstrings.

"The gardens all connect. We can run over to the training arena. There's a loop we can run around there," Zuri replied before darting away.

I chased after her, the movement already bringing me a bit of relief from the thoughts spiraling in my head. I couldn't tell if I was any closer to getting out of the arrangement with Kaizer, but I'd yet to figure out what the other option would be. Killing him was short-sighted, unfortunately my mother was right about that. Regardless I needed to be able to leave this stupid fucking place when I pleased. Seeing Kaizer and Athena last night, even if they didn't have sex, awoke something in me. I didn't exactly blame him. We all needed blood.

I wondered if I'd been going about it wrong. Maybe I should have been embracing the fact my mother thought I could handle this, that she thought I could save our people from centuries of more war. Maybe I'd actually make her proud for once in my life. I was born to rule, so that wasn't an issue, but I was born to rule brujas. Where they mostly handled discourse themselves and fought it out until one of the parties either died or got over whatever the issue was. My people weren't catty, didn't play games, not like they did here.

I wasn't prepared to handle politics in a way that cared for such varied people. The Acna's word was law in Caldera—you either agreed with her or got the fuck over it. Most witches weren't dumb enough to defy her; if they did, it was the last thing they ever did. My mother ruled with an iron fist, and I'd been sent many times to deal with those who turned against her. But here, Kaizer seemed to play both sides, like he needed to ensure that both parties still believed in him when it was all said and done. Was I really to sit in a room and try to handle squabbles about chickens? Surely that was a waste of my time. Not to mention we'd be ruling both of our lands, so there was a whole other factor of what that looked like. Would the witches intermingle with the vampires?

It wouldn't be the first time; almost all of us had vampires for fathers, but bruja blood trumped anything that it mixed with. It would be the first time that they lived together, though. Vampire men liked to test their limits and look for new challenges. Many times that led to them crossing over our borders to see what it was like to be with a witch. They surely didn't stick around after they were seduced by our mothers, typically due to our mother's getting rid of them. A good chunk of the witches didn't even prefer the company of men, but unfortunately for us, there weren't any other ways to procreate. We lived significantly longer than vampires, so we didn't choose to have babies all that often.

Most vampires weren't much better than the humans in Bonda. While the humans couldn't even wield the power of their land, the vampires could at least do that, some were much stronger magic wielders than others, but there were some who could barely conjure anything. Vampires were significantly stronger than humans, and lived longer, but they had no extra power like we did. I wiped some sweat sliding down my forehead and focused on each muscle moving my body. Marrying Kaizer didn't mean I had to love him or even like him. But I needed to make sure the witches remained well and in power. That had to be my focus.

Zuri came to a quick halt in front of me, pulling me from the whirlwind that was my mind. I nearly ran smack into her back before I realized why she stopped so abruptly. Kaizer stood in the middle of the path a few feet ahead, filling the area and leaving no room for us to go around him due to the walls of shrubbery on either side of the path. Zuri bowed at the waist and stepped back a few feet behind me, leaving me to face off against the vampire.

"I asked you to lunch," he said, closing the space between us.

His white hair was pulled up in the bun he wore this morning, still unpolished and slightly unruly. He looked like he had just finished training with his army but changed his clothes to appear a bit more presentable.

I arched a brow. "You demanded I meet you for lunch. There's a difference. I wanted to run since my training was cut short."

Kaizer crossed his arms. "Athena paid me a visit."

"I'm not surprised," I sighed as I rolled my eyes.

Kaizer turned his head to the side. "She said you threatened her while also telling her to continue letting me drink from her."

"That about covers it, yeah," I responded and tried to look around him.

Kaizer moved to stand directly in front of me and I peered back up at him to find his face pulled into confusion.

"I assumed you'd want me to find someone else," he stated.

I shrugged. "You make your own decisions. I just don't want you drinking from me."

"You were upset about it earlier. I didn't think you meant it," he said flatly.

"I think it would save both of us a lot of problems if you found someone else, yes. But I'm not going to tell you who you should be getting your blood from."

He surveyed me but didn't respond.

"Is this a monogamous situation?" I asked, the words slipping out of me before I could stop them.

Zuri coughed behind me and took a few more steps away from us before turning the corner past the wall of shrubbery.

"Are witches not monogamous?" he asked.

"We don't have a standard. It's up to the couple."

And if it was up to me, I wouldn't ever choose to be monogamous again.

"Vampires don't venture outside of their marriage," he responded.

"That doesn't exactly answer the question," I said, placing my hand on my hip. "This isn't a normal situation."

He took a step closer to me, leaving just inches between us. I tipped my chin up to look into his eyes, the warm light of the sky casting a glow on his white hair.

"If you're mine, you're mine alone. Does that answer your question?"

The timber of his voice sent goosebumps along my, thankfully covered, skin. If there was one thing the man did, it was surprise me in these moments where he became randomly attractive.

"It does. The question of if I'll be yours is still up for debate," I said, taking a step around his hulking form and gliding past him.

He caught up with me in a few strides and stood beside me. "We are to be married."

"That is true, yes," I said.

"So you will be mine."

"In the name of marriage. But if you expect more than a political arrangement, you'll need to work for that," I replied as the wind blew between us and shifted my hair in front of my face.

"What does that mean?" Kaizer asked.

"You'll have to figure that out, until then, you can do what you want, and I'll do what I want." I shrugged and picked up my speed into a jog.

"Okay. What about lunch?" Kaizer yelled from behind me.

"Maybe another day," I replied, waving my hand over my shoulder as I zipped away from him toward the loop Zuri was leading us to.

I didn't look back, but I could feel Kaizer's eyes on me as I ran away from him. I couldn't imagine a scenario where I would want to be with him outside of the arrangement, so I wasn't too worried about that. Regardless of what happened, I wouldn't be owned.

To be his and solely his—that sounded like a death sentence.

Chapter Ten

Dusra would be here in a few days, and everyone was starting to get flustered with the anticipation. I hadn't seen much of Kaizer since our time in the garden because he was out preparing at all hours of the day. The army secured the capital's borders, and Kaizer assigned guards to every few feet of the castle, ensuring every square inch of the place was guarded against wandering souls. Kaizer had planned every minute of the day, leaving no time for idle bodies. An itinerary he was now going over with me, his advisers, and my mother in his office, the red room. I'd met his advisers, Otto and Abel, a few times now, but they weren't exactly people I enjoyed being around. They were quite cold, but I did appreciate the fact that they didn't dance around the point like most people in Sanjry. Anytime they had something to relay, they got straight to it and left.

"We'll show him some of our lands and art and show him that we're doing well. But the most important part of this is to show him that we won't be trying to advance our borders with our added numbers," Kaizer exclaimed, his hands clasped together on his desk.

My mother inspected her pointed nails. "We can speak for the brujas. We don't have the same history with Dusra, so I doubt they'll be too interested in us."

"I think it would help if you presented as a true couple," Abel said dryly, causing my lip to pull back from my teeth in a scowl.

"The face you're making now is one you should try to avoid, Dayanara," Kaizer said.

"When you say true couple, what exactly do you mean?" I asked.

"Well, for starters, a bite mark," Abel replied.

I scoffed and rolled my eyes, my gaze landing on my mother, who had all types of disapproval written across her face at my attitude.

"It is the easiest way to show that this is true. While this was a necessary union to stop the battle between our people, it will look like the first steps in a move against them with our history," Otto added.

Kaizer sat back in his chair. "I agree. We need to present a united front. I'd ask that any issues be brought up away from their earshot."

"So you're asking me to be quiet," I stated, surveying him with a flat look.

"I'm asking that we practice some discretion," Kaizer responded.

My mother sat forward. "Just don't be an idiot, Dayanara."

"Noted. So when did this love affair start?" I asked.

"I don't think we need to go into the specifics," Kaizer dismissed me and picked up another piece of paper on his desk.

"No, she's right. You don't think he'll be interested in that?" Otto inquired.

Kaizer sighed and put the paper down, leaning forward onto his elbows to rest his chin on his hand as he looked at me. "Do you have any ideas?"

"Other than being struck by my undeniable beauty?" I teased as I tossed my hair over my shoulder.

My mother rolled her eyes and sat back in her chair before crossing her legs while Otto and Abel stared at me blankly.

The slightest smirk graced Kaizer's lips. "Yes, other than that."

"Is it vital for it to be anything other than a political union? They have to be aware of the war between our kingdoms?" I asked.

"Yes, it's necessary. How much of our history are you aware of?" Otto asked, and Abel perked up a bit, looking between Kaizer and Otto.

"Just that it took you centuries to recoup from it," I answered.

"The king prior to me," Kaizer started as he looked toward the map behind him. "He was overzealous. He tried to push Sanjry's borders into his land, as the island within Dusra's kingdom is said to be enchanted, holding magic that could begin and end a world. We have...particularly bad blood with the current king. He wasn't the king during the war, but it could be detrimental if he thinks we're only doing this to get our hands on his land again."

"So either this union fails, and we kill each other, or we make it work, and Dusra kills us both. How nice," I muttered.

"A lot is riding on this, yes," Kaizer said firmly.

"I think it makes the most sense to weave the truth in. It will make it more believable. Let's say that we were speaking of conditions for a truce and that during those meetings, we developed feelings for each other," I said with my gaze locked in Kaizer's.

Kaizer's lip twitched into a smirk as he nodded. "You are all dismissed. Dayanara, if you could stay, it would be appreciated."

Look who's catching along to not demanding things of me.

My mother, Otto, and Abel stood and left the room without another word, and I listened for the door shutting behind them.

Kaizer loosened the neck of his tunic and sat back in his chair, his biceps straining. "So, which parts of your statement are the truth?"

"The part where this was part of a discussion around a truce," I responded.

The corner of his mouth lifted. "Not the feelings part?"

I tilted my head to the side in surprise, and he chuckled darkly.

"I would like to say I'm glad you've dropped the seductress act," he followed up, not allowing me to deny having any feelings for him—feelings I didn't have.

I gathered myself and sat up straight. "Who said it was an act?"

He shrugged slightly. "You haven't made it seem like much more than an act, as it hasn't gone past you swishing your hips and gazing at me through your dark lashes."

"I told you if you wanted more than a political union, you'd have to work for it. You haven't done much since then," I responded, crossing my arms.

"I've been a bit busy. I apologize. But since you are dropping the act." He paused, waiting for me to rebuttal, and I said nothing. "I can get to know the real you better. Care to tell me what exactly makes you happy?"

Nobody had ever asked me that question before. I lived for my kingdom; it was my whole life. I was raised to become the Acna one day and to do the bidding of my mother. She pointed me in a direction to kill, and I followed directions. I had plenty of things that helped me de-stress, drinking, fucking, fighting, but happiness? I'd never given much thought to that. I could think back to my childhood, the parts and pieces I remembered when my mother was more than just the Acna. When we used to play outside in the streams and dance under the stars, what would have made that version of myself happy?

"I don't know," I admitted, "what makes you happy?"

"I don't know either." He chuckled. "My kingdom is my life, as yours is."

"What do normal people do?" I asked, the ease of this conversation put me in a more comfortable place than I'd ever been with him.

"I'd have to plead ignorance there as well. I spend most of my time in these walls, getting my information from my advisers and staff."

I stretched my arms out. "I like training, moving my body. Does that count?"

"I'm not sure. When we trained together, you didn't look very happy," he taunted.

"That was your fault," I said, rolling my eyes.

"Can I rectify that?"

"Now?" I asked.

Kaizer stood and removed his jacket. "I don't see why not."

The dress I wore had two slits running up the legs and didn't have one hundred layers like the dress I wore to tea with the ladies. It wouldn't be terribly challenging to kick his ass in it. I shrugged like I didn't care either way, and he gestured for me to follow him out of the room. We turned in the opposite direction of the training arena, and I looked over at Kaizer with a wrinkle in my brow.

"We're going to my courtyard. I learned my lesson sparring with you in front of my soldiers," Kaizer explained.

I laughed. "You're smarter than you look."

We walked at a leisurely pace, our footsteps the only sound in the hall.

"This is a rather big castle. I imagined it would be busier around here," I stated, trying to fill the blaring silence.

"We run very efficiently. Most of the staff works on the lower levels, and only a few trusted people work in this area."

This level housed his office, both our suites, an eating hall, and rooms that the generals and advisers used. I hadn't explored more since the first night, but some secrets might have been hidden somewhere around here if they didn't allow everyone free range. We reached Kaizer's suite, and he pushed open the large black doors with the flaming tree etched onto their surface. His suite was set up similar to mine, with the sitting room at the front, the room I peered into and found a naked Athena grinding in his lap. The door to his bedroom was open, his room just as immaculate as I would have guessed it to be. I didn't get time to study it too much as we breezed past the room and down a narrow hallway that I didn't have in my chamber. We walked down a narrow staircase and out a door into his courtyard. Walls of shrubbery ran high, his area completely cut off from the other gardens. Kaizer walked over to a large trunk along the wall and pulled out two vast swords. He handed me one of them, and I pressed the pad of my finger along the edge slightly.

"These aren't sparring swords," I muttered.

"They aren't, so try not to kill me," Kaizer responded as he set his sword down and tied his hair up into a bun.

"No promises," I muttered, shifting my hips and setting into a defensive stance.

Kaizer was a vampire through and through, the masculinity coursing through him, always pushing him to be on the offensive before the defensive. Something I'd noticed among most of the vampires over the years of fighting them. As expected, he charged me first, and I blocked his hit firmly; he pushed harder, testing my strength, but I was stronger than he thought.

He pulled his weapon away and circled around me. "Interesting," he muttered.

I tried to crouch slightly to get in a better defensive position, but my dress affected my mobility, even with the slits.

"Fuck this," I growled, taking my blade and ripping the bottom half of my dress off mid-thigh.

Kaizer looked down at the skin on show, his jaw and grip on his sword tightening. "Is this part of your battle strategy?" he questioned as he dragged his gaze back up to my eyes.

I shrugged. "Might be."

I took the advantage of his stunned composure and darted toward him. Twisting on my heel, I quickly changed direction before whirling around him with a slash of my blade directed at his thigh. He turned at the waist and blocked the blow as I took a step back from him. He smiled at me and licked his full bottom lip, and for some reason, it felt like his mouth was calling to me for a moment. Like I *needed* to kiss him. He chuckled like he knew what I was thinking and walked toward me slowly with his weapon hanging down at his side.

I looked him up and down, wondering how he turned the tables on me once again. He moved quickly, his weapon aimed for my shoulder, but with a blast of my air magic to the ground, I flipped over his head. Landing gracefully on his back, I wrapped my legs around him with my blade resting against his neck. He gripped my thigh, flipped us around, and pushed me up against the wall, knocking my wrist to the side with his forearm and sending my sword to the ground.

Kaizer twisted around to face me with his blade lifted, but I wrapped a tendril of air around it and yanked it out of his hand, sending the sword clanging against mine. He was still pushing me up against the wall, his grip on my thigh near bruising as his face got closer to the exposed skin on my neck. Our chests were rising and falling rapidly as we stayed there, his burning cedar scent wrapping around me, suffocating me in the best way. He dipped his nose into the crook of my neck, rubbing his cheek against the sensitive skin below my ear. His cheek was rougher than I thought it would be, the evidence that stubble was starting to grow.

He pulled back and looked into my eyes, and I found so much desire in his dark gaze it had a short breath escaping me as I held his stare. Kaizer pushed his hips deeper into mine, and I bit my lip at the pressure, the fabric of my dress ripping further, barely covering the heat that was gathering between my thighs. Any thoughts of him being too pretty or too put together for me disintegrated as I saw the power he held. I could feel how deep his magic ran everywhere our skin touched, calling to my own. He had taken his own throne by force, and I had no doubts he had the power to do so as it burned through me. I allowed mine to the surface, and his pupils dilated as he felt my own magic, not just the air magic of my region but my raw witch magic that was unlike anything a vampire would have experienced.

"You're exquisite," he growled, running his fingers lightly up my thigh and into the ragged edge of my dress.

Boots scuffed against stone somewhere behind us, and Kaizer whipped his head around to see who dared to enter his private courtyard.

Quinn stood in the doorway, a smirk gracing her lips. "We're supposed to be checking the outer wall," she said before backing up into the darkness of the hall. "But it can wait."

A rough guttural sound came from Kaizer's throat as he set me down on the ground and pulled down my dress to hide my skin from Quinn.

"I need to go. Our outer walls need to be locked down as soon as possible. I'll be out there until tomorrow morning," he muttered, his eyes dipping to my neck for a moment.

My breathing evened out now that his firm body wasn't pushing up against mine any longer. "I'll see you tomorrow at breakfast?"

"Yes, you will," he said as he stepped away and walked toward Quinn.

Quinn winked at me as she stepped to the side for Kaizer to get through and followed behind him. I looked down at my dress, some of the tears running almost to my hips now, and snapped open a portal into my room. I stepped through, and Zuri jumped back with her hand on her chest.

"Fuck, you scared me," she muttered, looking at my ruined garment. "What happened?"

"Fight with Kaizer," I explained, and she stepped closer to me.

"Do we need to leave?" she whispered.

"No." I laughed. "It was intentional. A training to make up for the other day."

"I can't tell if you won or not," she said.

I sighed deeply. "Me either."

Chapter Eleven

I had so much pent-up frustration I couldn't keep still any longer, so I decided to explore more while Kaizer was away from the castle. I was in the secret tunnels again, venturing into a part I didn't cover the last time. This stretch of hall felt longer than the others, and I was still determining where I would end up as there hadn't been any spy holes for a while. The air felt suddenly humid, and water rushed somewhere nearby. I took a turn to the right, following the sound until I reached the source. This far under the castle, I expected it to be some sort of sewage system, but the water was crystal clear, coming in through one grate and out another at the other end of the space. There was more tunnel on the other side of the water, but noise sounded outside the grate to the left, and I walked over to the edge to peek out.

The stream of water appeared to run out into the village, but a guard shifted into my view, and I stepped back quickly to avoid being seen. I had yet to go to the village, and I was really curious as to what the capital looked like outside of the castle. I listened for where the guard was and peered back out to see where I should transport. The inner wall around the castle wasn't too far, and there was a gate with more guards posted on watch. Kaizer wasn't kidding about making sure everything was on lockdown. The guards walked in opposite directions for a moment, and I took the opportunity to transport quickly into the darkness between them on the other side of the gate. I cleared my purple smoke quickly and pulled my hood down as far as I could so I couldn't be identified. I wished

I had some rose quartz for an identity spell, but I still didn't have any crystals. Moving some branches out of my view and crouching down low, I surveyed the surrounding area.

The edge of the village was a few strides away, the closest building to me appearing to be someone's residence as clothes were hanging to dry in the backyard. I hopped over the low fence and ran around the side of the house, staying close to the building so I could see what to expect around the other side. Even though the hour was late, people still walked up and down the street. I could easily stay hidden among the crowd. I didn't think anyone here would know who I was, but I didn't want to take the chance of the guards around noticing me from the castle. The group I was hidden among all were walking in the same direction, and I looked up to find a bar on the corner of the street. A beer sounded magnificent, and people would be drunk enough not to take too much notice of me. I loved places like this after my missions, or just when I wanted to get away and listen to music, dance, and find some man or woman to make me feel something.

I followed the crowd through the entry, and the smell of sweat and spilled beer assaulted me. The normalcy of such things brought a slight smile to my face. I'd been locked up in that castle for too long. I tended not to stay in one place for more than a few days as my mother sent me all over Caldera to deal with whatever issues arose. Needless to say, the possibility of me going crazy in those castle walls was soon imminent. My shoulders bumped into the patrons singing and dancing drunkenly in the center of the building as I weaved through the crowd. I walked up to the bar and sat my elbows on the wooden surface as the barkeep noticed me.

I kept my chin down, peering up through my dark hood. "Just a beer, please."

"Rather mysterious, aren't you?" the man chuckled, grabbing a mug from below the counter and filling it up to the brim. Foam spilled over the sides as he slid it over to me and held his hand out for payment.

Thankfully I never left the room without money, a habit I developed pretty early on as I could end up anywhere with a moment's notice. I dropped a silver into his hand, and he turned his head to the side at my over payment.

"Keep the change," I muttered before elbowing my way through the crowd to a dark, empty table in the corner of the establishment.

There weren't any guards that I could see inside the building, so I lifted my hood to the edge of my hair and sat back in the chair. No one paid me any attention as I sipped my beer and listened to the music the musicians played. I lifted the mug to my lips but realized I had drunk the entire mug of the shitty beer already. I sighed and pushed out of the chair, my body already feeling lighter from the liquid. I pushed through the crowd again, but a particularly drunk man stumbled into me, nearly knocking me on my ass.

"Watch it, bitch," he slurred into my shoulder.

I yoked him up by his collar and bared my elongated canines at him. "Call me a bitch again, and you'll regret it," I growled, pushing him off me to the ground.

He hit the ground hard but somehow managed to catch himself with his hands before his head hit, too. I continued my walk to the bar, but felt a presence rushing up behind me.

"*Bitch*, I'll fucking kill you," the drunk exclaimed, and I rolled my eyes and turned to face him.

I loosened the knife from the strap on my thigh just as he made it to me, charging me like a rabid animal. The alcohol in his system clearly affected his decision-making skills as I saw a weapon strapped to his hip. I grasped my knife in my hand and stabbed him in the shoulder, whirling around him and slashing him in the stomach as well. He was too drunk to feel the full effects of the wounds and turned to try to push me to the ground. The music suddenly stopped as I sidestepped him and kicked him in the back, so he fell on his front and quickly rolled over to defend himself. I straddled him, the smell of piss beer and actual piss wafting from the floor below us. I held the blade to his throat and slashed the blade across his face through his mouth.

"Have fun trying to say anything for a while," I grumbled, the blood rushing from the wound as he grabbed his face and wailed a muffled scream.

I stepped off him, my hood thankfully still on my head. A few of the people in the bar dragged him over to the wall and left him there to recover. The music started again, the whole crowd acting as if nothing happened at all as the singing and dancing raged.

At some point during the fight, I dropped the mug, but the barkeep already had a beer ready for me as I stepped up to the bar.

"He needed a lesson," he said with a laugh. "Serves him right. This one is on me."

I nodded and grabbed the beer to get back to my table before I had to stab anyone else for the night. The drunk man screaming and stumbling out of the building caught my attention, causing me to bump into a large man near my table. He twisted quickly, throwing his hands in the air. "Don't stab me," he begged, shifting to the side and flashing me a smile that had my stomach doing a flip.

This man was pulled out of all of my deepest desires, his short dark curly hair, dark olive skin, stubbly rugged beard, and dimple all working together to create the worst kind of temptation. I smiled back at him, raising my hood slightly to let him see my face better. "Don't call me a bitch, and we have a deal."

He licked his lips as his hazel gaze dragged up and down my body and landed back in my eyes. "I wouldn't dare. I've got a life I look forward to living," he responded as he turned around and watched me sit back in the chair I was using before the debacle.

"Oh yeah? What do you look forward to in particular?" I asked, taking a sip of my beer and moving my cloak to the side to expose my body.

He sat in the chair across from me. "Well, some of it involves a beautiful woman with a penchant for violence."

"I don't remember inviting you to sit," I said as I rested my elbows on the table.

The man lifted his cup to his lips and looked up at me. "Feel free to make me leave."

I rested my finger on my lip, drawing his gaze to my full mouth. "I'll allow it for now. What's your name?"

"Ax. You?" he asked.

"Daya," I responded, offering him part of my name. "What are you doing here?"

"Why is anyone here? The divine beer and entertainment," he answered, and ran his hands through his thick curls as his biceps strained at his white linen shirt.

"Fair enough," I responded.

I took another sip of my beer and Ax tracked each movement with a predatory gaze that had me biting my lip.

"Where'd you learn to fight like that?" Ax asked.

"There are a lot of idiots in this world, and unfortunately, I have a lot of experience with them," I answered, sitting back and toying with the buckle across my chest.

Kaizer could get his blood from Athena; I could flirt harmlessly with a ridiculously gorgeous man at a bar.

The man watched my fingers and chuckled darkly. "Unfortunately, I do too."

We watched each other for a moment, the odd feeling that I'd always known him sitting heavy on my chest.

He sat forward and rested his chin on his fist. "Tell me something."

"Like what?"

"What's your biggest fear?"

I turned my head. "A bit heavy for bar talk, don't you think?"

Ax shrugged. There weren't many people these days I could be honest with; a man in a bar I'll never see again seemed good enough for me.

"Failure," I answered.

"Interesting. Failing at what?"

I shrugged. "Everything."

I hid it behind so much confidence and theatrics, but deep down, I was worried I'd make the wrong decision. The wrong decision that would hurt my coven, and for a long time I was worried about failing my mother. For a while I tried to live up to her standards, practically begged for her love by doing what she wanted, but I'd failed time and time again. So many times that at some point I had to accept that I just wasn't what she wanted. As her daughter, I would always be a disappointment. There were some moments where she'd almost looked proud of me when I did something she asked, but it was never genuine. Outside of my little acts of rebellion that earned me punishment, I still did as she asked, always secretly hoping that it would be enough, and I wouldn't be a failure. It made me feel worthless, and sometimes I wondered if I was even doing anything right for my kingdom. Or if it was even worth trying, if all I'd do was fail, regardless.

I cleared my throat. "What's yours?"

"Same thing, actually. That I won't be enough. That I'll fail my family because of it."

"Now, you tell me something, preferably lighter than your question."

"What do you want to know, Daya?"

The way he said my name made me bite the inside of my cheek, but the conversation with Kaizer about happiness earlier came back to my mind. I wondered if this man had more to say about it than I did.

"What makes you happy?"

He surveyed me, the twinkle in his eye growing before he smiled.

"Getting what I want," he started, before shrugging. "That and taking care of my family. My fear and happiness seem to go hand in hand."

"Are you happy?" I asked.

"I could always be happier." He smirked. "What are you getting into for the rest of the night?"

"I suppose that depends on how the rest of this conversation goes," I offered, a lie, but it felt good to be back in my comfort zone, bantering with strangers.

He sat forward, leaning over the table with his dimple on display. "This conversation is going great, so I say we venture elsewhere."

"Do you? Where should we venture?"

"Somewhere a little less crowded would be preferred, but I'm open to public play," he said.

"Lucky for you, so am I," I said, leaning forward. Not exactly a lie.

He leaned forward as well, the magnetism between us almost palpable. His hazel gaze was so intense I froze as he ran a gloved finger down my jaw and tilted my chin toward him. Any previous thoughts on why I shouldn't be doing this flew right out of my brain. Ax got a breath away from my face as the front door slammed, and a tall guard stepped through the entry. The long black braid caused me to pull my hood back in front of my face and sit back as I realized it was Quinn. She ran her gaze around the room but walked up to the bar, not noticing me in the corner.

"Problem with the law?" Ax asked.

I stood from my chair. "Something like that."

"Surely you could fight your way out if you needed to. Stay," he demanded, grabbing my hand in his.

"Not worth the trouble," I responded.

"You wound me," he said as he clutched his chest. "There's another exit over there through the kitchen." He pointed to the corner across from us.

I made to move away from him, but he tightened his grip on my hand for a moment.

"I look forward to our paths crossing again, Daya," he said before letting me out of his grasp.

The chances of that were fairly slim, as I didn't think I could make this an often occurrence, but he didn't know that.

"Me too," I whispered, offering him one last smile before fighting my way through the crowd to the dark hall Ax pointed me toward.

I walked out of the pub and out into the dark streets. They were less populated than when I came in, but a blood curdling scream caught my attention a few streets down.

It was a woman's scream, and before I knew it, I was portaling down to where I heard the sound. A dark alley sat to my right, and I heard scuffling at the very end of it. I grabbed my dagger from my thigh and prowled into the darkness. A muffled scream sounded again, and I sent an orb of magic to float near the roofs of the buildings, the light illuminating a man and woman.

The man had his hand around the woman's mouth, as he was trying to pull his pants down, but looked up at me. Fear encompassed his being as my dagger flew blade over hilt and embedded right into his neck. The moment the blade hit his flesh, I was already there pulling the woman away from him. I yanked my dagger from his neck and plunged it into his chest as I held his gaze and watched the life slip from his eyes before he slumped down to the ground. Placing my hand on his shoulder, I pushed a spark of my witch magic into him and disintegrated him to ash.

"You're a witch," the woman mumbled as she scurried back from me.

Her pale skin seemed to glow under my magic, her blonde hair falling limply around her shoulders. I understood why she was scared, the vampires thought us to be evil beings who killed for sport, but no woman should ever go through what this one almost did. Witch, vampire, lobo, nobody deserved that.

"You have nothing to fear from me," I said as I wiped the man's blood from the dagger. "What happened?"

"I was just walking home. He grabbed me and pulled me into the alley. I froze...I didn't know what to do," she said before tears flowed down her cheeks.

My jaw ticked as I looked back at the bastard's fucking ashes. "Here," I said, offering her the weapon.

"I wouldn't know what to do with that. I'm weak, I'm a woman..." she trailed off, shaking her head, the movement sending more tears pouring down her face.

I grabbed her by her chin and made her look me in my eyes. "You listen to me. Being a woman does not make you weak. Anyone who ever told you that was trying to hold you back. You are strong, and you are capable. That," I said, pointing toward the ashes. "Will never happen again. You take this blade, and you sink it into anyone who tries to hurt you. In the chest, in the neck, in the groin, I don't care, but you don't let them fuck with you. Do you understand?"

"I...I understand," she replied as she wiped the tears from her face.

I took her hand and placed the dagger in it. "Stand up straight."

The woman listened, and I set her into a fighting stance before tapping her stomach. "Keep your core tight to maintain your balance, push the blade forward, and shift your weight."

She pretended to stab an assailant, and I nodded. "Very good. Don't lose that blade."

The woman looked at the dagger and up to me with a watery gaze, her lip quivering as she tucked it away.

"Thank you." She swallowed. "For saving me, and well, for saving future me too."

I nodded once as I extinguished my orb above us and walked out of the alley without looking back.

Chapter Twelve

"Daya," Zuri exclaimed, pulling me out of my thoughts about my activities the night before.

"Hm?"

"What's going on with you this morning?"

"Nothing, I'm just tired," I lied as I followed her out of the room.

"A lie, but I won't press," she said and bumped me in the shoulder as we walked down the hall to the dining hall for breakfast.

I chuckled while I tossed my hair over my shoulder to get a better look at her. "I appreciate that."

Zuri fished something out of her pocket. "Oh. Here," she said as she held her closed hand out toward me.

"What is it?" I asked.

She looked down at the ground. "I don't know if you can actually use it or not, but I saw this crystal in one of the older shops. I knew you were upset about not having yours, so I just grabbed it for you."

I let her drop it into my hand and inspected the crystal. "This is blue calcite," I whispered as I shifted it from one hand to another, "A decent chunk of it."

"So you can use it?" she said with a bright smile.

"I can. Not necessarily for fighting, but it's a calming stone—it can help someone sleep if they're having trouble." I swallowed and looked back up into her big gray eyes. "Thank you, Zuri."

Zuri shrugged. "You've been helping me with training. It's the least I can do, really."

Such a small token of appreciation, but it had me casting long glances her way as we continued moving. I was the only witch she knew, surely, but for her to use her own money to buy something that reminded her of me. Something she thought I could use to defend myself after seeing me upset about my mother not bringing me my crystals—it seemed so heartfelt. Like her being my handmaiden wasn't just her job, as if she really truly cared about *me*.

I slipped the crystal into my pocket as we walked the rest of the way to the dining hall in comfortable silence, and Zuri left me to do whatever it was she did while she wasn't with me before I pushed through the door. Kaizer was already seated at the table, back to the perfectly polished king in his burgundy tunic and sleek, wavy hair.

"Good morning," he smiled widely.

I was quickly reminded about our moment in his courtyard, as I'd nearly forgotten after the night I had.

"Good morning," I said, smiling back at him and taking my seat. I felt a little daring this morning and decided not to wear a dress. I had the seamstress make me some trousers and a few blouses to wear around the castle. She also made me a corset made of witch leather, which was far more comfortable than the stiff corsets worn here. Kaizer looked me up and down, not commenting on my wardrobe but surely marking it.

"How was the wall?" I asked.

"We are secure, ready for Dusra to enter tomorrow," he answered.

Some of the staff came over and set down platters of steaming hot food. The smell of the eggs, bacon, and pastries all mixing together into something that had my mouth watering. Above all those smells, the scent of blood wafted over to me as a small woman set down a chalice filled with goat's blood.

I could barely contain myself. "Thank you," I whispered as I lifted it to my lips and downed the whole entire cup.

I hadn't had any blood last night in favor of exploring, and all the transporting had waned down some of my reserves. The potent power in the blood trickled through my body, filling up my pool of magic to the brim once again. I had gotten much lower before, but I preferred to always be filled to the top. Some blood trickled down the corner of my mouth, and I used my tongue to lick it up, peering back at Kaizer across the table.

"I don't understand how anything could taste better than a person's blood, but you make that look like a delicacy," he mumbled.

"People taste like what they put into their bodies. Most people don't take care of themselves well enough to taste better than an animal that only feeds off the earth," I responded.

"And if they do take care of their body?" he asked, smirking.

I shrugged. "I suppose they may taste a little better."

"The theory could be tested," he teased and scooped some scrambled eggs into his mouth.

I brought the chalice to my lips. "I suppose, but I don't have a lot of interest in that when I have this."

"You might find you like it one day," he replied, but quickly continued. "Are you ready for tomorrow?"

"I am. You haven't given me the opportunity to be unprepared." I raised a brow.

Kaizer hadn't stopped talking about what to expect with the Dusrans after our initial meeting. He had an itinerary dropped off at my room and even talking points to make sure they believed we didn't mean them harm.

"Well, I'm sure I don't have to remind you," he started.

"But you will?" I quipped.

"Look at you, already knowing me so well," he laughed out. "They will arrive tomorrow. We will meet them at the outer gate and give them a tour of the capital. We'll have lunch in the great hall on the first floor, and then we will move into the more serious topics in the office off the throne room."

"I remember," I responded, taking a bite out of my bacon.

"I know you can handle yourself, but these are dangerous people. I'm having Quinn stay with you while they are here," he said.

I rolled my eyes. "That is not necessary."

"It isn't necessary, but I'm taking all precautions. If, for some reason, they tried to use you against me and they hurt you, I'd never forgive myself."

"They'd have to get me to hurt me," I responded dryly.

"All the same, Quinn will be your personal guard. Just until they leave our borders," he said absolutely.

"Fine," I muttered, knowing if I wanted to lose her, I could do so.

Kaizer didn't say anything, so I looked up to see him pinning me down with such an intense stare I sat back in my chair slightly.

"Something wrong?" I asked, and the predatory stare grew stronger.

"No." He shook his head. "I'm just on edge. I'll be glad when this is all over. I can't focus on what the future of our kingdoms is until I know they won't wage war against us."

I nodded, relaxing slightly

"I just..." he started, looking down at his plate. "I need blood."

"Where's Athena?"

"I don't want her blood," he snapped, his calm composure slipping. "I haven't had her blood since our conversation."

I knew he wasn't as collected as he made himself appear.

"You haven't had any blood since then?"

"No," he responded.

We all got our power from blood, but vampires needed it for more than just their magic. If they went too long without the substance, or used too much magic without replenishing, it threatened to drive them mad—into bloodlust. Whereas witches just didn't have access to our pool of power. That alone could drive you crazy, but not in the same way as the vampires. Kaizer stood from his chair and walked around the table slowly. He pulled out my chair and leaned onto the armrests, caging me in his body.

"I need *your* blood," he muttered.

"Why mine?"

His eyes ran up my scar free neck. "We talked about the significance of the mark."

"That's just a mark. Why do you need *my* blood?"

"I felt your power yesterday. Vampires search for the most powerful source and latch onto it. Before, I just didn't want any issues, but now?" He dipped his body closer to me. "Now your blood calls to me. It screams for me to come and take it by force. I don't want to do that. I want you to want me to do it, but at a certain point, I won't be able to contain myself any longer," he growled.

"I won't ever want it," I whispered, my heart beating so fast at his closeness I wasn't sure if it was the truth or a lie.

"I'm reaching that point, Daya. I'm creeping into bloodlust. If you don't allow me to do it, I'll just end up hunting you down and taking it."

"You'd have to overpower me," I mumbled.

"You're strong, but a vampire in bloodlust is strong beyond belief. The only thing rattling in their brain is to be fed, to get that power."

My throat bobbed and my lips parted slightly. "Does it take my magic?"

"No, it doesn't affect your reserves. It'll immobilize you for a moment, but once my venom runs through you, you'll be fine. You just won't have access to your magic until I pull my fangs out."

"I don't like the sound of immobilization," I muttered.

The sudden realization that he was so close to me, his breath brushing over my cheek and my face nearly in his own neck hit me. "What would you need your body for while I drink from you?"

I scooted away with some force and stood up from the chair. "Again, you'll have to overpower me," I offered, a rush of adrenaline coursing through my veins at the challenge.

"This isn't a game," he said through tight teeth.

Sounded like a fucking fantastic game to me.

"Seems like you'll be losing, then. If you can take it, you can have it."

I created a portal behind me and stepped through it with a wave to a furious Kaizer. He stepped forward to enter the portal, but I snapped it shut and ran through the middle realm. This castle was ridiculously minimalistic, and there weren't many great places to hide. I didn't want to go into the tunnels if he really could smell my blood. I still didn't know if that was literal, but I didn't want him to know I used them.

I hadn't done enough exploring outside yet, but I noticed a ledge above his courtyard that looked like it led to the roof, so I snapped open a portal there. My feet met the loose rubble of the roof a few inches from the ledge and I looked over to see his perfectly groomed courtyard below. My heart was beating so fast with the anticipation and thrill of being chased I could barely hear another hurried heartbeat getting closer. I stayed a few inches from the ledge as boots scuffed against the stones below, and I heard a growl emit from Kaizer's chest. I smirked and leaned closer to peer over, but jumped back immediately when he nearly barreled into me.

Fuck, I guess he really can smell me.

His eyes were bloodshot, his fingers were twitching slightly at his side as he slowly walked toward me. "I found you," he muttered, "give me your blood."

"Deal was you had to catch me," I said as I snapped open a portal and transported directly behind him.

I jumped down from the roof with my air magic blasting from my fists to soften my landing. His courtyard was completely isolated, so I ran toward his room. A loud thud sounded behind me and I looked back to see Kaizer extinguishing flames from his hands as he picked up his pace to chase me. Laughter escaped my throat, and I hated myself for enjoying this the way I was. He was truly into bloodlust now, only his primal instincts guiding him.

I kicked myself into a full run toward the door of his chamber, but he threw up a wall of fire I couldn't pass through. I lifted my hand to suck the oxygen from the fire as I felt him approaching from behind me. I twisted as he barreled toward me, and I quickly sidestepped him with a burst of air, forcing him into the wall behind me. He came for me again, and I slashed my nails across his chest, ripping his shirt and pulling blood from his body.

Interesting. I didn't think I could hurt him.

He barely flinched at the wound and grabbed my wrist before I could pull it back. I yanked my wrist, and found he wasn't wrong about the strength he possessed in this state. I flipped over his head with the help of my magic, dragging his hand with me as his arm extended above his head. He released my hand before I dislocated his shoulder, but he used his other arm to elbow me in the side, hard enough to knock me down. Kaizer turned around, and I swiped his leg, sending him tumbling over in front of me. I jumped over his body, but he grabbed my ankle mid-air and threw me over to his bed. I was thankful for the soft landing, but his blankets were made of silk, and as I tried to scramble to get up, it took me longer than I expected.

Kaizer jumped over onto the bed as I reached the edge, grabbing me by my wrists and pinning them above my head. He straddled me and shifted all of his weight onto my wrists and hips. I bucked, and he smiled, his hair falling in front of his face as the pieces of his shirt hung from him. He moved so fast I barely registered it, a sharp pain in my neck forcing a grunt from me as my power flickered away and I was momentarily paralyzed. The sharp pain transformed into a dull pain and then into a warm, tingling sensation bursting from my neck into every crevice of my body as I regained the ability to move.

Kaizer moaned into my neck, and I felt the fully hardened length of his cock as he pushed his hips into mine. My blood rushed from my veins and into his mouth, making me slightly heady as I squirmed underneath him, a movement that caused a moan to escape my throat as he rubbed against my pussy. He put more weight on my hips and my wrists, trying to force me to stay still as he continued drinking from me. Now so vigorously that I started to think this game wasn't a good idea. I didn't know how much blood vampires needed or how fast they came out of bloodlust when they did get blood. I couldn't see his face, just his corded arms straining to keep me in one place. An orgasm was building in my core, I wasn't sure how, but I couldn't help but grind up against him.

"Stop that," he muttered around my neck. "I'm not done."

I continued moving my hips slowly, and his weight pulled off from me slightly to allow me to move, showing he didn't really want me to stop. I ran my fingers up his arms and across his chest, then down his hard abdomen. He growled, seemingly stuck between wanting me to continue and wanting to get his full serving of blood, and I chuckled as I continued the torture. He slid one of his hands behind my back and pulled me close to him, twisting us around and sitting me in his lap as he sat us up with his mouth still on my neck.

The position made it much easier for me to move, and I dragged my hips at a faster pace as he gripped my ass with one hand and the back of my head with the other. Our clothes were painfully rough between us, and he pulled his fangs from my neck and immediately claimed my lips with his own. He slid his tongue into my mouth, forcing the taste of my blood onto my tongue, which I was oddly okay with. I ripped his tattered shirt off his body and slid my nails down his back, not hard enough to pull blood but enough to hurt. He growled, the vibrations in my mouth shooting pleasure right down to my core.

He licked the excess blood off my neck and ripped my shirt, which was already ruined with blood, a mixture of my own and his. My shirt hung around my corset, exposing my breasts to him, and he stilled for a moment as he took them in. He grabbed them both in his hands and took one nipple into his warm mouth as I ground against him once again, sending me so close to ecstasy I almost couldn't take it. Kaizer flipped me onto my back and pulled my pants down, my breathing heavy as I felt the heat of his face between my legs.

"I told you I wasn't done," he muttered before sinking his fangs into my inner thigh.

I screamed as the pain waned into pleasure again, and his fingers trailed up my legs. He pushed his fingers straight into me, gliding through the wetness already waiting for him. He pulled them out and slid them into his mouth while he continued drinking the blood from my thigh. "You're perfect," he muttered, the words muffled.

Kaizer ran his fingers back up my leg, but instead of pushing inside of me, he traced slow circles around my clit like he could feel how close I was.

"Kaizer," I moaned.

He groaned at the sound of his name on my lips and picked the pace up as he pulled his fangs from my thigh. The warm feel of his tongue licking straight up my pussy forced a scream that had to be heard around the castle from my throat. He feasted on me, licking and biting as he pushed his fingers in and out of me faster than before. His tongue ran up to my clit as he flicked and sucked down on it, and every spot of my body felt like it was lit with fire. Kaizer trailed one hand up my body as he grasped my breast and rolled my nipple between his fingers. My hips bucked again at the blissful pain, and he brought his hand back down, but put his forearm across my hips, pushing down on my lower stomach. The combination of his mouth and the pressure sent me over the edge immediately, and he drank up every last bit of my orgasm. He climbed over my body as I trembled beneath him, small aftershocks running through me.

"You lost," he muttered.

I looked down at my body, my legs still shaking. "Did I, though?"

"Well, I certainly feel like I won," he said, pushing himself off me and standing at the end of the bed.

His cock was still straining at his pants, somehow looking even bigger than before.

I sat up and pushed my palm against it. "Winners get to come," I said, as I looked up at him through my lashes.

"By those standards, yes, you are the winner," he laughed.

"I'll make you one, too," I whispered, before pulling his pants down and freeing the long, hard length of him.

I selfishly wanted to come about five more times, and I could give him one before he gave me more.

"You'll find no objections here," Kaizer said cockily.

I smirked and pulled him back onto the bed, climbing over his body and taking him into my hand, teasing him with a long drag of my tongue from base to tip as his whole body went tight. I pushed his tip between my lips and flicked my tongue around it before taking his whole cock in my mouth. I slid my mouth up and down, gripping the base of him.

"Just like that," he growled, his hand falling to my head as he gripped my hair.

His tip bumped the back of my throat as he guided my head, and I brought my other hand over, twisting and squeezing as I sucked. I felt the tension building, the pleasure he was experiencing getting me wet all over again.

"SIR!" a female voice yelled as they pushed through the door to his bedchamber.

I sat up quickly, nearly biting his dick off in surprise as Quinn stood in the doorway, once again catching us in an awkward position. At least last time, I wasn't throat-deep around a cock. *Fuck.*

"What the hell is wrong with you?" Kaizer boomed.

"I'm sorry, there's a riot approaching the inner wall. I would never charge in here like this otherwise," Quinn said, not looking either of us in the eye.

I wiped my mouth. "A riot?" I questioned as I grabbed my shirt, the shirt that was torn in half and certainly wouldn't be covering anything.

"Yes, some people are upset about your union still," Quinn explained.

"Fuck, I'll be right there," Kaizer mumbled as he went to his closet for new clothes, granting me a view of his sculpted ass.

"*We'll* be right there," I exclaimed, and Quinn nodded before she ran out of the room.

"I need a shirt," I said, walking over to the closet he had entered.

He pulled a white linen shirt over his head. "No, you don't. You're staying here."

"I'm not. Give me a shirt, or I'll go like this," I said, with my hand outstretched.

He yanked down a shirt identical to his and placed it in my hands before stepping into a pair of trousers. I put the shirt on while I ran out into the bedroom and pulled on my pants and the witch leather corset, the only significant protection I had. Kaizer walked out of the room with two swords and handed me one with what looked like a lot of reluctance.

"I thought I couldn't hurt you," I said, nodding toward his chest where I scratched.

"You didn't have intent to kill," he responded quickly. "Stay with me," he finished as we stormed out of the room, and he ran toward the closest exit.

I threw a portal out in front of us and transported us outside to the guard station in the inner wall. Quinn was just reaching the guard station as we appeared, and her eyebrows shot up.

I shrugged. "Witch shit."

"What are we dealing with?" Kaizer asked the guard in charge of this station.

"They're upset about her," he said, pointing to me with vigor. "They don't want our kingdoms to join peacefully. They want us to take it by force and not have to bend to any witch bitches."

"How eloquent," I muttered.

"Sounds like you agree with them?" Kaizer growled with a step toward him.

"I do," he said with a step toward me, his hand on his weapon. "She probably put a spell on you with her puss—" He was cut off by my blade dragging across his neck.

"Now that's been taken care of," I sighed, wiping my dagger down his shirt to remove the blood from it. "What else do we know?" I asked another guard nearby as I took a dagger off the dead guard's body and tucked it into a strap on my corset. Kaizer looked like he was going to explode, but I didn't care. The guard swallowed hard, and I took a slow step toward him as well.

"They're approaching from the east. It's not the entire kingdom by any means, but it's enough to be worried," he exclaimed before I could get any closer.

"Who is leading them?" Quinn asked.

"Lady Payne," the guard whimpered, and I couldn't stop the laughter from escaping my throat.

"Of course it is, the vindictive little bitch," I muttered.

"You don't speak a word of this," Kaizer said, pointing toward the dead guard.

The still living guard nodded rapidly as Kaizer turned the corpse into ash, and his remains flew away in the breeze.

"You can't just go around killing my men," Kaizer growled at me.

"Sure I can. Especially when they're siding with the fucking rioters," I snapped.

"Let's go," Kaizer said through tight teeth.

If Athena wanted a fight, I'd give her one.

Chapter Thirteen

"This feels like a moment I should say I told you so," I whispered to Kaizer as we ran along the wall to the east side.

"It's probably because I told her I didn't want to continue our arrangement when she told me you threatened to kill her," Kaizer responded.

"Well, now I get to fulfill that threat," I said with a smile that had Quinn looking at me sideways.

"You really are a dangerous little thing, aren't you?" she said with a chuckle.

"Let's try to talk to her first," Kaizer interjected, pissing me off so soon after he got me off.

We reached the east guard tower and climbed the stairs to get to the top of the wall. Just as the guard stated, a group of angry people approached the wall, screaming about me and the witches. Lady Payne stood at the front of the crowd, her red hair flowing behind her in the wind. She had a few guards between her and the riot, but the crowd followed her all the same.

"She works fast," I grumbled.

"Never doubt the power of gossip here, Dayanara," Quinn responded, placing herself between the wall's edge and me.

I looked over at Kaizer. "Don't tell me the personal guard shit is starting now."

He was staring down at the riot, his anger bubbling over as he gripped the edge of the wall so hard cracks splintered beneath his hold.

"I don't understand why she is so set against this," he growled.

"Because she wanted the power that came with this position. A woman like that thinks she's owed things," I said, rolling my eyes.

Athena separated herself from the group further as she walked toward where we stood on the wall.

"You know why we're here, Kaizer," Athena boomed.

"It's King Kaizer to you!" Quinn yelled.

"All the same. Get rid of the witch, take me as your bride, and we will stop the riot," Athena responded with a slight shrug.

"You honestly think he wants anything to do with you after this?" I asked.

"We all know that you are manipulating him. He'll realize that this was a mistake, and he'll be thankful I was there to fix it," she said, brushing her skirt down as if the conversation bored her.

I looked over to Kaizer, waiting for his response, but he stared out into the crowd, unmoving.

"There's only a few hundred of them," he muttered to Quinn. "Get soldiers to the gate and along the wall."

"I decline your proposal," Kaizer yelled loud enough for the crowd to hear. "Leave now, or there will be consequences."

"You won't kill me, baby," Athena exclaimed, and I laughed at the sheer confidence she spoke with.

A stampede of footsteps rushed up the stairs as guards crested the wall, the archers aiming their bows into the crowd. More soldiers appeared on the ground, forming a line between the gate and the riot. Athena didn't budge, just smiled at them as she glanced over at her guards. They all lifted their weapons, clearly not planning on backing down.

"I am what is best for this kingdom. A noble vampire, someone who knows the kingdom and its people. All of these people agree. We can bring Caldera down, kill her, and we can be together. We'll bring this kingdom back to its greatness," she said as she held her arms out in expectation.

Kaizer unsheathed his sword. "There's no going back, Lady Payne. Move on."

"Then we will kill her ourselves," she said, stepping back behind her guard. The riot moved forward, people screaming with their swords outstretched toward the guards at the base of the wall.

"I have to say, I feel pretty important right now. All this fuss just for me," I joked, and Kaizer looked at me with his brows high.

Quinn yelled out a command that had every soldier readying for an attack, and she looked over at Kaizer for a signal.

"This is great, the day before Dusra arrives—attack!" Kaizer yelled, sidestepping me to get to the stairs.

I followed behind him, and he held out his arm to stop me from following. "Stay here."

"No," I said before ducking under his arm and darting down the stairs.

Kaizer grabbed me by my shoulder and spun me around. "You are the reason they are here. If you go down there, you give them what they want. The opportunity to kill you."

"Don't forget who I am," I grumbled, "I can handle this."

"Can't you ever just listen?"

I snarled. "Can't you ever stop being a sexist asshole?"

"This has nothing to do with you being a woman. They want to kill you," he said, pushing me against the wall with his arm to get by.

"This will never work if all you try to do is protect me. I don't need the protection, and you can't stop me," I said as I opened a portal behind me and stepped onto the battlefield.

I left it open for Kaizer to come through, but I didn't wait for him to start attacking. One of the assailants charged me, and I smiled as the familiar sound of battle filled my ears, the sweetest song in existence. I ripped the oxygen from his lungs, and he gasped for air, holding his neck as I pushed my sword into his heart. I yanked out my weapon as someone else stepped toward me, and I whirled around to defend myself, but it was just Kaizer.

"Go back to the wall," he exclaimed before turning around and stopping a blade from slashing him in the gut.

"No," I yelled, running over to the next riot member.

I almost felt bad; most of these people weren't skilled soldiers, just regular people who had access to the average magic of their region. This wasn't a calculated attack, this was a last ditch effort that these people weren't prepared for. A ball of fire came for me, and I swept the flames to the side with a blast of air. I yanked the dagger from my corset and threw it at the attacker, hitting him in the neck. Blood poured from him, an indication that I hit the main vein as he fell forward. I grabbed my blade out of his neck and immediately threw it again at another attacker charging for me. The dagger embedded in his eye, and he screamed as he yanked it out and threw it to the ground. Another man approached, and I sent out a stream of my witch magic extending like lightning from my fingers and hitting him straight in his chest. He fell to the ground unmoving as Kaizer appeared beside me and dug his sword into the man's gut.

"I had that handled," I muttered before bending over to grab my dagger from the ground.

He growled and ran in the other direction at someone getting closer to the gate as he threw a stream of fire in front of the man to block him. I looked around, the battle now raging, but the castle guards were having no difficulty putting the riot down. A flash of red hair caught my attention as it blew in a breeze behind a building to my left. I chuckled darkly as I sauntered over to where Athena was hiding, clearing a path through the last two of her guards standing with ease.

Fire danced around her fingers as I stood before her and she yelled, "Stop!"

"Did you honestly believe you'd be able to bring me down?" I asked as I twisted the handle of my sword in my hand and grabbed my dagger.

"You don't deserve this. I do. If I don't have this, I have nothing!" she bellowed as she blasted me with more power than I expected from the proper little lady.

I stole the oxygen from her flames with a flick of my wrist and threw the dagger at her stomach, exactly where I aimed. She screamed and fell on her ass, and I pushed her down, yanking the blade from her stomach and straddling her waist.

I ran the blade down her neck. "Don't fuck with the brujas," I muttered as I lifted the dagger to end her life.

Someone caught my wrist, and I twisted to find Kaizer holding my arm back from killing the bitch.

"Let me go," I yelled and pulled my arm out of his grasp.

"She needs to be questioned," Kaizer said.

I growled and threw the dagger into the side of the building so hard fissures ran from the point of contact all the way up to the roof. Before I removed myself from Athena, I leaned down to her ear and whispered, "This isn't done. I know where the dungeons are."

She shrieked as I removed the pressure from her wound, and blood trickled down her leg onto the ground. "Don't you see she's crazy? She tried to kill me!" Athena yelled, crying and throwing herself into Kaizer's body.

Kaizer pushed her off him and over to Quinn, who appeared behind him at some point during my attempted murder.

"You brought this upon yourself. Look around. Every death here today sits on your head," Kaizer boomed, stretching his arms out around us.

"I did it because I love you! I love our kingdom! You'll see! She'll be the end of us all!" she yelled as Quinn dragged her away to the castle dungeons.

"Get this cleaned up!" Kaizer yelled to no guard in particular, but they all hurried to stack the bodies in a pile and pick up their weapons.

"Thank you for not killing her," Kaizer muttered, "we need to know if she had any other help and if this issue will arise again."

"I didn't promise I wouldn't kill her in the future," I grumbled.

"I don't understand how she was capable of this," he responded, ignoring the threat in my words.

"You should expect the absolute worst from everyone, then you'll never be caught off guard," I mumbled.

Kaizer looked at me like the words struck a chord in him, a crease lining his brow as he peered down at me. Rows of men were on their knees with their hands bound behind their backs as guards dragged each one toward the dungeons. A flame went up behind them; the dead being burned right outside the gate.

"Is this always what you do with your dead?"

"We're born of the flame in Sanjry. We die with the flame. No matter who you are," he replied sadly.

I wondered if he was starting to regret his decision to join our kingdoms now. Death still found its way into his land and by its own hand rather than Caldera's. Was one worse than the other? I couldn't be sure.

"Get the acolytes out here to perform the death ritual," Kaizer said to a guard nearby.

The guard hurried toward the temple I'd seen before, but this time I had a much better view of it. The building was massive, made of the whitest stone I'd ever seen. It had no windows, the only thing on the whole structure was a burning tree etched into the very tip of it. The grooves were aflame, making the tree actually appear as if it was burning. I didn't see the bell that was always ringing, but I was sure it was somewhere around here.

"Let's get back inside," Kaizer said before grabbing my hand and dragging me along with him.

Villagers came out of their houses to watch the commotion; some of them held my eye and nodded, appreciating my show of power. Some of them looked less than happy, but no one else attacked. Figures in dark orange robes left the temple and slowly walked over to the site. I heard mumblings as they passed us, but couldn't make out what they were saying. We walked through the gate and back into the castle as I looked down at my body. I hadn't been covered in this much blood and grime since the battle, an oddity to my typical life.

"How are your reserves?" I whispered as I ran my finger over the mark on my neck.

I didn't even have the time to look at the bite mark since we were dragged out into battle so quickly.

"I barely used any magic. I'm fine," he answered with a small smile.

"Are you okay?" Zuri yelled from across the room as she barreled into me and inspected my entire body. Her gaze ran up and down with a countenance in her eyes nobody had ever looked at me with. Her mouth was hanging open, her eyes wide and filled with...worry?

"Most of the blood isn't mine," I reassured her as my throat bobbed at the emotions radiating from her.

She looked over to Kaizer and took a step back to curtsy. "Your Majesty, I apologize," she said bashfully.

"No need to apologize," he said with a warm smile. "Please make sure she is taken care of."

"Of course," she said, turning and leading me away from him.

I looked back over my shoulder at Kaizer, who stood tall, but I could see in his eyes how affected he was about the events outside. Quinn ran over and whispered something to him; he nodded and followed her out of my line of sight.

"What happened?" Zuri asked frantically.

"Fucking Athena. She brought a riot to the gates to try to kill me and take the position of queen for herself."

Zuri looked up and down for injuries again. "She's delusional."

"Understatement. Kaizer stopped me before I could kill her so they could question her."

"She's threatening you. That makes sense," Zuri reasoned.

I growled. "She wouldn't be a threat if she were dead. Although, she did say something interesting, that she had nothing if she didn't have this."

Zuri cocked her head to the side. "She's a vampire of noble standing, even if she doesn't become queen, she still has plenty."

I shrugged as we made it to my room and Zuri ran to the bathroom to run a bath.

"Is that Kaizer's shirt?" she asked as she re-entered the room.

"It is," I muttered as I pulled it off my body and wiped away some of the blood on my face and skin with it.

Zuri gasped. "You let him bite you," she whispered.

"It's not a secret," I laughed. "Hence the mark remaining."

"I just didn't think you'd actually do it," she said as she took the shirt from my hands and gestured for me to take my pants off. I pulled my filthy trousers off and handed them to her as she threw them into a basket for washing.

"He was in bloodlust, and I didn't exactly get nothing in return," I chuckled as I walked over to the tub. The water was scalding hot, a cloud of dirt and blood escaping from my body as I dipped myself in.

"Bites can do that." She giggled and handed me the bar of soap. "Does this mean you're fully in now?"

I'd been fairly open with Zuri about some of my reservations, not all of them, but she knew that this wasn't my ideal situation.

"I think I have to be. There's no other way to ensure the longevity of my kingdom," I said before dipping my face under the water and resurfacing. "Besides, depending on how tomorrow goes, both of our kingdoms could be goners."

"True." Zuri huffed a laugh. "Are you prepared?"

"Kaizer made sure of it. We have the entire day planned. What I'm not sure about is the actual discussion around the kingdoms. It all depends on what he has to say," I explained.

I didn't express that concern to Kaizer as he already seemed to be on edge about the whole situation. But we couldn't plan for that part; we could come up with some hypotheticals until we knew how the king of Dusra felt about the union.

"I'm sure everything will go fine," Zuri offered before stepping away from the tub, a poor reassurance, really.

I watched as Zuri cleaned up around the bathtub and wiped down the marble sink in the bathroom. I knew Zuri cared for me, her actions thus far and the crystal made that more than evident. But the look in her eye when we came back into the castle shocked me slightly. She hummed to herself, like she always seemed to do mindlessly and I listened to the sweet tune, letting it calm me as I continued watching her. In a world of chaos, of doubts, pain, and blood, Zuri felt so...peaceful. She bent down to pick up something from the floor and her hair fell in front of her eyes; she tucked the curl behind her ear and looked over at me with a smile.

"What?" she asked.

"Are you happy?"

"Very random, Daya," she said with a laugh. "I suppose so, I'd say I've been happier recently, though."

I swore I saw some blush rise into her cheeks before she quickly looked away.

I cleared my throat. "I'm going to drain this water and sit in the bath for a while. Feel free to do something else if there are things you need to do," I said, hoping she would take the dismissal and not insist on helping me.

She nodded and exited the room as I unplugged the bath and re-ran the water until it was crystal clear again. I sat in the water, letting the warmth soothe my muscles. I dipped my face under the water, the lack of salts this time making it easier for me to open my eyes.

I had to be *the* queen tomorrow. Queen of Sanjry. 'Queen' of Caldera. Whatever this joined kingdom was to be. Staying under the water even longer than last time, I made to move when the sides of my eyes turned dark. I resurfaced and gasped for air, laying my head back against the side of the tub and watching the bubbles rise to the surface from my movement. Letting the burning in my chest fuel me, I reminded myself that my kingdom relied on me, and I wouldn't fail them.

Chapter Fourteen

I hadn't seen my mother in a few days. I wasn't sure if she was even in Sanjry or if she had returned to Caldera since the last time I saw her. She rarely found the need to let me know what she was doing unless it involved me. She popped back up today, though, just in time for us to *welcome* Dusra in at the gate. She wore a simple black dress that hugged her slight curves, the neckline high, and the sleeves long. Her hair was pulled into a low bun, showing off her beautiful face. While she wasn't a nice person by any means, she was stunning. She was the one who taught me to use my beauty to my advantage. Advice I did take into consideration today when getting ready. Unlike my mother's high neckline, mine plunged low; Kaizer would have had an issue with it had his mark not been more visible this way. The fabric was dark purple, the color of my kingdom, tight through the hips and loosening just at the top of my thighs. My sleeves were sheer and gathered at the wrist in a ruby cuff, as well as a ruby necklace to match my sizable engagement ring. I hadn't worn it too often, only during events with Kaizer, as it was heavier than I preferred.

My mother, Zuri, and I approached the foyer where we were meeting before going to the gate. Kaizer and his advisers already stood by the door, talking in hushed tones. Kaizer wore black trousers and a dark red tunic, matching the rubies I wore. Half his hair was pulled up into a knot, a style I hadn't seen yet. I wondered why today of all days he decided to try something new with his hair. He fidgeted with the hem of his tunic and looked up at me as we entered the space, his mouth dropping open slightly as he took me in. His eyes immediately fell to the mark on my neck, an arrogant smirk gracing his lips.

"Any update on the riots?" I asked.

"She only had one lord backing her, I think the effort was rushed due to her trying to kill you before the meeting with Dusra. I have some people going out to the other major cities to ensure there are no more connections or threats," Otto replied.

"You don't think the rest of them would have sided with her?" my mother asked.

Kaizer shook his head. "Most of them are avid Embers, they believe the Flame is guiding our way out of war."

"The Flame?" I questioned.

Otto clapped. "Time to go."

Nobody answered my question as they all moved toward the exit. Kaizer looked over to my mother, and she threw a portal wide enough for us all to step through in front of us. We appeared at the front gate and found Dusra waiting for us on the other side. There had to be at least fifty soldiers with them, dressed in impressive black armor that seemed to soak up any light around it. A group of five people stood in the middle of them with their backs turned to us, surely the king and his advisers. A sign they truly trusted the soldiers with them on watch.

"I'll go let them through the gate, you all stay here, and I'll come back and introduce you," Kaizer said, gesturing for Abel to follow him.

Otto stayed with us, his back ramrod straight. This was the first time I'd seen him with less than five weapons strapped to him, only his sword on his side. Zuri still stood beside me, her foot tapping against the floor.

"You okay?" I asked her.

"Just nervous," Zuri said, "I probably shouldn't have come out here with you."

"I'm glad you are," I responded with a gentle smile she returned.

My mother scoffed. "Quit your babbling. Here they come." Drawing my attention back to the group.

Kaizer turned on his heel as he led the group toward us and one of the Dusran men yelled to the soldiers to follow. My mother and Otto stepped forward in anticipation, but I remained by Zuri's side, a sudden burst of nerves overtaking me. The tallest of the group Kaizer was talking to turned toward us, and all my breath left my chest.

"Fuck me," I whispered, and Zuri scooted closer to me.

"What's wrong?"

"Nothing," I lied.

The man in the center of it all, undeniably the king by the authority he moved with was Ax. The man I flirted with at the bar, the man who had unknowingly lifted some of the weight off my shoulders for a few minutes. Possibly the most attractive man I'd ever seen before. He was the fucking King of Dusra. I stood stunned as Ax's gaze locked in mine, and he smirked just enough for me to catch it before turning his attention back to Kaizer.

"Fuck me, fuck me, fuck me," I whispered again, my stomach doing flips.

Zuri grabbed my hand. "Seriously, what is wrong with you?"

"Nothing, I'm just nervous," I lied again, and she gave me a sideways look that conveyed she didn't believe that for a second.

"King Kiaan Axel Vohra. I go by Axel," Ax introduced himself to my mother.

"It's a pleasure, King Axel. I am Lupe Amapola, the Acna of Caldera," she said, giving him one of her perfectly crafted smiles.

"This is my betrothed, Lupe's daughter, Dayanara," Kaizer said as they came to stand before me.

"Dayanara, that's beautiful. What does it mean?" *King Axel* asked me.

"It means forceful," I responded.

He chuckled darkly. "Seems like it fits."

Axel reached his hand out for mine and I lifted it, he held me lightly, bending over to bring it to his lips to place a kiss along my fingers. "A pleasure," he muttered, his mouth still on my hand.

Kaizer cleared his throat, and Ax, *King Axel,* winked at me through his dark curls before straightening and looking over to Zuri.

"This is my handmaiden, Zuri," I said, my voice cracking slightly.

He nodded. "A pleasure to meet you, Zuri."

Zuri shuffled on her feet like she wasn't sure if she should curtsy at him and offered him a partial smile. "The pleasure is mine," she muttered, blush blooming on her cheeks.

The others from his council came over, all of them just as ridiculously beautiful as him.

"These are all of my most trusted advisers." He held his hand out to the woman on the left, who I could guess was his sister based on their very similar features. "My sister, Ishani, the commander of my armies," he said before moving his hand to the man next to her, a man with ebony skin and cropped black hair. "Paxx, who is in charge of intelligence," King Axel said.

I had no idea what that meant, but I continued listening and nodding at each.

"Xavier, my second in command," he said as he pointed to another man who looked fairly similar to him. His hair was straight and long but with the same hazel eyes and light brown coloring as the king.

"Last, Akari, Ishani's highest-ranking general," he said with his hand stretched toward a woman with warm brown skin and blonde hair braided into what looked like hundreds of tiny braids.

I clasped my hands in front of me. "A pleasure to meet you all."

"We have the first half of the day planned," Kaizer exclaimed, bringing my attention back to him, who I actually forgot existed in the past few minutes.

"Lead the way," King Axel replied.

"We'll show you some of our lands and a few other things we are particularly proud of," Kaizer followed up as he led the group toward a few carriages lined up at the gate.

King Axel nodded and followed behind him over to the carriages. He wasn't particularly warm, but not as menacing as the Sanjryans described him.

"I'll see you when you get back to the castle," Zuri said, and I nodded as I turned to follow the group.

"I wasn't expecting so many soldiers," Kaizer lied, "there is only room for the ten of us between the two carriages."

"Can someone lead my men to where they'll be staying?" King Axel asked.

"Yes, Quinn," Kaizer yelled over to the line of soldiers on the wall. "Take them to the barracks. There should be enough room for them all."

Quinn nodded, directing the soldiers to follow.

"You all can take this one." Kaizer pointed to the carriage on the left. "The driver knows where to go."

They all piled into the carriage as we entered ours, the door slamming behind us.

"He is not what I was expecting," Kaizer muttered. "Is it going well?" he asked Otto and Abel.

They both nodded. "I think so," Abel replied.

The carriage started to move, rocking us slightly as the horses carried us over the cobblestone road.

"We're going to the temple first," Kaizer said as if we all weren't aware. "The art there is a good testament to our wealth."

We all nodded, and I was just thankful nobody but Zuri caught onto my raging anxiety when I faced the Dusran king. We rode the rest of the way in silence, Kaizer's foot tapping the only sound inside the carriage. As soon as the door opened, Kaizer jumped out of his seat and exited. I was the last out so the driver helped me down since my dress made it difficult to jump down like the others did. King Axel stepped out of his carriage at the same time I did mine. I found a smirk gracing his lips as he looked me up and down while the rest of our party had already started to move toward the temple. We met at the bottom step, everyone else already pushing through the door.

"I told you our paths would cross again. The bite mark looks good on you," he muttered, "I don't remember that being there."

"It's new," I whispered, wishing there were more stairs to climb so I could confront him about what the fuck was going on.

He held the door open for me, and heat rose into my cheeks as he undoubtedly checked me out from behind.

"This building is one of the oldest in Sanjry," Kaizer started, gesturing to the surrounding walls. "The art has been added over the years, but its essence remains."

King Axel stepped around me and joined his council as Kaizer walked over to me and offered his arm with a painfully fake smile. I looped my arm in his, and he moved to the first painting. This was my first time here too, so I was actually interested to see what the Sanjryans considered art. It was an abstract piece, so I couldn't tell what it was a picture of, a painting in blacks, grays, and whites void of any color.

"The Piedra," Kaizer said, pulling me toward him with a little too much gusto. "The barrier between Malva and Bonda."

The Dusrans all nodded before following along as he moved to the next painting and disentangled his arm from mine. I shifted to the back of the group for a better view of what was going on. My mother stepped closer to Kaizer in my absence, pretending to be interested in the art and whatever history this also particularly abstract painting held.

A marble sculpture of a woman drew my attention across the room, and I shifted over to get a better view while Kaizer continued talking. The woman was beautiful, the veins of gold marble running through her body somehow all flowing in directions that made her look like she was in motion. She stood with her foot on a rock, her hand pointing out like she was finding something for the first time. Her hair was beautifully crafted, her long curls looking soft to the touch. The metal plate beneath her said 'The First Queen,' with no further description.

"Interesting," King Axel's voice sounded from behind me.

"She's beautiful," I muttered.

"That's not what I found interesting, but yes, a beautiful vampire queen. Although my tastes seem to vary slightly these days," he muttered, coming to stand beside me with his hands behind his back. "The first Queen of Sanjry did not look like this, but the first Queen of Dusra did."

I turned my head to the side, surveying the statue. The arch of her nose was incredibly similar to Ishani's and her hair the same curl pattern.

"Holy shit," I muttered.

"Ah, yes, our first queen!" Kaizer exclaimed from across the room.

"Let's add that to our list of secrets, shall we? I wonder what else we can add to that list before I leave?" Axel whispered before Kaizer made it over to us.

"A magnificent sculpture," Kaizer said as he came to my side.

"Indeed," Axel agreed.

Kaizer gripped my fingers and pulled me along to the next painting, and I was unsure if he was jealous or if he was still nervous about making Sanjry look good. We walked through all the paintings in the space and ended up back in the carriages to take him to the farmland. Kaizer and his advisers spoke about how we were handling the rest of the day, and my mother watched me through slitted eyes as I was uncharacteristically quiet. I nodded to appear engaged in the conversation, and she looked away from me and chimed in on whatever they were talking about. I needed to get Axel alone at some point so I could ask how he was here so early without Sanjry knowing. Although I wasn't sure he would share that information with me. I just wanted to ensure he didn't mention seeing me, but that would give him away, so I was probably safe enough.

The carriage pulled to a stop again, and we exited out into a grassy area. I zoned out as Kaizer started going on about the crops we were producing, Axel's gaze remaining on him and not venturing over to me as I studied the group of people he brought. Ishani was the main one who spoke; the rest of them quieter, only speaking in when spoken to. Something about Paxx, their head of intelligence, set me on edge. His overall energy was intimidating, but he looked at everyone like he knew their secrets, and I was not too fond of that feeling as he turned that dark, piercing gaze over to me.

After we spent far too much time talking about wheat than necessary, we left the farmlands. Kaizer felt the need to stop a few times on the way back to the castle to show them the nicer parts of the village. By the time we made it through the inner wall's gates, I was more than ready to eat. Kaizer guided us over to our biggest dining hall, the smell of the already prepared food having my steps more hurried than before. The table was set for all of us; platters piled with more food than we could possibly eat in one sitting ran down the middle. Kaizer sat at the end in a chair more prominent than the others, gesturing for me to sit beside him.

"Please, join me down here," Kaizer said to King Axel.

Axel pulled out the chair directly across from me and scooted in, offering me an annoyingly polite smile. Kaizer waved over the kitchen staff, who scooped massive portions of the food onto our plates and then backed away quickly to return to the wall. One of them set down a chalice of goat blood beside me and walked to the other end of the table to set one beside my mother as well. I ripped a roll in half and ate it before grabbing the blood and sipping. Blood trickled down my lips and I quickly swiped it with my tongue before eating the other half of the bread. Kaizer was engaged in conversation with Ishani, but Axel watched me intently. I wasn't sure if he was confused about the blood or was just interested in how I ate bread, but I lifted my eyebrows at him in question. Axel smirked before he looked back at his plate and put a forkful of potatoes into his mouth. I ate until I was full, and finished the rest of my blood, the feeling of my magic recharging and my full stomach almost forcing a moan from my throat.

"Is everyone content?" Kaizer asked, standing from his seat.

Everyone nodded and stood from the table, and we followed him through the throne room. A power move for sure, because it was not necessary to get to the office we were going to speak in. I was getting tired of seeing the back of Kaizer's head, if I was being honest, but I was ready to get this conversation over with. We all sat around a round table, and I was thankful for Axel being a few seats down from me so he couldn't see me that well. Kaizer sat beside me and cleared his throat but didn't say anything right away.

"I'd rather us not beat around the bush," King Axel said, "if you don't mind me saying."

"No, I'd rather be direct as well," Kaizer said, folding his hands in front of him. "Would you like to start with any concerns you have?"

"My concern is that your kingdom is going to become double as powerful. That could cause you to become foolish enough to attempt to push into my borders."

King Axel spoke with a seriousness in his tone that wasn't there before, the timber and command in his voice making me shiver internally.

"We have no desire to do that. We showed you our capital—we have no need to move into your land," Kaizer said with just as much seriousness.

"What about the witches? Do you have the desire?" Axel asked as he sat forward on his elbows and looked over at me.

I had a desire to do something with him, but it had nothing to do with his land.

"No, we were perfectly content in our land before this union. We have no need to push your borders either," I exclaimed.

It dawned on me that this was the first time someone asked a question about the brujas directed at me and not my mother, as her mouth pursed and she sat back slightly. I looked away, but I felt her stare remain on me.

"Are you offering anything other than your word?" Xavier asked, King Axel's second in command.

"I would like to suggest an official treaty," Kaizer boomed.

"There already is a treaty," King Axel responded.

"There is one between Sanjry and Dusra, but not for our joined lands. That is what we're suggesting," Otto exclaimed.

"A treaty is just a piece of paper," Ishani responded.

"A piece of paper, yes, but a formality to back up our words," Kaizer replied.

King Axel sat back, resting his chin on his hand where it was propped up on the armrest. "Even with your joined lands, your numbers don't outweigh ours. If we wanted to, we could wage war on the both of you."

"Do we have a reason for war?" Kaizer asked.

"Not currently," he said as he sat forward again and looked directly at me. "Just thought I'd make it clear."

"I've written something up," Kaizer said as he slid a pile of paper over to him. "Feel free to review."

King Axel scanned the papers and pushed them over to Xavier when he was done.

"I'd like to speak to Dayanara alone," King Axel said.

"Why?" Kaizer questioned.

"I would like to hear from her directly, without the pressure of you around her," he responded.

"I can assure you there is no pressure," Kaizer said.

"I won't sign a treaty unless I can speak with her alone," Axel demanded, sliding the treaty away from Xavier and back to Kaizer.

Kaizer looked over at me, the battle of if he should allow this raging in his eyes. I nodded, and his mouth went tight, but he stood.

Kaizer gestured for the rest of the room to exit. "I'll allow it."

King Axel handed the papers to Xavier again. "Review these," he muttered before they all left the room.

The door slammed shut, the fact we were truly alone causing my stomach to flip once again.

"Daya, Daya, Daya," he said, standing from where he sat and scooting into the chair beside me. "What have you gotten yourself into?"

"I don't know what you mean," I exclaimed.

"Why are you marrying him?"

"We're in love," I said, the bitterness of the lie coating my tongue.

He laughed. "No, you are not. So I ask again, why are you marrying him?"

His stare was so intense goosebumps rushed over the exposed flesh on my chest, and I swallowed, trying to get the lie to sound more real in my head.

"It started as a conversation to stop the war between our kingdoms. It developed from that." Less of a lie, but Axel still watched me with a smirk that conveyed he didn't believe me still.

"There are other ways to stop wars between kingdoms," he said.

"Our kingdoms have been fighting for centuries without either of us coming out on top. A treaty would not have worked for us. You destroyed them. Thus, them agreeing to a treaty made sense, Sanjry and Caldera have been back and forth too long."

"You could marry me instead," he said, a joke for sure, but he leaned closer to me, making me question how serious he was. "I'm kidding, of course," he finished, sitting back in the chair again.

"Hilarious."

I snapped my fingers and sent a shield of air around us to block any sound from escaping the room, just in case.

"What are you playing at?" I asked.

"I like this side of you, so demanding. Whatever do you mean?"

"Are we going to pretend like you weren't here prior to your entrance or that we…" I paused, wondering what word exactly described what we did. "Knew each other?"

He ran his tongue over his bottom lip. "I don't see how that would play into either of our favor. But while we're talking about it, I had a wonderful time with you."

"You lied," I quipped, my eyes narrowing.

"Did you tell the truth?" he asked, his eyebrows raised.

We had somehow gotten closer and closer with each rally between us. "I'm engaged," I breathed.

"We've covered that," he said before sitting back and breaking the magnetic pull I felt. "I'm worried for my kingdom."

"I have no interest in your kingdom," I said.

He smirked. "You would if you visited. Might I suggest a visit in the summer? It's divine."

"Nobody is allowed in your borders," I responded.

"It is invitation-only, but you have an invite," he said, smiling and flashing his fangs at me.

"I'd rather us not beat around the bush, if you don't mind me saying," I taunted him with his own words.

"I have reasons not to trust Sanjry. I've found them trying to enter my lands several times over the last decade. I don't know what they're looking for specifically, as my kingdom holds many treasures, but I feel this is a step toward whatever it is they're trying to accomplish."

"I don't know of any plans. I wasn't lying," I reassured.

"I don't think you're lying at all, my dear Daya. I think your *betrothed* is. I'm not going to sign the treaty today. I plan on trying to get more information out of him. Maybe even push the stay until the day after tomorrow."

"He won't like that," I muttered.

"Oh, I'm betting on it. I'm also betting on the fact he is going out of his mind outside of these walls right now. A rattled man is a man who makes mistakes," Axel responded.

"I imagine you're going to ask me not to say anything?"

"I don't imagine anyone can tell you not to do something with full reassurance you won't do whatever is being asked of you." He chuckled. "So no, I ask that you act at your own discretion."

I turned my head to the side, the trust he was offering me after lying about who I was to him was strange, but I nodded all the same.

"I worry he's not who he presents to the world," Axel said, the seriousness in his tone returning. "Do be careful, Daya. I know you can take care of yourself, but please watch your back."

"So what are you going to say when we leave?" I asked.

"I'll say that I don't agree to the treaty now, but I'm willing to negotiate over the next few days."

I nodded, standing from the chair. "Did you know who I was?" I asked before disbanding the air shield around us.

Axel's jaw ticked. "I didn't, but I was drawn to you. I could sense your power. Powerful people tend to be drawn to each other. I knew I'd be seeing you again."

I snapped my fingers so I didn't have to answer that, my attraction and anger twining together. I wasn't sure if I was upset about him lying about who he was or if I was upset that I was in the situation. I had lied too, but he didn't know how much I needed that break from reality in the pub. Before we exited, Axel grabbed my hand, his power already at the surface, mine immediately coming up to intertwine with his without any effort. I felt it everywhere, in every crevice of my being, in my soul. The cool caress of his magic wrapped around mine, I couldn't place what was so unique about his power, and before I could figure it out, he pulled his hand back.

He blinked a few times as his chest heaved. "You are always welcome in my land, Daya. That was not a joke."

I pushed through the door as I pulled down a mask of indifference and glided over to Kaizer, who grabbed my hand immediately. The fact I didn't sense the same level of power from him as I did with Axel hit me like a brick wall. I thought Kaizer was powerful when I felt his magic before, but Axel put him to shame.

"I can't sign the treaty as it is. I must review and revise it. We can reconvene tomorrow after lunch," Axel boomed, leaving no room for questions as he and his council turned and exited the hall.

"He doesn't even know where he's going," Kaizer muttered, flagging down a palace staff and directing him to show him his rooms.

"What happened in there?" my mother asked, and Kaizer glared at me with the same question in his eyes.

No part of me felt it necessary to tell them the truth, as there were things I needed to look into myself now.

"He was worried it was fake." I looked over at Kaizer. "I reassured him it wasn't and gave him the story we agreed on."

"And?" my mother pushed.

"He's hard to read," I lied. "I can't tell if he believed it or not yet."

"You said something in there. He didn't appear as concerned before we left," my mother grumbled, stepping toward me.

"I didn't," I responded.

"I don't believe you," she said before turning on her heel and exiting the hall as well.

Kaizer looked at me like he was trying to figure out if he believed me as well, my knack for saying too much, something he clearly had caught onto already.

"I need to make sure the guards are prepared for him to stay longer. We thought he'd leave in the morning. I'll see you at breakfast," Kaizer stated and turned to speak to Abel and Otto.

"Well, alright then," I muttered as I turned and left.

Zuri stood outside the throne room and ran over to me as soon as I stepped away from the group. "How'd it go?"

"I honestly have no fucking idea," I replied.

"Want to train?" she asked with a tilt of her head.

"Yes, I do."

I needed to sweat and hit something; my feelings were so jumbled up that I could barely tell up from down in my brain.

Chapter Fifteen

I focused on a bead of sweat running from my neck down my spine into the band of my pants. The quiet in my head was more than welcome after the last few days I'd had, the last few weeks, really. Quinn was posted on the veranda, my 'guard' while the Dusrans were here. Thankfully she wasn't being obnoxious about it, just standing from a distance and watching. I'd opted for one of the soldier's training sets instead of my leathers. While it wasn't anywhere near as flattering, it was lightweight, and the breeze I was getting through the fabric was wonderful. I could barely hear Zuri's footsteps behind me, she wasn't keeping up, but I didn't mind too much. It made it easier for me to focus on the sweat, on the muscles working to move me at such a fast pace. I turned the corner of the loop and realized Zuri wasn't even running anymore. She was plopped down in the dirt on the side of the path I was coming around to.

"I quit on the last loop," she said, guzzling down water from the jugs we brought with us. "Just give me a minute. I can keep going."

Her chest was heaving, her breaths were coming in quickly, and her short honey curls were sticking to her forehead with the amount of sweat she had gathered there. I laughed internally, I knew she hated this, but she also knew how much I needed it and that little fact made me smirk slightly.

"It's okay. I think I'm good," I said.

I could have gone for hours, but the main thing I needed to do was center myself and figure out where to go from here. That I accomplished. I had decided that killing Kaizer was short-sighted, for now, but I was never going to go along with this union without finding out as many of the secrets this kingdom held. I'd done enough exploring that I was confident I could get into the more secure areas. If there were secrets that could hurt my coven, I needed to find out. I'd go along with everything for now, and make sure Kaizer knew I was 'on board,' but I wouldn't damn the brujas. Dusrans, before they shut their borders completely, were known for being ruthless, for being conniving, so I couldn't rule out that this was some play for Axel to use me against Kaizer. He could have known who I was, even though it didn't feel like a lie when he said it.

"Feel any better?" Zuri asked.

I filled her in on what Axel said to me in the room, outside of the fact we knew each other, and I was so thankful to have someone to be able to share these things with. I never really had that, I had tons of witches I could confide in, but I was never really sure if the things I said would get back to my mother. If Zuri ever turned against me, I'd have to gut her.

"I do. I just don't know who to trust right now. Everyone has something to gain," I responded.

"You don't trust Kaizer?"

"I don't know. We had a moment yesterday, he was in bloodlust, and he hunted me. It turned into some...other things. But I feel like that might have been a reaction to the adrenaline I felt. I don't really feel anything toward him today."

"Do you need to have feelings for him to trust him?"

"No, but I can't tell if he has any genuine feelings for me either. He could be using me to get something from my kingdom, outside of just stopping the war," I said, plopping down beside her. "I've been too distracted, I need to know what the magic he used was."

The dirt clouded around us slightly before settling, and I sat back on my hands to throw my face up to the sky. The sky was cloudier than it had been recently, the soft orange glow of it barely peeking through.

"Once you know what King Axel says tomorrow, you'll have more of an idea of what to do next," Zuri said.

"You're right. I just need him to sign the treaty so Kaizer can stop being a fucking nut case."

"I have never seen him so on edge," Zuri laughed.

"It's obnoxious." I chuckled and pushed to my feet to stretch my arms to the sky.

I'd suspected the cool, calm, collected Kaizer was all for show, but the nervous showboating Kaizer was going to drive me crazy. Zuri stood as well and picked up the water jugs we brought out, handing me one before we moved toward my garden.

"I know you have secrets, Zuri. But if you ever wanted to talk to me about it, you can. I feel bad I'm dumping on you all the time," I said, bumping her in the shoulder.

"I don't mind the dumping," she responded with a smile. "But I appreciate it."

I wanted to know Zuri, really know her, but she tended to not want to share too much, which I respected. I'd keep trying, though. Quinn ran over before we exited the training area and stopped us before we could make it out. "Where are you going?"

"Just back to my room, no need for guarding," I stated.

Quinn wasn't a bad person; as a matter of fact, she was one of the better Sanjryans I'd met. But I really didn't need a watchdog right now.

She bit her lip and looked past me. "I do need to check on something, so I'll just make sure to escort you to dinner."

She turned and ran to the veranda and I sighed as we walked through the narrow path connecting the training loop to one of the courtyards. But before we exited, muffled voices reached me from around the hedge wall. I grabbed Zuri's wrist, stopping her in her tracks and pulling her close to listen. I focused on the voices but didn't recognize them. Of course, there would be people out here as soon as I send Quinn away. There was rarely anyone outside in these courtyards other than the random gardener. I grabbed the dagger strapped to my thigh and handed a smaller knife from the holster on my ankle to Zuri. I moved in front of her, motioning for her to follow me closely and creeping up to the edge of the wall.

"It's ugly," a female voice muttered, and it took me a moment to recognize it as Ishani, Axel's sister.

"Everything is ugly here," a male voice, Xavier, responded.

I straightened and set my face into the uncaring glare I often wore around people I didn't know that well. I stepped out of the covered path and looked directly over to where Ishani and Xavier stood in front of a hedge sculpture that was cut to resemble a burning tree.

"Hello," I said flatly.

"Hi," Ishani responded before pointing back to the hedge. "A burning tree doesn't reflect power, more like defeat."

Her dark curly hair flowed in the breeze, nearly brushing her hips where she had a hand propped up in a judgmental pose.

"There was a forest close to the border of Caldera that used to burn freely without destroying the trees," I said and walked over to where they stood with my hands clasped behind my back.

"Ah yes, the forest of Incen." Axel's voice sounded from behind me. "As you said, it once burned, but the trees are black now, charred and stuck in their life cycle, never dying or growing. It's said to be where the Sanjryan's magic started, the Goddess of Fire gifting them the ability to manipulate the flame of the forest. It's long been extinguished, but they have kept the symbolization. I think a flame itself would be a better symbol of the power rather than this dying thing."

Axel stepped beside me, separating me and Zuri. His dimple was on show as he spouted knowledge about a kingdom that wasn't his own.

"Ax—" I cleared my throat. "King Axel, I didn't see you there."

"One of the staff that showed us to our rooms said we should take a look at this courtyard. They came before me," he explained with his hand outstretched toward Ishani, Xavier, and a slew of their soldiers.

"It's not much to see," Ishani grumbled.

"It's not," I agreed with a laugh. "The Sanjryans excel in their version architecture, but any other form of art they fall short."

Axel chuckled and looked over to where Zuri stood beside him. "What were you two doing?"

Our training sets were covered in dirt from kicking it up on the path and sitting in it when we were done. Not to mention that I was soaked in sweat to the point the linen shirt was sticking to my skin.

"Training," I explained, pulling the shirt slightly to release it from my body.

He looked me up and down. "Kaizer doesn't seem like the type to allow that."

My shirt ended up right back on my skin and I gave up on trying to fix it. "Took some convincing." I shrugged. "We have to go. I'll see you later," I said before grabbing Zuri by the wrist and pulling her along with me.

Axel's low chuckling sounded from behind me, it sounded like his sister called him an idiot, but I was moving too fast to focus on it.

Zuri pulled her arm from my grasp. "Why are you so weird around him?"

"Okay, there is one thing I haven't told you yet," I started, looking around to make sure nobody was around once we entered my garden. "I met him."

"What do you mean you *met* him?"

"He was here a few days ago. I was exploring and ended up in the village."

Zuri's eyes went wide. "You didn't tell Kaizer?"

"No, it would give my nighttime activities away," I responded.

"So what happened?"

"Well, some drunk was fucking with me, so I got into a bit of a bar brawl. I ran into him when I was storming away, and we talked."

"Talked?" she asked, her eyebrow raised.

I had to hold back the smile pulling at my lips. "Yeah, we almost kissed."

"Daya! What if someone saw?"

I put my hand over her mouth and pulled her along with me. "They didn't. We didn't even kiss; Quinn walked in, and Ax helped me get away."

"This all makes so much sense now," she said, looking back toward the courtyard. "You didn't realize it was him until he introduced himself this morning?"

I nodded. "Something about him gets me all rustled," I said as I rubbed my temples. "I'm usually able to play it way cooler than that."

"You mean something other than his chiseled jawline, god-like body, dark curly hair, and dimples?" she asked sarcastically.

"Yes!" I exclaimed, "you're right. He is exactly my type of man, and Kaizer is exactly not. Even though sometimes I feel like he could be if I tried hard enough." I dragged my hand over my face. "I'm usually the one who knows things before everyone else. Being caught off guard has my brain not cooperating with me."

"I can say you don't feel well and need to skip dinner?"

"You're a genius," I said before grabbing her forehead and kissing it. "I can't be in the same room as both of them so casually. Even if no one else notices something is off between me and Axel, my mother might."

"Let's run your bath, and you can sleep all this off," she said.

I nodded and threw a portal out in front of us to get us into my room.

"He is here for a few nights. You might be able to..." Zuri trailed off.

"What are you suggesting, Zuri?" I asked.

"I'm just saying you have found ways to get around the castle without anyone knowing. *If* you did want to try to talk to him while he's here, you could."

My mouth hung open in a small smile. "You aren't supposed to tell me to cheat on my fiancé, your *king*."

"I'm not saying you *should* cheat. I'm merely saying you only live once," she laughed.

"I mean...Is it *really* cheating? This is technically just an arrangement, I made it clear that I'm not his yet..." I stopped, pulling my shirt over my head. "No, I don't need any more complications. Especially not solely based on the fact he's attractive."

"Gorgeous," Zuri corrected me.

I waved my hand. "Yeah, yeah, yeah. Go tell them I'm sick or whatever it is you planned on."

Zuri laughed and left the room quickly, leaving me alone, still, and with my thoughts. Just when I was convincing myself it was a good idea to attempt at embracing the marriage to Kaizer, Axel came in and made me second guess myself. While having to force myself into things with Kaizer, outside of our little bloodlust fun, felt unnatural and uncomfortable, I had to do what was best for all of Caldera. I didn't regret getting physical with him; if anything, it helped me know that there was some sort of attraction in there. I still wasn't sure if it was the thrill of being the hunted instead of the hunter, though. I should really look into the fact I had only been attracted to him when he was bloody or acting like a fucking psychopath.

Axel really did seem genuinely concerned for his kingdom, so I just hoped he figured out whatever he needed to before tomorrow's meeting. And I hoped I could last another day without my secret being found out.

Chapter Sixteen

"Dayanara," Kaizer exclaimed from across the breakfast table.

I wasn't sure how many times he called my name. I was too lost in my thoughts from last night. "Hm?"

"I asked if you had anything you wanted to discuss before the meeting later today?"

"You should just tell us whatever it is you discussed in private. I know you're not telling the truth," my mother added.

"I told you the truth," I bit back. "I am not the one at fault here. King Axel doesn't trust us because of *your* history with him," I said with my gaze directed at Kaizer.

"My predecessor's history," Kaizer corrected.

I took a bite of my toast. "Either way, that is what is holding him back."

"I don't know how else to reassure him I don't want to move my borders into his land," Kaizer said, sitting back in his chair.

I took another bite of my toast, knowing that Axel knew about Sanjryans trying to get into his land. I wasn't sure if Axel would bring it up in the meeting later, but I wanted to know more about why that would be happening myself. Giving up that information could allow him to prepare, to hide what the real reason might be.

"What is the plan if this doesn't work?" my mother asked.

"Then we'll be joining our kingdoms in war rather than just in marriage," Kaizer replied.

"The whole point of this arrangement was to avoid further war," I groaned.

Kaizer banged his fists on the table. "You think I don't know that!"

I leveled a look at him with my eyebrows high as my mother watched him through slitted eyes.

"I'm sorry, I'm stressed," he muttered.

"Do something about it before the meeting," I snapped, standing and scooting my chair in.

"I need blood," Kaizer said before I could exit the room.

I stopped with my hand on the doorknob and turned around to grab the chalice with which I drank my goat's blood this morning. Shifting the slit of my dress over, I yanked the dagger from my thigh and cut my wrist deep enough for the blood to flow out of me rapidly. I held his gaze while the blood filled the chalice and my head started to get slightly woozy but I ignored the feeling. My mother muttered something behind me, but I ignored her as well. Once the chalice was full, I scooted it over to him, rubbing my finger over the gash and pushing healing magic into it. The wound stitched up quickly, and I mocked a curtsy before gliding toward the door without making eye contact with either of them.

Quinn moved from where she stood along the wall, ready to follow me wherever I went again.

"Not today," I said, pinning her down with a firm stare.

She looked to Kaizer, and he shook his head before he reached for the chalice and brought it to his lips as I stormed out of the room. If he thought I would be his punching bag in this union, he was mistaken. I took no shit from anyone—outside of my mother—and I wouldn't start now. I could feel pieces of me fading away since I'd been here, too lost to the masks I'd been wearing. It was exhausting, always having to be 'on,' always trying to be one step ahead of everyone around me. I walked toward the courtyard, and a figure in a dark orange hooded robe, one of the acolytes, walked toward me. They were walking on the wrong side of the hallway, and I could hear them muttering something, but they didn't look up.

"Hey," I exclaimed as I jumped out of the way.

Their head snapped up, their gaze not meeting my eyes but lingering on my forehead. "May the Flame light the way, may the Flame return before dismay," they continued muttering.

"What the fuck," I whispered.

The acolyte looked away from me and continued down the hall, and I shuddered at the oddity of the experience. *Fucking weird-ass vampires.* I really needed to ask more about whatever this Ember thing was. Nobody seemed to want to answer me the last time I asked. I rushed down the stairs to the lower level where the courtyards were, needing to feel the air and smell the earth. I turned the corner out of the stairwell and nearly ran into Ishani.

"You're always on the go, aren't you?" she laughed as she sidestepped to allow me down the hall.

"I can't sit still, or I'll go crazy," I responded a little too honestly.

"You and I are alike in that," she laughed out. "It's hard to do too much here, though," she pointed her shoulder toward two guards who were doing a terrible job at being discreet in following her.

"They're under strict orders not to let any Dusrans out of their sight," I said with a wave of my hand to dismiss them. "I'll escort her wherever she's going."

They both looked at each other, the question of if they should take orders from me in their gaze. "*Now,*" I commanded with no room for questions, and they scurried away.

Ishani brushed her long curly hair over her shoulder. "Impressive."

I shrugged and started to walk with her. "Where were you going?"

"I actually don't know. I just didn't want to sit in a room with my brother any longer," she mumbled as we walked toward the courtyard.

"He is rather intense," I joked.

"You don't know the half of it," she responded as we stepped into the fresh air.

We both sighed, turning our faces up into the breeze whooshing by us.

"It's so stuffy here," Ishani muttered.

"In Caldera, we are always outside. Even our buildings are made to let the air flow throughout," I responded.

"It is similar in Dusra," she responded.

Ishani seemed kinder than the others in her group; something about her felt warm and inviting. A small smile from her seemed to put most people around her at ease. I wasn't sure if it was a ploy or if she was actually a genuinely good person. Axel had trusted me, and I wondered if I could trust Ishani too.

I snapped down an air shield around us to keep our conversation private. "How do you feel about all of this?"

"I've been around long enough to know when someone isn't telling the truth. I don't think we have the whole truth here. Axel told you about the Sanjryans we've found in our land?"

I turned my head slightly, wondering just how much Axel told her, but nodded along.

"I know that this is not your kingdom, that you are joining it to stop the war between you. I hope we're wrong as we have no interest in another war, but we have to be sure," she added.

"You're a rather trusting bunch. Both you and Axel have told me far more than I would have expected."

"As I said, we've been around long enough to know who people truly are." She shrugged. "This is all new to you, is it not?"

"Is it that obvious?" I asked.

We walked into the courtyard and sat on a bench near an immaculately manicured bush of roses. "It's not necessarily a bad thing," Ishani suggested.

"My mother always focused on the politics. I was the one who went out and made sure things were executed. I sat in on plenty of meetings, but it always came down to her. Witches aren't as finicky as vampires, though. We deal with our issues upfront, and we're stubbornly loyal creatures."

"It gives you a different point of view. It could be helpful," Ishani replied.

I sat back on the bench. "You two aren't exactly what I expected," I muttered, crossing my arms.

"Oh, don't be mistaken. We are a ruthless when it comes to protecting our kingdom. We aren't the beings of pure evil that the Sanjryans believe us to be, though," she assured.

"The rest of your group is pretty much what I expected, however," I said.

Ishani laughed as she sat back as well. "You got me there."

We sat a little while longer in comfortable silence, watching the clouds go by, until Quinn found me and stood at the entrance back to the kingdom.

"My personal guard," I muttered, unable to hide how annoyed I was with it.

"From what I've heard, you don't need much protection," Ishani whispered with a wink.

My eyes went wide as I disbanded the air shield and stood. "I'll see you at the meeting," I declared loud enough for Quinn to hear.

Ishani's chuckling traveled over to me on the wind as I made it to Quinn, and she followed behind me.

"Thought you weren't following me today," I muttered.

"Kaizer sent me to make sure you made it to the meeting safely," Quinn responded.

"Of course he did. How long do I have?"

"He wants Sanjry to be there before Dusra, so...now."

I sighed and switched directions. "Great, let's get this over with."

I pushed through the doors, and to my surprise, Kaizer and Axel were both seated around the table already. I sat down beside Kaizer, and he made a big show of kissing my hand, and I had to stop myself from rolling my eyes. The rest of the participants in the meeting strolled in a bit later, the sound of their chairs scraping against the marble floor loud in the blaring silence.

"You're all early," Ishani said as she took out the treaty and slid it over to Axel.

Nobody responded, and Axel shuffled through the treaty, aligning the pages with a tap on the table before him. "I'd like to start this conversation with the fact I don't have interest in going to war with you." He set the pages down, his mouth turning from his casual smile to a flat line. "That doesn't mean I won't. The treaty is not the issue. I double-checked where you drew the borders. They are correct with your combined kingdoms. It's a simple agreement, agreeing to the borders and the lack of entry both ways outside of an approved visit. The issue is that you aren't even abiding by the current treaty Dusra has with Sanjry."

Kaizer didn't flinch, didn't make any movement to show that he was guilty, only sat forward on his elbows. "I can assure you are incorrect."

"You'd do well not to call me a liar," Axel growled.

The pleasantries were gone; their true merciless selves on display. They stared each other down, not breaking eye contact, until Kaizer sat back and laid his hand on top of mine.

"I'm sure you can produce proof?" Kaizer asked.

Axel's stone face softened, his mouth turning up into a smile. Not a warm smile, but a smile meant to warn, a smile that would send a weaker soul running away from him on a battlefield. Which this room was. Axel looked to Paxx, and he lifted a bag from beneath his chair and plopped it onto the table with a thud. Kaizer's hand squeezed mine for a second, the only sign that showed he was worried about what was in that bag. I immediately knew what it was; I'd done enough killing to recognize the way the bag hit the table. Paxx reached his hand in, pulled out a head, and threw it onto the center of the table. The head rolled across the surface and didn't cease until Kaizer lifted a hand to stop it from hitting him. Paxx pulled out a severed hand and tossed it over as well, landing directly next to the head with a fleshy smack.

"I've frozen its insides to avoid decay, so you are fully aware of who it is," Axel said.

Short dark hair fell limply in front of unseeing eyes, and the pale skin had a particularly gray hue, but it wasn't decaying, so it was hard to tell how long the man had been dead. The hand was covered in blood, but I picked it up and rubbed the sticky substance off the ring around the finger.

"This is a general," I muttered.

A wide steel signet ring was on his finger, the flaming tree etched into its surface. All the generals were given that ring when they were assigned the role. Quinn stood along the wall, hers gleaming in the light of the chandelier. I snapped my gaze over to Ishani, and she nodded ever so slightly, just enough to confirm this was why they didn't trust Sanjry.

"What does this prove?" Kaizer asked, sending a flame into the deceased flesh and turning it to ash before us.

"He was on my land, hence his death," Axel said flatly.

"He was acting on his own accord. He had no orders from me to cross your borders. You were within your rights to kill him."

"I find that hard to believe. Although I'll give it to you, Kaizer, he held up well under torture. Didn't utter a word about what he was doing or who sent him."

The corner of Kaizer's mouth lifted in an arrogant smirk. "Well, there you have it."

My head was bobbing back and forth as they rallied, not knowing what to believe or even *who* to believe. If Kaizer was already trying to get into Dusra, we could be signing a death wish for half the kingdom, including the witches, should we go to war with them.

"What is it you're looking for in Dusra?" Axel asked.

"I'm not looking for anything in your kingdom. I have plenty here," Kaizer responded.

"What does this mean for the treaty?" I asked, and they both snapped their heads in my direction.

"What does this mean, Dayanara?" Axel answered, flashing me his teeth in a devilishly flirtatious smile that caused a growl from Kaizer. "It means I need more. I'm not reassured that this was not Sanjry's doing."

"What is it that you want?" I asked.

I didn't want to feed into the behavior that was getting Kaizer riled up. Axel opened his mouth, his smile saying he would say something that would send this conversation in the wrong direction, but Xavier, Axel's second, spoke before he could.

"Every person that comes through will be killed. There is no way into Dusra that isn't guarded. You should put more men at your borders to avoid those deaths if they are *acting on their own accord*. The space between our borders remains untouched, but the moment someone crosses over, we will deal with them."

"That is what the current treaty says?" Kaizer questioned.

"And we want this agreement sealed in magic," Ishani added.

Kaizer scoffed. "That is wholly unnecessary."

"It is necessary. At this point, the only thing we have to go off is your word that this general was acting on his own. Not to mention he wasn't the first. The others we just outright killed before it began to feel like a pattern. Should you not agree to this, you'll be waging war," Axel exclaimed.

The authority in his voice made my throat bob, and I watched as every person not of Dusra stilled, including Kaizer. He looked over at Abel and Otto, who hadn't muttered a word thus far.

"What are the terms?" Otto asked.

"They're simple. If you send anyone across my borders knowingly, the magic will enact a price," Axel said.

"A price?" Abel asked.

"Could be death, could be the loss of a limb, of a loved one—this kind of magic is a little unpredictable. However, the price will be taken regardless, and the price will be steep."

"Done," Kaizer exclaimed, and Abel and Otto both snapped their heads in his direction.

"Sir, we should discuss this," Otto said in hushed tones.

"I told you I'm not sending anyone over there. Do you want reassurance? I agree to your terms," he said before holding out his hand to Axel.

Axel smirked, gripping Kaizer's hand as magic sparked between them. I still didn't know what kind of magic Axel had, but the magic felt ancient. It bloomed where their skin met, a rush of warm air extending from their hands and blowing my hair behind me. I swore I saw the faintest hint of black magic rolling down Axel's neck, but it was gone in the blink of an eye.

Kaizer's eyebrows shot up. "That is old magic."

"I'm old," Axel replied.

I looked at Kaizer's wrist, but it was blank. "No marking?" I asked.

"I'd rather not have his sigil on my skin," Axel grumbled as he sat back down in his seat. "The rest of the treaty we agree with. It can be signed today. We will stay one more night as we prefer to travel in the morning," he finished.

Kaizer lifted his hand in question for a pen from one of the staff. "Very well."

Someone scurried over and handed him the pen; he signed his name on the last page and scooted it over to Abel and Otto for one last review. The treaty made its way around the table to Axel, where he signed his name as well.

Kaizer stood, and Axel lifted his hand. "Dayanara," he said as he pushed the paper over to me.

"Of course," Kaizer muttered, sitting back down.

I took the pen from Axel's hand and signed my name above Kaizer's on both signature pages. My mother reached for the paper, but Axel took it from my hand and stacked them on top of each other.

"I'll have a copy of the details made for myself also," Axel said, leaving our signature page on the table for Kaizer.

My mother scoffed. The disrespect Axel showed was surely about to send her on a tangent.

"Dayanara represents the brujas in this union, does she not?" Axel asked.

"She does," she said through tight teeth.

Axel nodded. "See you all at dinner."

The Dusrans stood and exited the room in the blink of an eye. Kaizer let out a long breath after the last one left.

"It could have been worse," Abel muttered.

"Yes, a magical agreement that could kill him is obviously the best course of action," Otto responded.

Abel shrugged. "We avoided a war. That will have to be enough."

I stood up without a word to anyone and closed the door behind me as they all continued the debriefing of the meeting. I had no interest in listening to how they thought it went; I knew how it went. Kaizer was lying, and I needed to figure out what he was lying about, and I needed to figure it out before I married him. Caldera's future depended on it.

Chapter Seventeen

Dinner was just as awkward as expected; I didn't say much, opting to observe everyone around me. Kaizer made more attempts at showboating about our joined kingdom, but Dusra didn't seem to care much. I was sure that Axel still believed Kaizer sent that general into Dusra on a mission, but he kept it pretty cordial. The dinner was growl- and threat-free, thankfully. I was also thankful for the abundance of wine and blood, the mixture the perfect end to a shitty week.

It took effort to attempt to take my dress off as my bedroom was spinning slightly from the effects of the beverages I'd enjoyed. Zuri advised that she had to take care of some duties she was responsible for after dinner, so since she wasn't here I had to loosen the buttons myself.

I felt a sharp zing in the back of my mind, an indication that someone was trying to transport directly into my room, and I quickly pulled on a pair of trousers and a linen shirt. My mother watched me down the wine and blood with a glare. I thought she was just judging me per usual, but it seemed she was plotting that I'd be less than sober tonight. She was more powerful than me, so she'd be able to push through the barriers I set, but at least I could be prepared. Another zing and a snap sounded; green clouds and the familiar tang of her magic filled the air as her henchwoman came through the portal.

They stepped toward me with their hands outstretched, and while normally I just accepted whatever punishment she had to give me, the wine flowing through my veins had me a little more daring. I punched the woman on the left in the face with every ounce of my witch strength, and she fell backward into the open portal they were trying to drag me through. I reached for my weapon on the bed, but the second woman blasted it away with a gust of air. She wrapped me in a tendril of her magic, pulling my arms to the side. I broke out of the hold, but my steps weren't steady from the wine, and I stumbled toward her still. She pushed me through the portal, and I cracked my forehead on the cold, hard stone floor.

My mother flipped me over with her foot, and I groaned, my head wasn't spinning anymore—it was *screaming*. I didn't know where I was. Everything around me was a blur of dark gray color, but the damp scent hit me at the same time I realized I was in the dungeon. I put my hand on my head to try to push healing magic into the wound, but before it was wholly stitched, my mother blew the magic suppression over me, and the bleeding picked back up again.

"Fuck," I muttered as the blood ran down in my eyes and into my mouth.

"I know you did something. I know when you're lying, child. You've been disrespectful for days. This punishment is overdue."

"Be real, mother. You're just mad they're already starting to see me as queen over you," I said as I spat the blood out of my mouth onto the floor. "This is all your own doing. You're the one who put me in this position!"

She scoffed. "I thought I taught you enough lessons over the last century and a half to respect me regardless of your position, but clearly I was incorrect."

"There's a first for everything," I muttered, as I didn't think those words had ever left her mouth before.

I could barely see through the blood dripping into my eyes, so I didn't have time to react before she slapped me across the face hard enough to knock my jaw to the side. The impact ricocheted through my body, sending me into the wall.

"You don't even deserve for me to be the one to give you your punishment. Add an extra three lashings on for that comment," she said to one of her henchwomen.

"Yes, Acna," she responded.

My mother's heels clicked against the stone, the sound growing further away until I heard the drag of a heavy door shut behind her.

"You two are pathetic! You don't even know why she's punishing me!"

"We don't need to know," one said before clasping my left wrist in the cuff and moving to my other side.

"What will you do when I'm Acna? You think I'll forget this?"

Neither said anything. Their movements paused briefly before I felt the cuff clasp onto my other wrist. I lifted my hand to wipe some of the blood out of my eyes, but was barely able to reach my face before they pulled the chains, and I was suspended. My shirt was ripped open and tossed; the pieces floated to the ground as rustling started from behind me. I tried to clear my mind, to go to the place I went to during these 'lessons,' but I couldn't. The wine just made me angry, so fucking angry. I pulled at the chains as every muscle in my back and arms strained with the movement, and I felt my restraints pull from the wall.

"Stop that!" one of them yelled.

The chains were pulled again, and I heard the click of the lock they used to hold them in place this time. The snap of the whip sounded, and I braced myself, but nothing ever prepared for the pain the braided wires served. My flesh was ripped open, my back arching as the sting traveled from the point of contact into every square inch of flesh on my body. I couldn't help the scream that escaped from me before the next snap of the whip landed horizontally across my back. *The bitches can't even aim properly.*

I screamed again with the next lash, my head falling limp in front of me as I felt the warm blood rushing down my legs. I heard the fourth snap, but no pain followed, and I wondered if I had already made it to the place between consciousness and unconsciousness, where I went numb. A muffled scream sounded, the crunch of bones and squish of flesh following as somebody undoubtedly died behind me. I pulled on my chains, yanking them enough to get to my feet. I strained my neck to try to finally get the blood out of my eyes, but still couldn't fucking reach. A presence moved closer, and I kicked backward, connecting with something as I heard a grunt.

"It's rather rude to kick someone who is trying to save you," Axel muttered.

Fucking fuck. What is he doing down here? How did he find me? What will he say about this to the rest of his kingdom? To Kaizer? He pushed the key into my left cuff, and I fell forward into his arms before finally clearing the blood from my eyes. The henchwomen's contorted bodies lay on the ground. Limbs were pointing in the wrong direction. A pool of blood surrounded them, and something was sitting beside them, but I couldn't make it out. The other cuff fell, and I rubbed the last bit of blood from my eyes to see their hearts had been ripped clean out of their bodies.

"What did you do?" I asked.

Axel wiped the blood from his hands onto his pants. "What did *I* do? What the fuck is happening in here?"

"Punishment from my mother," I answered, looking down to realize the top half of my body was uncovered.

My skin was covered in blood, and my hair hung in front of my breasts, but I was extremely exposed.

"She'll fucking die for this," he muttered before handing me the pieces of my shirt to cover myself with.

It was *almost* comical how used to these punishments I was. I almost forgot that this wasn't a normal thing for most people.

I shook my head. "No. I just need to get back to my room."

I tried to move toward the door, but my body locked up, and I fell back into Axel's arms. He lifted me to his chest as he carried me toward the door and tried to keep me as still as possible, but the movement sent pain shooting through my back.

He stopped for a moment. "Let me heal you," he mumbled.

"Not yet. She'll be back. She can't see you did this. It could be an act of war. We just signed the treaty," I responded, my face tight and my breathing heavy.

"How do I get to your room?" Axel asked.

"Um..." I trailed off, trying to think of a way that we could get back without anyone seeing.

"There are tunnels," I whispered, and wondered for a moment if it was a bad idea to share. "There are secret tunnels. Take that right, there's an entrance at the end of the dungeon."

One I was glad I found during my exploration. I didn't know how it opened from this side, though, just that there was an opening somewhere near the last cell.

"There should be grooves somewhere in the wall," I said.

He sat me on my feet, and I leaned against the wall, running my finger over the surface as he did the same, the pain almost unbearable. Our fingers met at the button, and we both pushed at the same time. The wall shifted away, and he picked me up quickly. I directed him down the winding halls and up the stairs until we made it to the entrance into my closet. I put a magical block on it when I found the entrance to ensure anyone who wished me harm couldn't make it through. Axel didn't know this was a test for him, and I didn't know it would be so helpful when I cast the spell. I pushed the button to the opening, and we walked through. Axel groaned like he'd been zapped, but it didn't kill him. I wasn't really sure what that meant in regard to his intentions.

We moved into the bedroom, and he set me down on a chair near the fireplace. I was glad that Zuri either didn't hear or wasn't in her room right now. He placed his hand on my back, the contact pushing another groan from my throat. The pain quickly ebbed into the cool feel of his water magic and healing magic twined together. The water flowed over my skin, washing away the blood from my body and the healing magic stitched the wounds together simultaneously.

"Wait, don't heal them all the way," I groaned.

"I'll do no such fucking thing," he snapped.

I tried to move, but he didn't allow me. "She'll know something happened," I muttered.

"The dead fucking witches might give that away. I won't be leaving you in pain."

The last of the wounds fused before I could finish my argument, and my body relaxed at the lack of excruciating pain the lashes gave me.

Axel grabbed my face and pulled it toward him. "Say the word, and I'll take you with me."

"I can't. You were right. Something is off," I said, sitting up with ease. "I don't know what it is, but I'm not going to stop until I figure it out."

Axel's face softened, like he was sorry that he was the one who had to tell me that this union might not be in my best interest. He lifted his hand and washed the blood off my face and hair as he pulled all the water away in a bubble and dispersed it in the fireplace. I stood and walked over to my chest of drawers, pulling on a long black tunic and taking my blood-soaked pants off since the top fell to my mid-thigh. I turned to find Axel's eyes already on me, not in the same manner he'd looked at me for the last few days. He joked and flirted, his face always in an agonizing casual smile around me.

Right now, his gaze bore down to my soul, like he wanted to burn the world for me. He didn't truly know me, so I wasn't sure how he could achieve such a look. We had fun in a pub for a few minutes and had been going back and forth about a treaty between kingdoms. But at this moment, he looked at me like he knew me. Like he'd been there for every other time my mother punished me. As if he held the same rage I did for all the shortcomings this life had served me.

"Why does she punish you?" he asked, his body tight.

I laughed, walking over to the fireplace and crouching down beside it. I scratched the flint, and the fire bloomed to life as I sat in the chair beside it.

"I've been punished for so many things in my lifetime that they all blend together. Disrespect mostly, saying the wrong thing, straying from her precise instructions."

"This time?"

"She doesn't like that I'm going to become more powerful than her soon. She's trying to beat respect into me that I don't have for her."

"I thought witches revered the Acna above all?"

"We do—I did," I huffed. "I don't know. It's complicated. Being in this position I'm in now has me second-guessing her even more. I thought these lessons were for my own good at one point, and I've followed her lead, but respect—I'm not sure I respect her anymore."

Axel didn't respond, just continued to watch me. I would have been more comfortable if I found lust in his gaze, but I couldn't place what this look was. *Was it pity?*

I cleared my throat. "You all should leave first thing in the morning before shit goes sideways."

Axel nodded his head, his soft curls shifting in the movement. The flames were dancing in his hazel eyes and illuminating his light brown skin in a way that made him appear godly.

"You didn't deserve that," he started, and I looked away from him into the flames.

He stood in front of me and forced me to look into his eyes. "You didn't deserve that. Remember who you are, Dayanara. You are a force to be reckoned with," Ax stated, moving the hair in front of my face behind my ear. "You will always have a place among my people. I hope to see you again one day."

"Hopefully not on a battlefield," I said jokingly to break the seriousness.

"I wouldn't want to put my soldiers in your path," he chuckled with a slight smile.

His hand lingered on my neck as he licked his lips and gazed down at me with soft eyes. "Goodnight, Daya."

"Goodnight, Ax," I responded.

He pulled away, and I longed to live in those few minutes where we both gave up our identities. When I was just Daya, he was just Ax, and we were just people in a pub drinking shitty beer. He went back into the closet and left through the tunnels. None of me regretted showing them to him; if anything, maybe he'd be able to find more answers. I sighed and walked over to my sitting room to pour myself another glass of wine.

The night started with wine. It might as well end with it, too.

Chapter Eighteen

Zuri advised me Dusra was gone when I woke up this morning, thankfully heeding my warning. The castle was already quieter; guards had gone back to their original posts, and the castle staff on this level thinned out again. My mother hadn't come to my room yet, and I wasn't sure if she went back to the dungeon or if she thought it was me who killed the witches. She couldn't exactly ask me in front of anyone, or the fact she had me in the dungeons in the first place would be known. Kaizer summoned me to the red room, and Zuri said my mother and the advisers were summoned as well, so the answer would come to light soon. I was first to the room, so I sat as far away from Kaizer's desk as I could in a window seat surrounded by bookshelves. A few of them caught my attention as they were the books he had stacked on his desk when I looked through the spy hole from the tunnels. They were pretty noticeable, black with gold letters etched into the spine. I listened for if anyone was approaching and didn't hear anything, so I scooched closer to the book and pulled it down from the shelf.

I ran my finger over the title, *Magic of the Old.*

What was with this man's fucking obsession with old magic?

I flipped it open in hopes it might have some answers, and there were a few pages with the corners folded down to mark their spot. *Fucking psychopath.*

I turned to the first marked page and found the history of our world. A beautiful image of the Creators was sketched across the first page: Cama the Goddess of Fire, Coleb the Goddess of Earth, Zalvoh the Goddess of Water, and

Naom the Goddess of Air and Essence, the only dual powered goddess. They created a balanced world, each section of the land dedicated to an element, and the goddesses gifted their patrons with the power to wield that element. Witches, vampires, and lobos existed during the night, and the fae, sirens, and humans existed during the day. The goddesses were happy with their creation and went to rest.

Without them in the world to help create balance, the creatures turned against each other. The beings of the day accused those of night of stealing their children and feasting on them due to their need for blood. Accused them of murdering any of the creatures of day that dared leave their homes after sundown. The battles were ruthless, with such potent power running through everyone's veins. The Creators returned one thousand years after their rest, erecting the Piedra in the middle of Iteria. The barrier went straight through air and water, leaving half of the territories split, fire alone in Malva, and earth alone in Bonda. They separated our nations and the very fabric of the world, allowing the sun to remain in Bonda and not grace the sky of Malva.

The Piedra stretched for miles in every direction, an impenetrable force to ensure we didn't mix again. None of us would want to go to the other side and face the sun, and none of them would want to come here solely for fear of what we were. There were rumors that the humans, the only powerless creatures in our world, found their way here a few hundred years after the Piedra was built, forming some sort of tunnel system, but there was no proof of that.

The next tab was about the elemental stones, the artifacts made by the Creators after forming the Piedra. There was one for each of the elements: air, earth, water, and fire. I heard the steady sound of a heartbeat and footsteps moving toward the red room, and I slid the book back into its spot and pretended to gaze out the window just as the door opened and Kaizer walked through.

"Dusra left before I could see them out," Kaizer started, his face set into a scowl already. "I'm not sure if that's a good sign or not."

He sat down in his chair, finally making eye contact with me.

"I think you should just be happy they're gone," I muttered as I carelessly inspected my nails.

"You're still upset," he said flatly.

Our fight about his terrible fucking attitude seemed so long ago now, as I had literally been fucking whipped, physically by my mother and emotionally by Ax. Not to mention I knew he was lying. I didn't know what exactly about yet, but I had a hunch it had something to do with his obsession with the old magic.

I looked him directly in the eye. "I won't be treated as less than I deserve."

"It wasn't my intention. I apologize for my behavior while Dusra was here," he said, sounding fairly sincere.

The door opened, and Abel and Otto walked through, sparing me from having to reply to his apology.

"They're gone," Abel said as he sat on one of the chairs directly across from Kaizer, neither of them acknowledging me.

Fucking men.

"Hello," I exclaimed, and they both turned and nodded to me.

"We'll have to work on that when I'm queen," I muttered.

"Where's Lupe?" Otto asked.

"I don't know. She should have been here by now," Kaizer answered as he looked over at the clock on the shelf.

I wasn't sure if I should have been relieved or not that she wasn't here; my mother could be a wild card when she was caught off guard.

"We can get started," Kaizer said, gesturing me over to the table closer to them.

I rolled my eyes but got up and sat down before raising my eyebrows at him to tell him to say whatever warranted me to move closer.

"We will be addressing the kingdoms. We will address Sanjry first and then Caldera. This will be our first official announcement together as betrothed."

"Is this to discuss the treaty?" I asked.

"Yes, and it will do for both kingdoms to see us together. Seeing that we plan on ruling as one can help reinforce their trust," Kaizer answered.

"You will need to present as true royals," Otto said with his gaze on me.

"Say what you want to say, Otto," I responded.

"I'm suggesting that when in Sanjry, at least, you act as the people would expect from their queen."

"Make your fucking point," I snapped.

"That." He waved his hand in my direction. "That is not what the people will be expecting."

I rolled my eyes and sat back in my chair. I wished I would have kept the dumb seductress facade up sometimes, as that was a much easier way to deal with the people in this kingdom.

"I think what Otto is trying to say is that all the queens in the past have been of noble birth. Raised in Sanjry and accustomed to our traditions and our expectations. While you are of noble birth in your own right, witches are raised to be a little more...rough around the edges," Abel added a poor attempt at playing devil's advocate.

"She will be fine," Kaizer exclaimed, "I don't think she'll be stabbing anyone if that's what you're worried about."

No promises.

"You'll need to present as a true couple as well," Abel added.

"Yes, we've talked about this," I groaned.

"When it came to Dusra, yes, but Sanjry is a little different. Marriage is sacred here, a union of love and commitment, a political union would be shunned," Abel responded.

"What is going to be expected of me?" I asked Kaizer.

"You will need to address them. I will give the speech around the treaty and what our plans are. But Abel is right. We've made it known that this was not a political union, otherwise it wouldn't be accepted. Them seeing any evidence of it being...love will help." He cleared his throat. "But I think it would be best if you spoke to why this will be good for the witches as well in Sanjry. I'll let you lead in Caldera," Kaizer said as he pulled out a piece of paper.

"Thank you for allowing me to address my people how I see fit. Is this sacred union stuff regarding the Embers?" I asked.

Kaizer nodded. "Yes, it is our nation's religion."

"Who is the Flame? I heard one of the acolytes mumbling about it."

"It is who they worship," Kaizer responded.

I tilted my head. "Not the Goddess of Fire, Cama?"

Kaizer sat forward and looked to Otto and Abel before returning his gaze to me. "Yes and no. The forest of Incen burned even after the goddess went to rest. The Embers believed that the people of Sanjry were seen as blessed since it remained on fire. They worshiped the forest and the flames within until one day it went out. They believed that they were suddenly cursed, that the Flame itself found the people unjust after thousands of years of it burning."

"You'd think the forest going out would have stopped the belief in it all together," I responded.

"It is believed that if the Sanjryans are found as just again, the forest would reignite. It's what the faith is based around," Abel added.

"And you all believe this?" I asked.

"To a certain extent, some of the beliefs are a bit extreme, only the acolytes have to take vows of purity and what not. We don't go to the temple three times a day, but, yeah, we believe," Otto replied.

Kaizer stood to hand me the parchment he pulled out of the stack. "Anyway, I drafted this but feel free to make it your own. We will address Sanjry tomorrow and leave for Caldera right after. The men we sent to make sure Athena didn't influence them have notified the noble houses across the nation and will be meeting here in the capital. None of them seemed to have been part of the revolt, thankfully, so hopefully this will go smooth. Your mother said she was going to notify your sanction leads after you left the meeting yesterday."

As if summoned by the mention of her, my mother busted through the doors, her gaze falling on me immediately. Her face was stone-cold, the usual lack of emotion she wore, but her eyes squinted slightly at my position leaning against the chair. Something I shouldn't be able to do with ease after the beating I took, or she thought I took.

Her lip twitched. "Dayanara, you look well."

"You're late," Kaizer stated.

She took the seat directly next to me. "I had some...witch troubles."

"Something that needs to be discussed?" Kaizer asked.

"No, it's been taken care of," she answered.

Otto leaned toward her. "Did you notify the sanction leads that they'd be coming to address them?"

"I sent notice last night. They will be prepared," my mother responded.

Kaizer looked at me. "Good. Zuri should be packing your things as we speak for us to leave promptly after we address the people."

I nodded and stood. "I have some things to attend to if I will be leaving first thing tomorrow," I lied, trying to get out of the possibility of my mother bringing anything up.

"Oh yes, I'll come with you," my mother said as she stood.

Fuck.

We exited the room, and my mother threw out a portal in front of us the moment the door closed, pushing me through with force. I found myself back in the dungeon Ax had saved me from the night before, the witches were gone, but the blood still stained the stones.

"What the fuck happened here last night," she snapped.

I slowed my heart beat down. "I don't know."

"The witches were torn apart. You don't appear to be in the amount of pain you should be. What happened?"

"I don't know," I bit out. "I woke up in my room with a bloody rag beside me. Someone healed me. I don't know who. The last thing I remember is that I passed out after the fourth lash."

I hoped my years of omitting truths would pay off, but she didn't say anything, just looked back at the blood of her two most trusted witches.

"It was probably Kaizer. Did you notice how standoffish he was in the meeting? Someone must have tipped him off. He wouldn't have taken kindly to the beating I was getting," I growled.

My mother looked at me, her lip pulling back from her teeth as she tried to find the validity in my statement.

"I haven't ruled out the possibility it was you," she snarled.

"They immobilized me and used your magic suppressant. I wouldn't have been dumb enough to leave them here for you to find out if it was me."

She tapped her foot on the hard stone. "Don't embarrass the brujas while you're out acting like a vampire."

"I won't be acting like a vampire. You're the one who wanted me to marry one."

"A decision I'm still weighing the benefits of. You're dismissed," she said with a wave of her hand as she opened a portal back to the hall near the red room.

I stepped through and sighed deeply, thanking the goddesses that she believed my story enough for me to escape unharmed. She'd still be investigating, but the fact she didn't mention Dusra eased some of my concerns. My mother would wage war against the kingdom for the disrespect he brought the witches. As backward as it was. The brutal punishment of her daughter wasn't the issue; it was the fact her henchwomen were dead. I hated how deeply the loyalty to her was ingrained in me. From birth, we're told she is the beginning and the end of everything. We're told never to question her methods or her opinions, and as her daughter, it was even worse for me.

I prided myself in being a badass, but my mother still had the ability to beat me senseless without me lifting a hand to her. It was fucking pathetic. Like I told Ax, for years I actually believed that what she was doing was for my own good. I took each beating, every lesson, and honestly tried to be better. After Ximena, it was like a switch went off in me. I lost all respect for her, I still did what I needed for my kingdom, but it was never for her.

I would be in her position soon, and the pressure of being the very lifeline to thousands of people was far too much to handle. I wanted to be me, to move freely in the world and do whatever it was I decided I wanted to do when I woke up. That would never be the case for me, though. I was tied to Kaizer, for now at least, and he was up to something as well. Everywhere I turned, there was someone else who had the possibility to betray me, and I didn't want to deal with it a minute longer. Not to mention I'd be stuck in close quarters with him while we traveled. Tonight was my last chance to see if I could figure out if he could be trusted.

Chapter Nineteen

I was starting to think I was an expert on getting around here without being seen. I wasn't sure if I was the only person who knew about the tunnels, but it surely felt like it. Kaizer seemed meticulous in his study of histories, so I found it hard to believe he didn't know about them. Either way, I hadn't been caught yet, and tonight I'd use them to my advantage. It was well past midnight, and I passed by Kaizer's room to make sure he was asleep. I could hear his slow resting heartbeat, so I made my way over to his office to look at those books. I slid into the entrance of his sitting room and tiptoed to the bookshelves, running my finger over the books. The book wasn't in the same spot as it was when I left, so I searched the shelves until I found it much closer to his desk. I flipped open to the last marked page about the artifacts and found the paragraph I left off on.

The artifacts formed a circle of stone, each quarter of the stone belonging to one of the elements made by the Creators. I'd seen the stone the witches held for the air element in our treasury. It was held in a glass case, and one thing I do remember was the odd material it was made of. While witches held a connection to many stones and crystals, this stone felt more alive; it had streams of color running through it that felt like veins flowing through a body. My mother forbade me from touching it, for once, I listened immediately. The stone was thousands of years old, and just being near it caused my body to be on high alert, the potency of the magic so strong and revolting.

After the Piedra was erected, the goddesses formed the stones, taking their essence and some of the world's magic and putting it into each sliver. We were left less powerful than before but still able to wield the elements of our region and order. Each stone could only be used by a person that held that element so that no one person could become too powerful. The stones were useless alone, but together they could be used to remake the world, or so the legends say. All parties would have to agree to use the stones, and since we were separated, they were never used again. The fae, sirens, and humans all lived in Bonda. From history, the earth stone should be held by the fae. I wasn't sure if the water stone was in Dusra or in Bonda, as the water territory split across Bonda and Malva just like the air territory. The next page Kaizer marked had words written in the margins, possible locations of each stone.

Air—Caldera

The witches knew that the airstone was in Caldera and not in Bonda, but I didn't know that the vampires knew that as well. Kaizer had written enough handwritten instructions for me to recognize his handwriting. While definitely his, it seemed like he was rushing when he wrote it, the lines a little sloppy, the 'i' missing the dot.

"What could you possibly need with the stones," I muttered.

Footsteps sounded in the hall, and I backed up into the shadows with my magic at my fingertips in case I needed to create a portal out of there. The person walked past the room and continued down the hall, and I let out a breath of relief.

I sat back down at Kaizer's desk and tried to see if there was any more information I could use, but the only thing I could find was more history about the creation of the stones. I slid the book back onto the shelf, making sure that it was in the spot he had left it, and grabbed the next book I had noticed on his desk before. This one seemed significantly older than every other book in his collection; the spine was barely holding itself together, the edges curling in.

Malva's Original Beings

This book might as well have been a nightmare written in ink because the creatures that roamed this land thousands of years ago could only be described as monsters. The much smaller, still as disgusting, ancestors of some of these still lived in some of the less populated areas. One of them being the horned scorpions of the desert that I'd had to take down more than once while getting to the Sand City. I didn't consider myself to be a fearful person, but those things *I* didn't even want to mess with. While they were smaller than the original ones that stood as tall as a house, they were still the size of a cow and had pinchers as sharp as my blades. A shudder ran through me as I kept flipping through the pages, passing the Triori, a section about the creatures in the Inbetween, only stopping when I saw a section about the Creators, starting with Naom.

Now this history I had been taught plenty of as a child. While Sanjry got their regional magic from the Goddess of Fire, Cama, we got ours from the Goddess of Air and Essence, Naom. She was a being of great power, holding the strongest of magics. Her body burned with pure essence; purple, blue, pink, and green streams of magic pulsing through her, much like how our magic presented itself in jewel tones. While most of the creatures couldn't trace themselves back to creation, the witches could. We were connected to Naom through and through, as she created the brujas as well. The evidence was in our magic. When she gifted a kernel of her power to the first Acna after erecting the Piedra, and before going to rest, I always thought she wanted to give her creation an extra edge against the others.

I ran my finger over her wings and down the curves of her feminine frame. She disappeared with the other goddesses and more ethereal creatures at the time the Piedra was erected. There were many other beings not quite as powerful as the Creators that also disappeared with them, and no one really knew why. A few of them were better off gone, but some scholars had theories that so much magic was used to separate our worlds and create the stones that it pulled from the very source that fed them, and they fell into their final rest.

The next page was about Sanjry's creator, Cama, the Goddess of Fire. Much like Naom she burned, but with orange and red flames adorning her body. There was the start of a sentence at the bottom of the page, the word 'urn' was circled and underlined, and I ran my finger over to the next page, but it was about the water dragons of Dusra. I splayed the book open with a little more force and saw the raw edges of a torn page extending from the spine.

I shuffled through a pile of papers on Kaizer's desk, but none of them were nearly as old as the paper in this book. I tapped my foot, bit my cheek, and scanned the office for any other signs. This really only confirmed what I already knew; he was interested in old magic and wanted access to more than the scraps he used in the battle. But how he would go about it and what he would do if he was successful was still up in the air. I looked over every shelf, every drawer, but found absolutely nothing of use. I returned every item I touched to its original location and slipped back into the tunnel, weighing my options. I was close enough to Kaizer that I could monitor any moves he made. If he trusted me enough, he might give away whatever it was he was trying to hide.

The familiar feel of my magic lapped over my skin as I stepped through the block I set up into my room. I peeled off my leathers and pulled a nightgown on before crawling into bed. I'd have to address Sanjry tomorrow as the future queen, and I wasn't looking forward to it.

There were so many goddess damn vampires here that every square inch of the streets were covered. We stood on the terrace far above everyone, waiting to address them. Otto advised that there were still people filtering in, where I had no idea, but we couldn't start until they thought everyone was here. Zuri was behind me, her head on a constant swivel like she was my bodyguard. Quinn, my actual bodyguard, was beside her, never removing her hand from her sword on her side. Abel pushed through the doors and whispered in Otto's ear; he nodded once and walked over to where Kaizer and I stood.

"We're ready," he muttered between us.

I looked back at Zuri one more time, and my chest tingled to find her already watching me with a small smile that had me returning one of my own on instinct.

Kaizer nodded and stepped up to the edge of the terrace, placing both his hands on the railing.

"My kingdom," he started, and the crowd raged with excitement.

He lifted his hand after a few moments of the commotion, and the crowd silenced.

"As many of you know, Sanjry and Caldera have ceased war and unified. Today, we would like to formally address you."

He turned around with his hand stretched for me to grab, his mouth set in a pleasant smile. I placed my hand in his and stepped forward with him, moving over a few inches so we weren't as close as he wanted us to be.

"Dayanara and I found love, and through that we are able to stop the centuries of fighting between our kingdoms."

His words made me want to barf, *love,* there was no such thing, and he surely hadn't found it in me. But everyone around us thought it would be the best way to sell the union. So here I was *in love.*

"Outside of the obvious cease of the war, this union will have minimal impacts on our people. Our kingdoms become one, but I will still ensure that no harm comes to Sanjry or its residents. We have also ensured there will be no problems with Dusra and have signed a formal treaty between our kingdoms. This is the start to a great and fruitful future for our people. Dayanara," he finished, looking for me to say my part.

"I would like to formally introduce myself to you all. I am Dayanara Amapola, daughter of the Acna of Caldera," I exclaimed; some of the crowd clapped, but a lot of them just watched me with intent.

Kaizer shifted closer so our arms were touching, and I continued. "My people are happy that the war has ended between us, and we are excited to be joining this kingdom. Just like you, we look forward to peace. I would also like to invite each of you to our wedding ceremony," I boomed.

"It will take place in a few weeks. You can expect formal invitations in the coming days. May the Flame light the way," Kaizer yelled with a smile.

The crowd went wild, screaming and clapping and dancing in the streets. People climbed up on the roofs of their homes on the other side of the wall, jumping up and down with excitement. Kaizer's smile stretched wide as he took in his people, the people that would become mine soon. I knew one thing for sure; this would not be how the witches received the formal message. They already had their reservations, rightfully so, because I did too. Kaizer lifted my hand in the air and waved to his people as we took a step back from the rail.

"We'll walk through the kingdom so they can see us together, and then we'll head to Caldera," Kaizer exclaimed, his smile still shining.

"I expected...more," I said.

"More what?" Otto asked.

"I don't know. They were happy just to be invited to a wedding. I was expecting to need to say more for them to give that kind of response," I replied.

Otto shrugged. "The people here are fairly easy to manage, give them a reason to celebrate, and they forget about half of their troubles."

"Don't expect that to be the case in Caldera," I responded, descending the stairs beside Kaizer.

Zuri muffled a laugh directly behind me as we made it to the ground level near the door to the courtyard where the thousands of vampires waited for us.

"Ready?" Kaizer asked with his chest puffed out, offering me his arm.

I nodded and looped my arm in his as Zuri and Otto walked around us to open the doors. Zuri looked at me and smiled dramatically, reminding me that I probably should look less murderous than I was sure I did at the moment. The doors were pulled open for us, and a line of guards had already split the crowd to create a path for us to walk down.

The dress I was wearing was a Sanjry style fashion, the long sleeves bunching in the crook of my elbow stiffly as I waved out into the crowd. They all shouted for Kaizer like he was some kind of god, trying to touch his hand and get his attention. I felt my face pulling into a scowl at the behavior and quickly painted the fake smile back on.

We walked through the border wall gate, where more people were waiting to see us, people shouting from their rooftops. I heard my name shouted, but the tone of the shout had me on immediate alert. A ball of fire came from deep within the crowd aimed toward me. Putting up a shield of air around me, I stole the oxygen from the flame and looked out in the direction the attack came from. Someone shifted through the crowd, and I charged toward them but was yanked back by my wrist.

"Let go of me." I yanked my arm from Kaizer's grip, but he held tight.

"Let them deal with it," Kaizer mumbled.

The crowd went silent, all eyes shifting over to me and my magic pooled in my hands. Kaizer didn't move, didn't look bothered at all, he simply pretended it didn't happen and turned to speak to one of the patrons lining the street politely. The others surrounding us watched as Kaizer carried on without missing a beat and started cheering and yelling again.

Guards pushed through the excited vampires to get to the attacker as I stood there watching them until they ran out of sight, the only person seemingly concerned about what happened. Kaizer stepped back toward me and we walked forward again.

"They were mine to deal with," I growled.

"Not today," Kaizer said through his teeth.

I balled my hands into fists and extinguished my magic before biting my lip with frustration. Zuri stepped beside me and put her hand on my arm, to guide me to follow him.

"He's right. You attacking them the first time they see you probably wouldn't go over well," she whispered.

"I don't fucking care. He should have at least said something. Him not defending me or allowing me to defend myself is going to let others think they can attempt it to," I snapped.

I was owed blood for what that vampire attempted. My insides were on fire with the need to exact revenge, and the fact that Kaizer said absolutely nothing pissed me off even more. Zuri idly rubbed the inside of my arm where she had her hand looped and the small movement calmed me enough to continue. I carried on a few steps behind Kaizer for the rest of the way until we made it back onto the castle grounds. Only Otto, Abel, and Zuri followed us back through the border wall, and I didn't want to discuss how my first appearance went. I stormed past Kaizer, and he yelled for me to stop, but I kept walking toward the door. The guards blocked me from entering the castle, and I whirled around to Kaizer on my heels.

"Dayanara," he started, but I cut him off quickly.

"Why aren't *you* upset? Why didn't you try to defend me? Would that not have been more of a show of unity?" I asked.

"It wasn't the right time for me to react," he answered.

I rolled my eyes. "I expect to be able to handle the situation myself or for you to do *something*. What would have happened if it was directed at you?"

"The guards would have handled it," he responded flatly.

Otto and Abel shifted beside us while Zuri's face was set in a scowl behind Kaizer.

"Bull-fucking-shit. You would have handled it yourself," I snapped.

Kaizer turned to his advisers, his jaw ticking as he searched for a response. Otto looked away from him, and Abel surveyed me with a disgusted stare.

"That's what I thought," I mumbled.

"We are due to leave shortly," Kaizer exclaimed, gesturing for the guards to let us in.

I scoffed and entered through the doors, my patience was wearing thin as it was, and now I had to travel with the fucking bastard to Caldera.

Chapter Twenty

Unlucky for me, Kaizer decided that we'd be traveling in our own carriage, so I didn't even have Zuri to act as a buffer on the ride. I could have created a portal for us to get there instantly, but Kaizer insisted on bringing a bunch of guards and horses so he could 'see the real Caldera as we traveled.' I smoothed out the lightweight fabric of my dress, thanking the goddesses that I decided to change before we left into a dress fit for Caldera. A beautiful black gossamer dress allowing all of my tattoos to be on show, which was something I had missed dearly. Kaizer was eyeing me as I looked out the window, which I'd ignored for the last few hours, but he cleared his throat to draw my attention to him.

"I understand that things are handled differently where you're from," he said, breaking the silence.

I scoffed and looked back out the window.

"Sanjry is a lot about...appearances. How royals should and shouldn't act," he added.

"You're the king. You set the rules, Kaizer. You not doing anything at all and pretending like it didn't happen sends its own message," I responded.

"I am the king, but I have to make sure everyone is happy," he reasoned, his gaze burning into my face.

"Everyone will never be happy. But you are right. Things are handled different-ly where I'm from. You're more...civilized, but at least we don't have to pretend for the delicate sensibilities of our people. When you fuck up, you get fucked up. That's just how it goes. Had that happened in Caldera, I would have had the attacker's head, and my people would have praised me for it."

"That's how it was at one point in Sanjry. We can't move backward," Kaizer responded.

"I wouldn't call it backward," I quipped. "I was owed blood; I should have made them suffer for daring to kill me."

I looked back out the window as the river bordering our kingdoms came into view, and I could already feel my soul reconnecting with my land. It had been too long since I stood on Calderan soil, and my body was screaming with the need to get back home with it being so close. The carriage jerked as the horses pulled it onto the bridge, their hooves knocking against the stone until we came to a stop. I couldn't see ahead of the carriage, so I scooted over to the door and swung it open.

Kaizer followed me out of the carriage. "Dayanara, what are you doing?"

"Seeing why we stopped," I responded as I walked past the horses and around the carriage in front of us.

A line of witches stood at the end of the bridge near our watchtower, and a familiar head of long black hair caught my attention as Cat, my childhood friend, practically ran over to me. For a moment, I thought she was going to attempt to hug me, but thankfully she stopped just short of where I stood and bowed.

"Daya, they told us you'd be crossing soon, so I came to the border to see you through," she said, lifting her head to meet my gaze.

"Why'd they stop the procession?" I asked.

Her eyes cut over to Kaizer before returning to me. "They didn't see you."

"Are my people not welcome here?" Kaizer asked.

"Are mine welcome in Sanjry unannounced?" Cat asked.

"Lupe should have announced our arrival. Besides, we will be one kingdom soon, one people," Kaizer replied.

"All the same, they didn't see you, so they stopped the carriages until we knew you were among them," Cat responded.

"Well, I'm here," I said, lifting my hands in the air.

Cat smiled and brushed her hair over her shoulder as she glanced back and waved to the soldiers to allow the carriages through. Kaizer turned back to the carriage, and I went to follow, but Cat grabbed my wrist. I looked down at her hand on my body and back up at her face with eyebrows raised.

"I'm sorry," she muttered, "why aren't you traveling by portal?"

I pulled my arm from her grasp. "He wanted to see the land."

"The brujas are still uneasy. I just thought I'd warn you that you're walking into a potential bloodbath. Your mother hasn't been very present, and people have concerns."

"Do you have concerns?" I asked.

"I don't like that you are separated from us, but you know I will follow you wherever you go. But something about them does put me on edge. I don't know if it's the years of animosity or if there's something...off."

I looked over my shoulder at the soldiers on horseback and the rows of carriages carrying our companions and sighed.

"You're not alone in that," I replied.

"Has something happened?" Cat asked quickly, her voice shifting into that of her newly appointed general position.

"Not yet, but I want you to keep an eye on them while we're visiting. Don't tell my mother or anyone you can't trust, but I want them monitored," I replied.

"It's done," she responded with a bow.

I turned to get back to Kaizer but stopped and looked back.

"Cat," I started, and she whirled back around. "Always bring me your concerns—as general."

She nodded and moved back in the direction of the watchtower at the end of the bridge as I walked back to my carriage. I hopped back in, and Kaizer was tapping his foot, drumming his fingers on the back of the seat he was on. I slid into the bench across from him and looked out the window, nodding to Cat as we passed the watchtower. Kaizer was still tapping his finger, and I snapped my neck toward him with a scowl, his face pulled tight, his skin slightly sheen.

"What is your problem?" I asked.

He looked over at me, biting his lips and looking away from me. "I need blood."

Of course he did; he hadn't had any blood since I cut my wrist into the chalice a few days ago. I didn't think I'd get used to the fact he *needed* my blood; I wondered if I could convince him to start drinking animal blood like me.

"I know you aren't used to giving it, so I don't know how to ask you," he followed up.

"How long until it's a problem?" I questioned.

"Soon."

I sighed, biting my lip, wondering why I ever fucking agreed to let him drink from me in the first place. He started the tapping again, and I shot up and sat beside him. "I swear to the goddesses if you tap that finger one more time...Fucking do it," I snapped, leaning toward him. "Before I change my mind."

He slid closer to me so his thigh touched mine, and I turned my head to pull my hair away from my neck. He lifted his hand, hesitating for a moment, but before I could turn back, he gripped my bare shoulder, and I felt his fangs slice into my flesh. My muscles relaxed, his venom immobilizing me for a moment until he started pulling the blood into his mouth with force. His venom transformed into a warm sensation coursing through my veins, sending me flashbacks from the last time he drank from me. I clamped my thighs shut, cursing my body for the unwanted reaction to the fucking bastard. He groaned into my neck, and his thumb started to rub circles on the exposed flesh on my arm. I wasn't so thankful now for the fact that I had changed out of my long-sleeved gown.

He was still pulling in mouthfuls of blood; I could hear it rushing down his throat with every gulp he took. My core was pulsing, and I crossed my legs, hoping that Kaizer couldn't sense what was going on inside of me. I separated my thighs, feeling the evidence of my desire between them. I turned my chin toward Kaizer, but all I could see was the top of his head, his hands still in the same spot as before. I ran my fingers up my legs, every point of contact like a million tiny fires under my skin. I gasped sharply as my fingers reached my inner thighs, and I wondered if it wasn't the worst idea to shift my hands slightly higher to the area of my body begging to be touched.

My fingers grazed the fabric at the apex of my thighs, and I muffled a moan of my own just as Kaizer pulled his fangs from my neck, his head hovering above my skin. He licked the drops of blood that escaped the wound, both our chests heaving, the sexual tension so thick in the carriage I was practically choking on it. He tilted his chin up before licking his lips as his gaze fell to mine and then up to my eyes. He moved closer, his mouth only inches away. The carriage rolled over a rock, shaking me enough to get a grasp of myself and move back to my seat. He cleared his throat, and I watched as he adjusted himself in his pants in my peripheral vision and I pretended to be very interested in the land outside the window.

"Thank you," Kaizer muttered, breaking the tight air around us.

I didn't look him in his eye. "Mhm."

I needed some kind of immunity spell to vampire venom, and I needed it fast.

"Take a lover who looks at you like maybe you are magic."
– Frida Kahlo

Chapter Twenty-One

While I may have been slightly biased, there wasn't anything better than being in Caldera. The sights, the smells, the food, it was all so much more superior to Sanjry. We set up camp for the night, but I went off by myself for a walk, trying to figure out my next move. I was half tempted to portal myself to the palace to see what we'd be walking into. I wasn't sure if the agreement stopped me from that. I was thankful that I saw Cat, and that she warned me that people might not be happy. If there was anyone in this world I could trust, I knew it was her. While we weren't nearly as close as we were growing up, I knew she was loyal to me. To my mother as well, but she'd always had my back, no matter what situation we were in. I knew it would be likely that they'd be upset; I would have been just as upset if I were them.

As Abel so kindly reminded me, my people were rough around the edges and could be unpredictable at times. The majority would follow my mother's word, but there were always those outliers—the ones I'd always been sent out to deal with—that would be the problem. I was the second most powerful being in Caldera, so I wasn't worried for my life necessarily. Not to say I wasn't always on edge and ready for a fight, as always. I was concerned that there would be enough strife that Kaizer would back out of the agreement, and we'd be back in war, or use whatever he did in the blast to just kill us all. We were practically built for battle, and had no problems with a fight if it was presented, but I knew my people were tired of fighting solely to defend our land. I was tired of fighting myself; I'd never known a world at peace. If I wasn't on a mission, I was out on the battlefield or preparing the armies for war. I was curious, who I might be if I wasn't always fighting for my life. A snap of a branch had me whirling around with a ball of air ready in my hand to throw, but Zuri peeked around a tree and stepped onto the path I was following.

"Hey," she exclaimed.

"Is something wrong?" I asked.

"No, I just wanted to make sure you were alright. It's late, and I noticed you hadn't come back yet."

"You don't have to worry about my safety here," I replied.

She shrugged, looking up at the moon. The witches' connection to the moon was something so substantial, it felt like I knew her, like I'd danced in her craters as a child. I could sense the push and pull of energy from the moon; it brought me such wholesome peace. Being out in the open air, with the moon above me and the stars twinkling in the dark sky, was one of the few times I felt that. Zuri hadn't said anything else; she stood beside me with her chin tilted to the moon, taking in the beauty of it just as I was.

"I've never been to Caldera. I like it here. I feel...alive and free," she whispered.

"Me too. The Sanjryans have forgotten what it's like to be out in the wild, to live the way we were meant to. They're so worried about being civilized and proper to bring back the Flame that they have no idea what they're missing."

She sighed and turned to face me, the moonlight casting silver on her brown skin. Zuri was beautiful, beautiful in a way that sometimes had me staring when she wasn't watching. Her dark gray angular eyes, the fullness of her mouth, and her short, bouncing curls all worked together to create a work of art. I could never fully appreciate her beauty, even if I tried. She was like a classic painting, where you found something new to admire every time you looked at it. There wasn't a single thing out of place with her, the closest thing to perfection I'd seen in a long time.

She turned to face me with a small smile gracing her lips. "Will we reach the palace tomorrow?"

I nodded. "Yeah, probably in the late afternoon. I forgot what it's like to travel for such long periods."

Since my magic awakened, I rarely ever traveled by anything but a portal. I had to know where I was going to open one, or I'd be stuck in the middle realm. Still, I'd seen every part of this land at this point in my life, so I usually arrived at my destination in moments.

"Well, you should probably get some sleep," she said, bumping me in my shoulder.

I wasn't sure when Zuri became my friend; I'd trusted her for a while, tolerated her presence, and appreciated her spark, but somewhere along our journey, she'd weaseled her way into being my friend. I didn't have many friends; Cat was the closest thing. I had a whole kingdom of subjects, of people who would be loyal to me, but not people I really cared for the way I'd come to care for Zuri. Sometimes when I'd catch her already looking in my direction, when she smiled on instinct just in my presence, or seeing the worry in her eye every time I showed up bloody, I thought it could maybe be more than just friendship. Regardless, I'd kill for her if it ever came to it. I nodded and followed her back to the camp, dreading every step as I had to share a tent with Kaizer.

"You know you can stay with me? You don't sleep in the same room in the castle. I don't think people would talk about it," Zuri whispered.

"That's actually a good point," I muttered with my gaze on me and Kaizer's tent.

"I'm over there"—she pointed to a tent on the other side of camp—"if you decide you want to stay with me, just come by."

My feet dragged through the tall soft grass as I slowly made my way to my tent, casting one more look at the moon before opening the flaps and dipping my head in. Kaizer had his back turned to the tent entrance, sitting on the bedroll—a mistake I'd never make. I wasn't sure if it was because he'd been made to feel comfortable enough in his land that he wouldn't expect a threat or if he just had that much confidence in himself. I couldn't see what he was doing, so I took another step toward him, but he whirled around and looked up at me with his eyes wide in surprise.

"I didn't hear you come in," he muttered.

"You should really be more cautious. You aren't in Sanjry," I responded.

He had a small journal and a pencil in his lap and quickly put it in his bag before standing before me. "Should I be worried about that?" he asked.

"If you ever feel safe, you're either an idiot or you've gotten too comfortable." I shrugged.

"You don't even feel safe here?"

"Seeing as I'm not an idiot, no. I feel safer here than anywhere else, but I always assume someone is going to try to hurt me. It's how I stay one step ahead of everyone."

"That is...sad," he replied with his head tilted.

I shrugged again and grabbed my bag with my clothes from our pile of things.

"I need Zuri to redo my hair before tomorrow," I started, not making eye contact. "I might just stay with her if it gets too late."

Kaizer didn't respond, so I glanced over to find him looking up at me through narrowed eyes. His gaze was on my well-manicured purple locks. "Your hair?"

"That's correct," I responded, turning to exit the tent.

"Dayanara," he exclaimed, and I stopped in my tracks. "What do I need to do?"

My head tilted in confusion. "For what?"

"To get you to forgive me. What must I do to get back to where we were before?"

An idea sparked in my mind, and I smiled devilishly.

I stepped toward him, replying sharply. "Grovel."

He looked up at me with his brows drawn together, not responding.

I put my sharp nail under his chin and tilted it up to me, digging it in a bit and glaring down my nose at him. "Grovel," I repeated, "if you want my forgiveness, that's what you need to do."

He bit the inside of his cheek, his gaze not leaving mine as he stared me down, presumably weighing if it was worth it.

When he didn't respond or make any moves, I released my hold on his chin and tsked. "Didn't think so," I muttered as I walked out of the tent.

I probably wouldn't have forgiven him if he did grovel, but it would have been quite the sight. I chuckled to myself as I made my way over to Zuri's tent and burst through the flaps. I saw a lot of skin as Zuri pulled her pants over her ass and spun around quickly.

"Fuck, you scared me," she muttered.

"Just me," I said, laughing with my hands up.

She folded her leathers and placed them beside her bedroll. "I wasn't sure if you were coming, so I was getting changed."

"Yeah, I had to talk to Kaizer," I sighed as I laid out my bedroll beside hers.

"What did you tell him?"

I side-eyed her. "That you're doing my hair."

"How did I end up having to work in this arrangement?" she laughed.

I shrugged. "That's on me."

She gestured for me to sit in front of her, and I sat between her legs, the feel of her running her fingers through my hair soothing me. "I saw Cat talking to you," Zuri said.

"She warned my people may not be offering the warmest of welcomes," I whispered.

"Are you worried?"

"I'm worried Kaizer bit off way more than he can chew with the brujas. I don't think he knows what he's getting himself into. When they show their faces, he might go back on his word of the deal."

She ran her pinky nail down the center of my head, separating my hair and humphed.

"What?" I questioned.

"Just doesn't seem like you'd be against that."

"As much as I hate to say it, my mother was right. This is our best option right now. I do want peace. Or however much peace we're capable of," I muttered.

She weaved the left section of my hair into a braid. "That's understandable."

"I know we've been training, and you can hold your own. But when we get there, try to keep your head down. My people don't take kindly to any disrespect. If they think you're a threat for a second, they'll gut you before I can even get to you."

"Comforting," she muttered as she finished the braid on the right side of my head.

"Also," I started, wondering how to word what I needed to say. "We've gotten close, and I've let you see a side of me that they don't typically see. I may be more...cruel."

"I won't judge you," she said as I felt her knotting the two braids together at the center of my skull.

"Would you judge me if I told you part of me enjoys it? The cruelty, the feeling of power I have. The taste of fear before I crack down on someone," I said, wondering just how far our friendship would stretch.

The only other person I ever felt comfortable enough to talk to like this was Ximena, my first and only girlfriend. Much like what I had with Zuri, what started as a friendship blossomed into so much more. The closest thing to love I'd ever had, and my mother made sure that I suffered for the weakness she brought out in me. The memory of her made me regret even opening up this much to Zuri; I hadn't known her long enough to feel this comfortable. I had to admit it was nice; it had been nearly a century since I lost Ximena. Lost wasn't the right word, but thinking about what happened to her hurt too much. Still, I was supposed to be a cold-hearted bitch, and that's what I needed to present in front of the sanction leads.

Zuri still had her hands in my hair, but she hadn't moved them since I made the comment. She hadn't responded, and I worried that maybe I really did take it too far.

"Was that—" She cut me off and lifted her hand before sitting beside me.

She put her hand on my leg and squeezed. "When I said I wouldn't judge you, I meant it. You never have to explain yourself to me."

I looked up at her, and for a second, Ximena looked back at me. I blinked, and her features were her own again, but it shook me enough that I scooted over to my bedroll and opened my bags. Zuri had a candle burning at the center of the tent, illuminating the small space, and I grabbed out my sleep clothes. I stood facing away from Zuri and pulled off my leathers as I looked back at her and she shuffled through her own bags to drag out a blanket. I pulled on my soft nightgown and placed my folded leathers next to hers before blowing out the candle and laying on my bedroll beside her.

"Zuri," I whispered.

"Yes?"

"Thanks," I said quickly, rolling to face the tent wall and pulling the blanket over me.

It was hard to allow myself to be vulnerable with her; it was probably a mistake and I just hoped it wouldn't come back to bite me. Something about Zuri was so soothing, I almost couldn't help myself. I closed my eyes, knowing I wouldn't get much rest after thinking of Ximena. I hadn't thought about her this much in a long time, as I'd never felt anything close to the feelings she invoked in me. I tried to completely forget about who I was when I was with her, the things I did because of her, the outcome of allowing myself to be that...exposed. I lay there staring at the canvas of the tent, listening to Zuri's deep breaths in and out.

After what felt like an eternity, I felt sleep calling to me, but it came with the sounds of pained screams, of muffled tears, and of daggers tearing into flesh.

I felt myself waking up, but this morning was different I was...warm. I blinked awake to find myself directly behind Zuri, her head full of curls splayed out between us. My arm was around her waist, and her chest rose and fell in deep, even movements. I couldn't remember the last time I woke up so content, and I wanted to stay here, breathing in her scent. I still couldn't pinpoint what exactly it was about her scent that was so unique, so I inched my nose closer to her and took a deep inhale. The smell was subtle, floral, but earthy. I couldn't help how relaxed I felt every time I got a whiff of it. She groaned and wiggled her hips, and I raised my eyebrows, unsure if it was intentional or if she was still asleep. Footsteps sounded from outside the tent, getting closer, and I rolled away quickly, the movement jolting her awake.

"What happened?" she asked, her voice gravely.

I sat up and stretched my arms as I pretended to just wake up. "Nothing, camp is just waking up."

"It's time to go," a male voice boomed from outside the tent.

I quickly changed, casting glances over at Zuri to see if I could figure out whether she knew how we woke up this morning. She wasn't acting awkward or looking at me weirdly as she hummed and packed up her things, so I was pretty sure I was in the clear. She strapped her bag onto her shoulder and looked over at me. "Ready?"

"Yes," I said quickly, before stepping out of the tent.

The moment my feet hit the grass, I looked up to find Kaizer's eyes already on me across the camp. I wasn't sure why I felt like I did something wrong, but I did. I didn't really owe Kaizer anything, alliance or not. Wasn't my fault Zuri was a better option than him. I stepped into the carriage with Kaizer already seated inside.

"Hair looks nice," he said.

"Thanks," I responded, sitting across from him and looking out the window.

I wasn't sure if there was something more to this thing with Zuri, but one thing I knew was that I needed to get a hold of myself before I met with the sanction leaders and my mother. They were ruthless, and any weakness would be snuffed out quickly. I closed my eyes, shifting myself back into the frigid witch I needed to be later today.

Chapter Twenty-Two

We'd sat in silence for hours, Kaizer read a book, and I pretended to be asleep for most of the ride. I opened my eyes and looked out of the window, and the sparkling jewel-toned leaves swaying in the breeze had me sitting up straight and scooching closer. Those trees lined the path to the gates of the palace, and their sweet cinnamon scent wafted over to me through the open window. A smile stretched across my face as I craned my neck to see how close to the gate of my home we were. Grass and flowers as far as the eye could see surrounded us, the rolling hills of the land going on forever. The carriage came to a halt, and I jumped out to find Cat already back and waiting at the wide golden gate with wings painted across the doors.

Fuck, I missed portal traveling.

The excitement I had at being home quickly faded as a puff of green formed beside Cat, and my mother stepped out of it. As always, she looked perfectly put together. Her dark green hair pulled back tight in a simple bun, her bronze skin clear and bright. I remembered who I needed to be and slowed my walk, pushing my shoulders back and setting my face into an uncaring glare. She didn't make a move to get any closer to me as she kept her feet planted with hands clasped in front of her. Heavy footsteps sounded from behind me, and I remembered that Kaizer was also here, but I kept moving until I was before my mother. I dipped my head and placed my hands behind my back, the way my mother preferred to be addressed, even by her daughter.

"Acna," I said.

"Dayanara, Kaizer. I'm glad you all made it safely," she said, her voice sounding sincere.

I hated that part of me wanted to know if she meant it, if she actually cared for my safety. She'd done enough during my life that I should have known she was merely making a show of being friendly, but I couldn't help the slight lift of my chin at her words.

"Once you two get settled, I'd like to meet with you before we address the clan. Catalina will show your people where they will be staying," she said just before she went up in a puff of smoke and was no longer before us.

"She wants them in the East Wing," Cat said with a wave of her hand for the witches stationed atop the wall to open the gate.

"That is where most of the empty rooms are," I agreed, looking back at Kaizer.

He'd be sharing with me, I presumed. While the thought surely didn't excite me, I was on my land now, and something about that had me more secure than before.

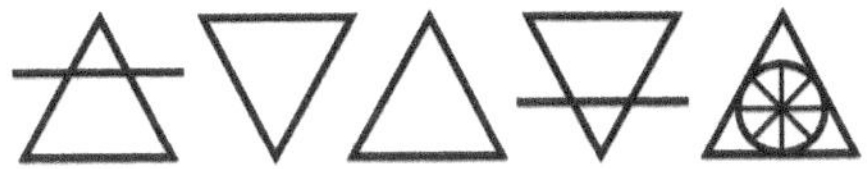

I was 99 percent sure now that Zuri didn't know what had happened this morning. She had been precisely herself as she rushed around my suite, trying to get my things set up. I didn't typically have much assistance here, so it was odd. My bedchamber was usually where I could have some solitude, but both Zuri and Kaizer were in the room.

"Zuri, you really don't need to do all of this," I said as she unpacked my things and put them into the drawers in my closet.

"It's quite literally my job," she responded, pushing the drawer shut.

I rolled my eyes but smiled as I turned to face Kaizer where he sat on one of the chairs near my fireplace. The breeze rolled into the room and shifted my hair slightly; I couldn't help but savor it. The fresh smells of the flowers in the courtyard outside of the permanently open doorway flowed into my room, so different from my chamber in Sanjry. I was quickly reminded that I needed to adjust the magical barriers in my room to allow Kaizer and Zuri in when I wasn't here, or they'd be in a world of pain.

Taking a deep breath, I closed my eyes. Bruja magic was really just tapping into the essence all around us. It was always there—in the air, in the ground—we just had the ability to guide it into something tangible. So I let myself feel it, let it vibrate until the room lit with a soft purple glow, and the magic rolled over everything in the room. I rubbed my hands together, the magic pulsing between my palms, and whispered the spell into my hands. They glowed as I threw the magic into the air, watching it spread to each wall and settle. I lifted my hands and closed them into fists, the magic glow dissipating and returning to the natural lighting in the room. I felt eyes burrowing into me, and I looked over my shoulder to see Zuri and Kaizer staring at me with wide eyes.

I turned around to face them. "First time seeing bruja magic?"

"That kind, yes," Kaizer muttered as Zuri nodded.

"Well, get used to it. You're in Caldera now," I said with a wink directed at Zuri.

"What did you do?" Kaizer asked.

"Oh, I just updated the protection spell on my room so that if either of you tries to come in without me, it doesn't burn you from the inside out." I shrugged, tossing my hair over my shoulder.

"You can do that?" Zuri asked.

"Oh, you two have no idea the things I'm capable of, do you? You should see what I can do with the help of crystals," I laughed out. "I'm the second most powerful being between our kingdoms, and you aren't number one, Kaizer."

Kaizer watched me, and I couldn't quite read his expression. It wasn't fear or reverence, but something maybe between the two. He knew I was powerful; I was sure it was one of the things that drove him to the agreement. I'd decimated battlefields time and time again, taken down hundreds of his soldiers, even though it was never quite enough to tip the win in our favor. They had the numbers;

vampires bred far more often than we did. But witches were powerful enough to withstand the centuries of war.

Zuri looked between the two of us multiple times before stepping toward me. "You two are due to meet with your mother, yes?"

"Yeah, we should probably get going. She didn't give a time, but I'm sure she has one in mind, and she'll be pissed if we don't meet her by then," I responded.

Kaizer blinked out of his shock and stood to his feet, offering me his arm, and I looped mine in his reluctantly.

"Catalina said there'd be a gathering after the council meeting, so I'll meet you there," Zuri said, crossing the sitting room to the empty suite she'd be staying in.

The door shut behind her, and Kaizer opened the door into the hallway, the movement making his bicep flex and squeeze my hand where it was resting.

"Tell me about your palace," he said as we turned the first corner in the hall.

I looked up at him, wondering if he was asking for any malicious reason, but his gaze was soft as he surveyed the beautiful architecture that was my home. "We are in the West Wing, where my mother and I stay. The palace is just one level, so most of the rooms can be open to the outdoors. It was built by my great-great-grandmother. It's been updated over the years, but the main structure remains."

"It's much more open than Sanjry," he responded, looking up at the lack of ceiling in this part of the hall.

"Now you understand why I spend so much of my time outside training," I replied.

He humphed, and we continued down the halls, passing a few staff that looked to be heading toward the dining hall for our lunch. It was significantly busier here, and all the witches we passed dipped their chins at me, some of them at Kaizer as well, but most of them watched him warily.

"There's her office," I said as I pointed my chin toward the door at the end of the corridor.

Kaizer stopped, not looking at me, but down at the floor.

"Wha—"

He cut me off. "You asked me to grovel. Is that what you truly need?"

My lips parted in surprise. I didn't think he would mention that again, as he didn't have a response for me when I said it. The question remained heavy in the air between us as I weighed my options. Pushing him too far could hurt the 'union,' and I needed to stay close enough to him to make sure I could see what he was up to. I might as well have some fun while I was at it. I flicked my finger out and turned his face toward mine with my nail.

"Mhm," I responded, with my lips pursed.

The door to the office was pushed open, and my mother stood in the doorway with one of her eyebrows raised.

"Do you plan on making me wait all day?" she snapped.

"Not a terrible option," I muttered under my breath, and Kaizer blew air out of his nose in a subtle laugh.

She turned on her heel back into the room, and we followed behind her through the dark door. I was always convinced that her office was built as an intimidation tactic. Every other room in the palace was open and airy, but this room was closed off and dark. The room was shaped in a circle with a spiral staircase in the back of the room to a tower she could use to look out into the capital. Her desk was large and made of obsidian, the chair she sat in a few inches taller than the ones in front of the desk. There were no windows, the only natural light coming from the tower window far above the space. Sconces sat on either side of her head behind the desk, illuminating her and only her.

I sighed. "What is it that needs to be discussed?"

She looked down at me, her lip pulling back slightly at my brashness. "There has been some discourse. I want you to be prepared," she muttered, and I felt Kaizer tighten beside me.

"Around?" I asked.

She pointed her lips toward Kaizer. "Him."

"What about me?" he asked.

She tapped her finger on the desk twice. Something I'd come to learn was her sign that she was forming her thoughts. "We knew there would be push back.

There hasn't been a time when we coexisted or were ruled by anything but our own. They are worried about our land's riches and what you might do with a combined army," she said as she folded her arms on the table.

"That is expected," I said, tilting my head, waiting for the other shoe to drop.

"Two of the sanction leads have been more vocal than others. There have been whispers that they plan on revolting against the union."

"Rosa?" I asked, the crotchety old bitch always the one with something to say.

She'd kept her life over the years by the skin of her teeth, always saying enough to gain my presence in her sanction but not enough for me to gut her like I wanted. My last meeting with them was quick, not even an official meeting, just a briefing before sending them home, and she had been pretty vocal then.

"Yes, she is the main one. Adriana has been wavering back and forth, but last I heard, she's leaning more toward Rosa's views."

"How long has this been an issue?" I asked.

"Since the initial meeting," she responded.

I leaned closer. "You didn't think to mention this until now?"

She shrugged one shoulder. "I was waiting to see whether it would turn into more. Neither of us expected them to roll over and accept the new predicament."

Kaizer looked between the two of us, not speaking, and I rubbed my temple as I tried to figure out the best way to explain to him what we'd be walking into.

"You should try to remain quiet unless spoken to directly in the meeting," I said to Kaizer.

His eyebrows rose, and he opened his mouth, but I cut him off quickly.

"Whether you like it or not, you are the issue at hand. Sauntering in with all of that machismo you exude will only make matters worse. Let me speak to them and handle them in our way," I said, my voice steady and powerful.

"I did say I'd let you lead here. If you think that is best, then I will try," he responded, and I saw a ghost of a smirk on my mother's lips in my peripheral.

I didn't prepare anything because I figured it would be pointless, that assumption being solidified at my mother's news. I could handle Rosa, and with any luck, she'd be just the right level of ornery so I could end her once and for all.

Chapter Twenty-Three

It was unfortunate that the meeting was expected to be shitty because the coterie room was easily my favorite space in the castle. Sometimes late at night, I'd come here to escape the chaos of the palace as a child and even as an adult when I was actually home. The structure sat nestled in the expansive garden at the very center of the palace compound. The ceiling was in the shape of a dome, but it was open to the sky between the beams that held the shape. Rows of stained-glass windows lined the bottom half of the dome, so no matter how bright it was in the sky, colored light poured into the space. Even at night, it was beautiful, the moon shining through the glass, giving off a softer light as the stars sparkled above.

I could hear all the witches in attendance already seated within as Kaizer and I walked up to the entrance. I took a step ahead of him as we pushed through the doors between the stone columns, and the space went deathly silent. I walked down the stairs slowly, passing each ring of witches until we got to the smallest ring at the bottom, where the coven coterie sat with their sanction behind them.

Letting some of my magic slide between my fingers, I stood at the center, turning in a slow circle to look each person in the eye. After I'd glared at each of them I took my seat at our table beside my mother, with Kaizer by my side. The tension in the air was thick as I made them sit in silence. I wasn't the Acna yet, but I would become her soon, and each and every one of them knew it. Rosa sat beside Adriana. I wasn't sure if it was the official sign that she was siding with her, but I did know that they weren't aware we knew of their idea to revolt. We had so many spies within the sanctions that none of them could get away with anything without it being whispered back to us. Catalina sat directly across from me with Sara, the highest-ranking general. Yesenia and Elena, the last two and youngest sanction leads, sat beside them.

Rosa looked like she was going to start steaming from her ears, so I turned to my mother, and she nodded her head for me to begin.

"I don't think it's any secret of why we're here today," I exclaimed as I sat forward on my elbows. "The last time we spoke, we advised of the union. Kaizer wasn't present, so I'd like to introduce you to him officially."

None of them spoke, but all eyes darted to Kaizer, and he lifted his chin under all of their gazes.

"Such a warm welcome." I grinned, and Catalina smirked across from me. "I've heard there has been some discourse among the sanctions," I finished, my gaze landing on Rosa.

Her lip pulled back, but she kept her mouth shut, knowing that she needed to wait for permission to speak.

"Speak, if you must," I muttered, as if the thought of hearing her speak annoyed me—which it did.

She cleared her throat. "As you all know, I am the oldest witch in Caldera," she said, her gaze on me. "For thousands of years, we have remained. Now, you invite this foreign sanguijuela onto our land, give him access to our riches, to our armies. What will become of all of us? Of the brujas? Will we be washed away from history? Will we start drinking each other's blood like they do?" she finished, pointing her lips toward Kaizer in disgust.

Kaizer's entire body was tight. He wasn't used to anyone speaking to him in this manner, and it showed. His jaw ticked, and his knuckles were white atop the table we sat at.

"Rosa, do you think I'm stupid?" I asked as I stood from my seat and came around to the front of the table to rest my ass on it.

She cocked her head to the side. "Those were not my words."

I let my nails out to their full sharpened length, inspecting them as the air got tight in the council room. "It appears to me that you think so. Either me or my mother has to be an idiot if your little speech is to be taken into consideration. Is it my mother you think is the stupid one?"

Rosa's eyes darted over to my mother, and her sanction started to squirm, sweat beading on their foreheads.

Her mouth opened and closed a few times. "I would never."

"You've been a thorn in my side for some time, Rosa. You think because you are the oldest, it makes you the wisest among us," I said as I slowly walked toward the table she was seated at. "I know about your little idea of rebellion. I know that you have other sanction leaders backing you."

Adriana sucked in a breath, shifting in her seat as I looked over at her.

"Decades of me having to come and deal with you and your clan. Their faith in you is misplaced. So give me a reason, Rosa," I said as I placed my hands on her table and leaned toward her.

"A reason?" Rosa inquired.

I smiled cruelly before whispering, "Give me a reason to end that long life you like to brag about."

The sound may as well have been a scream as the coterie was completely silent; I could barely hear anyone breathing as I stood face-to-face with Rosa. I ran my nail across her cheek, a single drop of blood spilling from the cut. I watched as it ran down her cheek and stood back up.

"Rosa, have you fought in the recent war?"

"I haven't," she growled.

I moved to walk down the line of witches. "Adriana, have you?"

"No, I haven't," she whispered.

"Catalina, Sara, you have fought beside me in those battles, yes?"

They both nodded.

"Elena, Yesenia, have you?"

"We have," Elena responded with her chin high.

I turned back to Rosa. "Rosa, how many people in your sanction did you lose in just the last battle?"

"A few thousand," she muttered.

"Adriana?"

"The same," she responded.

"Thousands from two sanctions alone in a single battle. We have been at war for *centuries*, thousands upon thousands lost over the years," I said, turning back toward Kaizer. "Kaizer, how many has Sanjry lost?"

"Since the war started originally?" he asked.

I nodded once.

"Tens of thousands. If not hundreds."

"Is that what you two want? For us to lose thousands more, so you can continue with this narrative that he is coming to steal our riches and resources?"

Neither said anything, and I saw a single tear fall from Adriana's eye. I never really liked Adriana. She stood for nothing in particular; she was so easily swayed and manipulated it was almost laughable. Anytime I had to come and put down some problem witches in her sanction, they swore she felt the same as they did. But when it came down to it, she always fell right back in line, worried for her own life.

"We have run out of options," I said before taking my seat again. "This is what we must do to save both of our people. If there are specific questions about it, I'm open to hearing them."

Elena sat forward. "The armies, what is to come of them?"

"I would hope we wouldn't have to use a joined army, but they will become one."

"Has Dusra heard of the union?" Yesenia asked.

I'd nearly forgotten about the meeting with Ax, as so much had happened since then. The thought of him had my chest warming slightly, and I squeezed my hands together. "We have met with their king, and a treaty has been signed saying we will not cross his borders, and he will not cross ours."

All of them looked slightly shocked at the notion, but nodded their understanding.

"Our borders," Adriana's voice cracked. "My sanction borders on Sanjry's land. Will that change?"

"No, the borders for sanctions will remain as they are."

"And their borders?" Rosa asked.

"We are becoming one kingdom. People won't be killed for crossing borders anymore. However, if a vampire wants to live in witch lands, they must have it approved."

No witch would ever want to live in Sanjry, so I didn't bother to mention they'd need approval as well.

"But they could come in and travel if they like?" Adriana asked.

I smirked. "Expect an uptick in brujitas."

The younger witches smiled, their canines on display as the fun they'd be getting into excited them.

"Are our laws changing?" Elena asked.

"No," I answered, and I felt Kaizer tense, like he wanted to add something, but I ignored him.

I knew how he felt about some of our laws around...murder. The law was that there wasn't much of one. If someone did something to warrant being ended, who were we to step in? He was probably concerned about the arrogant assholes who would come and father bruja babies, as they often ended up dead or *wishing* they were dead. But they knew what they were getting themselves into when they laid with a witch. They all thought they could be the ones to tame the beast, but that would never happen.

"Are there questions for Kaizer?" I asked.

Every row of eyes shifted over to him, some of them with their lips pulled back, some with a cautious glare. No one said a thing. I was certain that there were plenty of questions, but after my threat to Rosa, I doubted any of them would question anything else. My mother had been quiet, so quiet I almost forgot she was there before she cleared her throat and sat forward slightly so I could see her.

"The wedding will be in a few weeks in Sanjry. They have invited you all. The Ritual will happen the day before, and everyone is expected to show," my mother said absolutely.

"There will be a gathering tonight. You're all expected there as well," I exclaimed.

Each sanction lead dipped their chins. Rosa not dipping as much. I wasn't sure if it was because she was old as fucking dirt or if it was a slight.

"You're all dismissed," I bellowed.

The witches all stood together as one, filing out of the room until I was left with Kaizer and my mother.

"That went great," I said, leaning back in my chair.

Kaizer's eyebrows shot up. "That was great?"

"Giving the lack of too much blood, yeah," I replied.

"You did well," my mother exclaimed, and I just about fell out of my fucking chair.

My head snapped in her direction, and she walked around the desk as if she didn't just praise me for the first time in my adulthood. My mouth hung open, but no words came out.

"I'll see you all at the feast," she said as she walked out of the council room.

I was still staring in the direction she went when Kaizer leaned into my eye line to snap me out of my shock.

"You okay?" he asked, looking me up and down.

"Yes," I replied quickly, "the feast will be in a few hours. I need to get ready."

"What will be happening at this gathering?"

"Blood, wine, dancing, the usual salacious events of Caldera." I shrugged and stood.

His brows drew together. "But you're all females?"

He stood to follow me out, and I turned to face him, stopping us in our tracks. "Surely you don't think men are *needed* for salacious activity?"

"Well..." he trailed off and looked out into the space behind my head like the answer to my question was floating in the air.

I stepped closer to him, only an inch away from his chest. "Why don't you tell me at the end of the night if you feel the same," I muttered, putting my finger on his chest.

His muscles tightened under my finger, and I pushed slightly before turning and exiting the council room with him on my heels.

"The thing about the laws," he started.

"What about them?" I asked as I stepped out into the courtyard.

"You know there will need to be changes," he muttered.

I shrugged. "We've existed this way for centuries. I think it will be fine."

"There needs to be rules in place. One-half of our kingdom can't exist in bloodshed and the other civilly."

"Existing in bloodshed feels like a stretch. What happens in Sanjry when someone is killed?"

"A trial is held, a panel of vampires reviews the case and deems them guilty or not. The vampire in question is held in the dungeon until their sentence."

I tilted my head. "If you know they are the ones who killed them, how would they not be guilty?"

"Well, it's more so if the killing was justified. Self-defense and things like that," he responded.

"That's stupid. They should have simply done a better job keeping themselves alive," I muttered.

The courtyard ran the full length of the palace, and my room was at the very end; we could have gone inside and walked the halls, but I was more than happy to stay out in the fresh air. I missed the flowers that ran the border of the courtyard, the chaos in which they grew. They weren't planted in any particular order, just hundreds of different flowers wrapping around each other and growing up the walls. The courtyards in Sanjry were so well-manicured they almost looked fake, but here the wild did as it liked, and I loved it.

Kaizer walked beside me, not pushing any further about the witch laws.

"Are you worried about being around that many witches at once?" I asked to bait him.

"No, I did bring quite a few vampires," he said as he flicked his gaze over to me and then away quickly like he was reconsidering if it was a good idea.

"Don't worry, I'll make sure everyone knows to be on their best behavior," I laughed out.

My courtyard was lined with tall hedges to keep people away when there were big parties out here, and I flicked my wrist, allowing the barrier to sense my magic and banishing them from existence for us to pass through. Kaizer's eyebrows rose the same way they did before when seeing my magic, and we stepped through the opening. I flicked my wrist again, and they settled back into place behind us.

"I need to go check in with the vampires we brought," he exclaimed.

"You realize you just walked in the complete opposite direction?" I asked as I looked over my shoulder at him.

"Yes," he said without further explanation.

"Okay." I flicked my wrist yet again. "You can go back the way we came. Just keep going until you reach the other side."

He nodded his head and exited my courtyard, the hedges settling behind him after he stepped through.

"Fucking weirdo," I muttered, walking toward the open doorway.

Zuri was already in the room, and I watched her with a smile as she floated around the space, gathering things to prepare me for tonight. I had a whole entire closet full of gowns I hadn't worn yet, and I asked her to pick one for me when I passed her on the way to the coterie meeting. I stepped into my room silently. I figured I could turn this into a training opportunity since we hadn't done any over the last few days.

She had her back turned to me, her caramel curls bobbing around her shoulders as she shifted some things on the vanity she stood before. There was a mirror in front of her, and I avoided stepping into its reflection as I moved directly behind her. I lifted my hands, making to slip my forearm around her neck, but she quickly grabbed it and whirled around to face me with my wrist in her grip. I yanked my arm from her and punched her in the side with about half of my strength. She groaned but lifted her leg to knee me in the gut, her rallying getting much quicker than it was before.

Look at my little trainee learning.

I swiped her leg out from under her, catching her by her hand before she hit the ground all the way. "Not bad for a surprise attack," I muttered, pulling her back to her feet.

"You're not as quiet as you think you are," she laughed.

"Psh, I *am* stealth," I said as I let go of her hand. "What did you choose for me to wear?"

She walked over to my vast four-poster bed, where she had two dresses laid out. They were two of my favorites, actually. I was sad that I didn't get a chance to wear them before the battle. The first was a deep red; it was really just one long panel of fabric, overlapping in a way that covered the most important parts. It crossed at the breasts and around the hips, leaving two high slits on either side that made it impossible to wear any undergarments, with some fabric bunched together at the front and the back. The second was a rich cobalt; the heart-shaped neckline was connected to two thin straps that hung off the shoulders. Unlike the red one, it only had one slit that ran up the left thigh, the pleated skirt flowing from the tight bodice, different shades of blue nestled in its layers.

"They're both so beautiful in different ways I couldn't choose one," she said with her hands folded together under her chin.

"I'll wear the red one. You should wear the blue, the straps around the bodice make it adjustable," I said as I grabbed hold of the hanger attached to the red dress.

"What? No, I'll wear one I brought. This is too much for me," she gasped.

"Don't make me call it an order," I said with my hand on my hip.

She sighed and grabbed the dress.

"You put up a real fight there," I joked as I hung my dress on the wall hooks beside my large mirror.

"It's one of the most beautiful dresses I've ever seen. I couldn't get myself to argue too much," she laughed as she did the same. "What do you want to do to your hair?"

"Nothing, I'm just going to leave it down. You're not working tonight," I responded as I walked over to the miniature wine cellar beside my bed.

"How did the coterie meeting go?" she asked.

"As expected, they aren't happy, but they'll fall in line," I responded.

I pulled out two glasses and poured the dark liquid into each cup, definitely higher than what was deemed socially acceptable, but fuck it.

"You aren't worried about how tonight will go?" she asked.

I scoffed. "No, if there's one thing witches know how to do, it's party. The problem witches will only stay for a little bit, and they wouldn't make any moves against me with so many of us in one space."

"Well, I hope they don't eat the vampires alive," she said with raised brows.

"I'll have to make an announcement for them to refrain from that," I said with a chuckle, handing her the cup of wine.

She brought the cup up to her full lips and took a sip, a smile pulling as soon as she brought it back down.

"Fuck, that's good," she whispered as she went back for more.

"Everything is better in Caldera," I said, sitting down at the vanity.

I rummaged through my drawers finding everything in the same exact place as I had left it. I shouldn't have been surprised, nobody could get in here if they wanted, but something about it had me wishing I could stay here longer. I pulled out some pressed glitter and ran my finger across the compact, rubbing it on my eyelids and down my cheekbones. Pulling my fingers through my hair, I looked in the mirror to see Zuri taking off the dress she wore today. She stepped out of it and walked to the mirror beside my vanity, where we hung the dresses.

"Your comfort with nudity has me thinking you could be a witch," I laughed, keeping my gaze ahead.

"You should know by now I'm not nearly as uppity as the other Sanjryans," she responded as she stepped into the cobalt dress and pulled it over her slight curves.

Zuri was slender, and the clothes I'd seen her up until this moment never did her justice. This dress fit her perfectly, accentuating every dip of her body in a way that had me running my eyes up and down her and my chest tingling.

"Don't just look at me like that. Say something," she said, her face pulling into an embarrassed grimace.

I stood to help her with the straps running around the bodice before I started openly drooling on the floor. "You look amazing."

The back of her dress sat below her shoulder blades, and I tied each one, fluffing up her curls before going to pull my dress from the hanger. I dropped my dress and pulled on the exquisite red gown. The dress was so light weight and open I almost felt naked, and I loved it; how free I could move after being in Sanjryan fashions for what seemed like an eternity. She grabbed out some heels for each of us to wear, and I slipped them on, loving the few inches they gave me.

We stood before the mirror, and I couldn't help the smile pulling at my lips. "Damn, we look good," I muttered.

"Better than good," she added, tossing her short curls to the side with a smirk.

I winked. "Let's go have some fun."

Chapter Twenty-Four

We passed witches looking Zuri up and down as we made our way through the halls, and I had to bite down a growl at their eyes on her. I'd never been possessive, and I didn't know where the feeling came from, but something about the way they raked their gazes up and down her had me ready to pounce. Kaizer turned the corner, almost running into us, and he looked at our joined arms and over to me a few times before opening his mouth.

"I was just coming to see if you wanted an escort," he said, straightening his jacket.

He had his white hair pulled back into a bun, my favorite style that he wore. His dark blue jacket was trimmed in gold, complimenting the rich tan of his skin. I looked over at Zuri, and they actually matched more than he and I did.

I tightened my grip on Zuri and smiled. "We were already on our way."

"I can escort you both," he said as he stepped toward us and offered us both of his arms.

I sighed internally and let my hold on Zuri go as I looped my arm in his and she did the same on the other side.

"How were the vampires?" I asked, breaking the awkward silence.

"Good. I told them not to provoke anyone tonight," he responded.

"Easier said than done," Zuri whispered, and Kaizer looked over at her in surprise.

Zuri didn't really show her snarky side to anyone outside of me; Kaizer was technically her employer, so she tended to stay as quiet and invisible as possible around him. I laughed as we made it to the corridor of the great hall, music raging inside already. My mother was waiting by the door with her arms crossed across her chest.

"Finally," she muttered, and I let go of Kaizer's arm as we stood before the doors. Zuri came up to my side and Kaizer on the other as my mother motioned for the doors to be opened.

The music stopped after the doors shifted an inch; everyone inside quieted and stood straight as we walked to our dais. My mother had perfected the slow power walk, and I'd seen her do it enough that I had as well. Our heels clicked against the stone of the floor, the only sound in the space. Brujas glanced from me to Zuri to Kaizer, surely wondering what exactly the arrangement between us all was since we arrived together in such a manner. The looks weren't judgy by any means, as there wasn't much that our people judged, but they watched with intent until we made it to the velvet stairs lining the dais. Three vast chairs sat atop it, and I internally cringed at Zuri having to stand behind me until the party started.

My mother and I sat in unison, Kaizer slightly behind us, as the witches kept their gaze on the dais, waiting for us to speak. The room was packed to the brim, as every high-ranking witch in Caldera was in attendance. The air was tight as no one dared to move or mutter a word until we allowed it.

"May the Acna rule long," my mother started, and I saw a few shoulders sag as they allowed themselves to breathe.

The brujas continued our mantra in unison. "May the brujas remain loyal."

"Tonight, we celebrate the union of my daughter and the King of Sanjry. We celebrate the end of the war," she said, and most of the room clapped.

I eyed each one that didn't, mentally noting their faces.

"There are a few other Sanjryans in our presence," I said as I eyed the line of soldiers by the door. "Do play nice," I finished with a devilish grin.

The witches echoed my smile, and I waved my hand for the music to begin again. The Sanjryan soldiers weren't wearing their full armor, a move surely to show that they had something resembling trust with the witches. A few of my clan sauntered over to where they stood, and I bit back a laugh at the poor Sanjryan souls who had no idea where their nights would be ending. I was almost entirely sure that they came into this thinking the witches were terrifying creatures. Which we were, but the ones who hadn't seen us like this before most likely had no idea just how beautiful and tempting we could be.

It was a curse of our kind, our undeniable beauty. Even in our old age, our beauty was indisputable; part of me thought it was because there were no male witches. We needed the extra edge to try to seduce the males of our land into procreating with us. Regardless, they were already losing some of their resolve as the witches rubbed against them, some already draping their bodies across the stiff men. I stood as the music reached a crescendo and pulled Zuri with me over to the table of food and drink. Blood and wine sat in barrels at the end of the table, and I filled a cup of blood as I hadn't had any since we left Sanjry. Zuri filled herself a cup of blood as well, and I tilted my head at her.

"Figured I'd give it a try." She shrugged, taking a sip. "Mmm, what is that?"

"Goat, my favorite," I responded, taking a sip of my own. "Do you dance?"

She looked out onto the dance floor, the witches winding their hips and moving like water around each other.

"Not like that," she joked.

I downed the rest of my blood. "Oh, come on, just let the music take you. It's fun."

I could feel the blood recharging my power, the sensation tingling through my limbs as I backed up slowly, beckoning for her to follow me. My mother hated that I did this, danced like the common witches, but I didn't care. It was one of the few things I had that gave me the illusion of being normal. I'd forgotten how good music made me feel after being away, and I wanted to take advantage. Zuri followed reluctantly, her feet dragging in her heels. I swayed my hips, putting my hands on hers and guiding her to follow along. She laughed and started to do it on her own, and I let go, throwing my hands in the air and spinning around.

I felt a rush of air, the high slits of the gown threatening to expose a little more of me than I expected, but I kept moving. I shifted behind Zuri and danced with her, looking up to find Kaizer's eyes burrowing into me. He was so stiff he could have been mistaken for a statue, jealousy bubbling up in his gaze. I smiled wide and ran my hands from my hips up to my breasts and over my neck before pulling through my hair, tossing it over my shoulder.

One of the staff brought me and Zuri each a glass of wine, and we both tossed them back and handed the cups back with a thank you. Zuri's cheeks were starting to flush, and *damn*, did she look like the cutest fucking thing I'd ever seen. She twisted to face me, stepped into my space, and continued dancing with me, taking a note from the witches doing the same nearby.

I wasn't sure just how far she'd take the witchy behavior, but I tested the limits by running my hands up her arms and tossing them around her shoulders to pull her closer. She laughed as she continued dancing, and I flicked my gaze over to Kaizer, or where Kaizer was the last time I looked up. Zuri turned around and rubbed her ass against my legs, the slits in my dress leaving just the fabric of hers between us. The wine had me not thinking too much about it, and Zuri was pulled away by another witch to dance with. She looked back at me, and I nodded with a smile so she knew not to be worried. I threw my hands in the air again, spinning around and dancing by myself, when I felt a presence behind me. A non-witchy presence. I bent over slightly as I continued dancing, turning around and pretending like I didn't know Kaizer was standing right there.

"Come to dance?" I asked as I ran my finger down his muscled chest.

He waved his hands out. "I don't dance like *this*."

"Well, then, you're definitely in the wrong place," I said as I turned around and rubbed my ass across his legs in a taunt.

I looked back at him over my shoulder. "If you aren't going to dance, why are you over here."

"You were putting on quite the show," he muttered.

"And?" I said, turning around to face him and winding my hips, running my fingers up my sides.

He stepped closer. "It felt like it was for me."

"I don't know why you'd think that," I laughed out.

I was taunting him, sure, but I was having such a good time dancing that I wouldn't say it was for him by a long shot. One of his soldiers nearby was sandwiched between two witches; he wasn't exactly dancing, but he was having a good time, regardless. I laughed as I watched them, and Kaizer snapped his gaze in their direction.

He shifted on his feet like he was going to say something, and I caught him by the wrist. "Don't stop their fun," I said, pulling him off the dance floor and over to the outskirts of the space.

We watched the chaos of Calderan festivities together for a few moments. Brujas with their bodies pressed against each other, some making out, some dancing more seductively than others. I followed Kaizer's gaze to a couple of witches in the back corner; one straddled over another as she ground her hips against the woman beneath her.

"Have any thoughts about the need for men at an event like this?" I asked with my arms crossed.

He yanked his stare from the brujas he was watching and shook his head.

"Didn't think so," I laughed.

Kaizer returned to the dais as he mumbled something under his breath, and I scanned the area for Zuri, finding her now on the completely opposite side of the hall. She laughed as she danced between a few witches, her smile practically gleaming even from so far away. I was glad she was having a good time. I hated that she had to wait on me hand and foot in Sanjry, but if it wasn't her, it would be someone else. I damn sure didn't want to spend my time with anyone else.

I went to grab a snack from the table, and the hairs on the back of my neck rose as soon as I put my hand on the pastry I was aiming for. Turning around, I scanned the area, but nothing appeared out of place. The feeling remained, and I walked over to the dais where Kaizer sat, hoping if I was elevated, I could figure out what was awry. My foot hit the first step, and the sensation was now overwhelming; I snapped my gaze back into the crowd with my violet magic already pooling in my hand.

People had indulged a great deal at this point; some witches were slipping out of the room together, some with the Sanjryan soldiers. My mother must have left a while ago as she wasn't on the dais any longer; she didn't tend to stay at events like this for longer than absolutely necessary. I settled slightly, pulling my magic back into my palms as I made it in front of Kaizer.

"What's wr—" He was cut off as a burst of air knocked me in the chest.

I pulled my hand back, blasting air into the floor to set me on my feet, and whirled toward where the attack came from. Witches from Rosa's clan emerged from jewel-toned smoke as they stepped through portals into the room. Nobody could portal directly into the palace unless they were already here, and I didn't see any of these people here during the festivities. She knew what she would do at the coterie meeting, and my fists tightened. I didn't give them a chance to take in their surroundings before I sliced through the first two with the dagger that I had strapped to my thigh.

I heard a battle cry from across the room and found Catalina pulling her sword from a witch's belly, their body slumping to the ground, lifeless. Witch magic was pure magical essence, hotter than the flames of Kaizer's people. I shot a stream of it into the two witches charging me with their swords raised, the power shooting straight through their chests and into the witches behind them. I continued forward, cutting into them for good measure as they fell on top of each other. I felt a presence behind me and whirled with my dagger raised, but Zuri's big gray eyes stared back at me.

"I need a weapon," she exclaimed.

I pulled the other knife strapped to my ankle out of its holster and placed it in her hand.

"Stay with me," I said as I felt a witch coming for me with my back turned.

I put up a wall of air between us as the attacker ran smack into the invisible force, sending her weapon crashing to the ground. I scanned the room for Rosa, but she wasn't there. A stream of flame shot past my head and straight into a witch to my left, and I looked over to find Kaizer in the middle of the room fighting with two other witches. He nodded to me as he kicked a witch in the chest, she used her air magic to bounce back toward him, but he expected the movement and had his sword ready for her, impaling her in the heart. He pulled his sword from her and turned to slash into the next witch behind him.

Zuri grunted, and I turned to find blood splattered over her face as she slashed the neck of a witch that was charging her. Between me, the witches already here, and Kaizer, all the attackers were on the ground. The witch Zuri cut was groaning near my feet, her wounds not yet fatal.

"Where the *fuck* is Rosa?" I said, pulling her up into the air by her shirt.

Kaizer came to stand beside me, and the wounded witch spat blood in his face. "We are not your equals. We should not be yoked to your kind," she growled at Kaizer.

"I asked you a fucking question," I said as I let my long nails extend into her chest where I held her.

"You'll bring an end to all of us," she said as her gaze saddened slightly and she looked at me.

Her head lolled to the side as she took her last breath, and I dropped her onto the ground with a wet thud.

"Sara! Catalina!" I yelled at my generals, "Get this shit handled. You know what to do with any traitors still living," I growled, stepping over a dead witch.

Kaizer called after me, but I was blinded by the absolute fucking disrespect shown. Zuri ran over to Catalina and asked if she could help as I pushed through the doors and closed my eyes. I listened for Rosa's ancient fucking heartbeat, but I didn't hear it; my mother portaled directly in front of me, her hair more disheveled than I'd ever seen it.

"Explain," she said, looking back at the great hall I had just exited.

"Rosa's clan," I bit out, "the first shot was directed at Kaizer. I assume that's who they were trying to get to."

"I heard the screams. Where is she?"

"I don't know. She must have returned to her sanction. I don't sense her here anymore."

"Handle it," she demanded before portaling away immediately.

Kaizer burst through the doors, but I didn't feel like dealing with him. I turned on my heel to go back to my room so I could grab more weapons to go and put an end to Rosa and her *revolution*.

"Daya!" Zuri yelled from behind me, and I looked back to see her moving around Kaizer, who was also following me.

"I'm going to deal with Rosa. Stay here with Catalina," I snapped.

"You're going by yourself?" Kaizer asked.

"Yes, I always do," I grumbled.

"That doesn't mean you should," Zuri said, grabbing my arm to slow me down.

I bared my teeth at her, but she didn't even flinch, showed no signs of fear at all. I was too far gone to my magic; it seeped out of my hair and my hands. I could see the violet glow of my eyes in Zuri's as they were lit with my power. But Zuri didn't care; she stood in front of me, staring me down, telling me she wasn't going to let me do this alone.

"Zuri, you don't want to see this," I muttered before looking back at Kaizer, who watched the two of us like I would bite off Zuri's head.

"I do," she whispered back. My magic flickered, settling slightly at the tone of her voice.

"Fine, you can come," I said and pulled out of her grasp to continue walking to my room.

"Me too," Kaizer exclaimed.

"You're not going to like what I do. You can't come with me."

"All the more reason for me to be there," he replied, picking up his pace with me as I sighed and accepted that he would be coming.

When did I sign up to have two sidekicks? I pushed through the doors, my magic starting to rage in irritation at the fucking vampire asshole. He had done fine in the great hall, he only had minimal scratches on him, and he took down quite a few witches, but that didn't mean I wanted him with me in this fight. I didn't even really want to bring Zuri, I had no idea why I agreed to either of them coming with me. Kaizer already didn't approve of my methods, and if I had to argue with him and fight, I would probably lose my mind.

"I swear to the goddesses one word about how I handle this, and I portal you back here with a snap of my fucking fingers," I said, looking up at him in a fierce stare. "You protect Zuri above anything else."

He nodded and grabbed his chest plate to strap it on and sheathed his sword on his side.

I pulled down two short swords from my excessive number of weapons hanging on the wall and placed each of them in Zuri's hands. "Just like we practiced. Don't initiate if you can avoid it," I said as I grabbed a leather sword belt and clipped it around her waist.

She tucked both swords into the belt and nodded, her short curls bouncing around her shoulders. If she got hurt today...I couldn't think about it. I needed to leave now before Rosa got too far underground. Rosa's sanction was one of the biggest, and there were thousands of places she could hide before I found her.

I didn't even bother to change my shoes or put on any armor before I snapped my fingers and opened a portal to the heart of Rosa's sanction, the city of Sabia.

Chapter Twenty-Five

The city of Sabia, to my ever-growing displeasure, was actually really beautiful. Nestled between the Piedra and the great silver lake, there was something picturesque no matter where you looked. I stepped through the portal with Kaizer and Zuri on my heels at the edge of the lake, away from most of the eyes of the city. The great body of water stretched out far. While just a lake, it was the biggest lake in Malva and ran as far as the eye could see. Its silvery water sparkled under the night sky, looking like liquid starlight itself. The water was always warm and rejuvenating, but I didn't have time to swim in its depths today. I was on the hunt.

My sharp heels sank into the grass, and I immediately regretted my choice not to change my shoes, but I shifted my weight onto my toes and tracked into the line of trees, crouching low between some shrubbery to look around. The city was unnaturally quiet, not a soul walking its cobblestone streets. Rosa's estate sat at the center of the city, lines of smaller homes lining the way.

"Fuck it," I said, pushing through the trees.

Kaizer and Zuri followed behind, and the click of my heels against the stone bounced between the houses as I made my way to the center of the city, swiveling my long sword in my hand. All the shops were closed, the pub that quite literally never closed was dark and empty, and I still hadn't seen anyone yet. I closed my eyes and crouched low to place my hand on the ground and tap into my witch hearing. I knew there were tunnels running under the city thanks to my spies, they hadn't been used in decades, but it sounded like they were in use now. I heard many heartbeats and rustling feet against the dirt, and smirked.

"Gotcha," I muttered.

Shifting my sword into my other hand, I stood and gathered magic in my hand, balling it into a fist and smashing into the ground. Zuri stepped back a few steps, running into Kaizer as the dust settled and a huge crater sat in the middle of the street. I hopped down gracefully as I moved my sword back into my dominant hand, and listened for where they were hiding. The tunnel was pitch black, and Kaizer hopped down with Zuri, some fire in his hands to illuminate the space. A maze of tunnels sat before me, none of them looking more inviting than the other. I could still hear the heartbeats, but none of them sounded close.

"If my spies are correct, there should be a bunker somewhere down here," I said as I stepped into the right path.

I kicked up dirt as I shuffled down the tunnel, keeping tapped into my witch hearing and following the sound of the people. It took some time, but I felt us getting closer to where they were located. They must have felt safe in these tunnels because it sounded like they were celebrating the further in we got. Witches laughed, and music rang out on my right, but to my left, I heard one single weak heartbeat surrounded by four strong heartbeats.

I licked my canines and followed the sound, but I felt a detection spell ahead and dismantled it with a flick of my wrist. There was no door where they were located, but I could hear them just on the other side. I whispered an anti-portal spell into the wall, letting it seep into the stone and encase the room. The spell wouldn't hold up forever, as magic on magic spells were temporary, but it would make sure nobody could leave for a few minutes. I balled my hand into a fist and punched the stone wall, wide cracks spreading from the impact, and one more punch had the stone falling into pieces on the ground. Shrieks sounded in the room as I walked through with the most wicked of smiles stretched across my face.

"Hello, Rosa," I muttered.

Rosa sat at the end of a table; four witches stood flanking her, two on either side. Rosa flicked her wrist, trying to create a portal, but the magic sparked out.

"Oh, no. This will be ending here," I said, slowly walking toward the end of the table opposite Rosa.

Kaizer stood in the hole I created in the wall with Zuri beside him, both of them with their hands on their weapons.

I stabbed my sword into the wooden table. "Explain yourself."

"You'll kill me regardless," Rosa spat.

"True," I laughed out. "I am curious, though. Was I your target, or was he?" I said, pointing over my shoulder to Kaizer with my thumb.

Rosa's lips pulled back, her canines on display. "Him."

"Ugh," I sighed. "We've already been over this, Rosa. We're stopping a war. Sounds like you don't mind that the coven is dwindling among the deaths."

"I would rather die than be led by that fucking vampire," she spat.

"Well, that can be arranged," I said with a smirk.

The witches by her side charged me, and I rolled my eyes, shooting my violet magic from my hands and piercing through two of their chests. I wanted to have fun with the last two, so I pulled my sword from the wood and twisted it around my body before the first witch got to me. She tried to strike me with her own less powerful magic, the pale blue color showing just how much weaker she was than me. I deflected it with one finger, licking my lips as I pulled the blade across her belly, her insides bulging at the wound. She pressed her hand to her stomach as she fell to the ground while I spun on my toes to block the sword coming down toward my shoulder.

Our blades crossed, and I stepped closer to her as she put every ounce of her strength into the blow. I blew her a kiss before pulling back my strength and letting her fall forward slightly, kneeing her in the stomach and dragging my blade across her neck. Her warm, dark blood coated my hands, and I dragged them down the table as I walked closer to Rosa, leaving streaks of red behind.

"Any last words," I said, sitting on the table in front of her.

My dress was hanging in pieces, and there wasn't much of it in the first place, but I brushed my hands down the skirt as I crossed my legs. Rosa went to lift her hands, but I tsked and cast two tendrils of air to lock her wrists in place.

"None of that," I said as I placed my hands behind me and leaned into them on the table. "See, you've annoyed the shit out of me for years, so this really doesn't bother me too much. You think because you are old as fuck, you know better, but you don't," I said, moving my head onto my shoulder.

"You don't know anything, child," she growled.

"I know enough," I said and sat forward to run my sharpened nail down her cheek to give her a matching gash to the one from earlier today.

"You think you're saving us from war, but all you're doing is whoring us out to a vampire who will get rid of us when he gets what he wants," she said, spitting blood with every syllable.

"What does he want?" I asked with a smile.

"Power, Daya, he wants power. As all men do, they'll stop at nothing to get it."

I looked back at Kaizer, who had fury burning in his eyes and shrugged. "If he thinks he can overpower me, he's mistaken."

"All the same, he'll destroy us on the journey. All I want is for the brujas to thrive. We'll never do that while he has access to our lands, our magic, our treasures," she said with her eyes snapping up to him.

Kaizer stiffened, pulling his blade from his sheath, but I waved him off. "I said it once, I'll say it again. I'm not an idiot. I'm tired of war, Rosa. This scenario is the only one that keeps us alive. You should have had faith in me. You could have seen us prosper. Everything I've done has been for Caldera, always for the brujas," I said, hopping down from the table and leaning into her face. "But you decided to disrespect me, disrespect the Acna," I whispered in her ear.

I wrapped my taloned hand around her neck and lifted her in the air, squeezing the life right out of her.

"You...don't know what's...coming," she gasped between breaths.

"Ugh, just shut up," I said, crushing her windpipe and dropping her to the floor.

I wiped my hands on my dress, the already red fabric camouflaging most of the substance, and turned around. Kaizer looked at me like I was a monster, his lips pulled back and his chest heaving. But Zuri...She looked at me like I was the Goddess of Death, and it didn't bother her at all.

"Don't start with the judgments," I said to Kaizer, "You knew what you were getting yourself into when you followed me," I finished as I pushed him to the side to get back into the tunnels.

"She should have stood trial," he exclaimed.

"And said what?" I snapped.

"She could have been sent to prison," he replied.

"What's the point in imprisoning someone for life if they're just going to die in a cell?" I asked, and Zuri laughed.

He didn't respond, or maybe he did, and I ignored him. I wasn't sure, but I walked over to where the people were celebrating earlier. I punched through the wall again, my knuckles already raw and bloody, but I didn't know where the fucking doors in this place were, and I didn't want to portal into anything unknown. I stepped through, and the music stopped, the witches all shrieking and standing straight in my presence.

"What the fuck is going on in here?" I asked.

No one said a thing, and I walked up to the closest witch, lifting her chin up with my nail to look her in the eyes.

"Speak," I growled.

"Rosa told us to come down here for the night. She didn't tell us why, just that we would be here until the morning," she bit out.

I released my hold on her chin and looked around, it wasn't anywhere near everyone in her sanction, but it looked to be a few hundred, the amount of people just within the city.

"Where is Juana?" I yelled, looking for Rosa's second in command.

"She went to the capital with Rosa. We haven't seen either of them today," another muttered with her gaze on the ground.

"Who's the highest-ranking here right now?" I asked.

"Me," a red-headed witch said as she stepped forward from the back of the crowd.

"Ana, right?" I asked, trying to remember her. I'd seen her a few times but didn't know her well enough to judge whose side she'd be on.

She tipped her chin down. "Yes, Dayanara."

"Do you want to kill me?" I asked.

Gasps sounded around the room, and Ana quickly shook her head.

"Do you want to kill my betrothed?" I asked.

She looked over at him and shook her head only once.

"That wasn't too convincing, but I'll take it. You're the new sanction lead, Rosa is dead, and if Juana isn't dead already, she will be soon."

"What happened?" Ana asked.

"A piss-poor attempt at rebellion," I said, turning my back and exiting the tunnel.

A shout sounded from inside the room directed at Ana, presumably trying to figure out where to go from here.

"You're a fucking legend," Zuri whispered as she looped her arm in mine.

Kaizer scoffed behind us, and I rolled my eyes as we made it to the original hole in the street I made. I gripped Zuri's side, pulling her tight to me as I shot us out of the opening with a blast of my magic to the ground. Kaizer landed beside me with his flames playing around his fingers, his body was still tight, and he opened his mouth to argue some more.

"What's done is done. No point in arguing your point," I muttered.

"That is not how things will be handled in Sanjry," he exclaimed.

"I'll follow your rules there, but we're on my land right now. I make the rules," I replied.

Kaizer's chest was heaving as he flailed his arms around. "That type of behavior is unacceptable, you all have no morals, you're no better than anim—"

I flicked my gaze to him and he stopped with his mouth open.

"I only mean that there's a better way, I..." he trailed off, trying to find a nicer way to convey exactly what he had already said.

I snapped a portal open and walked through without looking back.

Chapter Twenty-Six

I had portaled directly into my room and changed into my witch leathers and boots before checking on the status of the palace. I'd officially ruined the dress and heels I wore earlier tonight, and I was fucking pissed about it. I now stood in the great hall where Catalina had the dead piled up, Juana among them. I wasn't sure if her sanction really didn't know what she was up to, but for now, most of the people who followed her were gone. Catalina also put Adriana in cuffs at the foot of the dais after having my mother suppress her magic, waiting for me to ensure she wasn't part of Rosa's plan. Holding my hands behind my back, I walked toward her, looking down at the blood-covered floor.

"Oh, Adriana. What are we going to do with you?" I asked, stopping directly in front of her.

"I wasn't part of it, I swear," she said, her voice full of panic.

I crouched down in front of her. "That's not what my spies tell me."

She brought her watery gaze up to mine, and I smiled, licking my canines. "Care to share?"

"I didn't know she was going to do this!" she yelled, her long brown hair flying around her face. "I agreed that we shouldn't be getting into bed with the vampires, but I never wanted it to get this far!"

I grabbed her chin and looked into her eyes, searching for the lie, but there was none. "Tell me what you know, and I won't kill you," I muttered.

I left Kaizer in my room for this and portaled directly here. I was fairly sure he was running down the halls to get here, but I really didn't want to hear his mouth.

"She thought if she killed him, the witches could take over since you're already seated at their head. She didn't want to kill you, just him. I don't want us to fall back into war, I really don't, but she convinced me that if we went through with this that the witches would fall. I agreed, but I didn't go along with her plan. I swear," she said, tears running down her face.

Fucking pathetic. I released my hold on her chin and shoved her face to the side before standing back up. "Any of Adriana's clan attack?" I asked Catalina.

She shook her head. "Nope, just Rosa's."

"Hm," I said as I looked back at Adriana on the ground. "Let her go," I commanded.

Catalina signaled for one of our soldiers to remove the handcuffs, and they fell to the ground in a loud clank before Adriana stood up.

"Adriana," I said as she made to walk past me. "This is your last warning. You will meet the same fate as Rosa, should you betray me."

"Yes, Dayanara," she said before scurrying out of the doors.

Kaizer walked in just as she walked out, and he scanned the area rapidly.

"I didn't kill anyone. Get the stick out of your ass," I muttered.

"Deal with the dead. I need to go talk to my mother," I said to Catalina.

I walked around Kaizer and out of the room and felt him following behind me.

"Were any other sanctions involved?" he asked.

"No, just Rosa. We should be in the clear," I responded quickly.

Kaizer loomed at my back until we made it to my mother's office, and I knocked on the door twice before opening it. My mother sat behind her large desk, flipping through some papers, and looked up at me under her brow.

"Dealt with?" she asked.

I sat across from her and nodded. "All dead."

"Adriana?"

"Says she wasn't involved. I believe her. I can't believe Rosa had the audacity to attack us in the palace. That's never happened in all of the centuries here."

"We've never been in the current situation before," my mother said, looking over to Kaizer. "You disapprove?"

"Of all the killing? Yes."

"Do you not kill on the battlefield?" she asked.

"That wasn't a battlefield. War is different," he responded, sitting forward.

I sat back and crossed my legs. "Every day is a war. Every room is a battlefield. You'd do well to remember that."

"What would you have us do?" my mother asked Kaizer.

"Ugh, please don't get him started on trials and prison again," I responded before Kaizer could.

"How long are you staying?" my mother asked, looking back down at the pile of papers.

"Original plan was for a few days. He wanted to see more of Caldera," I responded.

My mother raised only her eyes. "What do you want to see?"

"Just the land, the people. If we're to rule *together*," he bit the word out, glancing over at me. "I'd like to see what I'm ruling."

"Where will you take him?"

"I don't know. I hadn't gotten that far yet," I responded with a shrug.

"Keep me updated," she replied.

"Don't trust me, Lupe?" he asked, his tone teasing.

Her lips turned down at the informal use of her name, something most people didn't get away with. "I don't trust anyone," she said with a wave of her hand in dismissal.

We stood from the chairs and left the room, walking back in the direction of the great hall. I peeked my head in to see how much progress they'd made, and the room looked almost exactly as it had before the attack. There were still a few spots of blood, but all the dead had been removed. Most likely incinerated where they lay and cast out into the wind. Traitors didn't deserve to be buried with the rest of us. Not all witches were strong enough to incinerate with their magic, but Catalina was, and I was sure she would have been the one to do it.

"Wow," Kaizer muttered from behind me, his arm on the door frame above us. I ducked under his arm. "We're efficient."

"Dayanara, we really need to talk about all of this," he said, his pace matching mine.

"Goddess, you can be so fucking persistent," I mumbled.

"I just need you to know that if you act like that in Sanjry, we'll both be overthrown by the Sanjryans. I need to be sure that this behavior remains in Caldera," he exclaimed.

"I'd like to see them try," I replied.

"You are not invincible, Dayanara. You are powerful, yes, but you can be killed just like the rest of us."

I pushed open the doors to the courtyard, the grass rustling beneath my boots as I marched away from Kaizer. "I know I'm not invincible. I just don't understand why you need me to be someone I'm not for this to work. I am not clay for you to mold. I am who I am. You should have done your fucking research before tricking me into marriage."

His brows drew together. "Tricking you?"

Well, I guess we were doing this.

"I was barely conscious when you made that *magic binding* agreement with me. You had to know I didn't know what I was getting myself into!"

"Your mother said you'd agree to it regardless to save your people," he said, his brows even tighter, like he really had no idea where I was coming from.

"Oh, yes, my *mother* said I'd give away my life, so it must have been okay."

"Do you not want to end the war?" he asked.

"That's not the point, Kaizer," I bit out, "not to mention that bullshit that happened in the courtyard. And you're hiding something. I don't know what the fuck it is, but I know you are," I said, pushing my finger into his chest.

He looked past my head and his nostrils flared slightly. "Daya," he started.

"Don't fucking call me that," I said as I turned and headed toward my room.

"Can we just talk like civil people, please?" Kaizer asked.

"Instead of like animals?" I snapped.

I waved my hand in dismissal and created a portal directly in front of me to my bedroom. I tried to close it behind me, but he was right on my heels and stepped through into my room.

"I want this to work," he mumbled at my back.

I walked over to my cellar and pulled out some wine. "Try not being an asshole for a start."

I popped the cork from the bottle and put it right to my mouth, skipping the cup entirely. Today was a disaster, or was it yesterday? I couldn't tell what time it was, but it had to be late into the night. I went into this knowing it would probably go left, but I never expected them to actually try to kill him in my presence. They were idiots to think they'd be successful. Rosa was always passionate. She had more than enough ego, and the fact she felt she was doing the *right thing* sealed her fate. There was no right or wrong in this world; you did what you had to do to survive. Anybody playing the hero wasn't going to make it far. Villains ruled this part of the world, and I wouldn't try to be anything else.

Kaizer was seated by the fire again, his knuckles white around the arm of the chair. I rolled my eyes and walked out of the door into my courtyard. The moon was still high in the sky, so it wasn't quite as late as I thought it was. I sat down and threw my feet up onto the wrought-iron table, tossing back my wine. Zuri's door was closed, so I was sure she was fast asleep at this point. We'd had a hell of a night, and if this didn't have her going back on our friendship, I didn't think anything would. She didn't waiver once. She fought with the ferocity of a bruja, and didn't balk from the blood or gore. She'd had my back from the beginning of the night to the end, and I couldn't thank her more for it. Not to mention, seeing her covered in blood and dragging my knife across the neck of a traitor turned me on more than I cared to admit.

A smile pulled at my lips as a shadow loomed over me, quickly sending my smile out of existence.

"What do you want?" I mumbled, not looking at him.

"Your forgiveness," he muttered.

I looked over my shoulder at him and watched him as he fell to his knees, and a slight smirk graced my lips. "You're prepared to grovel?"

"If this is what I need to do, I will," he sighed.

"Well, go on, then," I said, taking my feet off the table and sitting up straight.

"I don't actually know what you want me to do," he mumbled.

I swished the wine in my cup. "Say that you should have had my back. Say that you're sorry you were being such a fucking asshole."

His jaw ticked, and he looked away from me. "I should have had your back. Sorry, I was an ass," he repeated.

"Oh no, baby. Say it like you mean it. Give me some eye contact, too," I said, grabbing his chin and pulling it toward me.

Was I going to forgive him? Probably not. Was I enjoying this more than I should have? Definitely. He tried to move his mouth, but my grip was too tight on his chin. I looked down my nose at him as I loosened my hold to allow him to speak.

"I should have had your back in the courtyard. I should have made sure the crowd knew that I wouldn't stand for someone trying to hurt you. I'm sorry about what I said earlier. I shouldn't try to force you to be something you aren't."

I sat forward. "Fuck, you really do want this to work, don't you?"

"I do, I just...we're so different, it's hard to navigate," he mumbled, his white hairs shifting in front of his face in the wind.

"Hm," I muttered.

I sat back in my chair, wondering where exactly I should go from here. We were fundamentally different. He was right, and it had clearly been a problem thus far. I also didn't know what to do about it, if he meant to hurt me with the things he had done or if he thought what he was doing was the right call from his life experience. He was on his knees for me, something I knew vampires didn't take lightly. He was drinking me in, looking me up and down. His gaze settled on my neck, the stare so intense that I could feel my carotid artery flexing on the flesh there. I was unbelievably fucking horny. I didn't need to actually *want* him to fuck him, and the memory of his mouth on my pussy a few days ago had me clenching my thighs. I smirked as I wrapped my fingers around his neck, squeezing enough that I could see it made him uncomfortable.

Pulling him closer to me, I leaned in, just a breath away from his face. "Words are nice, but why don't you use that pretty little mouth for something a little more tactile," I whispered, letting go of his neck.

He grunted and spread my legs wide as he pulled me to the edge of my seat in one quick move. Kaizer unbuttoned my pants, and I bucked my hips enough for him to peel them off my legs. He ran his knuckle over my panties, the light touch somehow setting my whole body alight. I arched my back into his touch, unbuckling the straps of my top and pulling it off my body. He used his canine to tear my underwear right off, the pieces of black fabric falling gracefully to the floor. He nestled his face between my legs, the slight stubble on his cheeks rubbing against the softness of my thighs.

"Tactile, I can do," he muttered against my skin, the vibrations of his voice against my clit making me wrap my hands tight around the armrests.

I thought back to the last time we were in this position, somehow forgetting the pleasure he pulled from me then. He flicked his tongue in one smooth motion right up my pussy, and I rolled my eyes into the back of my head. He moaned at my taste before he pushed two fingers right into me, pulling them out and dragging the wetness up to my clit to rub circles around it. A cool breeze blew through the courtyard, pebbling my nipples as small flower petals flew by in the air. It distracted me enough to hear a heartbeat nearby, a heartbeat that was only a few yards away from me. Kaizer pushed his fingers back into me, and I muffled a cry as I tried to find the source of the heartbeat. I closed my eyes, the sound getting faster and faster. It was coming from my room.

Zuri. The heartbeat continued to crescendo. She wasn't in her room, she was standing somewhere in mine. *Was she...watching?* Fuck, the thought had me about to orgasm already. Kaizer hooked his fingers inside me, hitting a spot so fucking perfect a moan escaped me. Zuri's heartbeat was still going crazy, and I ran my hands over my body, stopping to squeeze my nipples, biting my lip. Her heart had to be nearly about to explode at that moment, and right then, I knew she *had* to be watching me. Kaizer picked me up and laid me on the table, my head hanging off the edge slightly so I looked directly into my dark room.

Her heart skipped slightly as my gaze caught with hers. She looked like she was about to run away, but I shook my head slightly to stop her. She peered at me with wide eyes, but I ran my hands lightly all over my body, keeping eye contact with her as Kaizer feasted on me. I squeezed my breasts again, kneading them as I watched her fingers gravitate toward her pussy. I nodded, letting her know that that's exactly what I fucking wanted from her. Kaizer didn't seem like he noticed any of this, so lost to giving me his tactile apology. She slid her nightgown over as she leaned against the wall for leverage. She opened her legs, and I could see how fucking wet she was from here, the candles nearby illuminating everything she had exposed for me.

She pushed her fingers in, and she moaned, forcing an even louder moan from me as Kaizer pumped his fingers in and out so fucking fast I was about to see stars. Zuri pulled her fingers out, rubbing circles around her clit as she bit her lip so hard, I swore I saw blood spilling. She pushed them back inside of herself with force, pushing and pulling at the same rate that Kaizer was going. By coincidence or on purpose, I had no idea, but *fuck* was it fucking hot. Zuri threw her head back, hitting the wall behind her as she brought herself to orgasm. I screamed; I screamed so loud that Kaizer thought he was the one I was screaming for.

"That's it," he muttered as I came so hard that everything around me went bright.

When I opened my eyes and looked back into my room, Zuri wasn't there anymore, and part of me was wondering if I had imagined the whole fucking ordeal. Kaizer pulled his fingers out of me and kissed up my stomach, leaning over my body as the moon illuminated his white hair. He lingered there on my neck, raking his sharp canines over my skin, asking for blood.

I couldn't fucking care less at the moment, so I nodded to him as I looked back into the empty room again. His teeth sliced into my neck, warmth rushing through my body. Before, it felt amazing, but nothing compared to the insane fucking orgasm I just had. He drank deep, his throat bobbing as he moaned into my neck. He ran his hands over my naked body, lingering on my right nipple as he rolled it between his fingers. I moaned at the contact, my body still sensitive, forcing a dark chuckle from him.

Kaizer pulled his fangs from my neck and licked his lips and looked down at my body. "Am I forgiven?"

"What?" I asked, forgetting why this started in the first place. "Oh, sure, you're forgiven."

My chest was heaving, and he looked at me like he just gave me the best fucking orgasm of my life, which he was part of, but he wasn't the one who made it so fucking mind-blowing.

Chapter Twenty-Seven

I rolled over on my side, waking up from the deep sleep that consumed me last night. Between the fighting and the orgasm, I was worn out; I was pretty sure that I fell asleep before my head hit the pillow. Warmth radiated from beside me, and my brow pulled together, my eyes still closed. I wiggled a bit, trying to figure out what it was in my sleep haze. When I opened my eyes, I found Kaizer half-naked in my bed and yelped. I didn't even think about where he would end up after the events yesterday. My original plan was to make him sleep on the floor, but there he was beside me.

I poked him in his firm bicep until he woke up. "Hey, big guy, what do you think you're doing?"

He groaned and looked over at me. "You told me to sleep here before you fell asleep. You just said not to touch you or you'd '*fucking gut me.*'"

That checks out.

"I don't remember that," I said, pulling the covers closer to my chest.

Thankfully I had on a nightgown; I typically slept naked when I was home.

He propped himself up on his elbow and leaned forward seductively. "Do you want me to get up?"

"No, it's fine. I was about to go check on Zuri," I said as I stretched my arms out wide. Kaizer watched me stretch, and I figured I should probably set some expectations.

"To be clear, that was just sex. That doesn't make me yours," I stated.

Kaizer smirked, like he thought it was a joke, and nodded before laying back down. *Well, I did my part.*

I wasn't exactly sure what would happen today with her, but not having Kaizer shadow me during our first interaction would be preferred. Stepping out of bed, I slipped my feet into my slippers and walked toward Zuri's room on the other side of the sitting room. My stomach was tight, and my breathing was uneven, like she was the first person I'd ever been attracted to. The worst part was she was really my only true friend in Sanjry, so thinking that I might have fucked that up had me more nervous than I would have liked to admit. I took a deep inhale, wrapping my fingers around the golden door knob, the cool feel of the metal sending goosebumps up my arms.

"Zuri, I'm coming in," I said before turning the knob and pushing open the door.

It was still dark, but I could hear her even breathing. I flicked a small orb of witch magic near the door, and the soft purple glow fell over Zuri's sleeping figure. She was on her side; the blankets were pulled up to her neck as she cradled a pillow in her arms. Her short curls fell on her silk pillow around her head, one curl thrown over her face. I walked over to the side of her bed, watching as she slept with her mouth slightly ajar for a few moments.

"Zuri," I whispered, sitting down on the bed.

She shifted slightly but fell back asleep a moment later. I picked up the curl that hung over her eyes and tossed it to its rightful place behind her ear.

I put my hand on her shoulder. "Zuri, it's me," I said a little louder.

She shifted again, but this time her eyes blinked open, and she looked up at me through heavy lids. I pulled my hand back and leaned against it beside the pillow she was cuddling.

"Hi," she said with a small smile.

I grinned from ear to ear. "Hi."

She scooted closer to my hand, her nose grazing the inside of my wrist slightly. A smile pulled at my lips instantly at the contact, and I had to bite my lip before it got too big, and I embarrassed myself.

"Why are you awake?" she asked.

"Woke up to a mountain of man in my bed and decided I should leave," I sneered.

She smiled again, but it faded slightly, and she looked away from me. "About last night..."

"What about it?" I teased as I snapped an air shield around us so no sound could escape.

"I wasn't snooping. I came out for wine after our day, and then I saw you through the open door and..."

I smirked. "Then you were enamored with my naked body?"

"Well, sort of, yeah," she laughed out.

"The other day in your tent, I felt...something. I didn't really know what it was, but then when we woke up, you were cuddled up to me. I wasn't sure if you knew, so I didn't say anything."

"I knew," Zuri said with a breath of laughter.

I tilted my head. "Well, let me say you are a fantastic actress."

"The situation is a little...messy."

"Understatement," I muttered.

As if the mess knew we were talking about him, Kaizer walked over to the bathroom and closed the door behind him.

"I need to escort him around Caldera today," I sighed, lying down beside her.

"Want me to come with you?"

I smiled and turned my head to meet her gaze. "Yes." I nodded. "I'm sure he'll want to bring a few soldiers too."

"When?"

"The sooner we go, the sooner we get back," I said.

Zuri sat up, her silk nightgown clinging to her frame as she rustled through her bouncing curls. "Okay, let me get dressed," she said around a yawn.

She stood from the bed and made to walk to her dresser but ran smack into the air shield I had left earlier.

"Oh no," I said, dissipating the magic as soon as her ass hit the ground and standing to my feet.

"What the fuck, Daya!" she shrieked.

I put my hands to my face and peeked through my fingers. "My bad."

"Well, I'm awake at least," she responded as she pushed to her feet.

"I'm going to go get dressed," I said as I ran out of the room.

A pillow flew through the air and hit the side of the door frame before I made it out, still laughing. I rounded the corner out of the sitting room and back into my room as Kaizer walked out of the bathroom with a towel hanging low on his hips. His hair was pulled into a high bun, and I watched as water droplets fell from his shoulders and down his chest.

"Good morning again," he said with a grin.

"I'm going to get dressed, and then we can go," I said, trying not to let my eyes linger on any of the skin on display.

Kaizer was attractive like this, but his personality was equivalent to the rear end of a horse half the time, so that was unfortunate.

"Sounds good," he said as he walked to grab his clothes off the bed.

I turned my back to him and heard the towel drop on the floor. The bathroom door was open, and the large mirror behind my sink reflected a muscled back and ass as he grabbed his underwear. *Fuck, I need a cold bath.*

I stood in the East Wing where the soldiers were with Zuri and Kaizer, waiting for them to adorn their armor so we could leave. I talked him down to just two soldiers, as taking all fifty we brought with us would put a strain on my magic and was extremely unnecessary. He chose two men I didn't know, their names rhymed or something, but I couldn't bring myself to care what they were.

"Where are we going?" Zuri asked.

"I don't actually know. What do you want to see, Kaizer?"

"Whatever you think holds the most importance. What makes Caldera, Caldera?"

"The brujas," I responded flatly.

"No landmarks or great wonders of your kingdom?"

I smiled. "Sure, I can think of a few."

"Elias, Enzo, are you ready?" Kaizer asked his soldiers.

Alliteration, not rhyming, oops.

"Yes, Your Majesty," they boomed, and I rolled my eyes.

"Ever traveled by portal, boys?" I asked the soldiers.

They shook their heads in unison.

"Well, allow me to be your first," I said with a wink before snapping open a portal in front of me.

"We just...step through?" the one on the right asked. *Enzo?*

"That's all there is to it." I shrugged, grabbing Zuri by her arm and pulling her into the portal with me.

Purple smoke and shadow encompassed us as Kaizer stepped through, then the two soldiers fell over top of each other onto the ground in front of the portal. I made it *slightly* unstable when they walked through, and Zuri looked over at me like she knew what I was up to. I shrugged again and pushed through the smoke as my feet squished into the hot sand.

"A desert?" Kaizer asked.

"It's one of our jewels," I said with a sarcastic smile.

"Do people live here?" Zuri asked.

"More than just people," I joked, looking out over the rippling sand.

The two soldiers put their hands on the hilts of their swords and scanned the area, and I laughed. "Oh, those won't do you any good here. The monsters that roam this place can't be cut down with your blades."

"What kills them?" one of the soldiers asked.

"Better weapons and witch magic." I winked. "Come on. There is something I want to show you here."

We pushed through the sand, all the others losing their footing and sliding around the mounds of blazing hot particles. My foot hit the hollow ground, and I held my hand up for them to stop as I crouched down. As much as I hated this fucking place, I really loved this one small part of it. I placed my hand in the sand and pushed it down until the substance fully covered it, and I felt the grooves I was looking for. Letting my magic seep from my fingers and into the channels, I looked back at Zuri's face. Her brows pulled together, looking at me as if I'd lost my mind. The lock clicked, and I smirked as the ground beneath us shook. Erect stone emerged from the ground and sand poured down like liquid as the mural I brought them here to see came to its full height. I turned around to face my companions, their faces lit with surprise, and laughed.

"This is one of my ancestors, Mariana," I explained.

While I was pretty sure Kaizer was going to lose his mind at the very realistic nudity on display, I always loved this mural. It depicted my grandmother, many generations ago; she stood tall with her shoulders back, her long waves pulled back into a half-up hairstyle. Her violet magic blasted from her hands and lit everything around her. She was fucking terrifying, and I loved it. Something about the fact she held no weapons, no armor, not even clothes, and still looked as powerful always resonated with me.

"She's beautiful," Zuri said, her head tilted to the side as she examined the sculpture.

"Got a thing for witches, Zuri?" I taunted.

She waved her hand in a dismissal, and I laughed internally. Kaizer hadn't moved; he just stared like he didn't quite understand what was happening.

"Why is she naked?" he asked.

"It's art, Kaizer, don't be such a bore," I replied with a hand on my hip.

His gaze softened slightly, like he was starting to understand what the art was supposed to be conveying.

"You look so much like her," Zuri said as she came to stand beside me.

"I always thought so, too," I whispered, looking back at my ancestor.

I'd never met her, but something about her always felt like she called to me. If our histories were correct, she was the first Acna, the first true witch to wield the extra power gifted by the Goddess of Air and Essence. She created the sanctions and brought a resemblance of peace to the witches. Be that as it may, she was fierce and so powerful the texts said she could barely contain her power sometimes. Her magic was the same hue as mine, the same rich violet color. She was the only other person to have it. There were people with lilac and plenty of other colors, but we were the only two to have such a deep purple. Clicking sounded from somewhere nearby, and I knew we wouldn't be able to stay much longer. This mural was placed here because it was where she died, but it was a great distance from the closest city and, unfortunately, was in monster territory.

"We gotta go," I exclaimed, snapping open another portal behind me.

Giant horned scorpions crested a hill with their claws clicking together, their dagger-tipped tails pulsating in the air with poison dripping into the surrounding sand. They burrowed into the sand out of our view, and I turned to the others as they watched with panic.

"Fucking go!" I yelled.

The men barreled toward the portal, and I tackled Zuri through as I closed it behind me. A severed claw crashed down on top of me, leaking black blood, and I jumped up, pushing it off me as my skin crawled.

"Well, that was eventful," Zuri joked.

I reached behind me and stuck my fingers into the sticky substance I was covered in, shaking my hand to try to get it off me.

"Fucking disgusting," I growled.

"Where are we now?" Kaizer asked.

I waved my hand in the air. "You don't recognize the lake?"

Their heads swiveled as they took in the silver lake we had visited the night before. We were on the other side, so the city wasn't in view, but the sparkling liquid was a sure tell.

"The water is always warm. Some say it has healing properties, but I've never known it to be true," I explained.

Foliage lined the lake's border, and I separated the typhus plants enough to get to the bank on the other side. The wet sand was packed tight, a line of tiny footprints extending from the plants down into the water. There were a few amphibious creatures that lived within the lake, the salamanders being my favorite. They appeared to be lizard-like creatures with slick blue skin but had iridescent wings when they burst from its surface and hit the air. I looked around to see if any were nearby, but the water was utterly still. I toed my boots through the ground until I met the water's edge next to Zuri. She dipped her hand into the water, and the liquid surrounding her fingers glowed bright white.

"What the fuck," I muttered as I leaned in closer.

She yanked her hand out of the water and looked back at Kaizer and the soldiers to see if they noticed, but they were looking in the opposite direction.

"What do you think?" she murmured.

I shook my head. "Not here," I whispered.

"It's beautiful," Kaizer exclaimed as he turned to face us.

It *was* beautiful, but the stench of gore on me was going to make me nauseous if I didn't do something about it as soon as possible.

"I'm gonna clean off," I said to no one in particular.

I went to pull off my clothes and was reminded half of the people here were prudes when Kaizer's eyebrows shot up as he stepped toward me.

"Ugh, fine. I just need to get this blood off me," I said, rolling my eyes.

I could dry off with my air magic so, while annoying, it wasn't the end of the world. I stepped into the water, but all three of the men stood on the shoreline watching me.

"You can go look around," I suggested.

Kaizer and his soldiers turned quickly and pushed through the foliage out of sight, and I rolled my eyes and dipped my body under the water.

Zuri crouched down near the water's edge. "What was that?" she whispered.

"Remember I said the water was rumored to have healing abilities?" I asked.

She nodded, dipping her fingers back into the water. The glow seeped from her fingers, and she pulled her hand through the water, leaving a luminescent stream behind.

"You're a gifted healer. I think it has something to do with that," I whispered.

"Weird," she mumbled.

I tried to scrub the substance off me, but I couldn't reach the center of my back, and the water wasn't doing enough for it to clean me by itself.

"Can you help me?" I asked. "I can dry you off after."

Zuri nodded and stepped into the water, every spot her skin touched glowing as she pushed through the water gracefully. I turned, and she ran her fingers over my back, pulling the blood from my leathers with just a few swipes of her hand.

"Good as new," she said brightly.

I turned to face her, the glow now radiating a few feet from her body. "You're...beautiful," I whispered, taking her in.

She smiled wide as the silvery gleam sparkled in her eyes. I stepped closer to her, the water sloshing around us as her glow encased the both of us. The tips of my hair were wet, and she moved them over my shoulder as she looked from my lips to my eyes. A salamander burst through the surface beside us; their wings spread wide and glittering as they glided over the lake. We both watched in awe as it disappeared, and I eyed the smile gracing her lips at the magical little critter. A branch snapped nearby, and we both jumped back from each other and quickly got out of the lake before Kaizer pushed through the shrubbery.

"All done?" he asked.

"Yeah," I muttered.

I put one hand on Zuri's shoulder and the other on my stomach as I blasted us both with enough hot air to dry off our clothes in a few moments.

"Thanks," Zuri whispered.

"Where to next?" Kaizer asked.

"One last place," I said, unsure if I should take them to the next place on my list.

I snapped open a portal at the shoreline as the other two soldiers met us, and I held out my hand, directing them toward the opening. We stepped through into the violet smoke, and my heart started to ache slightly as the smoke cleared around us.

"This is Cape Coven," I mumbled, "where we're laid to rest."

Malva was a dark place in general, but even the odd light of the sky didn't seem to reach this part of Caldera. Fog so thick it was hard to breathe encompassed the area. You couldn't see more than a few feet in front of you, and the edge of the cape was a fall that could kill even the strongest. There was always a constant warm breeze here, the spirits of our beloved wrapping around us, embracing us from the spirit world. I had my eyes closed and my chin pulled down as I felt that sensation; some people claimed they could tell who was visiting them, but I never could. All the same, I could hear their whispers on the wind. They all blended together, but it felt good to know that when we died, we didn't just stop existing.

It was morbid, but I loved it here. On days I felt so numb that I could barely function, coming here and letting the emotions of the dead overcome me reminded me that I was still alive. I opened my eyes, Kaizer and the soldier's gaze looking out into the distance, or as far as they could see anyway. Zuri was looking at me like she could feel the sensations bubbling up in my chest, the warm breeze moving through her curls.

"When we die, we're cremated, and half of our ashes are buried in the land. The others are scattered into the wind. We leave something that marks our lives behind," I muttered, crouching down to move the dirt off the stone beside my feet.

I didn't recognize the name etched into the headstone, but I did recognize the precious gemstone that was set into it.

"What's the gemstone mean?" Kaizer asked.

"It's moonstone. This witch was from Catalina's sanction," I said as I ran my finger over the white stone.

Each sanction had its own stone that represented them, moonstone, sapphire, ruby, amethyst, and the capital's: bloodstone.

I didn't bring Kaizer here to make him feel bad originally, but I wasn't hating how sad he looked while he gazed over the thousands of headstones that were put here from the war.

"There's so many," he muttered.

"We've been using this space for burial since the beginning of Caldera, but, yes, lots have been added in the recent centuries," I responded, taking a deep breath.

He nodded and crouched down to inspect the surrounding stones. Zuri stood by my side, her fingers grazing mine ever so slightly. I smiled at her as I walked closer to the edge of the cape. She followed me, and I used some air magic to separate the fog to make sure she could see the edge. Raging water boomed around us as our toes met the edge of the Cape, and I pushed some more magic out in front of us so she could see the water. The dull grayish blue water moved, streams of white foam pulsing through as it crashed against the sharp rocks at the bottom.

I closed my eyes once again to feel the spirits of the dead caress my skin and run through my hair. The sound of the waves and their whispers grew so loud, I couldn't hear anything but them. I could sense Zuri's presence still beside me, and I opened my eyes to see hers closed and her brow pulled together.

"Can you feel them?" I asked.

"I feel something. I don't know how to describe it," she responded.

"It's an odd place, but I really like it," I said as I turned back toward where we left the others.

Zuri followed behind me as we bobbed and weaved to avoid any of the headstones, which was hard due to the sheer quantity laid on the earth.

"Tour's over. Let's go home," I exclaimed.

I opened the portal, the purple glow of my magic radiating in the thick white fog, making it look double the size. Kaizer nodded and stepped through, the soldiers and Zuri following behind him. I peered over my shoulder one more time with a small smile before I stepped through the portal back into the courtyard in Caldera.

Chapter Twenty-Eight

"Where did you take him?" my mother asked, her nail ticking on her obsidian desk.

She called me here this morning after I didn't update her immediately about where we went yesterday. I wasn't in the mood to talk to her, which, if I was being honest, I never was, but all the same, I didn't want to talk to her. I didn't even talk to Kaizer this morning; I woke up before he did and came straight here after eating breakfast.

"Just to the desert, Silver Lake, and Cape Coven," I explained as I sat back in my chair and crossed my legs.

She looked down her nose at me and stopped tapping her nail against the stone surface. "What did he have to say?"

I leaned forward with intrigue. "He didn't really say anything. He just wanted to see some of the land. Do you suspect something is going on?"

I knew he was up to something, but I hadn't figured out what it was quite yet. If my mother was concerned, it made me think I was actually onto something, and it wasn't all in my head.

"No, he's a man. I always suspect they'll double-cross me," she hissed.

"If you know something, I'd like to be informed. I am the one living with him," I growled.

"I don't know anything. You know you should always keep your head on a swivel. I taught you that."

"Is there anything else you need from me?" I asked.

She set the papers she was looking at down and snapped her gaze up to me. "Your handmaiden."

My chest tightened; I tried to keep my heartbeat even because I knew that she could detect any small flicker in my emotions.

"What about her?" I asked in an apathetic tone.

"She's interesting," she said.

It took effort not to flinch. "She's a handmaiden. How interesting can she be?"

"They said she fought during Rosa's revolt," she stated with the slightest tilt of her head.

"She did. I've been training her. She's always with me. I figured she should know how to defend herself."

"That's smart. Having someone you know is on your side," she said as if she didn't expect me to be all that smart at all.

I looked into the light behind her head. "Mhm."

"Let me know when you plan on leaving. You're dismissed," she demanded with a wave of her hand.

"Always a pleasure, mother," I muttered.

I rose from my seat and smoothed out the fabric of my skirt. I was wearing an orange silk gown today. The cowl neck and high slits one of my favorite designs as it accented the curves of my body beautifully. I came here alone, knowing my mother wouldn't want Kaizer with me in case there was something she wanted to talk about privately. We'd done the tour yesterday, and Kaizer seemed satisfied enough with what we'd seen, so I wasn't sure if we needed to stay much longer. I wouldn't argue to go back, that was for sure, but it felt like a cruel vacation. My life with him still remained in Sanjry. So, as nice as it was to be here, I didn't want to enjoy it too much, or I'd be even more disappointed when it was time to go home.

Home, ugh. I referred to Sanjry as *home*. I didn't think I'd ever refer to anywhere other than Caldera as home in my life. Especially not Sanjry, where the fucking vampires lived. Well, all the vampires weren't so bad. Zuri may have been the only one that didn't make me want to kill them at one point or another. I still needed to figure out how to go about that situation; the likelihood of Kaizer only wanting to be married for namesake and letting me go about what I wanted to do was slim to none. I had some leeway for now as I made it clear he had to work for me, but once we were married his stupid conventional conservative views were sure to make that difficult.

Any attraction I'd had to him thus far had been purely sexual, and just in those moments. But Zuri... Zuri was something else. She was like a bright star in a night where none shone, the warmest fire on a relentlessly frigid evening. She'd been there for me from day one after I woke up in that fucking bedchamber without an idea of what was going on. She listened to me to understand, not just to respond. I hadn't been fully honest with her at first because I didn't know who I could trust, but she'd proven herself over the weeks. I didn't want a world where she wasn't always with me, but these feelings that had blossomed between us were something I was sure I wouldn't be able to hide forever.

I was already irritated that I was engaged to begin with, when I had no other unselfish reason not to want it, but now...I didn't know. She made me feel alive in a way I didn't think I was capable of. I wanted that opportunity to be with someone who saw me and didn't try to change the parts most said were too much. The fact I even wanted Zuri the way I did was evidence enough that I was changing. I'd said for decades I would never do that again, never let someone in. But she was doing it without me even fully realizing, and that had to mean *something*. The thought that I had the chance to be genuinely happy, and wouldn't be able to reach it because of Kaizer and the agreement had fury bubbling up in me.

Would I risk war just for the chance at happiness? Real happiness? The answer was undoubtedly yes, but I didn't think it should have been. As a leader, you were supposed to put your people first. Make sure they were taken care of, but fuck, I just wanted to run away with her by my side and forget everything else. I was to be the Acna in a few short weeks, truly having the power to change the things I wanted to, but I'd still be linked to Kaizer the day after.

I was powerful; some days, I felt even more powerful than my mother. *Could I overthrow Kaizer myself and take Sanjry?* Rubbing the stupid fucking tattoo on my wrist that marked our agreement, I sighed and turned the corner to the treasury. I kept most of my expensive jewelry there, and as I was dropped off in Sanjry with only the tattered clothes on my back from battle, I was in dire need of bringing back as much shit as possible with me. Some may have described me as vain, but I didn't care. I liked nice things, and while I was covered with blood for more than half of my life, when I wasn't, I wanted to look fucking good. That was not a crime.

The treasury was hidden in plain sight, sealed by magic to appear like a wall with a tapestry on it, but me and my mother knew where it was and were the only ones who could open it. I made it to the giant hidden vault door and put my hand on it, but before I unlocked it with my magic, I heard footsteps coming my way. Taking a step back from the wall, I turned to make it look like I was walking toward the person coming my way. A few days ago, I'd say no one would dare steal from us, but with Rosa's attack, I didn't want to be too careless. Kaizer turned the corner by himself, and I raised my brow as his gaze met mine.

"What are you doing?" I asked.

"Just looking around while you were busy," he said. His heartbeat was steady, but he could have trained it like I had to hide any lies.

"When do you want to go back? Was the tour sufficient?" I asked.

"It was. We can leave tonight if you like?"

"I'm not saying I want to leave," I mumbled under my breath.

He smiled and stepped toward me. "You eager to get back for wedding planning?"

"I just don't want to spoil myself too much here and then return to your dreary excuse for a castle," I joked, but was it really a joke? It definitely wasn't.

"We have much to do when we return. We'll need to figure out the specifics with the event team around the wedding, and we need to draw out some plans for combining the kingdoms officially."

"We haven't figured that out already?" I asked with my hand on my hip.

"The lands are technically joined with the treaty, but it will help to have the rest on paper," he expressed and looked around past my head.

I raised my eyebrows. "Looking for something?"

"No, I just haven't been over here yet. What's down here?"

I turned and pointed around the corner. "That way to the dungeons. They're typically empty for reasons you're well aware of."

"Mhm, interesting," he replied, glancing back at me. "I will go let the soldiers know we'll be traveling back tonight."

I nodded, and he walked away back around the corner. I waited until he was far enough away that he couldn't turn back before I placed my hand on the vault door. Pushing my magic into it, I broke down the spell until the door appeared and the lock clicked open. I pulled the door and closed it behind me quickly before waiting for the spell to lock back in place. While I didn't have fire like Kaizer, we had a narrow crevice running horizontally across the wall that would contain magic enough to glow. I shot a stream of my violet magic into the space and watched the line of purple spread until it filled the entire opening from one side of the room to the other. The luminescence sparkled across all the jewels and trinkets forcing a smile across my face as I took in my treasures.

Lines of tables with protective glass bordered the room, other tables of trinkets were nestled in the center of the room, but those were mostly weapons and random items we found value in. I lifted the glass in the corner and pulled out a few of the necklaces on display, then walked over to the other wall to grab some earrings and rings. An amethyst bracelet laid on the velvet, seeming to scream *Zuri,* and I lifted it up, inspecting the purple stones. It was a golden cuff with oval stones set into it; tiny diamonds were peppered throughout the design that sparkled in the light of my magic.

Stuffing the bracelet and the rest of the jewelry I could take in one trip in my pockets, I made to turn back toward the door, but the airstone from Kaizer's books caught my attention. I opened the case and ran my fingers over the other stones until I reached it. Like I remembered from before, it felt alive, like it had a sentience.

I picked it up gently and held the sliver of stone in my palm, bringing it closer to my face to inspect. It had the air symbol etched into it and markings below it in a language I didn't recognize. The odd swirls and slashes seemed so foreign from the alphabet we used now. The bands of color pulsated with my heartbeat, the warmth of my hand bringing the stone even more alive.

"You don't seem that important," I muttered.

I grabbed a piece of old parchment, hopefully not something too important, and extended my pointer finger, letting some magic gather at the tip like a pen. I copied the markings, folded the parchment up tight, and put it in my bra. I had no idea what it meant, but it looked important enough that I should try to figure it out before Kaizer did. Listening for bodies out in the halls, I waited a moment before opening the door and stepping through the opening, letting the magic seal close before I left.

The jewelry was heavy in my pockets since the dress was made of silk, so I wrapped one of the necklaces around my neck, put in a pair of earrings, and slipped on all the rings around my fingers. Zuri was outside in the courtyard when I exited the palace, and I smiled as I watched her admire the wildflowers that were my favorite. She turned toward me, smiling as brightly as I imagined the sun would burn.

"Where are you going?" she giggled, her eyes dancing between all the ridiculously fancy jewelry I had on at once.

"Oh, nowhere." I laughed. "I just picked some of my jewelry up from the treasury. Actually..." I trailed off, pulling the bracelet I picked for Zuri off my wrist. "This one is for you."

I reached my hand toward her, and she looked at the bracelet and back up at my face a few times before she grabbed it gently, her skin grazing mine slightly.

"Daya, this is beautiful. I can't take this," she muttered with a shake of her head.

"It was just sitting in the treasury. I can't possibly wear all the jewelry in there. It reminded me of you. Seriously, it's yours," I responded.

She smiled and slipped the cuff onto her wrist; the gold and purple against her brown skin felt like art in and of itself. I really couldn't believe how perfect it was on her delicate wrist.

"Looks better on you than me," I joked.

"Somehow, I doubt that's true," she teased, peering behind me for a moment and stepping closer.

I grabbed her hand and looked at the bracelet with a quick tug to pull her as close as we could be out in the open.

"Daya," she murmured, but the laugh and smile that followed told me she didn't mind too much.

I rubbed my thumb across her skin. "I'm just making sure there aren't any stones missing."

She bit her lip, but I heard footsteps nearing one of the courtyard entrances and let go of her arm reluctantly and moved to stand beside her instead. One of Kaizer's soldiers walked by the entrance and nodded once at me before continuing past the opening.

"You like these flowers?" I asked.

"They're so chaotic. I love them," she responded.

"Me too," I muttered, "we have to go back to Sanjry tonight."

I couldn't help the sigh that escaped me at that declaration, a declaration that sent the corner of her lips down.

"I like it better here," she breathed.

"Unfortunately, we can't stay. If it was up to me, we would stay here forever and ditch those losers," I said with a bump of my hips to hers.

"I know the fate of both kingdoms lies on you and Kaizer," she swallowed.

"I haven't told you something," I started, looking around and snapping down an air shield. "Kaizer is up to something. I didn't trust him before, but he has these books in the red room that talk about old artifacts and magic. He's obsessed with it, and I don't know if he is trying to do something or not, but something tells me it's not good."

She scooted slightly closer to me. "What about it?"

"The books talked about the stones used to dampen our power after the Piedra was erected, the magic used to make that happen. The magic he used in the battle was old magic, but I don't know how he did it. He hasn't used it again, so I think it was a onetime spell he used or something, but I feel like he wants more of it. I think that's why his people were found in Dusra. I just can't figure out the why behind it."

"You think he wants all of Malva?"

"He's a man. I'm sure he wants all of everything." I rolled my eyes. "He seemed scared of Axel, though, so I don't think he would try anything just yet."

"How sure are you that it's not only an obsession, and he has no plans to do anything about it?"

"Like 75 percent." I shrugged.

Zuri bit her lip and looked back into the flowers. "I'm assuming you haven't asked him?"

"No, I don't want him to know that I'm onto him. But I found this," I said, pulling out the piece of parchment from my bra. "This was scribed on the airstone."

She ran her finger over it. "This is the old tongue."

"You know what it says?"

"No, but I recognize it from some books in my childhood," Zuri said, one of the few times she mentioned anything of the time before I met her.

I looked her up and down with my brows drawn. "You studied the old tongue?"

"My mother was..." Her throat bobbed. "I studied a lot of things, but the old tongue was one of them. I just can't remember how to decipher it," she huffed.

"You are such an interesting little vampire," I joked.

She laughed, but her eyes darkened like she was remembering things she would have rather kept buried. I wasn't sure if her family died tragically, or if they betrayed her, I never pushed. I had a feeling she didn't like the connection to whatever it was she didn't talk about, and that was something I understood.

Once I realized what my mother really was, I had a hard time doing anything that she taught me. Even though I still followed her for all these years, a piece of me hated that I was a part of her and her a part of me. I was no saint by any means, but my mother was a level of cruel even I couldn't get behind. I was honestly surprised I didn't wake up pulled from my bed last night for punishment when I didn't report directly back to her. The two vampires in my room probably saved me from that.

"Well, let's go get packed up. I'm going to try to convince Kaizer to let us portal back instead."

"Please, I don't want to ride in that rickety-ass carriage when you have the power to get us there with a snap of your fingers."

That's my girl.

Chapter Twenty-Nine

Kaizer didn't know it, but I was sizing him up to get him to agree to let me and Zuri portal back by ourselves. I laughed at all his jokes, rubbed his arm throughout lunch, and smiled wide like he was the center of my fucking universe. He was eating that shit up. We were back in my room, and I sighed loud enough to catch his attention.

"What's wrong?" he asked.

"I just don't want to travel for days. I really want to get back to our palace," I sighed, emphasizing the word *our*. "Do you mind if I just portal back with Zuri?"

He contemplated, rubbing his chin. "I don't see why not. You gave me blood at lunch. I'll travel back with the soldiers to ensure nothing goes wrong."

When he asked me for blood in front of everyone at lunch, I jumped at the opportunity. I could control myself enough when I was surrounded by people, and his venom only made me *slightly* horny.

I jumped up and hugged him. "Thank you!"

I may have been a bit over the top, but I got what I wanted in the end, so whatever. He rubbed my back, the touch getting more sensual as the hug prolonged. We still hadn't had sex, and I really wasn't planning on it right now.

"Let me go tell my mother," I pulled back, waving at him as I stepped through a portal to my mother's office door.

"Hell fucking yeah," I muttered as I rapped my knuckles on the door.

She yelled for me to come in, and I pulled the door open to find her in the same spot she was this morning.

"Have you not left yet?" I asked.

"I did momentarily, but there's a lot to catch up on while I was in Sanjry."

"Okay, well, I was just coming to let you know I'm heading back soon. I'm going by portal, but Kaizer and the others will be leaving this evening."

"Why aren't you traveling with your betrothed?"

"Have you traveled by carriage recently? It's fucking terrible," I muttered.

She looked up at me and rolled her eyes. "I will come on the morning of The Ritual. If you need me before then, you know where to find me."

She lifted the papers back up, dismissing me without even saying anything, but I was free of her, so I sprang out of my seat and practically ran out of the door to find Zuri. She said she was helping Catalina with something before I left, so I went over to the office Cat usually used when she was visiting. Witches came and went from the palace daily. I was always surprised it didn't bother my mother, but she never seemed to care too much. I thought that deep down she was still the person I knew in my early childhood who loved being around other witches, but she never let on.

I turned the knob into the office to find Catalina and Zuri laughing like they were old friends, and the sight warmed my heart. I wouldn't outright admit it to Cat, but I missed her. Being away from Caldera and not constantly on the move gave me a lot of time to think about what my life was lacking. I'd known her since we were toddlers, and me, her, and Ximena were inseparable as kids. It was hard to maintain friendships when I was always gone, and my mother had molded me into the perfect soldier. Someone who didn't have anything to lose outside of what she provided me.

This whole marriage to Kaizer opened my eyes to how little I had in life. As much as I hated it, all of that brought me to this moment, to Zuri and whatever it was between us. I was trying my hardest not to overthink it because the last time I did, I kept comparing the situation to Ximena. *Would she receive the same treatment if my mother found out?* I could keep it a secret, not allow her to bring any weakness out of me like before, but there was always a risk. A risk of Kaizer finding out, of my mother finding out.

My chest ached as I spiraled, and I looked up to find them both staring at me.

"Are you going to say anything or..." Zuri trailed off, her brows pulled together.

"Sorry, yes." I cleared my throat. "We can travel by portal whenever you're ready."

Cat's eyes danced between the two of us. "Not going back with Kaizer?"

"No, I would rather be shot in the chest with a poisoned-tipped arrow," I mumbled.

"I was just about to tell Zuri how beautiful I thought her bracelet was," Catalina said, her eyes sparkling knowingly.

"Shut up," I growled.

"Hey, I was just admiring the jewelry," Cat said as she threw her hands in the air.

Zuri looked at me with wide eyes, and I waved her off. "Do you have any concerns before I leave?" I asked Cat.

"Nope, it's weird not preparing for another battle. I don't really know what to do as general right now."

I crossed my arms and took another step forward. "Actually, can you keep an eye on Kaizer until they leave and then go check on Rosa's sanction in the next few days? I left the highest-ranking person in charge, but I don't know how much they know since Rosa and Juana were stupid enough to get themselves killed."

"Yeah, I'll get them up to speed," Cat responded, straightening into the general she was.

"Thanks, Cat. Let my mother know if there are any issues." I hesitated. "I...look forward to seeing you at The Ritual."

Cat grinned as we walked toward the door before shouting, "Be safe, Daya!"

I tossed one more look over my shoulder and smiled gently at Cat, and her smile widened as the door closed behind me.

"What is this Ritual?" Zuri asked.

"It's actually only been done two other times. Typically when one Acna dies, the next in line is automatically inducted. When it's passed on like it will be to me, there's a whole ritual that takes place. It's very…witchy."

Zuri's head cocked to the side. "What does that mean?"

"It happens at night. There's an altar that's lit with fire, we lay our stones out on the border of the altar, and we chant a spell. I'll have to be naked, blood is spilled by both my mother and I, and in the end, the power is transferred to me."

"It's a tangible power?"

"Yeah, it's the power of Naom. Every Acna has a unique power that comes with it. I don't know what it is until I get it. My mother's was just an enhancement of her powers, so she doesn't need the stones to perform complicated spells. But in the past, some had persuasion, necromancy, a few other things."

"Witches are so fucking cool. I can't wait to see," she exclaimed.

"I'll have to hide you, only brujas are allowed present, but we can probably work something out," I said, bumping her in the shoulder.

We made it back to my room to grab our bags, and I threw a few bottles of my wine, my stash of crystals, and the jewelry I grabbed earlier into one of my bags before going over to Zuri's room.

"Ready?" I asked.

"Yes, can I take this pillow with me? I don't know what it is about it, but I swear it's the most comfortable pillow in all of Malva."

"You can have whatever you want," I said, gesturing to everything in the room.

She laughed and tucked it under her arm before she followed me out of the room, and I set my bag down to write Kaizer a note.

"See you in a few days, XOXO, Dayanara," I said aloud as I wrote it.

I set the parchment down on the table by the door and created a portal back to my room in Sanjry with a snap of my fingers. I looped my arm in Zuri's and grabbed my bags from the floor, tossing them through and stepping through the portal with her. My heels met the hard stone of the floor in my chamber, and I looked back into my room in Caldera and sighed before closing it off. Zuri walked over to her room and put her bags down while I threw mine into my closet.

"Do you report to someone here?" I asked.

"Yeah, there's a head of staff, Mia. She's the one who typically tells me what to do outside of my duties to you."

"Well, before you head back to her, do you want to come to the library with me before Kaizer gets back?"

She nodded excitedly. "Yes, let's do it."

The library here was huge, with so many levels I wasn't even sure how many it was made up of. Two spiral staircases sat on either side of the library to access the other levels with rows and rows of books in every place possible. There were books on shelves on the walls, standing shelves lined the main floor, and there was even a stack of books at the end of each shelf.

"Fuck, how are we going to find what we need," I sighed.

"We'll just ask Lina," Zuri said, walking around shelves and over to a small elderly woman sitting behind a desk.

"Oh, hey, Zuri. What can I do for you?" the old lady said with a warm smile.

She had wire-frame glasses, her silver hair pulled back into a tight bun at the nape of her neck.

"Hey, Lina. Can you point us in the direction of the books about language?"

"Sure thing, sweety. You're going to want to go to the east staircase over there." She pointed toward the furthest staircase. "Take it up to the sixth floor, and then you'll find those books on the fourth bookcase to your right. There are some rooms up there where you can go to read what you need."

Zuri smiled warmly. "Thanks, Lina."

"She really knows her shit," I mumbled.

"She's been here for centuries. She knows everything about this library," she responded with a shrug.

We followed Lina's directions and found a bookshelf full of books that looked like they would fall apart if we touched them.

"Look for anything that has to do with the old tongue," I mumbled, running my fingers over the tomes.

"Here's one," Zuri exclaimed as she carefully pulled a dark red book from the shelf before cradling it to her chest, and glancing around. "The rooms are down that hall," she finished, pointing to the other side.

I looked up as we walked and noticed at least four more levels filled with books as we made it to the corridor. The rooms were all empty, and we walked down to the last one on the right and entered. There weren't any windows in the room, which I was thankful for because I didn't want anybody to see what I was up to. I closed my eyes and tapped into my witch hearing; there wasn't anyone else in the space outside of us and Lina right now, and I was hoping it would stay that way.

"Do you have the paper?" Zuri asked.

I nodded and pulled it out of my bra, unrolling it and laying it flat between us. Zuri scooted it over to herself for a moment before opening the book and looking at the table of contents.

"This says this is a study of the old language. I imagine it will talk about these symbols somewhere," she said as she flipped through the pages with one of her nails in her mouth.

She pushed the book between us as symbols were laid out similar to what was written on the stone. Zuri flipped the page, and I looked between my paper and the book, the first symbol reflected on both.

"Here," I said, pointing to it. "This is the first one."

"It means *to move*," Zuri said, skimming through the paragraph below it.

I pointed to the third symbol "This one means *like the*."

"Second one is *swift*," Zuri said as we both ran our fingers over the last page of symbols.

"*Wind*," I said, tapping the last symbol.

"To move swift like the wind? That's...not helpful," Zuri said.

"I wonder if it was just part of the spell they used when the stones were created. It might just be a dead end," I sighed, pulling my hand over my face.

"Hey." Zuri grabbed my hand. "It was just our first lead. We'll figure it out."

"*We?*" I asked with a smile pulling at my lips.

Zuri shrugged. "I mean, it seems like the fate of the kingdoms relies on us, so sure, I'll help."

I chuckled and brushed her arm with my hand. "Do you want to pretend to be commoners and drink and dance until we pass out?"

"Daya, I am a commoner," she laughed out. "But yes, yes to all of that."

"Fucking fantastic," I beamed.

We walked back out of the room and put the book back in its spot, waving bye to Lina as we made it out of the library.

"Let's wait until it's dark, and then we can sneak out," I whispered as we made it down the halls.

I want to take advantage of every second Kaizer wasn't here before he made me start *wedding planning*.

Chapter Thirty

Night fell, and Zuri and I stood in my room as I worked through a spell to hide our identities. It was one I'd only used a few times, as my identity typically helped me. I needed a particular crystal for it, one that would have been very handy the last time I snuck out of the castle.

"Ah, here it is," I said, pulling out a rose quartz from my stash I brought from Caldera. "Okay, come here," I finished and motioned for her to stand in front of me.

I muttered the spell, rubbing the quartz over her forehead until I felt the spell settle into her. She turned to look in the mirror behind me.

"I look the same," she mumbled as she poked herself in the face.

"It's a spell for outside sources. Your appearance will be different for every other person who sees you. I made it so we can still see each other, though," I replied.

She nodded, and I redid the spell on me, feeling the warm sensation of the magic spread from my forehead down to my toes.

"We'll take the tunnels," I stated, guiding her over to the entrance in my room.

I lifted the protection spell to let her through, and we entered the dark space. I cast a violet light between us so we could see and walked us toward the village edge.

"I know you said there were secret tunnels, but seeing them now is kind of crazy," she muttered.

"Look out for the spy holes. You can see all types of things," I laughed in a hushed tone.

We came up to one of them, and I pointed to it for her to peek in.

"Holy shit, this is the staff quarters," she whispered as she pushed her face into the wall like it would help her see better.

"There's a hole in almost every room here, even in Kaizer's," I explained with a shrug.

Her eyebrows raised. "Well, that makes me want to be a bit more careful."

"I've never seen anyone in the tunnels. Maybe the royalty used them before. I don't think Kaizer knows."

"Let's keep it that way," she laughed out as we made it to the spot I'd used to get into the village the last time.

"Do you want to portal or have some fun?" I taunted.

"Fun," she replied quickly.

"Okay, so there's usually two guards on either side of the wall," I said, pointing in their direction. "I'll make a distraction, but you have to run before they realize it's not real."

"Deal," she replied.

I smiled something devilish and crouched down to the ground. Just like before, there were two guards; there wasn't much around but dirt and rocks.

"Got it," I whispered.

I sent a tendril of air magic under a boulder nearby, lifting it in the air and flinging it on the other side of the wall.

"What was that?" a guard exclaimed.

"It came from over there!" another guard answered.

"Run," I whispered.

We took off running as I tried to muffle my laugh. Zuri was slower than me, but not by too much. The guards were still by the rock, and I saw a flame-lit hand in the distance as we passed the gate.

"Hey!" a guard yelled, and I looked back to see Zuri a few feet behind me.

I grabbed her by her arm and pulled her with me as loud footsteps charged in our direction.

"Fuck," Zuri trilled.

"Come on, slowpoke!" I exclaimed.

We jumped over some shrubs and rounded around a house, the people-filled streets just a few feet away. I pulled her behind some crisp white sheets hanging out to dry and put my hand over her mouth as I pressed her body into mine. Her chest was heaving from the run, and I heard heavy boots pass us and busted out laughing when I heard them exclaim, "Shit!" and run back the other way. Zuri folded over, laughing, and we stayed behind the sheet for a few more moments to make sure the guards were gone. I didn't realize I was still holding her close to me, but neither of us made the move to separate.

"Okay, this way," I said, releasing her body, gripping her fingers in mine, and pulling her with me.

"Is this where you met Axel?" she asked.

"Uh...Yeah," I said awkwardly.

"Oh no, don't do that," she urged, "do not be ashamed."

"I'll take it," I laughed.

I pushed through the doors of the pub and was met with the same shouts of wasted vampires and beer as I was the first time I came to the establishment.

"Piss beer?" I asked Zuri.

"Yes, please," she said mockingly.

I put my elbows up on the bar and flagged down the barkeep, holding up two fingers. They nodded and grabbed two glasses that had seen better days and filled them with the amber liquid. He scooted them over to me, and I slid two coins onto the wooden bar for him before he went to the next customer. Music raged, the musicians playing a song so upbeat half of the drunks weren't able to keep up with the tune as they danced.

I weaved us around the bar patrons doing my best to avoid any extra intoxicated ones to ensure I didn't get into another mishap like before. There was an empty table in the far corner near the exit, and I guided us over to it. Zuri slid onto the bench next to me so we could both face the commotion happening in the bar.

"So," I started, taking a sip of my beer. "Should we talk about our...predicament since we're outside palace walls."

"Sure." She shrugged.

"What is this for you?" I asked.

I'd never been one to beat around the bush unless it was for performative reasons.

"I...don't know," she chortled.

"Me either," I agreed.

"It wasn't always like this for me. I cared for you from the moment I met you, but I slowly started to care more and more. I just didn't want to say anything and ruin our friendship, I really didn't think you'd feel the same way. Now, I don't know where to go from here. I wasn't prepared. Do we just sneak around forever?"

"Forever? Geez, you really do like me, don't you." I stuck my tongue between my teeth.

"Hush," she said, bumping me on my shoulder.

"I think we worry about that when we really know what this is. I'm not easy. I wouldn't want to implode your life for you to realize I'm not worth it," I said with a shrug.

Zuri looked at me solemnly, her lips pulling tight for a moment before she looked out into the pub.

"Let's go dance," she said as she grabbed my hand and pulled me along before I could answer.

I nearly spilled my beer as she tugged me, but I managed to down it all before being dragged to the dance floor. My face was tingling as she let my hands go and threw them into the air and danced like it was just the two of us here. With the spell, we really could do whatever we wanted; nobody would be able to report back to Kaizer. I danced in sync with Zuri, our hips moving back and forth at the same rate as we tipped our heads back and laughed.

A real laugh, a true belly laugh, something I didn't find myself doing often. Honestly, I couldn't remember the last time I had laughed this way. She grabbed my hands again, and we danced hand in hand, spinning each other around like we were doing some fancy ballroom dance. She let go of my hands again and turned around, rubbing her ass to my lap as I pulled at her curls. She spun around, but a man grabbed her by the waist, and she looked up at me with wide eyes.

Zuri tried to pull away and groaned, "Get off me."

"It's my turn. Why don't you come and dance with a real man," he slurred.

Fuck, why were the people here such fucking idiots?

Before I knew it, my fingers were around his neck, and he dropped his hold from Zuri immediately. I had to refrain from letting my nails dig into his flesh, or it would be a dead giveaway that I was a witch. I lifted him a few inches from the ground with my canines on display.

"Touch her again, and you'll fucking die for it," I growled.

He nodded rapidly, and I threw him down a few feet away from us. The music didn't stop this time; people shifted out of his way as he scrambled to his feet and went back to the bar. My chest was heaving, my insides screaming to draw blood from anyone nearby. I should have just killed him; any man who thinks they're *owed* a dance from a woman is as good as dead in my eyes. I whirled around to find Zuri watching me, it wasn't fear in her eyes, but I could tell she was trying to figure out what my next move would be. She stepped closer to me and wrapped her fingers around mine, her skin grounding me and pulling me back into myself. She brought her face close to mine, her lips just a breath from my ear.

"I'm fine," she whispered.

I nodded and swallowed, my eyes still darting around for potential danger.

She put a single finger on my chin and pulled my face in her direction. "Why don't we head back?"

"Okay," I said, the muscles in my face relaxing slightly. "There's an exit right there," I finished, pointing to the hall by the table we were just at.

I led her in that direction, my hands gripping hers so tight her fingers were being crushed, but I couldn't help it. Once my blood got boiling like this, I couldn't come back down right away; I didn't know if all witches were like that. I didn't want to ask, as it felt like an admittance of weakness, a lack of control. This was so much worse than it had been before for some reason. I could still hear the ringing in my ears, and the desire to turn around and kill that man was so close to overcoming me.

"Daya," she exclaimed as we got to the dark hallway.

I heard it but didn't really register that she was trying to get me to stop until she paused mid-walk, forcing me to jerk back a step.

"Daya," she said again.

I whirled back to look at her, but she was only an inch from my face, my hair almost slapping her across hers.

She leaned into me and stopped before our lips met, whispering, "You're not in battle right now. I'm not in trouble. We are both okay."

I might have stopped breathing, but I didn't offer her a response. I was always in battle, always needed to be ready for a fight, but maybe right now...maybe I could relax.

"Okay," I muttered in one single breath.

She pulled her face back slightly and ran her fingers up my tattooed arms, watching as the hairs stood on end until she made it up to my neck and wrapped her arms around it. Zuri looked at me with those big gray eyes of hers, and I just about melted under the intensity of her stare. Her gaze bounced between my eyes and lips, and I lost any restraint I might have had. I turned our bodies and pushed her up against the wall, her arms jerking in the air at the quick movement, and crashed my lips into hers.

Fucking fuck.

Her lips were softer than anything I'd ever touched. They were slightly fuller than mine, and I felt them completely cover my mouth as she pressed into me. I pushed my hips into hers, our chests pressed together as she let out the breathiest moan. I turned my head, darting my tongue into her mouth, the taste of her so foreign, just like her scent. Whatever it was, it was fucking perfection. She opened her mouth a little more, giving me access to explore as she ran her fingers through my hair and pushed her tongue into my mouth. She ran it over every crevice, my thighs tightening every time she went back for more.

I pulled back and ran kisses down her neck, sucking and letting my canines drag over her skin as she threw her head back and pulled me into her neck even more. I ran the pad of my tongue back up, biting and tugging at her earlobe until she moaned loud enough to draw attention. I muffled her moan with my mouth as I pulled back the aggression and kissed her slowly, taking my time as our tongues met each other between movements. This wasn't a lust-fueled kiss any longer—it was my very being reaching out to hers. As if our souls had been separated for centuries and were finally coming back together as one. I could feel it down to my core, that this was right, that we were right.

She pulled her hands out of my hair, running them down my arms until her fingers tangled with mine. Zuri drew her head back, her lips swollen and darker than they were before. We stared at each other for a few moments, and I noticed the faintest of dark golden freckles across her nose and splattered among the blush on her cheeks. Her lashes were so dark and curly that they were almost caught in the eyebrows framing them. Layers of light brown curls fell beside her heart-shaped face in a way that was just *her*. I had a feeling she woke up like this, that she didn't have to manicure every lock of hair or make sure her lashes all curled in the same direction.

A small smile pulled at her lips as she studied my face too. "You have a lot of beauty marks," she muttered.

She was right; they were all over my face, my chin, my cheekbones, my forehead; I even had one on my lip. They always felt like imperfections to me, but the way she smiled as she said it made them feel a bit less imperfect.

"You have a lot of freckles," I whispered.

The corners of her lips pulled down, and shadows ran over her eyes. "From my mother," she mumbled.

"Why don't you talk about her, any of your family?" I asked.

"Hurts too much," she murmured.

I nodded, stepping away from her body. "Let's get back."

We pushed through the back exit, the stars sparkling high in the black sky, the moon casting silver on the small homes of the village. I said that we shouldn't worry about anything until we knew what it was between Zuri and me, but I felt like that time was going to come sooner than later.

Chapter Thirty-One

Here I was engaged to a king, in bed with my handmaiden. We bathed, changed into our nightgowns, and Zuri lit a few candles in the room instead of using the brighter lamps. It was really late, but neither of us was tired enough to go to sleep. I sat on my bed and pulled my blankets out for her to sit beside me. I made sure all the doors were locked and reinforced the magic to make sure nobody could get in if they somehow had a key.

Kissing her in the pub was an experience I hadn't had in centuries. I'd kissed and fucked plenty, but that kiss…it was far above what I expected. The thing that was messing me up even more was that it felt even better than when I was with Ximena. I thought I had reached the peak of the emotions I was capable of with her, but I was wrong. It scared the fucking shit out of me. My thoughts kept spiraling back to it, to Ximena. I hadn't told anyone about what I did, not even Cat, but if Zuri was going to be an even more significant part of my life, she should probably know.

"I have to tell you something," I murmured, pulling the covers over my lap and close to my chest.

Zuri scooted beside me and threw her elbow on the headboard as she turned in my direction. "What is it?"

"It's about my ex, Ximena, the last person I really let get close to me," I said as I stared into the candlelight beside me.

She nodded, encouragement for me to go on, but the words were stuck in my throat. She'd seen me do terrible things in the short time we'd known each other, but fuck, this was so much worse.

"My mother, well, you met her. She has been cruel and cold for over a century now. She didn't like me to be distracted or to have any other opinions outside of hers. Ximena and I were friends first, like us, but we'd been friends since childhood. Me, Cat, and Ximena were glued to each other as kids. Ximena was kind, confident, and pretty vocal about her views." I paused, looking over to get a read on Zuri's features.

"Was?" she asked quietly.

I nodded as my throat bobbed. "My mother didn't like it, especially when our friendship started to develop into a more romantic one. I challenged my mother on a point that Ximena brought up in a coterie meeting. She thought I was disrespecting her and said that I needed to learn a lesson. You saw the wounds on my back, the punishments I've received from her." I paused and took a deep breath.

Zuri gripped her fingers in mine and smiled gently.

"That was the first time. The first time I'd been punished that way, some of those wounds are from that. I thought it was done the next day. But I was wrong. She brought me back into the dungeons when I was healed. Ximena had been down there since I'd been beaten—almost a week. My mother had lied to me initially and told me that Ximena left to help another sanction. She was gagged and looked so frail, her brown skin ashen. She had so many cuts on her, some closed up and healing, some leaking blood. The moment I saw her, I lost it. For the first time in my life, I put my hands on my mother. I was too angry, and my moves weren't calculated. She stopped me from killing her and didn't kill me, but in that moment, I wished she had."

My nails extended, and I pulled my hand from her grasp. Not in a way that said I was upset with her, but that I just needed a second to gather myself.

"My mother subdued my magic and locked me up, made me watch her beat Ximena until she was barely breathing. She unlocked my chains, but my magic was still blocked. It took every ounce of my strength not to try to fight her again. She put a dagger in my hand and told me to kill Ximena."

Zuri flinched.

"I knew my mother would kill her if I didn't, and she wouldn't make it quick. I'd seen what she'd done to people who betrayed her. She would have let her heal enough so she could get a reaction out of her, and I didn't want that to happen. Ximena was in the situation because of me, because she...loved me." My lip quivered. "I did it. I killed her quick and clean, a smooth jab to her heart. She held my gaze until the life left her eyes. She didn't have an ounce of regret on her face, just resolve as I was the last thing she saw in this world. From that point on, I listened to my mother and did what she said, but fucking hated her and didn't respect her. I never let anyone close again. I didn't want her to have another chance to do what she did. I think that experience made me what I am today, the ruthless killer. My mother got what she wanted."

I looked at the dagger tattooed on my forearm, identical to the one I used to kill Ximena; I felt my blood starting to heat before a soft hand landed on my forearm.

"Look at me, Daya," Zuri whispered.

I raised my gaze to hers slowly, every muscle in my body screaming not to look at her, not to see the look of regret and hate that would surely be on her face after such a confession. Everyone knew I was a killer, but killing the only person in this world who loved me made me the worst kind of monster.

"What you did was a mercy," she whispered, scooting closer. "You won't have the threat of your mother for much longer. There won't be a person in this world who can control you. I know who you are. You don't scare me. You never have, you never will."

My face felt wet, and I looked up to see if there was a leak from the ceiling, but the movement made my other cheek feel wet too. I lifted my finger and ran my pointer finger through the liquid, rubbing it on my thumb. I was...crying. I hadn't cried since childhood; my mother made sure I knew it was a weakness. But at this moment, I couldn't hold back the emotion. Zuri didn't say anything as she watched me, but she moved closer and guided me to turn around away from her so my back was lined up with her chest. More tears fell from my eyes as they puddled on my pillow and Zuri rubbed smooth circles on my arms. As I lay beside her, embraced in her arms, I decided I didn't care what I had to do, who I had to kill, or where I had to go. There would never be a world where Zuri met the same fate as Ximena.

I woke up feeling lighter than I had in years, the dim morning light filtering in between the sheer black curtains in my room. Zuri's face was only a few inches from mine. I fell asleep in her arms, and we never said anything else, we just allowed each other's presence to say what we needed. Her mouth was slightly open, and her hair was thrown in every direction. The tiny snores that escaped her lips made me want to run kisses over all of her skin, but I didn't and allowed her to sleep. She was usually up before me, so I took the opportunity of her not waking up at the ass crack of dawn to let her catch up on some rest.

I sat up and hung my legs over the side of the bed, trying to figure out what I should do with the day. I had a hunch that without us, Kaizer would just push through without stopping to sleep, so I didn't want to do anything like last night. I really just wanted a lazy day before the chaos of the next couple of weeks picked up. Between the wedding and The Ritual, there was a lot to plan, and even though I didn't really care about the wedding, I knew I needed to at least appear interested. Zuri would be dragged along for most of the events and planning, and I felt bad for it. We both knew what we were doing, knew the reality of what we were getting ourselves into, but it felt like a jab to make her be around for it.

I glanced back as her arm idly reached into the spot I was in before and pushed a pillow toward her. She grabbed it and brought it close to her chest as she nestled her face into it with a smile. I laughed quietly and got up; the cold stone floor bit into my feet, but I couldn't find it in me to let it bother me too much. I lifted my gaze into the large mirror, stunned at the reflection. I looked so...bright. My hair was lustrous, the purple shade of it so rich and vibrant. My skin glowed, and I leaned in closer to see no evidence that I had stayed up so late. Fuck, it felt good not to wake up angry. I knew I shouldn't get too used to it, as I'd soon be waking up with Kaizer.

I turned on the water, put toothpaste on my toothbrush, and started brushing my teeth. I ran my toothbrush over my canines, thinking back to Kaizer's bite. I had no desire to drink from him, but if Zuri wanted me to...I might have tried it for her. I heard her stir in the bed and moan slightly; I spat my toothpaste into the sink and looked over my shoulder to see her sitting up. She pulled up the strap of her nightgown and set it back in its rightful place; her eyes scanned the room until they fell on me.

"Hi," she muttered, her voice thick with sleep.

"Hey, sleepy head," I said, coming back into the bedroom.

She looked out the window with wide eyes. "What time is it?"

"Like 10:45. I figured I'd let you sleep in."

"Fuck, I need to go check in with Mia," she said through panic.

She jumped up and took half of the blankets with her, running toward her room.

"Hey, calm down." I tried to reason. "We didn't advise any of the staff of when we'd be back. She's not expecting you."

"You're right." She stopped abruptly. "I still need to check in with her. I don't want anyone else to be inconvenienced by having to do my chores with me being gone."

She entered her room, leaving the door open so I could still talk to her.

"You're too good for this kingdom," I said as I grabbed the blanket off the floor and put it back on my bed.

Zuri came back out of her room with her staff uniform on. She didn't always wear it when we were out and about, but I had a feeling the head of staff preferred them in it. She ran into the bathroom and brushed her teeth, fluffing up her hair before exiting the bathroom. Zuri grazed my lips with a feather-light kiss and was gone before I could even say goodbye. It was such a normal morning, like this was our everyday life, making big declarations, falling asleep with each other, and rushing off to start our days.

I laughed and went to straighten up the room a bit so she wouldn't have to when she got back. I pulled my jewelry out of my bags from Caldera and put it on display in my closet. One of the bracelets was one I wore on missions, set with all the precious gems and stones we used for our spells. I hadn't seen it since the battle; I assumed it was destroyed by the blast that knocked me out. There hadn't been much of a need for me to perform spells since I'd been here, but I had a feeling that wouldn't be the case much longer. I put my other raw stones next to the jewelry and slipped on the bracelet before grabbing a simple black dress. My morning started off great, and it was only going to get better because I had to go make a visit to an unsuspecting prisoner.

I had to stop myself from recoiling at the dungeons of this castle, the scars on my back burning in the memory of being here. The feeling shifted into something else as I remembered the feel of Axel's body as he carried me away, the feel of his magic when he healed me. I pushed through, reaching the end of the hall and slowing my steps down. I walked carelessly as I turned the corner and counted the cells until I saw the one I was there for. I hummed a tune, an eerie tune that would unsettle most people, until the small red-headed woman came into my sight.

"Lady Payne," I said, with my hands behind my back.

She was rolled in a ball in the corner of the cell. I told Kaizer to kill her, but he refused. I'd been down here one other time just to make sure her living conditions were up to par. There wasn't anything in her cell but a bucket for her to use the bathroom; her red dress was tattered and nearly black with dirt.

"Fancy running into you," I muttered, the smile on my face heard in my voice.

She growled and turned to me, her face just as dirty as her dress. Her lips were pulled back, and her eyes were bloodshot, that tinge of crazy that came with bloodlust making an appearance.

"What do you want?" she snapped.

"Oh, nothing. Just was down here and figured I'd come to say hi. How are you feeling? You look just as beautiful as the day I met you."

I leaned against the wall across from her cell, the stench of her a little too much for me to be so close. She jumped up and grabbed the cell bars, squeezing so hard her fingers were whiter than usual.

Her hair hung limp in front of her face as her chest heaved. "You laugh, but this could have just as easily been you."

A laugh really did burst from my throat at that. "Oh please, Athena. Do tell," I said as I scrunched up my nose at her scent.

"If Kaizer had done what I said and beaten you in battle, you could have been thrown in a cell to rot like me."

"Is that why Sanjry didn't win? He was taking war advice from the sorry excuse that is you?"

She barked a laugh. "We didn't win because he wasn't man enough to use the full extent of the power he found."

That piqued my interest, but I kept the smug, uncaring look on my face. "Did you honestly think you could take me down?"

"I had to! You have no idea the things I've sacrificed. The things I've done." She looked down at the ground for a moment, but by the time she looked back up at me her face was set back in a scowl.

I pushed off the wall and fished a chunk of bread out of my pocket before I took my nail and pressed it into my wrist, letting a bead of blood bubble out.

"You look like you need blood?" I asked, stepping closer. "How often do they give you blood down here? Just before you go into bloodlust?"

Her nostrils flared, and she pushed her head even further into the bars she still held a deathly grasp on.

"I'll do you a little favor," I said as I dabbed the blood with the bread. "All for you," I finished, throwing the bread at her.

The bread hit the dirty floor, but she still pounced on it crouched down like an animal as she licked at the blood and ate the bread in one gulp.

I waved a hand over my shoulder as I walked away. "Until next time, Athena."

"He'll never love you! Don't get too comfortable! I know he'll come to his senses soon!" she yelled.

The sound of rattling bars and her screams followed me down multiple halls until I was far enough for it to be a faint whisper. It sounded like she may have known something, and I had enough experience with my mother getting information out of people. As fun as that sounded, I didn't know how I could do it and get away with it when there were guards who walked through periodically. I could have asked Kaizer, but I needed to figure out how to word the question to make sure he didn't get a whiff of my uncertainty.

Chapter Thirty-Two

Zuri hadn't found me yet, so I assumed whatever duties the head of staff had her doing were more extensive than she initially thought. On the way back from the dungeons, I'd run into a few people who had question after question about the wedding. I didn't know what to tell them, but I had to put my fakest smile on to ensure I *looked* excited about it. It was about time for dinner, so I made my way over to the dining hall. Being back in this palace really made it clear how dreary and monotonous it was. I missed the art and color of Caldera. I sighed and pushed into the room, my misery quickly turning into something else entirely as I laid eyes on Zuri. She was laying down plates on the table, just her and one other palace staff in the room.

"Good evening, ladies," I exclaimed.

Zuri jumped and dropped a plate, causing the side of it to chip slightly. The other woman jumped as well with her hand on her chest.

"You nearly scared me to death," the woman sighed as she hurried out of the room.

I stepped closer to Zuri. "You've been busy?"

"When the others saw I was back, they decided they didn't need to do the tasks assigned to them, including some of their own." She rolled her eyes.

"Is that something I can help with?" I asked.

I picked up the broken piece of plate from off the floor, looking up at her for her answer.

"It might look suspicious, like I'm your favorite or something."

"Well, you are, sooo…" I trailed off as I put the piece back into its place.

I rubbed the jade in my bracelet, whispering the spell for it to mend itself back into one. It was technically a spell to turn back time, not just a fancy adhesive replacement for witches, so the crystal was needed for it.

"Be that as it may." She laughed and grabbed the fixed plate from my hands. "It could present a problem."

I shrugged and stepped closer again as I pulled at the fabric of her dress. "Your uniform needs an upgrade. These are dreadfully boring."

"They want us to blend in here, so this is what they give us," she responded before her brows pinched together. "Is that blood on your sleeve?"

"Oh, yes," I laughed. "I visited Athena."

She took a step closer to me, the warmth of her body radiating and mingling with my own at the closeness. "Anything interesting?"

"She mentioned something about Kaizer not being man enough to use the power he found. I'm going to ask him more about the magic he used since I haven't found out on my own, just have to figure out how."

The skin on my hand tingled as she grazed her fingers over where it sat leaning on the table. "Let me know if I can help," she muttered.

I leaned into her, my lips brushing hers ever so slightly. "I can think of a few ways you can help."

She took a deep breath, the movement pressing her lips deeper into mine again before she grabbed a lock of my purple hair and twirled it around her finger. "Sounds fun."

I felt a presence walking toward the room, and I rolled my eyes. "Another time," I said, fingering her jaw.

I portaled to my seat just as Kaizer pushed into the dining room.

"I thought I'd find you here," he exclaimed, nodding once at Zuri.

"Find me you did," I said as I took a sip of the goat blood Zuri already had ready for me. "How was the journey? You're back earlier than I thought you'd be."

"Great, we pushed through without stopping. I'm ready to eat and go to sleep," he laughed as he scooted in his chair across the table.

Sounds like a great plan to me. The staff brought in the food and set it between us before scooping out our servings. Zuri handed me my plate, and I ran a nail down her hand before she pulled back. She smiled with her back turned to Kaizer, and I started eating as if nothing suspicious was happening at all.

"So, tomorrow," Kaizer said as he finished his bite of food. "We'll start preparations for the wedding. I have an event planner meeting us around 11:00 to get whatever information they need. The priest will be there as well."

"Sounds great," I replied, stabbing a piece of chicken and forcing it into my mouth.

"From what I understand, it's pretty much them just asking what we like, and they'll handle everything else. They just need to get a better understanding of who we are as people."

I nodded as I scooped up some mashed potatoes and brought the fork to my mouth.

"You okay?" Kaizer asked.

"Hm? Oh, yeah. I'm just thinking about The Ritual," I lied.

"What is needed for that?"

"Not much. It's just the day before the wedding, so I feel like I need to make sure both are taken care of."

"Let me know if you need a planner for that as well. The one for the wedding may be able to help," Kaizer responded.

I smiled weakly. "My mother should have it mostly handled, but thank you."

"What did you do today?" he asked, taking a sip of wine.

"Nothing much," I started, but looked at Zuri momentarily. "I did have a question for you."

"Shoot," Kaizer responded.

"I haven't brought it up yet because of the...nature of the event. But the magic you used in the battle. What was it?"

Kaizer tightened slightly and paused before he stabbed a piece of meat with his fork. He looked around the room and dismissively nodded to the palace staff, including Zuri.

They scurried out of the room, and he sat back in his chair, setting down his fork. "It's no secret that I've been interested in old magic."

I nodded. "Interested, yes."

"I found an old relic, something from thousands of years ago. I read about this particular relic in one of my books. It was said to have the power to create a blast so large that it could flatten a small village."

Not exactly an answer.

"Right, it killed thousands."

He nodded and bit his lip at the mention of the dead. "I used a fraction of the relic's contents, and you saw the damage. I was worried if I used the full thing, it would kill too many of my own."

Part of me regretted this already; listening to his logic about how he planned on killing off my people was starting to piss me off. Also, what Athena said checked out. Which was interesting; he talked to her more than I thought he did.

"So you are looking for more relics like this?"

"I just want to make sure my kingdom is always protected. The other kingdoms have great power. Sanjry doesn't; I want to at least level the playing field. It was...a risk, to say the least."

I looked down at the tattoo on my wrist. The tattoo I got from the deal with him on the day he spoke of—the fucking tattoo that spiraled my life in directions I didn't know were possible.

"Daya," he started, and I snapped my gaze up to him. "Dayanara, I didn't mean for it to upset you. I just wanted to answer your question."

"I asked," I said, the words coming out in more of a growl than I meant to.

I downed my blood as a knock sounded on the door.

"Dessert," a palace staff said from the hallway.

"Come in," Kaizer boomed.

They brought in some sort of cake with a chocolate drizzle over it and placed it in front of Kaizer. I could practically taste it from over here, the scent so strong in the room. Zuri brought in mine, setting it down with a curtsy that almost had me bust out laughing. Her presence alone pulled me out of the mood I was plunging toward, and I scraped my plate clean, getting every drop of chocolate sauce I could.

Kaizer stood, pushed his chair in, and leaned against it. "I really am sorry. I don't want the conversation to put us back where we were."

I stood as well and flattened out the skirt of my dress. "Don't worry about it. I might have done the same thing."

He smiled, his straight white teeth on full display, before walking toward me. Every step held intent, and I was slightly worried about what he was going to do once he reached me. I yawned dramatically as he made it in front of me and stretched out my arms wide.

He stopped and rubbed the side of my face with his hand, his calluses scraping against the softness of my cheek. "Did you not sleep well?"

I shook my head. "Had some trouble. I'm sure it'll be better tonight."

"Let's get you back to your room," he said as he placed a light kiss on my cheek.

I nodded, blinking slowly. "That would be great."

Kaizer walked me back to my room, stopping at the door. I pushed it open, feeling my magic caress my skin as I stood in the doorway. He leaned against the door frame, one of his hands gripping the top. The ridge of every muscle that lined his arms and chest pushed into the fabric of his shirt, and the light in the hall gave him a bright halo around his head I couldn't pull my eyes from.

"You going straight to sleep?" he asked, his voice husky.

I swallowed hard. "Yeah, I'm going to take a nice bath and then hop right into bed."

"Hm, pity," he responded, pushing off the door frame. "I have a breakfast engagement, but I'll see you at the meeting with the event planner."

He wrapped his large hand around my body and pulled me close to him, tipping my chin up with his other hand and pressing his lips against mine. Zuri may have ruined me for everyone because it didn't feel the same as when we kissed before. The other times were mixed with his vampire venom, so that was probably a big part of the spark I had felt. He pulled back and smiled at me like it was the best kiss of his life, and I smiled back as I stepped into my room and closed the door. Zuri busted out laughing behind me, and I whirled around.

"How did you get back here before me?" I yelled.

"I came back after I dropped your plate off. Lira was handling the cleaning up tonight," she said, stepping out of her bedroom.

"Well fuck," I laughed out. "I didn't even feel you in the room. I was too busy trying to figure out how to make sure he didn't come in."

She threw her hands in the air. "Don't stop on my account. I didn't exactly hate watching last time, as you know."

"Zuri!" I yelled, my mouth hanging open.

"What? Don't judge me!"

"I'm not judging. I just wasn't expecting you to say that." I laughed. "I'm not sure I could *just* watch."

"Let me know if you ever want to test the theory," she said as she leveled me with a look that told me she was only partly kidding.

We hadn't even done anything past kissing yet, but the thought of someone else enjoying all that she was while I had to stand by didn't sound exactly appealing to me.

"So what did he say?" Zuri asked.

"He basically confirmed what Athena said," I said as I dropped down into my chair near the fire. "He said he found a relic that gifted him some old magic, but he only used a part of it because he was worried about demolishing his own army."

Zuri scoffed. "So he does have a heart."

"I don't know if I go as far as that. But it does make me think he's going to be looking for more. Axel said his people were found on his land. I definitely believe him now."

"Fuck," Zuri whispered, "only question is, what side is the right side to be on."

Zuri sat in the chair beside me, putting the dark red pillow in her lap and squeezing it close to her.

"Exactly. He says he's just doing it to level the playing field. Sanjry doesn't have great magic compared to the other kingdoms. The witches are, well, the witches. Dusra has Axel, who claims he's extremely old; his magic is far more powerful than Kaizer's. I feel like I'm marrying the wrong king," I joked.

"You get to have fun planning the wedding tomorrow, too," Zuri laughed.

"Fuck, that's going to suck. What are weddings like here?"

"You don't marry much in Caldera, do you?"

"Nope, rarely ever. It's not frowned upon or anything—we just typically choose not to. There's not even a particular ceremony. There's a spell to bind souls, but that's it."

"Interesting," Zuri said, a glint of intrigue in her gaze. "It's very boring and traditional here. You have to wear a super plain white dress that I'm sure you'll love. You've seen the acolytes, right?"

"Yeah, they look creepy. They never make eye contact with me, and they're always mumbling under their breath."

"Yes, those are the acolytes of the Embers. There's a high priest they all practically worship outside of the Flame. He's the one who will do the ceremony."

"I still don't understand that, why they worship the Flame and not the goddess herself?" I responded.

"Yeah, I don't know. I've never actually been to a ceremony. Almost everyone here partakes in the religion to a certain extent, though the higher-ranking vampires make a big deal about it. But they've been known to break the rules in secrecy while scorning the lower-ranking families for the very same thing. There's a bunch of things they aren't allowed to do, rules set in place that if everyone follows, they believe the Flame will return once again. They've been known to be fairly extreme in the villages. They aren't necessarily violent, but very much in your face about what they believe."

"Sound like a fun bunch."

"Yeah, you're going to hate every second of it," she teased. "I'll be sure to get you a good gift."

She stood and walked over to me, dropping down into my lap with her arms around my neck.

"Are you going to be there at the wedding?" I asked as I ran my hands down the curve of her back.

The reflection of the flames danced in her eyes as she watched me, her skin glowing golden from the raging blaze as she leaned in and whispered, "I'll be where you want me to be."

"Let's just run away," I said, pulling her closer to me.

"You'd hate yourself if you left all the witches to whatever fate Kaizer has planned."

"It's getting harder and harder to care about anyone but a certain handmaiden in my lap," I breathed.

"It would catch up to you eventually," she replied as she curled up and laid her head on my chest. "I'm happy to be wherever you are."

She nestled her face closer to my chest, and I rubbed the bare skin on her shoulder with my thumb. I never really believed in fate, and the witches didn't worship any gods. We revered Naom, respected the earth, and drew our power from it. We didn't believe in any prophecies or beings controlling our lives from beyond the clouds. But...I said a small prayer just then to anyone who might have been listening. Asking that Zuri and I could make it out on the other side of whatever would happen in the coming weeks.

Chapter Thirty-Three

The event planner was late, so Kaizer and I sat in the red room together. He was filling me in on a new training technique he was looking to start, which usually would pique my interest, but I could barely hear the words he was saying.

"It'll be a game changer, don't you think?"

"Yeah, can't wait to see it in action," I replied.

He smiled and nodded eagerly, and I almost felt bad that I was ignoring him with the look on his face. The door was pushed open, and a man in a dark orange hooded robe walked through the door with a blonde woman on his heels. The man had his eyes on the ground until he stopped directly in front of me. He snapped his gaze up to mine and stared, tilting his head to the side like he was trying to see my soul.

"Dayanara Amapola," he said mystically, like I should be impressed that he figured out who I was.

Seeing as I was the one he was coming to meet, it wasn't exactly a revolutionary finding. His skin was pale, and his dirty blond hair was cut bluntly across his forehead under his hood. I startled slightly as I looked in to his blue eyes, an eerie light blue that almost made his irises look to blend in with the rest of his eye.

"High Priest," I muttered.

He didn't release me from his gaze for an unnatural amount of time before he turned to Kaizer. "My King." he bowed deep.

"Hello, Joseph," Kaizer said, nodding at him to take a seat.

"Hi!" a squeaky voice exclaimed.

I almost forgot that the event planner came in with the strange man and turned to greet her. She was practically jumping on her heels, her straight hair bouncing around her shoulders in the movement.

"I'm Misha! I'm so excited to meet you! This wedding is going to be the best either of our kingdoms has ever seen. You can trust me on that!"

She ran over to me, stopping just short of hugging me, and I jutted out my hand for a handshake instead.

I pulled my hand from hers and sat down. "Pleasure."

Her face drooped slightly, but her wide smile quickly snapped back into place as she looked over to Kaizer.

"I brought the samples you asked for." She stopped and grabbed a large bag behind her. "Let me get them out..."

"I think we should talk about the religious part of this before your party favors," the high priest stated dryly.

Fuck, this was going to suck even more than I thought it would.

Kaizer nodded for him to carry on.

"You'll need to be inducted into the Embers," Joseph said, his icy gaze piercing me.

"Not happening," I said with a straight face.

Joseph looked like I stabbed him in his chest, and he turned to Kaizer.

"I told you this is not a marriage between two Sanjryans. There will need to be some adjustments," Kaizer stated.

"You expect me to perform a ceremony for someone who is not an Ember?" the high priest bleated.

I sat forward and flashed my canines. "Are you the only one with the power to marry?"

Kaizer cleared his throat. "He is the royal priest, so he will be the one to marry us. Joseph, that is why we are here now. Things will need to be adjusted."

Joseph looked at me with so much disgust I almost laughed at how pinched up his face was. "Very well. No induction. The ceremony, though, there will still be the religious aspects, yes?"

"Yes, you can still perform the ceremony as is, but you shouldn't expect a conversion before that," Kaizer responded.

"Would you be open to converting eventually?" Joseph asked me.

"I wouldn't hold your breath, bud," I grumbled.

He sighed deeply. "I will have to pray about this, my King."

"You aren't the one who makes the decisions. This is a royal wedding, and you will perform your duties, or another can take your place," Kaizer snapped.

I tilted my head, impressed with the authority in his voice, and Kaizer looked over at me with a slight smile.

"Please tell me you two, at the very least, have taken the vow of purity since engagement?"

"The what?" I asked.

"From the time of engagement to the wedding ceremony, you are expected not to partake in intercourse. It's supposed to keep you clean and ready for the ceremony. You haven't taken it, have you?" he asked, his eyes wide.

"No, but we haven't fully, um," Kaizer started, looking over at me.

"We haven't fucked, no," I said, sending red all over the high priest's face.

"We will have to work on that profanity. Okay, well, we have that, at least. Please make the vow," the priest said as he sat back in his chair.

"Dayanara, we don't have to. This is a part of the tradition not everyone partakes in."

"Royalty does partake in this; you are not two commoners," Joseph scoffed.

"Still—" Kaizer started, but I cut him off.

"I can take the vow if it means I don't have to be inducted," I said.

I could almost scream with such an easy way to keep Kaizer from my bed. After the wedding, I'd have to figure something out. But for now, I didn't have to worry about him trying to initiate anything like he did last night.

"The two are not exclusive—" Kaizer started, but Joseph cut him off too.

"She said she would take the vow," he exclaimed.

Kaizer's jaw ticked, and it looked like the words were glass shards in his throat, but he got them out. "I vow to keep myself clean until the day of the ceremony."

"Yeah, me too," I responded.

"Being clean not only covers premarital relations. While it may be the most important one, it also covers the consumption of alcohol or any form of substance that can alter your mind, cursing, killing, really anything that could darken your soul. You should keep your soul as pure and bright as possible until the ceremony."

I crossed my arms. "Oh, Joseph. I don't think there's anything that could make my soul pure at this point in my life. I agreed to no sex with him, but you'll have to give up on the rest of it."

Joseph started muttering a prayer, rocking back and forth like the admittance of my darkened soul hurt his own. "And you, Your Majesty?" Joseph asked, finally coming out of his prayer.

"I'll do my best," Kaizer responded.

Joseph rolled his eyes. "Great. I'll leave you to talk about flowers and cake."

The high priest stood and bowed at the waist, he snapped back up, and his hood fell from his head, exposing a tattoo on his neck that I felt I recognized. He fixed his hood and walked out of the room, but before the door even closed behind him, Misha threw fabric samples into my lap and stood from her chair.

"What's your favorite color?" she asked.

She looked at me with her big doe eyes and hands grasped under her chin like it was the most exciting question she could have asked me.

"Black," I muttered.

"Ugh, no. We can't do that. Second favorite?" she exclaimed.

"I like purple," Kaizer said, throwing a smirk in my direction.

"Ohhh, purple! Purple we can do, lilac, violet, plum, periwinkle?"

"Fuck," I muttered under my breath without realizing I actually said it out loud.

"Whatever you think is best," Kaizer answered for me.

"Okay! What about cake?"

"I'm going to be honest with you, Misha. You can literally do whatever you want, and I will be fine with it," I replied.

"Aww! That's so sweet. It really is true love," she gushed.

Kaizer smiled and nodded as she rambled off all her ideas with so much excitement, I thought she might have been on some sort of mood enhancer.

"Will you have any bridesmaids?"

"Brideswhats?"

"Bridesmaids, there are typically ten. Ten of your closest female friends," she explained.

"You're close with Zuri. You could ask her?"

I pressed my legs together. "Do we have to have them?"

"No, in the old days, it was believed to protect you from evil spirits so that if a spirit came for you, it would be confused, and there was a possibility it would inhabit someone else. We don't believe that anymore though!"

"More morbid than I expected from your people," I muttered. "No, I think we can do without them."

"Okay, well, I think I have everything I need. Do you have any questions, Daya?" Misha asked.

"Dayanara," I corrected. "No, I don't."

She nodded rapidly and collected her things before she excitedly bounced out of the room.

"She's something," I murmured.

"She does all the palace events. She is...energized," Kaizer laughed. "About the vow," he started, and I lifted my hand.

"I'm ruining every other part of the tradition. Joseph might have a heart attack if I don't do something Sanjryan."

"That is true." He sighed.

"The ceremony is less than two weeks away. Surely you'll survive," I mocked.

Kaizer sighed and sat back in his chair as he ran his hands through his hair and broke the perfection of the style. "It's just...it's been a long few weeks. You're right. I will survive," he agreed. "What are you doing today?"

"I didn't have any specific plans other than this. I was thinking of going to the library to learn more about the kingdom," I lied.

I knew he would be happy if it sounded like I was taking an interest in his history, and just like I thought, a smile stretched across his face.

"I'll come with you," he exclaimed, standing from his chair.

Well, fuck.

"Okay," I replied quickly.

He offered me his arm like always, and I looped mine in his.

"So these Embers," I stated.

He chuckled darkly, the vibration from his chest meeting where my arm lay against his side. "They can be looked at as fanatics, but some of what they believe could be true. Do you not have religion in Caldera? Do you not worship Naom?"

"Not in the same way. We give thanks to the essence of the earth and revere Naom. The essence, the magic of our world, gives us life. We do what we can while we live before our bodies are returned to the ground. When we die, our spirits go to the spirit realm. As far as Naom, we have actual proof of her power. It still runs through my line's veins," I responded.

"There is proof of the Flame," Kaizer responded.

"There is proof of the Goddess Cama, yes. Her hand in creating the world, supplying your magic, helping form the Piedra with the other Creators. But the Flame cursing your people because the fire of Incen went out? Not really. I don't know much about what they believe, but given the shit Joseph was spitting, it all sounds made up by *people*. I guess that's the thing about faith; you never really know who's right until after you're already dead." I shrugged.

"That is...very true, I suppose."

I'd heard that some of the vampires in Sanjry were extremists, but I never took it upon myself to look too much deeper into it. I always believed that you could be spiritual without necessarily being *that* religious. You can feel the connections around you, the essence of the world, feed into it, and let it give back to you. Blaming everything that happened in your life on some invisible fate, some force, seemed like an easy way out to me. But who knows? I never really thought about death. You couldn't think about it in a life like mine, or it would drive you mad. My bloodline had necromancers, so there might have been some answers in Caldera somewhere. If that's how it worked anyway.

"Is there anything specific you think I should read about?"

I supposed we were here now; I couldn't go back on my initial lie at this point.

"I'll pull some books for you. I'd say that knowing the major cities and landmarks is a good place to start."

We pushed into the library, the smell of old books filling my nose. Kaizer didn't stop at the librarian's desk but took us straight up to the third level. He tapped his chin with his finger as he eyed the rows of books, making a noise as he found the book he was looking for. Kaizer flicked the book out of its place with his fingers and handed it to me before grabbing two others and piling them on top. I turned the books to the side, inspecting the spines.

"*The Great Land of Sanjry, Sanjry Royal Heritages,* and *Sanjryan Battle Tactics,*" I read aloud.

"The last one I figured you could use as a palate cleanser between the others," he joked.

It was always weird when he made jokes like that, actually funny ones. I laughed under my breath and walked over to the rooms for reading.

"You've been here before?" he asked as he followed me.

"Just once," I said, looking up to the sixth level, where I spent time with Zuri.

"I'm going to go grab a few books of my own. I'll be right back," Kaizer exclaimed.

I nodded and entered the small room with a large glass wall and three comfy chairs inside. There were small end tables beside each chair, but no large table like the one I'd been in before. Setting the books on the side table, I dropped down into the chair, sinking in just the right amount to make it comfortable.

"I need one of these in my room," I muttered before grabbing *The Great Land of Sanjry.*

I flipped open the book, landing on an intricate map of the kingdom. I'd seen a few of these places, the borders of Sanjry were easy to slip through from our side, something I'd be keeping to myself. There had been a few times when a vampire ventured into Caldera looking to see who we were and how we lived. One of them made the mistake of stealing from us, and I tracked them back here to deal them their punishment. The other times I'd just been bored and wanted to find an unsuspecting male to sate my needs. I didn't talk much during the trips; I didn't want to know anything about them or their people.

I ran my fingers over the cities and villages I'd been to. Mijra, Joriv, and Linj, stopping at the monoliths near the border of the forest of Incen. From the illustration, they looked huge, so huge I wasn't sure how people could have maneuvered them in the positions they were in. If the illustration was to scale, they were just as tall as the trees nearby. I turned the page, running my finger down the table of contents in search for the monoliths, finding it listed on page 341. I flipped to page 341; the title sat on the top of the page in bold black letters, *The Monoliths.* The paragraph beneath it detailed what was believed to be their origin.

The flames burned bright in the forest of Incen for thousands of years, even after the Goddess Cama went to rest. But the people of Sanjry fell into war, into bloodlust. The Flame found the people unjust and extinguished the fire within the forest. On this day, these stones pushed from the earth, forming a perfect circle. The Embers believe that you can go here and still feel the spirit of the Flame.

There were sketches below of the details on the stones, markings that looked similar to the ones on the air stone. The tattoo on Joseph's neck was one of the markings; the translation below it read *rebirth.* I heard Kaizer coming and flipped to a page about Cojmi, the capital, as he burst through the doors with his arms full of books.

"Oh, that's a good place to start," he said as he peered over my shoulder and dropped down in his chair.

We sat in the room in silence for a while as I read histories that were not nearly as interesting as the stones. Kaizer was tapping his foot rapidly as he read, flipping through the pages a little quicker than he was when he first sat down.

"You need blood, don't you?"

"Hm? Oh, yeah, I will soon," he responded.

"Well, I'm about to head back to my room, so if you need it, take it now."

I sat forward, sweeping my hair over to one shoulder and leaning in his direction. Kaizer was on his knees beside my chair before I even knew he left his. He ran his fingers over my neck before he sunk his fangs in, the jolt of pain waning. My throat bobbed as his venom took over, but it wasn't nearly as bad as it was the other times. He drank deep, rubbing my arm with his hand. Kaizer groaned slightly as the venom felt like it was building up. I bit my lip, trying to calm the sensation, and my toes curled. The thoughts running through my mind weren't about him, though; they were about a honey-haired handmaiden. The memory of our first kiss played in my mind on repeat, and just before a moan escaped my throat Kaizer pulled his fangs from my flesh. He licked the wound, lingering as his hair brushed my skin ever so slightly. He sighed deeply as he ran his nose up near my ear.

"I can't wait until our wedding night," he muttered before pressing his lips lightly to my earlobe.

I exhaled and smiled at him before exiting the room quickly and leaving the books behind for him to put away. Thank the goddesses for the fucking vow of purity.

CHAPTER THIRTY-FOUR

It had been over a week since the meeting with the high priest and event planner. The high priest had dropped me off a few books that he said, *'might make me come to my senses about converting.'* I opened one, curious as to what he thought could change my mind. It was some sort of text full of their teachings called *The Supreme Writ of the Embers,* and I had to admit it was entertaining.

Some of the things these people believed in and the things they didn't believe in were quite interesting. They forbid the act of fornication, drinking alcohol, bodily markings of any kind outside of religious markings, and lots of other things that were part of my daily life. The high priest wouldn't have survived a day in Caldera; he would have had a heart attack a few minutes after crossing the border.

I left the books in a stack right next to the surplus of wedding things Misha had dropped off. She involved me a lot for someone who was supposed to be handling everything. She asked me questions I didn't even think were relevant. What soap I'd be using the morning of the wedding, what color my underwear was going to be, and even said there was a special toothpaste I should use to make sure my fangs sparkled. I was so over it that I couldn't stop myself from yelling at her two days ago, telling her that I didn't give a flying fuck about any of it. I swore she almost cried, but I couldn't find it in me to care.

Thankfully, since then, she hadn't asked me a single question, and it was fucking blissful. Zuri and I had stolen a few kisses over the days, but we hadn't gone any further yet. Misha had the entire palace staff helping with preparations for the wedding, and I hated that's how Zuri had to spend her time. The wedding would be for both kingdoms; tens of thousands of people were invited, and apparently, that meant there was a lot to do. With only a few days left, I knew I probably wouldn't see her for more than a few hours until after the ceremony.

I was going to stay up tonight and wait for her no matter how late she got in. She'd been staying in her bed, but I really wanted to feel her close to me for the night. Sighing, I opened the door of my bedchamber and walked out into the hall to meet Kaizer. He hadn't tried anything else thanks to the vow; giving him blood was the most intimate thing we'd done, and I still hadn't figured out what I was going to do after the ceremony. Zuri had told me she didn't mind if I needed to sleep with him; she knew it would be part of my *marital duties*. I didn't even want to do that, though. There had been moments where I was attracted to him, even thought about fucking him, but since Zuri, I hadn't had any such urges. But as we were only a few days away, and I had no way out, I knew I wouldn't be able to fake a headache for the next few centuries.

I sort of suggested that we tried an open marriage situation, and Kaizer honestly full-belly laughed at that, so I pretended it was a joke. The problem was, he actually liked me. How, I had absolutely no idea. I was a fucking bitch, but somehow, he seemed to find my attitude charming. Honestly, I didn't hate spending time with him recently. We had things to discuss outside of the union, as he taught me about Sanjry. I had hopes he'd let something else slip about the magic he used, but that didn't pan out. Regardless it surely wasn't the same way he felt about me, but unlike before, when I wanted to avoid him, I found myself being okay with his presence. Part of it may have been that every other part of the day, someone was asking me about the wedding, and when I was with Kaizer, nobody asked me anything.

I rounded the corner toward Kaizer's office and stopped in my tracks as there was a new decoration on the wall across from the red room. It was a painting, the only painting in the entire palace. It was a landscape of Sanjry, but it was absolutely beautiful. The colors were deep and dark, with some pops of bright reds and oranges throughout. I smiled and put my hand on the door to Kaizer's office, but I heard a second heartbeat.

Both heartbeats were elevated, and I heard muffled screams. I couldn't make out what was being said for some reason, but I pushed into the room with my gaze on the ground, making as much noise as possible so whoever was within would hear me. I cleared my throat and raised my eyes to find Kaizer and my mother in what looked like a heated argument.

"What's going on?" I asked.

They both glared at each other but looked over at me.

My mother snapped her fingers and an air shield dissipated. "He's being stubborn about the accommodations for the witches before the wedding. The Ritual is the day before, so we'll need rooms before the ceremony."

"I didn't say there wouldn't be rooms, just that Misha said that the ones I originally told you about won't be available. We are opening another level of rooms, and the staff is working hard to get them ready for the guests. If they aren't available, I will find another option."

"I need a guarantee that when we arrive, we will have a place to stay. I will not have my people out on the streets of Sanjry because you couldn't do your job."

"There will be somewhere, I promise," he sighed.

"What are you doing here?" my mother asked me.

"I live here," I bit out.

Seeing her unexpectedly was not in my plans for the day, and she reminded me why I couldn't stand her within just a few minutes of being here. She leveled me a look but turned back to Kaizer.

"Have those rooms available, or I'll move the whole wedding to Caldera," she muttered before opening a portal and disappearing from the room.

"Always a pleasure." Kaizer sighed.

I sat down in the chair across from him, the chair I'd claimed as my own over the last week. Crossing my legs, I sat back and folded my arms, peering up at Kaizer.

"I ran into Misha, and she mentioned some...apprehension."

"I don't care what color ribbon will be draped across the aisle," I replied flatly.

Kaizer laughed. "Misha isn't used to the women she works with to be so uncaring. Most women around here have their weddings planned as children. They know every detail, down to the ribbon."

"Well, I surely don't care," I muttered.

I grabbed an apple off his desk and bit into it, the crunch loud as he glared at me with that look he always did. He was always trying to figure me out, figure out why I was so different from what he was used to. The truth was simple, the women of Sanjry had been so domesticated that most of them lost themselves completely. Some of them seemed happy to play that role, whatever floats your boat, but some looked incredibly empty. I wasn't sure if it was the lack of men in Caldera or just our way of life, but every person in our kingdom had a purpose. We were encouraged as children to find the things we were good at, home in on those skills, and use them. Even if the things we were good at weren't always necessarily *good things*.

"What's my lesson for the day?" I asked.

"No lesson. I thought we'd train today."

I'd been training by myself for bit now since Zuri had been busy; I had gotten used to training with her at night time instead of with the soldiers.

"I'm in," I said, "I just need to change into my leathers really quick."

"I'll meet you in the training arena," he exclaimed, bending down to get his sword from under his desk.

I snapped a portal open to my room and stepped through. I quickly closed it as soon as both feet hit the floor, but when my purple smoke cleared, Zuri stood only a few feet away, and I jumped back.

"Fuck, I didn't see you," I yelped.

"I had to come back and grab my extra apron. I accidentally left it here this morning," she explained as she held up the apron.

She had dark smudges on her cheeks, and I stepped toward her to wipe them away. "What happened to your face?"

"Wedding preparations." She sighed but then covered the emotion with a smile in an instant. "What are you doing?"

"Came to change into my leathers. Kaizer wants to train," I explained as I wiped away the last smudge from her skin.

"I miss training." She sighed again.

"I stand by me getting you out of all of this shit," I practically growled.

She tilted her head and pursed her mouth. "And do what? Hang out in your room all day until you come back?"

"I can get you a different position," I replied.

"If I'm not your handmaiden, I don't get to stay in your quarters," she said quietly.

"Fine, it's not the best plan," I breathed. "At least things will go back to normal after the wedding."

Zuri offered a weak smile. "Is Kaizer waiting for you?"

"Oh, yeah, I should probably get down to the arena," I replied before turning to grab my leathers.

The dress I was wearing had rows of tiny buttons running up the back, Zuri had helped me change into it before she ran off. If she wasn't here, I would have had to rip the thing off me.

"Let me help," Zuri exclaimed as she set down the apron.

She started at the nape of my neck and worked her way down to the base of my spine. Each button undone exposed more skin, her fingers grazing inch by inch until she reached the last button. The fabric of the dress was thick and heavy, the lack of support from the buttons pulling it down at my shoulders. Zuri slipped her hands into the opening and ran her hands up my back to my shoulders before sliding them over my arms and sending the fabric to the floor with a thud.

She kept her hands on my arms, her body only a few inches from mine. I could feel her breath on my shoulder as she lingered, the feel of her body heat getting closer with each brush of exhale on my skin. Zuri swiped my hair to the side and kissed the crook of my neck as she ran her lips up to my ear.

"How much time do you have?" she whispered.

"Probably only a few minutes until he comes looking, you?" I muttered, turning my face toward hers.

"Same," she replied as she rubbed her cheek against mine.

"Hm," I sounded.

Zuri placed both of her hands on my waist and spun me toward her, capturing my mouth with hers before I even adjusted to the movement. She walked us back toward the bed as I undid the tie on the back of her dress and plucked open the three buttons at the top that were holding it together. The dress fell from one of her shoulders, and I pulled back to pull it the rest of the way off her body. She pressed her body into mine, the warmth of our skin sending sparks at every inch that met.

The back of my knees hit the edge of the bed, and she kept pushing, forcing me onto my back. I was typically the dominant one in these situations, but fuck, I kind of liked this. Ironically, our underwear sets were matching, both black and silky. She crouched over top of me, the fabric from our bras rubbing against each other as she swept back in, crashing her mouth into mine. I ran my hands up the smooth skin of her thighs and slid my hands beneath her underwear to grip her round ass with both my hands.

She moaned in my mouth as I squeezed, letting my nails dig in just a little bit. I slipped them out before running my nails over the arch of her back and up to her shoulder blades. Her mouth pulled away from mine as she kissed down my neck and slipped her fingers into my bra. The soft skin of her small hands grazed my nipple as she cupped my breast, sliding it out of the fabric as she slid down my body a few inches. A moan escaped me as she squeezed it between her teeth and looked looked up at me through her thick lashes with a slight smile.

Zuri kissed her way to my other nipple, doing the same while she continued squeezing the other between her fingers. Her curls fell on the other side of her head, grazing my skin with each movement. I stuck my hand between our bodies and into her underwear, finding her slick and wet already. My fingers slid down to her pussy and I skimmed over her clit as I dragged my hand back out and sucked her off my fingers.

"Fuck," I muttered, "you taste better than I could have dreamed."

She sat back on my legs and dipped her fingers into my underwear to find me just as wet. She rubbed a few circles around my clit with a smirk, and I gasped before she pulled them out and stuck them into her mouth. She groaned as she shifted forward and sat her pussy right on mine. The pressure was enough to make me come at any moment. I was sure she knew it as she wiggled slightly, and my head jerked back as I bit my lip.

Zuri brought her chest back to mine to relieve me from the contact that had my head spinning. "Shame we don't have the time," she whispered.

"Fucking shame," I repeated and flipped her onto her back to lick down her collarbone.

Her back arched, and I ran my fingers over the length of her body as I stood up with reluctance. I removed my underwear and quickly changed into a dry pair as Zuri did the same and put her dress back on. I pulled on my leathers and tied my hair up into a high ponytail.

"Need me to portal you somewhere?" I asked as my chest still heaved.

"Actually, yeah. Can you drop me by the kitchens?"

I nodded and kissed her one more time before I opened the portal and stepped through with her. I watched as she ran away, her curls bouncing with every step, and ran toward the training arena. Pushing open the doors, I stepped in to find Kaizer and Quinn engaged in a sparring match.

Kaizer saw me and stopped, walking over to me and wiping some sweat off his forehead. "I was wondering where you went. You look flushed. Did you run here?"

"Just got a little warm-up," I replied with a shrug.

I pulled a sparring sword down from the wall and pointed it in his direction. I had more than enough pent-up energy I needed to get out, and Kaizer wasn't going to know what hit him.

CHAPTER THIRTY-FIVE

The witches were arriving for The Ritual later today, and I was getting a bit anxious about it. I'd been born to become the Acna one day, to be in this position of power. It was one of the few ways to ensure that Kaizer and I were equals as well. If I was just a 'princess' marrying a king, it still felt like he had more power. But a queen marrying a king, that felt equally matched.

Not to mention that my mother had been the Acna for half a millennium, and it was certainly time for her to move on. There were no rules on when it had to be done or when someone ruled for too long, but even my mother seemed okay with how it was happening. I hadn't seen her since that day in Kaizer's office a few days ago, but there really wasn't much for us to say. Today I'd officially become more powerful than her; I didn't think she wanted to talk about that. Part of me expected at least one more *punishment* before now, but she'd been eerily quiet.

She was still to oversee the day-to-day in Caldera as Kaizer and I were to stay in Sanjry, but all decisions would come to me...and Kaizer. Zuri hadn't looked me in the eye this morning when she was doing my hair and helping me dress, and I was starting to think the marriage was about to get to her. Selfishly, I sent a message to the head of staff and told her that any duties she had for the rest of the day needed to be sent to someone else. I needed my handmaiden for important queenly things. A lie, of course. I didn't want to go into The Ritual tonight without a clear mind or into the wedding tomorrow knowing she secretly hated me.

If I timed it right, she should have been heading back now as lunch had just wrapped up. I wasn't sure if she would be upset with me, but at this point, there wasn't any turning back. I sat outside in my courtyard, watching the clouds roll by and listening to the birds of Malva chirp and fly above my head. There wasn't much to prepare for The Ritual later today; I was literally going to be naked, so there wasn't anything Zuri would need to help me with either. The brujas would help with the other preparations and were probably already done setting up. The ceremony needed to take place outside, and we found a spot just outside the walls of the palace that would work. It would take place at midnight when the moon was at its highest, so I had a few hours before I needed to portal out there.

We were hosting a dinner with the sanction heads, though, and that was the excuse I was using when Zuri inevitably came back and asked why I had her work reassigned. I took a deep breath, savoring this quiet moment in the day before the chaos ensued. I had always been curious about what the power would feel like, what the special gift I would get would be. Nobody knew exactly how the magic chose what to give you in the moments it was transferred to the next Acna. Part of me wondered if whatever power I got would be enough to tip the scale in my favor and get out of the wedding before tomorrow. If it was something I could use against Kaizer, I could potentially take over his kingdom or make enough of a threat that we could go our separate ways. It was wishful thinking, of course.

Tomorrow I would be Queen of Sanjry and Caldera, or whatever it was our joint kingdom should be referred to as. Kaizer mentioned one time about renaming, and I nearly bit his head off, so he hadn't brought it up again. I heard someone walking toward my door and pretended to be stuck in a daydream as Zuri sauntered through the suite and found me out in the courtyard.

"Did you need me?" she asked, taking off her apron and fluffing up her curls.

"I always need you," I said with my most conniving smile on display.

She laughed. "More specifically, what did you need?"

"I need you to help me pick out a dress for the dinner later," I said before turning away from her so she couldn't read my face.

"The dinner in like..." She stopped, looking over at the clock. "Three hours?"

"That's the one," I replied with my gaze on the flowers at the border of the space.

Zuri stepped into my eye line with her hand on her hip. "Dayanara," she muttered.

I put my hand on my chest. "My full name, ouch." She kept staring me down, waiting for me to break, and I rolled my eyes. "Fine, I wanted to talk to you."

Zuri plopped down onto the chair beside me. "I told you I'm fine."

"So fine, you didn't even look me in the eye all morning," I responded, putting my hand under my chin and leaning it on the arm of my chair.

"You were ugly this morning," she joked.

I smirked. "Now I know you're lying."

She let a small chuckle form under her breath and looked over at me. "I really haven't been bothered by it until today. I guess it was all just hypothetical in my head up until now."

"So...you hate me?"

"No, Daya. I don't hate you. I hate this situation. I hate that I let myself get this deep into it. But I don't hate any part of you."

"I hate the situation, too." I sighed. "Do you still want to come to The Ritual?"

"Yes, if you can find a way," she replied.

"I have enough moonstone to be able to cloak you in the night. You'll just have to stay as still as possible to make sure it lasts."

She nodded. "Okay, yes, I can do that."

Zuri looked over at me, sadness written all over her features, and I just about went to find Kaizer and killed him with just one sorrowful bat of her lashes.

"You think it's time to figure out what we do from here?" she asked.

I leaned toward her and wrapped my fingers around hers, where they lay on the armrest of her chair.

"Probably," I whispered.

"I can't imagine a world not like the one we have now," she admitted.

"Me either. It doesn't have to change. I plan on keeping a separate room from him, so you can still stay with me."

"But you'll still have to...sleep with him sometimes," she muttered.

"I suppose I will, yeah."

She turned away from me, all prior jokes we shared about it gone, only the reality of our situation hanging between us. From the profile of her face, I could see what looked like regret, what looked like giving up.

"You can't leave me," I whispered, "I swear to whatever gods they believe in here that I will kill every person in this fucking castle if you do that."

"I'm not leaving you." She laughed, a small genuine smile gracing her beautiful lips. "I'm just thinking."

"We have the tunnels," I said. "There are ways to get around, and I have the portal magic. Once we're married, I can use it to leave the capital again. We can go wherever we want when there's time."

She looked over at me, and her watery gaze had my heart stopping mid-beat, the air in my chest tight. "I want all of you, Daya. I want every piece. I want to flaunt you on the streets and tell everyone that you're mine. I know I can't have that, but I do want it. I'll take whatever pieces you are able to offer me. I'll sneak around if that's what you want. I'll pretend to be your handmaiden during the day and have you in my bed when you're not in Kaizer's. I just need you, in whatever capacity I can have you."

I felt tears running down my cheeks, Zuri being the only one who had ever invoked the emotion in me. It felt...good. She wanted me, she wanted all of me, and I couldn't fucking stand that I couldn't give it to her.

"I'll kill him," I stated dryly, "after the marriage, I'll fake an accident."

Zuri laughed, but my face remained flat.

"Oh fuck, of course, you're serious," she muttered when she looked over at me. "And then what? You'll take some commoner as your wife?"

"If I run the fucking kingdom, who is going to tell me no?"

"Oh, Daya. You still have a lot to learn about Sanjry."

I sat up, grabbing her hand and pulling her as close to me as I could. "I want you too, Zuri. All of it, I'll find a way. I swear it."

She smiled gently, like she didn't really believe me, but I didn't care. I was completely serious. I had enjoyed my time with Kaizer recently in a wholly platonic way, but I would kill him as soon as the agreement was fulfilled and the magic stopping me was gone. I could drive my dagger into his chest, pull it out, and run right to Zuri.

She squeezed my fingers. "I look forward to it."

I couldn't wait until The Ritual now because the power I was going to receive would help me make sure I kept that promise.

I sipped the goat blood in my chalice, eyeing my mother from across the table. Something was off with her, but I couldn't tell what it was yet. She had been quiet for the entirety of the dinner, only speaking when spoken to. I could assume it was because she didn't want to give up the power; I honestly thought she would have gone back on her word at this point. She was as power hungry as Kaizer, so it had to be grinding on her.

"You ready?" Cat asked me.

She sat in the chair directly to my right, Kaizer in the one to the left, and I smiled at her.

"To have that fucking power? Hell yeah," I replied.

Everyone laughed except my mother, who looked at me like I was some child trying to play with the adults, but I just shrugged. Kaizer smiled and glanced down at his plate, lifting it and handing it to one of the staff behind him. The staff all hurried and took our dishes. I looked around for Zuri, but she wasn't there. I forgot I had relieved her of her duties for the evening, so she was back in my room waiting for me. A piece of me was missing; she'd been here for every meal since I'd been at the palace. I must have sighed louder than I thought because Kaizer leaned closer to me.

"You okay?" he asked.

"Yeah, I think I'll take some blood to go. I want to make sure I'm at full power tonight," I exclaimed as I handed my chalice to the staff member behind me.

Kaizer watched me warily, his jaw ticking a few times. He bit the inside of his cheek as he continued bouncing his anxious gaze all over my body.

"Don't worry. Nobody has ever died in this ceremony," I muttered.

I wouldn't tell him it had only been done two other times. Everyone started filtering out, and my mother gave me a slight dip of her chin as she walked past, leaving Kaizer and me by ourselves.

"You don't have to do it, you know," he mumbled.

"What?" I asked, not sure if I was hearing him correctly.

"You don't have to do The Ritual. You're still my equal even if you're not the queen of your people."

Kaizer leaned forward and put his hand on mine before bringing his face closer than before.

"It's a bit late for that," I stated.

He gripped my fingers so tight one small movement might have snapped them. "I'm just saying, if that's why you're doing it, don't."

"You don't want me to overpower you, do you?" I growled.

"No, that's not it. I'm just worried. What if something happens, and I'm left alone to rule both our kingdoms in chaos?"

"Nothing is going to happen," I said as I pulled my hand from his grasp. "You need to relax. Go find Quinn and train or something. It's going to be a long night for you if you are up all night worried."

I stood from my chair and scooted it in, walking toward the exit across the room. A force pulled me back, and I looked down to see Kaizer's hand on my wrist; I ran my gaze slowly up his arm and to his eyes as my lip pulled back.

"Daya, please," he pleaded.

"Why are you suddenly so against it?" I asked.

He didn't respond, only watched me as if I would fall apart the moment I set foot out of the room.

"It's happening. Deal with your ego before the wedding tomorrow," I snapped and opened a portal to step into my room.

"How was it?" I heard Zuri ask among the purple smoke surrounding me.

I stepped forward to find her in a chair by the fire with a book in her lap. She joked that she'd be waiting in my room for me, but I didn't exactly hate that it was what she was doing right now. I smiled wide, and she tilted her head quizzically.

"What?" she asked.

"You're just beautiful, that's all. Dinner was fine; my mother didn't speak to me. I think she's upset about making me Acna, but it is what it is now. Kaizer was trying to convince me not to do it. He thinks I'm going to die," I said, rolling my eyes.

She went still. "Is that a possibility?"

"No, he just doesn't understand witch shit. You tell him I'm going to be naked with blood spilled all over me, and he thinks there's no way I'll be coming out of it."

"Why do you have to be naked?" Zuri asked.

"I don't know, actually." I laughed. "It's just part of The Ritual, something about being fully connected to the magic or something."

She shrugged and looked me up and down, the same worry on her face as Kaizer.

I put my hand on my hip. "Oh, don't tell me you're going to start worrying now, too."

"I'll just be glad when you're done," she said before looking back at her book to stop from watching me with those worry-filled eyes.

"You'll be there to make sure I get back safe. Actually," I started as I walked over to my closet and pulled out the biggest chunk of onyx I had in my collection. "The cloaking spell will work, but I'm going to use this to make sure you're double protected."

I held the stone between both of my hands over a decorative bowl on the end table, sending my magic straight to its core and turning it into a powder. The particles fell into the bowl, and I picked it up, taking it over to the bathroom. I ran some water in it and turned it into a paste before coming back to the fire and sitting it at the base of the hearth. Zuri watched me as I sat down in front of it and whispered the spell, creating a dome of my magic around the top of the bowl. The purple dome turned white as it deflated and settled over the onyx paste. It seeped in, sending sparkles throughout the concoction, and I looked back at Zuri to find her smiling wide at my use of magic.

"I'll never get used to the shit you can do," she mumbled.

"It has to set for about an hour, but it'll be ready by the time we go. I'll rub it over your chest, and it will create a barrier against anything that means you harm, but it will only withstand a few strikes. So if something does happen, you need to get the fuck out."

"Not very reassuring," she muttered.

"Everything will be fine," I reassured.

I reached for her to sit with me near the fire, and we lay in each other's arms, not speaking until it was time to go.

Chapter Thirty-Six

The barrier spell worked. I rubbed it on her chest and tested it with a tiny spark that wouldn't drain much of the magic, and Zuri said she didn't feel anything. The area we chose for The Ritual was heavily wooded, so I set her up a safe distance away between a few trees that offered her enough coverage. I used the cloaking spell on her as well, so she was double, if not triple, protected, but I didn't want to take any chances.

"Please be careful," Zuri whispered, "I'm…just please come back. I need you to come back."

"I will, I promise," I murmured.

I set my forehead on hers, feeling our connection down to my bones, even if I couldn't sense her thanks to the cloaking spell. She tilted her chin up, catching my lips in a passionate kiss that I returned with every piece of me.

"I have to go, stay here and don't move if possible."

Zuri nodded, and I opened a portal behind me, not taking my eyes off her until I stepped back into it and stood beside the altar. The robe I wore was extremely heavy, an all-black garment with silver trimming that Cat brought me earlier. The hood was huge, pooling at either side of my head, but it covered my entire body, which was great because it was pretty chilly in this part of the forest. It wouldn't save me for too much longer, but I was savoring the warmth for now. I was the first here, so I took the opportunity to look around at what they'd set up.

I'd never been to one of these, as the last people who performed the ceremony were my grandmother and her mother hundreds of years ago. My mother had received her power when her mother died, so there was no need for The Ritual. The altar was black, so deep that you could barely see it in the dark of the night. The only clues that it was there were the torches set on each corner of it. All of our stones were set up along the border, each one gleamed in the firelight, freshly polished. The area around us was empty, as the witches would sit on the ground and join hands around us. I looked up, the clearing wide enough to show the moon straight above our heads. It was so big that none of the sky showed around it—a spotlight on me.

I felt the tingle of magic nearby, and witches started to portal in. Different colored smokes exploded in the area until it all settled, and they sat on the floor around me. They also wore robes, but theirs were varying colors, not the deep black that mine was. Nobody spoke; a rule of The Ritual. Only the spell would be chanted by the witches in the circle. My mother's jade smoke spilled from the altar as she stood tall in a robe that matched mine. For the first time in a century, her green locks weren't pulled into a tight bun at her neck. They cascaded down to her waist in thick waves; I hadn't realized her hair was that long.

She looked down her nose at me. One of the last times she'd be able to give me that look and have the ability to back it up. She motioned her hand to her side, beckoning me to join her. "We are here today to perform The Ritual. The power of the Acna will be transferred to my daughter, Dayanara."

The witches nodded, still not permitted to speak. My mother turned and nodded to me, her hand on the tie of her robe. She pulled hers at the same time I did mine. The garment fell open, exposing my bronze skin to the moonlight as I pulled my hood down and let it cascade to the ground. Nudity wasn't frowned upon in Caldera like it was here; none of the witches batted an eye as they took in our bodies on full display. While our bodies could be used in a sexual way, our bodies themselves weren't what made them that way. A witch could walk down a busy street naked, and nobody would think anything of it; nobody would think she was asking for any sort of sexual attention.

My mother held the bloodstone dagger in her grasp, the weapon that would be used to spill our blood. She shot the blade into the sky, and the witches around us began to chant. Their voices sounded in unison as they muttered the words, magic sparking from all of their chests. Streams of jewel-colored magic connected as they reached for us in a web of power. The first stream hit me in the chest, and my back arched at the impact. It wasn't painful, but the force of all their combined magic flowing through me had my legs shaking ever so slightly.

The stones at the edge of the altar started to vibrate, and they quickly shifted into a circle around me and my mother, as essence flickered inside them and they glowed in unison. Another stream of power hit my mother in the chest, forcing her body to jerk the same as mine. She took the dagger and ran it up her wrist, the movement choppy with the magic pushing through her. The chant grew louder and louder as the blood dripped from the wound, and she handed me the blade to make the same cut across my arm.

I dragged it from the base of my wrist up to the inside of my elbow. I couldn't even feel the pain as the chant grew so loud in my ears none of my other senses worked. I held my arm out toward my mother as she extended hers toward me. The blood dripped down to the altar, a pool around our feet that didn't seep past the stones encasing us. It was our turn to chant, and we tipped our chins up to the sky and spoke the words that would complete The Ritual.

"Acna. Essence. Magic. We call on the power of Naom. For we are the line of Amapola, the bloodline you blessed. We spill that blood to ask for the power to be transferred, for the power of you, of the first Acna to be gifted to another."

The very ground beneath us shook as the magic raged; my mother was lifted off the ground a few inches, her hair spread out around her. Glowing irises beamed in the darkness as her eyes glowed green, then purple, then blue, and pure essence shot from her fingers and into me. I fell to my knees as the power pushed through my veins. I had never felt so strong; this power was something I didn't think was possible. I felt like I could tear down this world and build it again, like I could end all life with a snap of my fingers. My head fell back as I screamed a primal scream, the sound of it sending the trees around us into movement. I opened my eyes, and I swore the moon was only a breath away from my face. I had to be floating somewhere in the atmosphere, and not on my knees upon an altar covered in blood.

My mother fell back to the altar, her body going limp as her hair covered her like a blanket. I stood to my feet, the sense that I didn't belong to this world still heavy. My special power wasn't evident yet, but I felt invincible. All the witches fell to face the ground and bowed for the new Acna. I bent down and grabbed my robe, wrapping it around my body, still covered in blood. I stood tall with my shoulders pulled back as I looked at all the witches around me who I was now to lead, whose lives were now in my hands. It made me slightly uneasy, but I would do whatever I needed to do to protect them.

I waved my hand, letting them know they were dismissed and could go back to the palace. Each of them nodded once, some smiling, some looking at me in reverence as they portaled away in unison. After the last one left, I turned back to my mother, who was still lying on the floor. She was trying to push herself to her hands, but her body was shaking with the lack of power that had run through her body for nearly five hundred years. I'd never seen her exude anything but pure strength, so it was odd watching her struggle this way. I bit my lip and decided to help her up. That tiny piece of me that always wanted her to love me peeking through the power coursing through my veins.

I reached out my hand, gripped her arm, and pulled her up to try to set her on her feet. She whirled toward me with a puff of magic suppressant in one hand and the bloodstone blade in the other. I felt the spell settle over me as my magic retreated deep within my chest, out of my reach. The unfamiliar feel of my Acna power felt closer, but still too far for me to access. My mother darted toward me with the blade, ready to kill.

"What the fuck!" I exclaimed.

I tried to sidestep, but the blood on the altar was so slippery that I went flying toward the floor, and she fell on top of me. My mother lifted the blade again as I tried to grab it and reason with her, but what I saw in her eyes told me she had made up her mind.

"You have to die to save us all!" she screamed. "Naom will return. You are the sacrifice that will allow it. I've seen it!"

Fuck. The blade was only an inch from my chest as she pushed in, and for the first time in my life, I was under threat and didn't immediately fight back. She was my mother, for fuck's sake. There was a time when she loved me, when she nurtured me and laughed with me. That woman was gone; there was no love in the gaze she held now, only a need for more power. My Acna power was so close, I reached down into my being, just barely grazing it, but still not able to get a hold of it. I tried to conjure anything, but I was completely powerless.

I wrapped my fingers around her wrists, lifting my feet to try to buck her off. My feet slipped on the blood, and she jolted forward, the movement sending the blade straight into my chest. It pierced my heart, shredding it into pieces with every beat it took. Until the organ stopped completely, and bright light encompassed my vision.

Chapter Thirty-Seven

Lupe

143 years ago

"Acna, we've found her."

One of my right-hand witches, Frida, came running into the room where Daya and I were playing with toys on the floor. I held up my hand for her to wait and she stopped and looked at the ground when she realized I was with my daughter. Daya was so brilliant. She was only ten years old, but she had nearly bested me in a game of chess. I smiled at her, capturing her king and ruffling through her hair.

"Checkmate."

She studied the board as she tried to figure out how I beat her and sighed when she saw what she had missed. "I'll beat you next time, Mama! I get better every time!"

"You're right, mija. Now run along. Mommy has some business to attend to."

She nodded and ran away, her little pigtails flowing like streamers behind her as one of her caretakers ran to catch up.

I sat up straight. "Bring her in."

The seer, Xuxa. Someone from her sanction had advised that she had a vision she'd seen that would save us all and put a stop to the war with Sanjry. I hadn't had much contact with her prior to this, but I'd heard she was kind, gentle, and fair. But even so, after she found out that we knew about the vision, she went into hiding. We'd been tracking her down for a while now, and we finally had her.

I had no idea why she wouldn't come straight to me with the knowledge, and my blood was already starting to boil at the thought of it. Frida and another one of my right-hand witches, Tirsa, pulled the hood from her face, exposing a witch with smooth brown skin. Her dark curls were matted, and her clothes were soiled and hanging off her in strips.

"Speak," I demanded.

"I can't, I can't, I can't do it," she muttered as tears streamed down her face.

I took a step toward where she knelt on the floor as my emerald magic sparked in my hands. She was terrified. Rightfully so, what she had done thus far had been far too close to treason, and she knew it.

My gaze ran up and down her shaking figure. "Why did you run?"

She looked away and Tirsa and Frida both grabbed her by her face and forced her to look at me.

"You don't understand, I can't. You'll kill me for it," she bleated.

"There are ways I can get information out of you, you know," I said as I took a step away from her and over to my plethora of blades. "Things that don't even include my magic."

Her lip quivered, but she held strong with her lips sealed shut. The witches holding her looked over at me in anticipation of what I'd do.

"Very well," I muttered as I snapped open a portal to the dungeons.

The witches dragged her through the portal and stuck her in the chair immediately, unlocking her handcuffs and strapping each of her limbs so she couldn't move. I blew my magic suppressant into her face and I watched as the cloud settled around her.

"Last chance to make this easy on you," I said as I twisted the blade in my hand.

Xuxa's eyes turned bright white as her head snapped back and I hesitated my next step as I watched her gift flow into her, even with the suppression, her seer gift was stronger than the spell used. She heaved a breath and doubled over as far as she could with the chair holding her and looked back up at me.

"Wait," she whispered, "wait, please, just wait."

I cocked my head to the side and watched as she caught her breath, looking over at Frida and Tirsa.

"I'll tell you, but you have to swear that you'll take my daughter in after you kill me. You have to swear that she can stay with you, that you won't kill her."

My jaw ticked. I needed that information. I could make her bleed, keep her without access to her magic and drive her insane for days. This was...easier. She wasn't very smart. She gave no other stipulations other than that I needed to take the girl in, and that *I* couldn't kill her. There was plenty of room for interpretation.

I lifted my chin. "Fine. Do we have the daughter?" I asked the other witches.

They nodded, and I turned back to Xuxa, waving my hand for her to continue.

"It will be easier if I just show you," she said as she strained her hand toward me.

Taking a step forward, I reached for her hand.

"Acna, this could be a trick," Frida said.

"Well then we'll kill her sooner than planned," I said as I wrapped my fingers around Xuxa's.

"I am...sorry for what you're about to see," Xuxa whispered.

Her eyes glowed white again, and my soul was pulled out of my body as I was taken into the spirit realm with her. We stood side by side. Xuxa was out of her cuffs but no harm could come to either of us in this realm.

A flash of the future started, and we were standing on a battlefield. A dark blast went off that sent thousands up in ash. I'd never seen anything like it.

"What is that?" I said as I took a step toward it.

My surroundings changed, and I watched as an older version of me ran to an older Daya. She was unconscious and covered in blood. I couldn't see why, but my heart skipped a beat as I tried to run to her as well, but the vision changed. I was inside a tent. A man with white hair stood in front of me, with his arms crossed and a glare that could kill.

"This isn't a war you started, but you can end it, Rey Falso," I stated.

"Why don't I just kill you now, and then take your kingdom," he growled.

Something about the man felt at odds. I wasn't sure why I called him False King, but he looked like he didn't belong in his role. He wasn't the largest man, although he did look incredibly strong, but he didn't seem like the type that would rampage a kingdom in spite as the previous king did.

"I am bringing back our goddess. Trust me, you don't want to be on the other side of this war when this happens. I'm offering you an out before that," I suggested.

The man's brow raised and his mouth hung open for just a moment before he regained his composure. "What are you offering besides words you have no proof of?"

I bit my lip. "I have seen it with my own eyes," I snapped. "But I offer you my daughter. We can join our kingdoms in marriage. There will be a...sacrifice. You won't have to put up with her for long."

His brows drew together. "You would kill your own daughter to return your goddess?"

"I would. Don't you worry about her, she won't be missed."

The man's fists balled, and he looked past my head as his jaw ticked. I turned around and realized I was in Sanjry's camp.

"Let me discuss it with my advisers. I will send a hawk to your kingdom with a response," he said.

Future me snapped open a portal and stepped through it back to Caldera with a devilish smile, and Xuxa and I followed.

"We will join our kingdoms. I will take your army, and then I'll take all of Malva when Naom returns. Nobody will ever come for the brujas again," I whispered to myself in the vision.

The vision changed.

I was atop Daya. She was covered in blood and I had a dagger aimed for her chest. I moved to push it in and end her life, screaming, "You have to die to save us all! Naom will return. You are the sacrifice that will allow it. I've seen it."

I plunged the dagger into her heart, and I watched as my only daughter died by my hand. Every candle blew out, and the moon and stars blinked out of the sky the moment her heart stopped, leaving us all in utter blackness. Suddenly pure essence poured out of Daya's lifeless body, a stream of every color of bruja magic twirling around each other until a winged figure appeared in the sky. Naom.

Xuxa let go of my hand and my soul plunged back into the mortal realm.

So many thoughts were running through my mind at once that my head started to spin and I stumbled.

"I...I can bring her back. When will that come to be?" I asked Xuxa.

Xuxa sighed and hung her head. "In the year of her one hundred fifty-third birthday. If this does not happen, Caldera will fall, permanently."

If Naom returned, she would protect us and put an end to the war, to all wars to come. I could ask for more of her essence. We could become unstoppable. We were her creation. She would stop at nothing to make sure we survived. Brujas were ruthless, one of the few things we held close was family and loyalty. If my kingdom knew that I killed my daughter, they would lose their faith in me. No matter how powerful I was, I couldn't stand against my entire kingdom. I had to play this right, entrust the knowledge with only my most loyal, and not let anyone else know what happened. Her death could be covered up, it could be blamed on the white-haired man who appeared to be the future King of Sanjry. With their potential union, it would be believable.

I swallowed as my mind wheeled back to what would have to happen for that to come to be. My daughter, my flesh and blood. Could I do it? Our numbers were dwindling with each battle, along with the fact that we needed the men of their kingdom to sire our brujitas. It had been difficult for the witches to lure any vampire men during this war. Crossing the borders undetected wasn't impossible, but it had been a much heftier task in these last few decades. I needed to stop the war, even it would take another 143 years. The war between Dusra and Sanjry lasted almost a millennium. There could be another way, but I needed the chance to decide where to go from here.

"What did you show her?" Frida asked.

Xuxa looked up at me and closed her eyes with her chin raised, already knowing what would come to be with this knowledge. I took the blade still in my hand and slit her throat. The blood poured out of the wound profusely as she gargled for a few moments, and I heard her heart cease beating.

"We don't speak of this," I commanded as both witches nodded. "Where is the daughter?"

"She's being held in the East Wing. Her name is Ximena."

10 years later

We'd done everything. No matter how hard we fought, Sanjry was inching closer and closer to victory. We held our ground. We were resilient, but I had to start taking that vision seriously. I'd been colder to Dayanara since that day. It was hard to look at her and know the weight she carried. The sacrifice that could be made with her. She'd gone through countless tribulations I formed to push her to her limits, and she'd come out on the other side each time. The punishments, though, those were more difficult. I forced myself to become detached from the situation, knowing that I ruled hundreds of thousands of brujas. I wasn't just a mother, I was *The Acna*. The mother to every single bruja in Caldera.

I sat in the courtyard, watching as Dayanara trained with Ximena, Xuxa's daughter. They'd gotten extremely close, they were the same exact age and had practically been raised together since that day. They were nearing their adulthood and both of their magic had manifested. Ximena didn't show any signs of seer power, and I kept a close eye on her to ensure that she didn't have her mother's gift. I'd had every known seer killed or banished to the Inbetween since then. We questioned Ximena after her mother died, but Xuxa didn't tell her anything. In that, she was smart.

Dayanara had been training hard. She had a natural talent with a blade; it was astonishing. I'd wondered a few times if she could be the tipping point in the wars, and if we could get out of this without her death. But I knew that the vision would come to be. I still held on to that sliver of hope foolishly, though. She would be used as a weapon, she would give everything she could for Caldera, and then she'd give her life for it.

15 years later

"That concludes this coterie meeting," I bellowed.

Brujas started pouring out of the council room, and I watched as Dayanara whispered something into Ximena's ear. She smirked and ran her hand down Dayanara's cheek with so much love in her gaze, my fists balled tight. Dayanara didn't need any distractions. She needed to focus. Dayanara was starting to stray from the path I set out for her. I could feel it. Ximena was soft and kind, like her mother. She was vocal about her kindness, too. Ximena wanted change, like everyone else. She wanted an end to the war, but her methods of truce and peace would never work. Dayanara was starting to believe it was possible, though. She was softening, and she *needed* that edge. She needed to remain ruthless.

They didn't know that the reason we were in this war was because of me. My mistake in helping Sanjry's royalty with a magic suppressant spell during their war with Dusra. I shouldn't have done it. It was one of my biggest regrets, and my coven would not have agreed to it. It was just after my mother died and I was made Acna. I thought it would help maintain peace between the kingdoms, but Sanjry demanded more of my assistance, hoping that we would offer them aid against Dusra again.

Their loss to Dusra was catastrophic. I never knew exactly what it was that came to their capital that day and demolished them so thoroughly. Dusra didn't even take his kingdom, offering a treaty to keep them apart officially, but Sanjry's king never quite got over the loss. I denied him, advising that I had to take care of my coven, and I thought that was the end of it. But they raged war on us in hopes of taking over me, my kingdom, and the power that we held. I wouldn't put my people in the path of Dusra, and whatever weapons they had that ended their war. This king was arrogant, and talks of peace would do nothing.

Dayanara left the room with one quick glance over at me. She knew I wouldn't have approved of her backing Ximena in the meeting, and there'd be a discussion about it when we were in private. Ximena was finishing up writing something in a notebook on the desk in front of her, and I stood from my chair to go in for lunch. Just as I walked past the row she was sitting at the end of, she took a loud gasp that caught my attention. I looked back to find her head thrown back, and her eyes glowing white, just like her mother.

She exhaled as her eyes returned to their dark brown color, growing wider and wider as she looked up at me with her mouth hung open. "You...You're going to..."

I grabbed her by her wrist and opened up a portal into the dungeons before she could make a move. I blew magic suppressant onto her and closed the door behind me as I stepped into the hallway. My heart was racing as I paced up the halls and into my office. Ximena was far too close to Dayanara. She'd tell her the moment she saw her. Dayanara couldn't challenge me. If she tried to kill me and became Acna, Naom would not return, and I'd be signing the deaths for my entire coven.

I felt that last bit of hope slip away as I decided once and for all she would have to die, and I would have to keep her beneath me. I'd been fairly lax in the punishments I'd given Dayanara thus far, but that would change. I had to do something more extreme, and then I'd force her to kill Ximena, and her very being—her very *soul*—would be changed. She'd return to my weapon, and I'd get all of my use out of her as I could for the next century.

I was no longer her mother—I was her executioner.

Chapter Thirty-Eight

Dayanara

I stood beside my lifeless body, watching as my mother yanked out the blade and looked up into the sky. I wasn't fully corporeal, there was a light emanating from my chest that sent a glow through my translucent body. I could only assume I was in the spirit world...dead. She killed me. I stepped behind my mother and tried to grab her, tried to strangle her and drag my nails through her neck, but my hands moved straight through her body.

"That won't do any good, my child."

I spun around ready to attack. Even though I knew nothing could hurt me in the spirit world, that was my instinct. My mouth fell open as I raised my eyes to a glowing being, a being sparkling with pure essence, a being with wings.

"Naom," I breathed.

She smiled and nodded once, as she moved closer to me and her purple dress swished with each step. She twined her fingers together before her and looked back at my corpse.

"Why would she do this?" I whispered as I followed her gaze.

Her voice came out smooth and ancient. A sound so powerful, yet so soothing in the same breath as she said, "She was misguided. I can't say much else, but I can tell you that you are not finished."

"What do you mean?" I said as I let the light in my chest shine through my fingers. "I'm dead."

"And I am resting with the other goddesses, but I was able to slip into this realm due to our connection, to come back and help my children one more time."

My head tilted, confused as to how the goddess planned on helping, if she was going to go back into the world and help my mother after what she'd done.

"I am here to guide you. You died with my essence in your veins. I can send you back just one time. You must find a way to stop what is to come. Your heart beats with many, and you must follow that sound."

"I—I don't know what that means," I said.

She smiled gently. "You will."

I bit the inside of my cheek. "If I go back, I'm going to kill her. That doesn't bother you?"

Naom sighed. "Morality has given you all a false sense of right and wrong. Things are not black and white, and you are not a singular thing, Dayanara. You do what you must. I am almost out of time."

I took a deep breath and nodded. "Okay."

Naom smiled and reached her hand toward me with her pointer finger extended and glowing. She pressed it into my forehead and I gasped as my soul poured back into my body lying on the cold hard altar. My heart beat once as I opened my eyes, and it was still complete darkness. I couldn't see my mother or anything around me. I gasped a breath as my heart beat again and suddenly the world became as it was. The moon and stars blinked back into existence and I saw my mother with her gaze still on the sky. Suddenly power beamed from my chest and into the sky, a swirling pattern of every color. My back arched as I was pulled toward the moon and my skin glowed in pure witch magic, purples, pinks, blues, and greens all ebbing together in a sparkling pool of essence. The tattoo of Kaizer's sigil on my skin burned and faded as my power was so strong it broke the magical agreement into a million pieces. My shoulder blades burned as if lava was being poured over my skin and I wanted to scream with the pain, but the sound was lodged in my throat. The burning sensation turned into a heavy weight and I looked over my shoulder to see wings unfurling and spreading wide.

My body descended as the power encompassing me waned and my feet settled on the ground.

"Naom," my mother whispered from behind me.

I turned around and my mother's features widened, all the white in her eyes showing as she took in my face.

"No, no, I saw it. This isn't right." She shook her head as she took slow steps backward.

"I don't care," I growled.

My skin flickered out, my wings vanishing, and I took a deep breath, hoping that I broke the hold the magic suppressant had on me. I screamed as I blasted her with a ball of air, sending her flying into the sky above me. She flew back toward the ground and I marched toward my mother.

"What the fuck is wrong with you!" I yelled, grabbing her foot and throwing her again.

She flicked her wrist to try to portal away, but I was quicker than she was and grabbed her again before she could step through.

"I'm your fucking daughter! I get you didn't love me, but I honestly didn't think you would fucking kill me!"

I grabbed her by her neck and lifted her in the air. She tried to fight back with her magic, but it bounced off me like it was nothing. She hadn't fought with the average power of a witch for so long she could barely create a spark that hurt. My nails dug into her neck, and the warmth of her blood rushed down my fingers as I growled in her face.

"Why?" I muttered, my voice cracking slightly.

With the amount of pressure I was squeezing, her voice was barely a rasp. "For...the...power. For...Caldera."

"You're fucking pathetic," I bit out.

Her eyes were starting to bulge, and I could already see the bruises forming around her neck. There was no going back; there was no saving her. There was nothing she could say that would take this moment back, nothing she could do that would make me trust her. A single tear fell from my eye as the rage inside me waned into sadness.

"I hope it was worth it," I mumbled.

With a single flick of my wrist, I snapped her neck. She peered down at me, the look of shock permanently etched into her face as the life slipped from behind her eyes. My mother fell to the ground, her head turned at an unnatural angle. I fell to my knees as my chest heaved and I crouched over her dead body. I wanted to do this for a century, ever since Ximena, and I couldn't even figure out how I felt about it.

She was cruel, she did unspeakable things, but...there was still that piece of me that was almost sad that I'd never make her proud. That I'd never be able to earn her love, the kind of love I yearned for before I had to convince myself it was useless. But still, I'd never have that chance. *Fucking pathetic.*

I grabbed my mother's robe and pulled it onto my body before grabbing her hand and slipping her ring off her finger and putting it in my pocket. A snap of a branch behind me had me whirling around to find Kaizer holding Zuri with a knife at her throat.

"I begged you," he said, his voice shaking. "I begged you not to go."

Zuri was crying as her chest heaved and she tried to fight to get away, but he was too strong.

I stepped forward. "You were in on this?"

He reinforced his hold on Zuri and lifted the knife closer to her throat, and I stopped my advancement.

"It was her idea. I tried to go back on it, but I couldn't," he said, using his teeth to pull back his sleeve and show another tattoo of my sigil on his skin. My mother must have had a cloak on it that I couldn't see, but now that she was dead before their agreement came to be, the usually iridescent ink turned black and permanent on his skin. "She came to me, said she was able to return Naom to this realm. I've been trying to return the Flame to the forest. If I did that Sanjry would be whole again, I would never be questioned. I wasn't expecting to fall in love with you."

LOVE? He actually thought he loved me. The thought itself was fucking ridiculous.

"When you found us in the office the other day, that's what we were arguing about. I told her I wouldn't do it, told her to let me out of the agreement, but she refused."

"Oh, how fucking nice of you," I said as I inched closer.

"I swear it, Daya. I didn't want to do this; she told me you were a sorry excuse for a witch, a terrible person, someone who deserved to die. In the middle of a war, I believed it. I'd heard of what you'd done to my army. Part of me wanted revenge for that. But you...you were nothing like she said. You were just alone in this world as I was." His voice cracked again, his throat bobbing. "Please, Daya. Please believe me, I want you. I still want to marry you."

I barked a laugh. "Let go of Zuri, and then we can talk."

"No, I know what she means to you. I know she's your only friend here. If you refuse me, I'll kill her."

"You think blackmail is the best start to a marriage?" I yelled.

"I'll do anything—if it means making you so alone that you need me, I'll do it. You'll forgive me. I know you will. You'll see that I'm doing this for us, for both of our kingdoms. One day you'll forgive me. One day, you'll love me the way I do you."

I looked over at Zuri and nodded once, hoping she would be able to read me like all the other times she knew what I was trying to tell her before I got the words out. The onyx would protect her for the first slice; it wouldn't break the barrier. She'd have a moment in his confusion where she'd be able to slip away.

"No. There's no world where I forgive this. You'll have to kill me to make go anywhere with you."

A sob escaped him as he plunged the blade into Zuri's neck. The onyx barrier held, and he looked down as he pulled his blade again to try to get it to cut her. His grip loosened, and she elbowed him in the groin and stepped onto the inside of his foot like I'd taught her in two quick moves. Kaizer doubled over as she ran to me, and I grabbed her quickly before shifting closer to him.

"That's my girl," I said to Zuri as I turned my predatory gaze back to Kaizer. "Now, we play."

Chapter Thirty-Nine

Kaizer trembled. "Please, Daya. I love you. We can have it all. We can have all of Malva soon, just stay with me. Don't do this."

"You don't love me, you fucking dumb ass. You love what we can do together, the power you'd control with me."

Fuck, that power was about to erupt from me without me even trying. It was bubbling up, about to pour over the edge, and I honestly didn't know how in control I was.

"Don't you want us to have it all? Don't you want to make everyone fall to their knees in our presence, knowing we could decimate them with a snap of our fingers?"

I smirked. "I can already do that."

I took a deep breath and let my Acna power loose. The pressure was building beneath my skin, until it burst from me so aggressively I stumbled a step. The robe I wore tore in two, the top half hanging loose over the tied string around my waist. *Fuck, I should have taken this off first.* Zuri gasped, and I looked over my shoulder to find a wing just like Naom's wrapped around her, protecting and shielding her. I flapped my left wing as I felt the air flow through the burning feathers adorning them.

"That's not possible," Kaizer muttered.

"Think again, bitch," I growled.

I pulled my wing from around Zuri, flicking my wrist and creating an air shield in front of her before charging Kaizer. My wings were still stretched wide, the position of them slowing me down as I ran. I pulled them in and my muscles groaned as they strained to listen to the new command of my body. Kaizer scrambled to grab his knife from the ground, but I wrapped a tendril of air around it, letting it float over to me and into my hand. I gathered some of my witch magic in my other hand, the power even more potent than before; I threw my hand out, sending a multicolored stream right into Kaizer's chest. It tossed him back a few yards into the trees as he was knocked out cold. I stalked toward him, and Zuri grabbed my wrist. I whirled to face her, too lost to the magic rushing in my veins to hear her.

"Daya! He has backup!" I finally heard her yelling as she pointed out into the trees.

Ember acolytes were walking toward us with balls of fire between their hands, illuminating their hooded faces in the dark of the forest.

"Of course, the fucking weirdos are part of this, too," I growled.

I readied more magic in my hand as I made to attack, but Zuri pointed to the other side of the clearing as more balls of fire popped up, surrounding us. They were...portaled here. There was a witch working with them. More than one, most likely, there had to be.

"There's too many," she muttered.

"I can take them," I responded as I called to the depths of my magic.

Zuri stepped in front of me. "Daya, there's too many. We need to go."

"Not for me," I snapped and handed her Kaizer's blade.

I extended both my arms to my side, my wings flaring out with the movement, and let a stream of my magic extend from each finger, taking out five of the acolytes on either side. More popped up behind them, and I readied my magic again, but Zuri grabbed my face with both of her hands and brought my gaze to hers.

"We need to go," she said calmly.

I looked around, now surrounded by hundreds of lights bobbing in the near black woods. Kaizer was knocked out by my blow, but he groaned and sat up slowly as he came back to consciousness.

"Please, Daya. Today is not the day we die," Zuri stated firmly.

I screamed another primal scream with my balls fisted at my side. The trees around us shook as power rolled off me, and the Embers stopped their slow-paced walk for a moment.

I snapped open a portal and heard Kaizer yell, "I'll come for you! There's no where you can hide from me anymore. You will be mine and we will rule it all!"

Grabbing Zuri, I jumped through it and snapped it closed behind me before any of the crazy fucking vampires followed.

"What the fuck!" I yelled as I slipped my arms into the sleeves of my torn robe. "There were other witches helping; the acolytes were portaled in. What the fuck was any of that?"

I threw my hands down, the ground around me erupting in witch magic as my body glowed bright again.

Zuri moved closer to me. "Daya...has anyone else had this power before?"

"No." I sighed. "Not that I know of."

"Are you...The Goddess of Air and Essence?"

"No, I don't think so. I just...I saw her when I died, she sent me back and gave me my Acna power."

"You saw her? What did she say?" Zuri gasped.

I nodded. "She didn't say much of anything that would be helpful, but I did. She was everything I would have thought she'd be."

It was still sort of unbelievable that I experienced that. It was hard to fully comprehend what she was, a being so powerful that she created the world, created my order. Even in the spirit world where she wasn't fully corporeal, I could feel her power, the root of the essence of our world.

Zuri pointed to a small pond nearby. "Look at yourself."

I portaled us to a forest within Caldera that sat on the coast the furthest away from Sanjry. The water here wasn't the sparkling silver liquid of the lake, but it was just as reflective as I bent down to stare into its surface. I gasped sharply, running my finger over the sparkling surface of my skin. My hair was burning with essence; it floated slightly around my shoulders, shifting like a flame as I moved closer. My eyes were lit purple, my wings peeking out above my shoulders, the multicolored feathers moving and shining the same as my hair. I didn't really get the chance to look at myself at first, but I looked just like Naom, minus my tattoos and face, I appeared identical to her.

"I don't know what this means," I muttered.

"Me either, but we need to get somewhere that Kaizer can't come for you."

I shook my head. "We'll be safe here. We're in Caldera."

"No, we won't. Technically Kaizer owns this land as much as his."

"Bullshit, this is *my* kingdom," I snapped.

"The treaty you signed with Dusra, you joined your land at that point. You were not the queen with that signature, but your lands were combined."

"Fuck," I whispered, "you're right, but the witches will have my back. We'll just go back into war. We've survived this long. We can keep surviving.

It wasn't ideal, but maybe if I could get a good handle on my powers it might be enough to win.

"Can you honestly say they will believe that your mother tried to kill you? There were witches helping her and Kaizer. There could be a plan in place for if they failed."

"*I'm* the Acna now. They will follow."

Zuri looked at me with her brow raised, pinning me down. "He will come for you, Daya. Probably with the power of his entire army. He thinks he's motivated by love, and that's more dangerous than his search for power."

"What other option do I have?" I yelled.

Not frustrated with her, but at the situation at hand. I hadn't had time to process, and my emotions were running the fucking gauntlet in my head.

"I don't know…" she said, trailing off and looking at the ground.

I sighed. "Dusra, we can go to Dusra."

"You think he was serious when he said you had a place within his kingdom?"

"I do." I sighed and looked up into the stars. "My people, I can't leave them."

"You won't do anything if Kaizer finds you and kills you. Dusra is the only place he physically can't go, thanks to that treaty."

"What about you?" I asked.

"We can deal with that when we get there," she replied, rubbing her hand to my cheek.

I felt my power relax with her touch, the burning magic inside of me waning and flickering out as my skin returned to its natural hue.

"He tried to hurt you," I growled.

"Well, thanks to you, he didn't. We will get him back for this. I'll do whatever I need to do to make sure that happens. But I need you alive, Daya."

"I've never been to Dusra. I can only portal us near the Inbetween. We'll have to travel by foot."

Zuri nodded and wrapped her fingers around mine. "Let's go."

I fucking hated the Inbetween.

I'd been here once before, and it was enough for me then. The land lacked magic, and that fact was evident everywhere you looked. Colors were muted here, and I couldn't feel any connection to any of my surroundings. You could never mistake the Inbetween for any of the other kingdoms. The moment you crossed the border you felt it. My magic recoiled under my skin, knowing that it was trapped inside of me while I was in this dastardly fucking place. Zuri felt it too, the moment we crossed into the land I saw her body jerk with the odd feel of this atmosphere.

I kept my head on a swivel; while the land lacked magic, it didn't lack danger. All creatures of Malva alike escaped here when they were on the run; some even chose to live here due to the lack of any law. The last time I was here was one of the few missions I had where I honestly almost ended up dead. I relied heavily on my magic then, and ever since, I made sure that I was as efficient with a blade as I was magic. I held Zuri's hand in a death grip, worried that someone or something would pop up around every corner. The monsters hadn't made an appearance when I was here, but I knew better than to think them a myth. I'd seen plenty of things in my years that others believed weren't real, and I wasn't going to let naivety be what killed me and Zuri.

"We need to be as quiet as possible. It'll take about a day and a half to walk through to Dusra's border from where we are. Let's try to push through without stopping, but if you need to sleep, let me know, and I'll stand watch while you rest."

She nodded.

"Okay. You stay with me the entire time we're here, don't go drifting off. Don't believe anything that calls to you, this land is evil, and it will try to kill you," I added.

"The *land* will try to kill us?"

"Do you know anything about the Inbetween?"

Zuri shook her head. "No, just that magic doesn't work here."

"The Inbetween is the one place in Malva even *I* wouldn't want to be. The lack of magic evens the playing field for whatever creatures crawl from its shadows. There's rumored to be monsters of nightmares lurking around every corner, and there are whole clans of people who live here to avoid any sort of law or royal."

"Fuck," she muttered, looking around her.

We tried to keep our steps as quiet as possible as we walked toward Dusra. The air was so stagnant here it was hard to take a deep breath without it feeling like an effort. There were noises in the distance, thankfully not in the direction we were walking, but I was still on high alert. I didn't have my typical plethora of weapons, just Kaizer's dagger, and without any magic, it would be the only thing between us and death until we made it to Dusra's border. Even then, I wasn't sure what would happen.

Axel was kind to me, but I didn't know how he would feel about me bringing a Sanjryan into his borders unannounced. Dusra hated Sanjry, so the odds were

50/50. I hoped he wouldn't toss her out on her ass, knowing she came with me, but it was a risk we had to take. We trekked up a rocky hill, and I stilled when I heard voices in the distance. I closed my eyes and could hear four heartbeats just on the other side. I grabbed Zuri and pulled her toward me as I motioned for us to go around.

She nodded and followed my movements, crouching low to the ground and avoiding the snap of any branches or loose rocks. All I had was the torn robe on, and it didn't make for very nimble movements, unfortunately. We rounded another hill, and I crawled on my belly to the top of it to peek over and see what was on the other side. Four people were sitting at the base of the hill we were climbing sharing some animals I didn't recognize from this distance. I couldn't tell if they were witches or vampires, but they were strapped to the teeth with weapons.

"Where there's a few, there's more. We need to be as careful as possible," I whispered.

Zuri nodded, her lip quivering slightly and her eyes wide.

"I won't let anything happen to you," I whispered as we slid back down the hill and continued in the direction of Dusra.

We walked for hours, not running into any more people who looked like they'd kill us without a second thought. My body felt heavy, and I tried to lift my foot over a rock and stumbled, shooting my hand down to use my air magic to balance myself out. I forgot for a moment we were in the fucking Inbetween, and my magic wouldn't save me. I fell to the ground as I barely broke my fall with the hand I had meant to use my magic. Zuri held onto me and tried to pull me up off the rocky terrain, but I could barely support myself.

She heaved me up with all of her strength. "Daya, you're exhausted. We can stop."

"I can't stop. We need to keep moving," I said, willing my feet to work.

"You used a shit ton of magic today, new, *very powerful* magic. Your body is going to need to get used to wielding it. You need to choose to rest now, or it's going to take away the option from you entirely."

I sighed and let my breath out of my mouth slowly as I looked around. There was nowhere particularly safe, but there was a hollowed-out tree a few yards in the distance.

"Just for a few minutes until I can defend you again," I muttered.

Zuri rolled her eyes but helped me over to the tree and set me down within the hollow before sitting beside me, closer to the entrance. I leaned my head back on the rough bark interior, and before I could make the decision, my body shut off.

Chapter Forty

I was being shaken, but the sleep that the magic demanded still had its grasp on me. I fought to open my eyes, sensing something was awry, slowly pulling myself out of consciousness. My eyes opened, and everything around me was blurred and slightly out of focus. I blinked a few times, Zuri's panicked face right in front of me, as she shook my shoulders as hard as she could.

"Wake up, Daya!" she exclaimed in hush tones.

She slapped me across my face, and the world suddenly became clear. She dragged me as far back as she could into the hollowed-out tree and stood over me with Kaizer's dagger in her hand.

"What's happening?" I whispered, rubbing the back of my eyes.

"Something or someone is out there; it has been for a few minutes now. I saw something pass the tree, but it looped back around," she mumbled.

I pulled her back and took the dagger from her hand as I shifted toward the tree's opening. I closed my eyes and listened. Something was definitely out there, but whatever it was didn't have a heartbeat. I could hear the creature moving in the grass, dried leaves crunching under them.

"It's not a person," I muttered.

"That doesn't make me feel better," Zuri said under her breath.

I smirked for the first time in the last twenty-four hours. My magic was pressing against my skin, a constant push and pull as it tried to escape me, but I still couldn't access it. I didn't know how anyone stayed here for any extended period.

Not being able to reach down into the pool inside of me was threatening to drive me mad in the few hours I'd been here.

The hairs on the back of my neck stood on end, my instincts still fully intact. I grabbed Zuri by her wrist and pulled her out of the tree with force as the top half of the tree was ripped off the base and tossed across the forest. I turned around to find one of the monsters of nightmares people said lived in the Inbetween. It stood on its back legs, nearly seven feet tall. It had no eyes, but its reptilian nose flared as it tried to scent where we'd gone. Its razor-sharp teeth were dripping with a liquid that sizzled against the ground with every drip that fell from its mouth. A fan-like membrane of skin was wrapped around the circumference of its neck, rattling and shifting as if it helped to enhance its hearing.

Zuri and I stood deathly still; the creature had four legs and was definitely going to be faster than we were. My chest heaved as I looked around for any sort of escape route, but the only thing I had was the dagger, and any small movement we made would alert the creature to our location. Its nostrils flared again as it climbed over the stump of the tree it had just demolished. The scales lining its body were thick, too thick to do any damage with the only weapon I had. Its forked tongue flickered as its collar flicked around until its face slowly turned to us, and while it had no eyes, I knew immediately it had found us.

I grabbed Zuri's wrist and pulled her with me as I ran in the opposite direction. I quickly bent down and grabbed a thick branch, tossing it away from us in hopes of throwing the beast off for at least a moment. It stumbled a step and shifted its face over to where I threw the branch as I looked behind us and continued pulling Zuri with me. It quickly snapped its neck back to us and trailed a few hundred yards behind.

"I fucking hate this place!" I yelled.

"What do we do?" Zuri screamed.

I was out of my element here with no magic, no weapon worth anything, and the only person I truly cared about by my side. The creature was gaining on us, and there was still nothing around but trees. It could snap us in half with its barbed tail like it did the tree if we didn't do something soon. We crested a hill, and I saw that the land was about to come to an end, a huge body of water just beyond the drop-off.

Zuri looked over her shoulder at me with wide eyes and sweat dripping down her brow. The water could have worse creatures; I didn't know if it was worth it to jump into its depths just to be swallowed whole. I stopped in my tracks and turned around as I decided to take the risk with the dagger.

"Stay here," I demanded of Zuri.

Without waiting to see if she listened, I ran away from her, leading the creature in the opposite direction. She screamed at me, but I didn't miss a step as I made it far enough away that I felt she was as safe as she could be. I turned around to face the creature with my dagger raised; it charged me, its jaws wide as it snapped at my legs. I jumped just as it reached me, stepping on its snout and onto its back. I let the dagger hang at my side and dragged it straight through the odd membrane that surrounded its neck.

The creature screeched, a sound so ancient and evil that every hair on my body stood, every instinct telling me that this wasn't a match I was going to win. I couldn't let it get Zuri. I *wouldn't* let it get Zuri. The animal bucked onto its back legs, and I held onto its neck, stabbing the dagger into its thick flesh. The blade didn't even draw blood and barely opened a wound between its scales, and I screamed as I continued stabbing. It made to fall onto its back to get me off, and I jumped to the side just as its body came crashing down to the ground.

Much like the horned vipers of the desert, its underside wasn't covered in the thick scales like the rest of it was. The only way that I was going to do any damage was going to be to aim for that. It righted itself back onto all four of its legs, its tail swiping back and forth behind it as it stalked toward me slowly. I yelled a battle cry as I charged forward, but dark movement to my right distracted me for just a moment. Its jaws snapped toward me, nearly taking off my arm before its entire head fell to the ground, severed. I whirled around, wondering what creature was about to kill me if it was able to kill this one so easily, but found a person covered head to toe in black, holding a huge obsidian sword.

"Come with me," they demanded.

Zuri was already running in this direction, and she made it to my side in a few moments.

"I told you to stay there," I snapped.

"And watch you die?" she bit back.

"Do you two *both* want to die? Because that's what will happen if we stay here, we're in their freaking nest," the person who saved me bit out.

We both nodded and followed them, winding around trees and rocks until we made it to one of the hills we had crossed earlier in the day. The person shifted a bush to the side to expose a wooden door that was carved right into the side of the hill. They opened the door and directed us in; Zuri and I had no better options, so we dove inside the dark space. The person attached the bush to the door and slammed it shut behind them. A flame flickered in the corner before it roared to life within a stone fireplace, illuminating the rest of the space. It was a small home somehow dug right into the hill. We stood in a living room with a small kitchen off to the side, a hallway leading to more rooms on the side opposite the kitchen. It was...cozy.

"Where's the smoke go?" I asked, pointing my lips to the fireplace.

The person pulled down their hood and removed the scarf from their face sending dark hair cascading from their head as it fell around their shoulders. They turned around to expose feminine features that looked so familiar to me that I put my hand on my blade. I couldn't place it right away, but I knew this woman.

"I have a tunnel system that forces the smoke far away from here so nothing comes looking," she replied.

She pulled her hair back into a low ponytail and removed the cloak she wore, exposing her wide shoulders and tattooed-riddled skin.

"Tirsa," I gasped.

I took the hood of the robe off my head, exposing my purple hair and pushing Zuri further behind me.

"Dayanara," she exclaimed, her eyes going wide.

"What the fuck are you doing in the Inbetween? I thought you were dead?"

Tirsa was one of my mother's right-hand brujas almost a century ago, and my mother said she died in one of the battles against Sanjry when I was still fairly young.

"Alive and not fucking well," she retorted.

She dropped down into one of the chairs, and I shifted myself to face her, keeping Zuri behind me.

"Why are you here?" I demanded.

"Ask your mother," she snapped.

"My mother is dead," I said flatly.

Tirsa shifted forward, placing her elbows on her knees as she studied me, looking me from head to toe predatorily. "Bull-fucking-shit."

I pulled my mother's ring out of my pocket, the only thing I took from her deceased body, and threw it over to Tirsa. "I killed her a few hours ago."

"*You* killed *her?*" she asked.

"Am I the only person in Caldera who didn't know she'd been plotting to kill me my whole life?"

Tirsa sat back with a deep breath. "Fuck."

"Fucking explain," I snapped.

Tirsa looked up at me defiantly, but I held her gaze, the years of being around my mother helping me perfect the scowl that had witches doing whatever it was she asked.

"You should sit down. Are you hungry?" Tirsa asked.

"No, and no," I responded.

"Okay." Tirsa blew air between her lips and sat back. "There was a seer who had a vision that foretold a way to bring Naom back."

I nodded. "My mother mentioned me needing to die for that to happen right before I killed her."

"I was there when the seer showed her the vision, she didn't tell us immediately what she saw, she just said there would have to be a great sacrifice," Tirsa responded.

Zuri flinched beside me and I leaned against her slightly. "Me?"

"We found out later, yes. She didn't tell anyone for years what the sacrifice was; part of me thinks she was debating how she could change the outcome."

"Doubtful. When did the seer bring her the vision?"

"The seer tried to get away, your mother had to hunt her down and threaten torture to get her to reveal it." Tirsa bit her lip. "You were about ten, I believe."

"That's when she started pulling away," I whispered.

I could never pinpoint when the change happened, but she slowly started to get colder and colder toward me until she reached the point she dealt my first real punishment.

Tirsa nodded. "She had to keep her distance from you, so she started training you and sending you away. She turned you into a weapon and made sure that Caldera got its use from you before you died for her."

"That's so far beyond fucked up," Zuri snapped.

"It is, that's why I'm here. I didn't agree with it, I thought there had to be another way to win the war. I told her that we should be doing everything in our power to protect you from that, but she was too focused on bringing back Naom. She didn't think..." She hesitated. "She didn't think that one life should outweigh the kingdom. Once I let my true feelings about it show, she banished me here to ensure I didn't interfere with the plan."

The vision she saw wasn't accurate, she must have saw my Acna power and thought I was Naom herself. It was all for nothing, a century of pain, torture, and loneliness due to her misinterpreting what the seer showed her. Not to mention the fact that now Sanjry had Caldera because of it, and I was on the run. I wanted to fucking kill her all over again. I needed to get out of this stupid magicless land.

"Well, thanks for this history lesson and for voting not to kill me," I said, standing to my feet. "We should really get going."

"You can't leave now. It's feeding hour. Those creatures and worse will be out and ready to turn you into their dinner."

I shook my head. "Just give us weapons. We will be fine."

"You really won't. Look, Daya. I know it's hard to hear, I wish I could have done more for you, I really do."

"My kingdom is gone, I need to get it back. I can't do that from here."

Zuri stood beside me and rubbed my hand, most likely trying to calm me down. I homed in on the feel of her skin touching mine, allowing the small contact to keep my rage at a reasonable level.

Tirsa raised a brow. "I'm telling you, if you go out there, you *will* die. Do you really want to survive your mother just to go and die in an attack?"

I bit the inside of my cheek and looked around without answering.

"I may have been banished, but I still respect you as Acna. I will protect you as best I can. I won't allow any harm to come to you while you stay with me. I swear it," Tirsa added.

My hands balled into fists at my side as I stared down at her, but she knew this land better than I did, and I really didn't want to put Zuri in harm's way if it wasn't necessary.

"Fine, we'll leave first thing in the morning. If you could still supply us with weapons so I can protect Zuri while we're out there, consider your debt paid."

Tirsa looked from Zuri to me, Zuri's proximity clearly showing we were probably a little more than best friends.

She nodded and walked over to the kitchen. "I have some bread and stew if you are hungry, you can have the last room on the right."

I grabbed the dagger from where I had it resting on the couch beside me and then Zuri's hand, dragging her to the room and closing the door behind me.

Chapter Forty-One

I paced the room, trying to digest the fact that my mother had been planning to kill me for more than a century. She hadn't been the warm-doting mother I had as a child for a long time. I had never thought her to be a saint, but fuck, I didn't think she had *this* in her.

"Daya," Zuri muttered.

The word barely registered as I continued pacing, and Zuri moved directly in front of me, grabbing my face the way she had done before.

"Breathe," she whispered.

I released a jagged breath. "I remember the day she switched, now that Tirsa mentioned it. We had plans to go on a trip to the silver lake that I took you to. She backed out, and after that, she never was the same again. She turned from my mother into my trainer. She didn't care about me, just what I could do for her before she got her final use from me."

I needed to kill something. I needed to slash my blade through *something* and feel the adrenaline that came with it, anything but what I was feeling. Maybe leaving now wasn't a terrible idea.

"She made a horrendous decision, and she died for it, Daya. By your hand, you did that," Zuri muttered.

"It wasn't enough," I sighed, falling back onto the floor.

Zuri lay next to me, put her head on my chest, and threw her arm across my waist. "At least you don't have to marry Kaizer," she joked.

A small smile pulled at my lips, and I looked down at her as I ran my hands through her thick curls.

"I'll take that win," I responded.

"We'll do what we have to do. No matter what happens, Daya, know that I'm choosing you. I'm choosing to stay beside you as long as you'll let me," she responded, squeezing me tight.

"We'll be fine." I sighed.

"Stew is done!" Tirsa yelled from the other side of the door.

I sat up and pulled at the tattered robe I still wore before I cracked the door open and stuck my head out. "You have anything I can wear?" I yelled.

Tirsa came down the hall with a bowl of stew in her hands, chewing the mouthful she had before responding. "Some of the stuff I brought with me should fit you before I bulked up this much," she said before walking into the first room in the hall.

She came back out with some folded clothes in her arms. "This is the closest thing to your size I'll have. Brought some for Zuri too. Everything else will be huge; not a lot to do here but train," she finished with a flex of the muscles in her arms.

"Thanks," I said as I slipped back inside the room.

Fuck yes, witch leathers. I pulled on the leathers and camisole. They were a little big in the arms, but they fit a lot better than what I was wearing previously, so I was grateful. Zuri and I walked back out into the living room, where two steaming bowls of stew sat on the low table in front of the couch we were sitting at originally. It smelled divine, and I grabbed the bowl as I sat, scooping the first chunk of meat I saw into my mouth.

"Where do you get the meat?" Zuri asked as she shifted through the ingredients with her spoon.

"Don't ask questions you don't want the answers to," Tirsa responded.

I shrugged. "Tastes good to me."

Zuri spooned some into her mouth and went back for more, so I supposed it was good enough for her.

"So...what's happened in the last century?" Tirsa asked.

"My mother shipped me off to marry the King of Sanjry. That was part of her plan on how to kill me. They were in on it together. So now Caldera belongs to him, and I have to find a way to get it back."

"You're going to Dusra?" Tirsa asked, her brows raised.

I looked up at her, not answering, and continuing to eat the stew.

Tirsa's head bobbed between me and Zuri through narrowed eyes. "What's the deal with you two?"

"Would you have asked my mother any of these questions, Tirsa?" I asked.

"I don't get a lot of company here. My social skills may be lacking," she responded as she scratched be back of her head.

"Understatement," Zuri muttered under her breath.

"Well, I'll leave you two to it. There's a washroom at the end of the hall. Just don't use too much water back-to-back, or it won't drain properly. I'll be in my room if you need me," Tirsa stated.

She stood up and placed her bowl on the counter before going over to her room and shutting the door behind her.

I let out a breath and sat back on the couch. "I feel like I could sleep for three days," I murmured.

"You didn't sleep very long before the attack. I'm sure you need more."

I nodded and slurped the last bit of my broth up. "Well, I'm done eating."

"Me too," Zuri said as she stood with me, and we put our bowls next to Tirsa's.

We walked down the hallway to the room Tirsa gave us for the evening. The bed looked incredibly inviting, but I was still covered in dried blood and dirt from the events of the day.

"I need to bathe," I said as I inspected the clumps of dirty hair that lay on my chest.

"Me too," Zuri admitted.

"Well, she said not to use too much water back-to-back. Might as well do it together," I said.

A smile stretched across Zuri's face. "We're only following directions," she added.

"Our specialty," I winked.

I laughed and opened the door to our room, stepping out and heading toward the bathing room with Zuri on my heels. When I turned the knob to the door and pushed, a room far bigger than I expected came into view.

"Wow," Zuri muttered.

The room definitely didn't look like it belonged in this house. Dark tile lined the floor that sat at a slight slant, and troves dug out at the base that seemed as if they would act as drains. A toilet, bench, and sink were on the wall to the left, but I didn't see a bathtub anywhere. Zuri walked over to the wall on the right and turned a silver knob that stuck out in the middle of it. Water cascaded from the ceiling, and she jumped back.

"Fuck that's cold," she yelped.

The water continued pouring as steam twisted between the streams; Tirsa had branches of eucalyptus tied to the mechanism, and the room started to relax me almost instantly. Zuri came over to where I stood away from the water and faced me, tugging at the leathers I had just acquired. She undid the buckles across my chest and pulled the hem over my head as I unclamped her pants and pulled them off her slender hips. Zuri stepped out of her pants, and I slid mine off quickly before tossing them into the pile near the sink so they'd stay dry.

I turned around and found Zuri completely naked, her tawny skin already glossy from the moisture in the room. She hooked her finger in the air, beckoning me to join her as she took careful steps back into the water. I could barely breathe as I trailed my gaze down her body. Her small perky breasts, the slight curve of her hips, and fuck, her pussy felt like it called to me, and before I knew it, I had my hands on her, pulling her close to my naked body. The water poured over our heads as our lips crashed together, our hands sliding over every inch of exposed skin.

I pushed my tongue into her mouth, meeting hers as she swept hers into mine. I nipped at her bottom lip before she pulled herself away and grabbed a bar of soap off a wired shelf on the wall.

"Let's get that blood off you," she said, smiling.

She ran the soap over my body, every touch feeling more and more sexual as she got the last bit of blood from my legs. She pulled her fingers through my hair, working out the knots and breaking the clumps of grime until they were back to their shiny purple luster. Zuri put the bar of soap down and ran her bare hands over my body, working with the streams of water to get rid of the suds. She stood face-to-face with me as she pulled me in and pressed her lips to my neck. Sucking slightly and running her canine over the spot before she dipped her head lower and ran the pad of her tongue around my nipple.

She didn't linger there like she did last time but pushed me against the wall as she descended my stomach until she was crouched on the floor beneath me, her face hovering right between my legs. Zuri looked up at me through hooded eyes, water running down her back as she smirked once, sticking her tongue out of her mouth and sliding it right up my pussy. She moaned and grabbed my leg to put it over her shoulder for better access before going back for more. I knew I was already soaked for her; from the moment I saw her naked body, I had been ready.

I'd been ready for weeks, but neither of us had crossed that line until now, and fuck me if I was ever going back because her mouth was something I didn't think I could live without. Zuri licked around my clit before closing her mouth around it and sucking; my knees threatened to give out at the feel of it alone. She moaned again, the sound was the most perfect fucking thing I'd ever heard in my life. I felt her fingers running up the thigh that wasn't resting on her shoulder, trailing higher and higher until she pushed them right into me.

I pressed my hand to my mouth as I screamed, biting down on the base of my thumb so hard I had to be drawing blood. She pushed and pulled her fingers so fast that another scream climbed up my throat. But with the last push, she held there with force, creating pressure and hooking her fingers inside while she ran her other thumb in smooth circles around my clit. Her tongue danced between the two points of contact, and I couldn't hold on any longer. The sound that escaped me might have been a moan, might have been a scream, but I couldn't hear it as all of my senses reared to a max.

She licked the inside of my thighs, unhooking my leg from her shoulder, and ran her tongue straight up my body until she reached my neck again. My legs were shaking from the orgasm, but I pulled myself together and grabbed her chin to pull it to my face. I captured her mouth with mine, the taste of her and me mixing together between us before I kissed up her jawline and over to her ear.

Bringing my lips right to her earlobe, I whispered, "Your turn."

The water was starting to pool at the drain, so I turned the knob to stop the water from pouring in. I watched her throat bob as I turned us around and pushed her up against the wall. The sound of our wet flesh smacking together rang between us as she pulled us down to the ground with her back to the wall. I straddled her hips with my thick thighs, and Zuri ran her fingers up my legs, squeezing my ass and pulling me closer to her. I dragged my hips against hers, the friction already almost too much due to how sensitive I already was from my orgasm. Zuri tried to bring her hand up to rub my clit, ever the giver, but I smacked her hand away and pulled back, standing up and bringing her with me.

I picked her up by her ass and wrapped her legs around me. I could feel how wet she already was as I walked us over to the sink and set her on the edge. Dropping to my knees, I spread her legs open, her pussy gleaming, and fuck, it was beautiful. I kissed up her thighs, running my thumb up through her wetness and rubbing her clit. Zuri's grip on the sides of the sink tightened, and her back arched, forcing her pussy closer to my face. I pushed my tongue into her, the taste of her sending my eyes rolling back and a moan reverberating from my throat. Pushing and pulling my tongue, I continued rubbing my fingers, pulling back and using my tongue instead to lick up to her clit. I took it between my lips, sucking as I pushed two fingers into her. I nipped at her lips, tugging at them slightly as her body already started to clench around my fingers.

I pulled them out, running them up and down at a tortuously slow pace as she clamped her thighs around my head in frustration. Laughing darkly, I spread her legs again, pushing my fingers back inside and pumping so fast that Zuri screamed. I looked up at her to find her squeezing her own breast, biting her lip with her eyes closed, and fuck if it didn't have me about to come again myself. I feasted, not letting up even when she clamped down again on my fingers or when the rush of wetness escaped her and she tried to pull back to reach for me instead. Zuri's hand wrapped around my hair, giving up on stopping me as I continued running my tongue around her clit until I was satisfied with the amount of pleasure I forced out of her.

I stood up, and she wrapped her legs around my waist to pull me close to her, crashing her mouth into mine. I slid my hands under her ass again and sat on the bench between the sink and the toilet. She straddled me, immediately moving her hand to my pussy as I did the same to her. I took her nipple into my mouth and bit down on it as I moved inside of her, trying to focus as she rubbed over my clit again.

Zuri dragged her hips against my hand, and I met every push with a pump of my fingers. She threw her head back and closed her eyes. She was absolute perfection. Her wet curls bounced around her shoulders as she moved, her fingers still inside me. Zuri opened her eyes again and bit her lip as she looked into my eyes. My mouth hung open as the intimacy, the feel of us connecting on a level that surpassed what we'd done, on a level I didn't fully comprehend. She moaned a sound I wanted to hear a thousand more times, forcing one from me as well.

She was starting to tighten around my fingers again, and I felt myself close to orgasm as well. We both continued pumping our fingers at the same rate, the both of us finishing one last time together, staring into each other's eyes as we screamed and our chests heaved. I grabbed her face and pulled her into another rough, bruising kiss, but our rushed passionate kisses turned slower, sweeter. We took our time, running our hands through each other's wet hair. I pulled back, smiling at the fucking perfection that was Zuri. Her hair was already starting to curl back up, her lips were full, her cheeks flushed, her dark eyes sparkling as she studied my face.

She licked her lips and sighed. "That was unbelievable."

Her chest was still heaving, mine moving at the same pace as I ran my hands up her back.

"I think we need to do that like five more times," I said as I pulled her flush to my body again.

"You need to rest if we're going to make it to Dusra," Zuri reasoned.

"Psh, I'll rest when I'm dead," I retorted.

Zuri rolled her eyes and pulled her body off me, grabbed two towels, wrapped one around her body, and handed the other one to me. She opened the door and looked back in expectation of me following; I sighed and trailed behind her back into our bedroom. We didn't have nightclothes, so we slept naked. The urge to taste her again was almost too much for me to handle, but Zuri turned me around and rubbed her fingers through my hair. Something in her scent blossomed. It felt stronger, but before I could think too much about it, sleep took me.

Chapter Forty-Two

Tirsa was making a hell of a lot of noise out in the kitchen, clearly not used to having sleeping guests. My internal clock told me it was about time to wake up anyways. The lack of windows made it pitch black in the room outside of a sliver of light from under the door, so it was hard to know for sure. Zuri's head lay on my chest, her curls mixing with my hair on my shoulder. She was still sleeping, and I didn't want to wake her until she absolutely needed to be up. It was nice being able to sleep together and not worry about anyone finding us. One of the few upsides of everything that had happened.

I shimmied from under her, catching her head with my pillow before she fell to the mattress. She shifted slightly, but I pressed a gentle kiss to her lips and stopped her movement. Running my hands down the bed I tried to find where we threw our clothes before going to sleep. The leathers were in a pile on the floor by the foot of the bed, and I slid them on quickly, buckling and clasping them closed before I quietly opened the door and closed it behind me gently. Tirsa was in the kitchen, as I suspected, with pots and pans all over the counters. She was crouched down and looking inside one of the cabinets, and I cleared my throat.

"Good morning," I muttered.

She jumped straight up and looked over at me. "Acna."

I recoiled slightly at the title. I hadn't had a chance to hear anyone call me that yet, and after it belonged to my mother for so long, my feelings were mixed about it.

"Just call me Dayanara," I responded. "Are you looking for something?"

She sighed. "Yes, I was going to make a Calderan breakfast, but I can't find the pan I needed."

"We're fine with whatever you have," I replied as I ran my finger down the stone counter.

"Zuri still sleeping?"

I nodded. "Yeah, we had a long day yesterday. I won't force her up quite yet."

Tirsa looked at me the same way she had before when she was inquiring about me and Zuri, and I rolled my eyes.

"Why are you so interested in what we are?" I asked.

"You know how our people are. We don't do the whole commitment thing often, but you two...you can feel your connection, like your very souls are one. It's curious."

I shrugged. "I don't know about all of that."

"Seems like it has probably been going on longer than your *break up* yesterday," Tirsa responded.

"She was my handmaiden. We've had a friendship for a while now."

"Hm," Tirsa said, crossing her arms and looking at me.

"Really not your business," I snapped.

Looking back at it, I wasn't one hundred percent sure if I was in the wrong for my feelings for Zuri. I felt a hell of a lot better now that I knew Kaizer was plotting to kill me, but still, hashing out the specifics of me and Zuri's relationship wasn't something I wanted to do. Not to mention—even if I was in the wrong—I didn't really care.

Tirsa threw her hands up in the air. "Didn't mean to pry."

"Do you really not have any company here?"

"There are a few witches who were banished or chose to live here, but no, we don't get together and have Inbetween parties or anything."

"Sounds miserable," I muttered.

"It's been my reality for a hundred years, doesn't really bother me much anymore."

I walked over to the couch and sat down. A shimmer from the fireplace caught my attention, and I followed it over to a pile of weapons.

"Those for us?" I asked.

"Yeah, you can take your pick. You should leave in the next half hour to get there before nightfall, or you will have to deal with the feeding hour again."

I nodded. "Okay, I'll go wake up Zuri."

I walked down the hallway and eyed the smooth walls that Tirsa had created as I ran a hand down them. If I didn't know that I was underground, I might not have ever known. She'd been here for a while, and it seemed like she had a lot of time to make it home. I made it to the room we were using and put my ear to the door to listen to how slow her heartbeat still was.

Turning the knob carefully, I tried not to scare her awake and pushed into the room. I lit the lamp by the door and tiptoed over to the bed before pulling the blanket off her gently. Her nipples pebbled from the cold air, and I smirked, placing my knees on the bed and crawling over to her. I straddled her body, kissing her neck gently, but she didn't stir. I ran my tongue up her neck, and she shifted slightly.

"Wake up. We have to go soon," I whispered.

She nodded, and I started crawling off her body, but she grabbed me and pulled me close. I had already descended a few inches, so the movement lined my face right up with her breasts. I smiled devilishly as I stuck my tongue out, flicking her nipple with the tip of it. Zuri released a breathy moan and shifted to get her nipple closer to my face.

"Won't find me saying no to that," I mumbled.

I wiggled, making her lose her grip as I got back onto all fours. I squeezed her nipple between my teeth enough to sting before I wrapped my lips around it and sucked the small hurt away. Taking her other nipple between my fingers, I rolled it before kissing over to it and making sure they both got equal treatment.

"I fucking love these," I said as I squeezed both of her breasts and sat my body on her hips.

"They're small," Zuri laughed.

"They're perfect," I responded as I ground my hips on hers.

"Why are your clothes on?" she asked, her voice graveled with sleep.

I sighed. "We need to leave soon. I was just coming to wake you up."

Zuri shifted her hips and flipped us over, putting me on my back. The glow of the lamp fell softly over her naked body, and I was wondering if maybe leaving a few minutes later would really damn us. Zuri brought her lips down to my ear, rubbing her soft cheek against mine.

"Pity," she whispered.

"Pity indeed," I sighed.

Zuri crawled off my body and stood. I sat up and made the bed, looking back over at Zuri to find her fully dressed when I was done. The leathers were significantly bigger on her, and I had to stop myself from laughing at the image. I walked over and helped her tighten all the buckles. The ones around the waist and hips pulled as far as they could go.

"As long as they stay on," Zuri laughed.

We walked back out into the living room to find a few bowls of some sort of porridge ready for us on the counter.

"Thank you," Zuri said warmly.

"No problem, you all should eat that pretty quickly and then choose some weapons. I can take you to the border of my zone, but then you guys will be on your own."

"Zone?" I asked.

"It's how it works here. We stay in our zones to avoid any unnecessary fighting. The Inbetween is broken into about eleven zones. You made it through about three yesterday, so now you just have to cross five more. The others aren't on the way to Dusra's border."

"Anything we should know?"

"Just don't linger anywhere for too long. Keep moving and keep your head on a swivel. There are other witches who might choose to help you, but some of them might take the opportunity of you not having access to your magic to get their revenge on your mother."

I spooned some of the porridge into my mouth. It was bland, but it would give us enough energy for the day's trip. "Okay, that was pretty much my plan anyway."

Zuri finished her bowl before me and walked over to the weapons. She shifted through the blades, lifting up a black short sword that glimmered in the light.

"I like this one," she whispered.

"Grab a knife too," I said as I scooped the last bit of porridge into my mouth and joined her. "We'll strap it to your ankle, just in case."

She grabbed a small silver knife with a red hilt and then threw it from one hand to the other smoothly, and I smiled at my little soon-to-be warrior.

"I'll take these," I said, looking over at Tirsa.

I chose three blades, one great sword, one dagger, and one small knife. Really as much as I could carry on my body and still be nimble.

"Good choices," Tirsa replied.

"Here are a few snacks, just some dried meat, and nuts for your journey," Tirsa said as she opened the door for us.

We walked through the doorway, the muted colors of the Inbetween taking my eyes a few seconds to adjust to. Feeding hour was over, but the land was riddled with blood, chunks of smaller creatures lying around sporadically.

"Damn, you really saved us more than we knew," Zuri muttered.

"Let's make sure we're not still here for this tonight," I replied.

Tirsa led the way, back in the direction we were heading before she found us. None of us said anything as we all continued looking around, making sure nothing was coming for us on all sides.

I saw a line of small white flags tied to the trees ahead, and Tirsa stopped a few yards away from them.

"This is the end of my zone. Good luck," Tirsa exclaimed as she took a step back.

"Thank you for your hospitality," Zuri told Tirsa with a warm smile.

"Yes, and thank you for your honesty," I added.

Tirsa nodded once, looking away from my gaze quickly, like there was something else she wanted to say.

"Your debt is paid. Should you ever want to return to Caldera once I take it back, you may," I stated.

Tears lined Tirsa's eyes before she turned immediately and headed back to her home without another word. Zuri and I moved back in the direction we were heading, crossing the trees marking the beginning of the next zone. I looked around to see if there would be an unwelcoming committee, but the space was as quiet and empty as it was before.

We trekked over the terrain, some rocky, some grassy, and one zone seemed to be solely sand. We still hadn't seen any other living creatures, and I was pretty sure we were only one more zone to cross through as the light in the sky dimmed. Zuri and I had been near silent the whole time, only whispering occasionally when necessary.

"We should be almost there, right?" Zuri asked.

"Yeah, we should be," I responded.

I felt something and grabbed Zuri by her wrist to stop her movement. She reached for her weapon as I did mine, looking around.

"Where is it?" she whispered.

"I don't know. I can just feel something nearby. Just keep your weapon in your hand and try to stay quiet."

Zuri nodded and followed my directions as she stayed close to me. We were back in a forest, and the leaves in front of me rattled slightly, but there was no wind blowing through the trees. I stopped and directed us to move in the other direction, but whatever was stalking us saw and leaped from a hole in the ground that was covered in leaves and branches. We picked up speed immediately, and I looked back as the leaves settled, and a man chased us with a black sword in his hand.

"Keep going," I yelled to Zuri as they gained on us.

I turned to face the assailant, taking a deep breath and keeping in mind this would just be a battle of steel, and no magic. The man didn't let up and continued charging me until his sword hit mine, and he pushed me back a couple of steps. I growled as I pressed back and stopped him from getting any closer. Our blades groaned where they met until I tipped the end of my blade, and his went cascading off mine.

I went on the immediate offense and swung my blade, slashing it across my body and into his side. He screamed, but it didn't stop him as he elbowed me in the side, and I took a step back. I locked my blade with his again and turned us around so I could make sure Zuri was okay. I found her a few hundred yards away, waiting for me. Another figure was charging her from the side, and panic filled my entire body.

"Zuri! Your left!" I yelled.

She whirled around just in time to meet their blade, and I let out a battle cry, needing to get to her. I let up slightly, letting him press into my blade with all his force as I quickly retreated my sword and spun around him with it at my side. The sword cut through the wound I'd given him previously, but significantly deeper, and he fell to the ground face first. I pushed my blade through his back and into his heart, ensuring he was dead and wouldn't chase me.

With the bloodied sword in my hand, I ran toward Zuri, where she was locked in battle with a woman a few inches taller than her. She had a small cut on her arm, but she was holding her own, and I was damn proud. Zuri was facing in my direction, so the other person couldn't see me as I ran toward them. She smirked at me while she slashed her blade for the woman's shoulder, the sound of blade crushing bone meeting me as I made it to them. The woman fell to the ground, and Zuri looked up at me triumphantly. She groaned, not quite dead yet, as she rolled over onto her back. I kicked her sword from her hand and pinned one arm down with my blade in her wrist, digging my boot into her other wrist to keep her immobilized.

"You need to aim for her heart to kill her," I started, pointing to the spot inside her left rib cage. "Here. It takes more force than you'd think. Don't hold back and push through until you feel the bone crack on both sides."

The woman screamed for help, and I kicked her in her head to knock her out so she wouldn't alarm anyone else. Zuri's throat bobbed, but she nodded, the fact that this might not be the last time she'll have to do this shifting between us. She lined the tip of her blade up with the woman's heart and pushed through in one swift move, the sound of bone crunching I told her to listen for evident.

"Good girl," I said with a smirk.

She smiled widely. "I'm not sure if I should be so excited for your praise for this, but here we are," she laughed.

I shrugged. "What can I say? I like my women a little murderous."

"Apparently, I like my woman murderous too, so no judgment here," she responded.

Sheathing my sword across my back, I surveyed the area, ensuring no more threats were nearby. I grabbed Zuri's hand and held it as we weaved between trees quicker than we were before. We pushed through some thicker shrubbery, having to cut some down to clear a wide enough path for us to walk through.

I dove through first, tossing my hand back for her to grab so I could lead her out. We both stood and stopped in our tracks. There was one last row of white flags, and just beyond the land was the brightest green I'd ever seen. A vast river separated the Inbetween from the land, a large stone bridge floating over it. And on the other side sat Dusra.

Zuri was shifting on her feet as we took in the land of Dusra ahead of us, and I squeezed her hand, reminding her I was with her. I could see the guards standing on the far side of the bridge next to two watchtowers on either side.

"I'll stay here. You can come back when you know if they'll take me," Zuri whispered.

"We're still in the Inbetween. I'm not leaving you. If they don't let you through, you can stay at the tower until I talk to Axel," I responded.

Zuri's steps were heavy as we made it to the bridge, and the guards spotted us and formed a line on their side with their weapons raised. I felt my magic return as I took the first step onto the bridge and sighed with relief as the pressure that was building under my skin finally waned a bit. I could feel the magical barrier just behind them. It was such pure energy, I wasn't sure how they kept it up all the time.

"State your business," a male guard bellowed.

"I'm Dayanara Amapola, and this is Zuri..." I looked over, realizing I didn't know what her last name was.

"Furaha," she mumbled.

"And Zuri Furaha. Ax—" I cleared my throat. "King Axel advised that I could come to Dusra without an issue. I'd like to see if he'd allow her in as well."

The guards motioned for us to meet him where they stood. The magic of the barrier had all the hairs on my body standing on end as we came to stand right before it. It wasn't necessarily visible, but every few seconds, you could see static sparking somewhere in the air. He looked over his shoulder, nodding toward the barrier. "If you're telling the truth, it will let you in."

"I need to know if Zuri can come with me. Can you notify King Axel that I need to speak with him?"

He surveyed Zuri. "It'll let her in."

"Why are you so sure?" I asked.

"She's Dusran."

I laughed. "She's from Sanjry. She was my handmaiden. Just notify Axel."

"I'm not going to waste his time when she can get through just fine," the guard snapped.

Zuri stood behind me, not speaking, and I looked over my shoulder at her to find tears brimming her eyes and sweat sparkling on her forehead.

"He's mistaken, isn't he?" I asked.

Zuri's throat bobbed, and she bit her lip as she looked out past me and into Dusra. She sidestepped me as she avoided making eye contact and moved closer to the end of the bridge.

"Zuri," I muttered.

She still didn't look back over me, but she stepped into Dusra and the barrier sparkled around her body as she walked through unharmed.

"Feet, what do I need you for when I have wings to fly?"
– Frida Kahlo

Chapter Forty-Three

My mouth hung open as the guard looked over at me. The sudden realization that I'd never seen Zuri use magic, even when fighting, hit me.

"Told you. Go on, I'll let the king know he has guests coming to the castle," the guard barked.

My body felt numb as I looked at the woman who had become my friend, taken my heart, and tricked me into trusting her with my whole being. It was all a lie. It had to be. She lied to me from the very moment we met and continued lying until this moment when she was forced to tell the truth. I walked through the barrier, and it let me through, just like Ax said it would. I didn't look at Zuri but stormed past her with my magic seeping from my fingers. It really wasn't a good time to have such strong emotions. I had so much pent-up magic I felt like I could explode and flatten everything in a mile radius in a blink of an eye.

"Daya," she exclaimed.

I could hear her footsteps coming closer, but I didn't turn in her direction. Instead, I turned toward one of the guards. "How do I get to the castle?"

He pointed toward the door of the tower on the left. "Just walk through that door. It'll take you right to the castle."

"How?" I asked.

The guard shrugged. "Some kind of magic, I don't know."

"A portal is witch magic," I responded.

The guard shrugged again and returned to his post, looking out into the Inbetween and ignoring my questions.

"Daya, can you wait a second, please," Zuri said as she tried to grab my hand.

I yanked it away from her and walked over to the door to pull it open and found a swirling pattern of magic I didn't recognize. I dipped my finger into it. It was definitely witch magic, but I didn't recognize what clan it could be. I didn't think Axel would invite me here just to kill me, and I needed to put some space between me and Zuri, so I stepped through. My boots met the hard stone floor as what I assumed was Axel's castle stretched out before me.

Everything in the castle seemed to be black—the floor, the walls, the ceiling. But where Kaizer's castle was dark and closed off, Axel's was bright with outside light pouring in from large windows and skylights. I looked to my right to find none other than the king leaning against the wall with his arms crossed, looking just as fucking beautiful as before.

"I—I didn't have anywhere else to go," I mumbled.

He was dressed head to toe in black, his pants and shirt tailored perfectly to his muscular body. His dark curly hair shined in the light, while his hazel eyes practically glowed as they looked me up and down. His smile stretched wide, his fangs on display as he pushed off the wall and walked toward me.

"Hello, forceful," he muttered.

Zuri stepped through the portal. Her footsteps hurried while she tracked me to where I stood before Axel.

"Interesting," Axel said, rubbing his chin.

"Daya, can we please just talk before we get into all of this?" she begged.

"So she knows who you are?" Axel asked Zuri.

"*You* knew who she was?" I spat.

Zuri looked to Axel as tears ran down her frustratingly beautiful face. They looked to be having some sort of wordless conversation, and she nodded once before Axel turned to me.

"She's one of my spies," he said flatly.

"You were fucking spying on me this whole time?" I yelled.

"No, Daya, I wasn't. I was there to monitor Kaizer, but we weren't expecting what happened with the two of you. I wasn't expecting for us to…" she trailed off and looked at Axel.

Axel's eyebrows raised, and he crossed his arms, looking down on the both of us. "That wasn't in any of your reports."

"I know," Zuri sighed.

"I don't give a fuck what you were *supposed* to be there doing. You lied to me. I told you things I never told anyone, and the whole time you hid who you really are," I snapped.

"Everything between us was real. Can we just go somewhere and talk alone for a minute?"

"No," I said flatly. "I need to talk to you, Axel."

Axel looked over to Zuri, who was approaching me again, and shook his head. "Zuri, go to your quarters and check in with Paxx. Daya, I'll take you to my office to talk."

I heard Zuri swallow a sob, but she turned away from us to go find their head of intelligence I had met previously. Axel gestured for me to follow him and I remained at his side as we walked down the great wide hallways of his castle.

"You've been busy since the last time I saw you," he said as he looked over his shoulder with that smile that made my gut tight.

"Your *spy* has been busy lying," I retorted.

"It was her job, but she never reported any of the more intimate things you two apparently have been up to."

"Is that supposed to make me feel better?" I snapped.

"No, it is just a fact."

Axel stopped before two tall doors and pushed them open, holding one for me to enter his office. I sat in a chair near the window, and he sat directly across from me. He studied me, his eyes trailing up and down. His gaze didn't feel salacious like it had before in the pub. He looked worried, like he knew me better than I realized. He probably did, thanks to Zuri.

"What happened?" he finally spoke.

"Fuck, where do I start?" I said, crossing my legs and rubbing the side of my face.

I told him everything, everything that I learned about Kaizer, everything that I learned about my mother, and all that happened in between. I was taking a risk trusting him with so much information, but I really had no other options. Outside of taking on Kaizer's entire army by myself, he was my only other option. Axel listened intently, only asking a few questions for clarity throughout my speech, never second-guessing anything I said.

"Our suspicions were correct, it seems," Axel said as he scratched his jaw. "We knew he was up to something. Zuri couldn't figure out everything, but we knew it was no coincidence his people were found trying to cross my borders."

"Is that even possible? Crossing your borders without you knowing?"

"I live my life never assuming anything is impossible. Our magic is strong, but I'm sure with the right spell or counter-power, it could be broken for enough time for one or two to slip in unknowingly. There aren't many strong enough, but I wouldn't rule it out."

"If my mother was helping them, I'm sure she would have tried."

"Don't have to worry about that anymore, do we?" Axel said with a smile.

"I suppose not," I laughed.

Axel's gaze was heavy as he looked like he was having an internal conversation about what to do next. "If he gets access to whatever it is he's looking for, this could present a problem. There is the treaty, but there are ways around such things." He stopped, looking past me before bringing his gaze back to mine. "I'll help you how I can, but we'll need to bring this to my inner council to discuss."

I nodded. "I understand that."

"Daya, I really am sorry for everything that has happened to you since I left. I wish you would have come with me. You could have been spared some of the pain."

"She'd been planning this for over a century. I'm sure she would have found a way."

"You are probably right. As far as Zuri—" he started.

I lifted my hand and cut him off. "I don't want to discuss her. I don't trust many people, and she just reminded me why that is."

"But you're trusting me right now," he retorted with a smirk.

"Don't make me regret it," I responded.

I didn't have anything to lose at this point, I had no kingdom, no family, no...Zuri.

Axel chuckled. "We're going to have some fun, you and I."

I smiled, my fangs on full display. "I like the sound of fun."

I didn't know what it was about Axel that made me forget about my problems. Talking to him in the pub had the same effect as it did now, and I was secretly thankful for it.

"I'm having a room near me prepped for you. I took the liberty of having some clothes made for you after our meeting, just in case you took me up on my offer. They should be in there momentarily," Axel said before standing to his feet.

"A little forward, isn't it, Ax?" I asked as I stood and brushed his side to walk past him.

"What can I say? I had high hopes, although I might have misjudged your...preferences."

"Oh no, I'm very much a *why choose one side when I could have both* type of girl." I shrugged.

Axel laughed and opened the door for me. "I respect that approach."

My fingers were twitching on their own accord as we walked, and Axel looked down, noticing the movement. "You need blood?"

"I need blood, and I need to release some magic as soon as possible," I responded.

"Goat? If I remember correctly?"

I nodded eagerly.

"I'll have some sent to us outside. You can let loose some of your power."

He held his arm to the side, advising me to head in the opposite direction we were initially going. I took in the castle, it was astonishing. The walls seemed to go on for miles, the ceilings were so high it almost felt like I was outside. I didn't feel cooped up at all, and my breathing came much easier with the feeling of safety I felt after months without it. Axel pushed open a door, the fresh air of outside hitting me instantly, my magic ready to explode.

"Don't you need to tell someone about the blood?" I asked.

Axel smirked. "I did."

"We definitely didn't see anyone on our way out here," I responded, wondering if the king was actually crazy.

"I didn't need to see anyone to let them know," Axel stated plainly.

My brow pinched for a second, the sudden realization that his mouth wasn't moving as he said the words.

"You're a mind speaker," I muttered.

Mind speaking was something that was almost solely a Dusran gift. I had no idea why, but there weren't very many across the other kingdoms. Like the gift of seeing, nobody really knew why the magic chose who it did.

"I am," Axel said aloud and cleared his throat. "Let's see what this magic is you were talking about."

I pulled the buckles across my chest open and took off my leathers, leaving the camisole I wore underneath tucked into my pants. I needed to see the magic on my skin. Axel smirked again as he watched me undress and sat down on a wrought-iron chair nearby before he crossed his ankle to his knee. He waved his hand, motioning for me to get started. I wasn't exactly sure how to call to that magic. It happened so effortlessly before, so I took a deep breath, trying to ease the magic to the surface.

The magic was too backed up, and the moment I let it rise it blared like a star in the night sky. My body glowed, my wings fell heavy on my back, and my hair started to shift around my shoulders again. I threw my hands into the air and let all of that power shoot into the sky. A column of pure essence rushed into the clouds at such a rate the trees and flowers around us bent away. It poured out of me, the sensation making my head spin as I had never released such power at once. It spewed from every crevice of me until I felt the power inside of me return to a comfortable level, and I fell to my knees. Axel was on his feet with wide eyes looking more rattled and surprised than I'd seen him look before.

He jogged over and offered me his hand. "I haven't felt magic that pure since..." he trailed off. "I don't even know. Maybe when my mother was alive."

"It's my Acna power. I don't remember ever reading about anything like this in my ancestry, though. I don't know what it is."

"Naom, wherever she is, seems to have given you more than she has others. Instead of giving the power to your mother, who wanted to kill you for it, she bestowed that on you."

I left out the fact that I saw Naom when I died. That felt like an experience I should have kept to myself, and it wasn't something I wanted to share with anyone else yet.

"I always felt more powerful than everyone around me. It's like I always had this inside, but becoming the Acna just released it."

"That's likely," Axel responded as he ran his hands over my wings.

I jerked my wing out of his touch. "That tickles."

"I bet it does." He laughed. "Stretch them as wide as you can."

I did as he asked with some effort, the muscles still straining as I still hadn't had much experience with them. The tips of my wings stretched wide, maybe seven feet between each side. My magic was still burning throughout them, but it didn't hurt Axel as he touched them again.

"Impressive. Can you fly yet?"

"I haven't tried," I replied.

"We'll have to work on that. You'll be unstoppable," Axel said, stepping around my wings and facing me.

I raised an eyebrow. "We?"

"We're working together, aren't we? You'll be training with me."

Axel was powerful, maybe the only person left in Malva whose magic rivaled my own now. If there was anyone who could match me in training, it would be him. I smiled, but it faltered as I looked past Axel and saw Zuri standing in the window watching us. I rolled my eyes and stepped in front of Axel so she couldn't see me anymore.

"You're going to have to deal with that at some point," Axel stated.

"Sometimes I like the whole, *I feel like I've always known you* thing, and sometimes I really don't," I snapped.

"Oh, so you feel that too?" he said with his dimples on display.

"From the moment I met you, unfortunately," I replied.

Axel shrugged. "Doesn't feel unfortunate to me."

Someone ran out to meet us and handed me a wine glass of goat's blood. I downed the entire glass in one go and handed it right back to the man. I licked my mouth clean and looked back over at Axel, who was watching me with amusement.

"If I would have left the pub with you that day, would you have told me who you were? If you found out who I was, would you have told me who Zuri was?"

Axel sighed, turning and gesturing for me to follow him into the gardens. I looked over to the windows, and Zuri was gone, thankfully.

"I'm not sure, honestly. I almost couldn't stop myself from finding you, from talking to you. Your power called to me like a song from a siren. I was powerless against it. I have a feeling I wouldn't have been able to hide myself from you even if I tried."

"Interesting," I said, mocking him with his own words.

We walked for a while in comfortable silence as we took in the gardens. Axel's sister was right; the Dusran gardens were far superior to Sanjry's. They were somewhere between Caldera's and Sanjry's, still wild and beautiful, but polished, like controlled chaos.

"Are you worried about harboring me?" I asked.

"No, there's not anything to fear from Kaizer yet," he responded.

I nodded and looked back into the garden. "Tell me about Dusra. We don't know much about it in the rest of Malva."

"By my design." Axel laughed. "We're a large civilization, larger than you guys know. Where we are now is the mainland, but I have a significant island off my coast that houses about a third of my people. We are a mixed bunch, vampires, lobos…" he trailed off, looking at me. "A few witches."

"Witches? That's how you were able to create that portal," I said.

Axel nodded. "There was a sanction of your people that came to my land maybe a few millennia ago. They've helped us greatly over the years. They've been mingling with my people since then. My mother was actually half witch, a hybrid of sorts. She got great power from both of her parents. Your magic reminds me a lot of hers."

"It's almost unbelievable. Witches are always so reclusive, not to mention the ones in Caldera only ever have female children."

"They have adapted over their time here. You will meet their leader, the one who speaks for them."

"When will we meet with your inner council?"

"If you're up to it, you can come to dinner tonight. We all eat together each evening," he replied.

We made it over to an entrance back into the castle, and I took one more deep breath of fresh air before walking back inside.

"So, is Zuri high in your spy ranks?" I asked.

"Do you really want me to be the one to tell you anything about her?" Axel asked.

I rolled my eyes. "No, I guess not. Where are we going?"

"To your bed chamber, you can get cleaned up and into some better fitting clothes before dinner."

I hadn't bothered to look at myself since we got here, but I looked down to find blood splattered across my body and my legs covered in dirt from my fight in the Inbetween. We made it to the room, and Axel pushed in the door, stepping in and spreading his arms out.

"This is yours. Mine is right there," he said as he pointed to the room directly across from mine.

"How convenient," I teased as I rolled my eyes.

The room was beautiful, and it also weirdly felt very...*me*. There were purple accents throughout the room. The bed sat on the far wall with an intricate arched stained-glass window behind it. From where I stood, I could see a bathroom and closet on one side of the room, and a vanity and sitting area on the other side.

"It's more than I could have hoped for," I said.

"Had it designed the day I came home." Axel shrugged. "Bathing chamber is stocked. You have plenty of clothes to choose from for dinner. We usually go somewhere between comfort and semi-formal, so whatever you wear is perfectly fine. I'll be back in about an hour to escort you to dinner."

I nodded, still inspecting my room as he walked out and closed the door behind him. For the first time in my life, I fell to the ground, held my knees close to my chest, and cried.

Chapter Forty-Four

I cried for what felt like an eternity, in reality only a few minutes, but the cry was so deep I had to snap an air shield around me so no sound would escape. I cried for the loss of my mother, for who she was when I was a child, for her decisions, for her death. I cried for the betrayal of Zuri, the one person who I thought would always be on my side. For the woman who broke down barriers without me even realizing, and made me care for her far more than I intended to. I cried for the disaster that was my failed engagement to Kaizer and for the repercussions for all of Caldera because of it.

For a few minutes, I let all of these emotions blare. I sobbed until I could barely breathe, until my chest got tight to the point of pain. When no more tears came and I caught my breath, I stood up, wiped my tears, and gave a big internal *fuck you* to all three parties involved. Unfortunately for me, Zuri's didn't stick nearly as hard as the others. I thought about her now while I finished drying my hair from my bath. She was usually here during this part, helping me get ready for whatever event I was to attend. While I didn't have a handmaiden prior to her, I got used to her presence and hated myself for missing her traitorous self.

I sighed as I finished drying my hair with a blast of warm air magic that had my hair falling into the well-manicured waves I usually sported. I had applied a little bit of makeup, just to make the fact I was crying my eyes out half an hour ago less evident. I set down the lip brush and smacked my now dark purple lips. Moving away from the vanity and back to the other side of the room, I pulled open the door to my closet, and my jaw dropped to the floor.

Axel had hundreds, if not thousands, of garments made for me in the short weeks since we'd met. They were astonishing, some intricate ball gowns, some casual dresses to wear day-to-day, and he even had multiple versions of the witch leathers I wore hanging in the space. I ran my fingers over the various fabrics, stopping on a black velvet dress. I pulled the hanger from the rod and hung it on a hook on the wall beside a floor-length mirror.

It was simple, simple enough for a dinner, but fuck it was beautiful. The neckline plunged low, trimmed in something that looked like diamonds, resembling a necklace. It had thin straps, and was tight through the hips, flowing down to the ground beyond them. I flipped it around and sighed when I saw that it was completely backless, the edge of it looking like it would barely graze the top of my ass.

My mother didn't like me to show the full extent of scars on my back, as there was only one person powerful enough in our kingdom to give them to me. Even though I presumed most people knew they were from her. I grabbed the hanger and went to put it back, but I stopped mid-movement. My mother was dead. She didn't rule me any longer. Axel had this dress *made* for me, and he knew about the scars my back was covered in. I bit my lip, trying to figure out if this would be the correct thing to wear to dinner.

I put it back on the hook on the wall and undressed, turning around to look at the scars. They were raised, some of them cleaner than others. Most were on the middle of my back and toward my ass, but a few of them curved over my shoulder, the only ones typically visible. There was something about the thought that I would own them, let these people see them, and not give a fuck what they thought that had me ripping the dress off the hanger and pulling it onto my body.

It fit like a glove, like Axel had memorized my measurements somehow. I slipped on one of the hundreds of pairs of heels he had stocked the closet with and heard shouting in the hall. I ran over to the door and placed my hand on the doorknob but stopped when I heard whose voices they were.

"How convenient that her room is right across from yours," Zuri snapped.

"Remember who you speak to, Zuri. I know you're hurting, but I won't tolerate it much longer," Axel growled.

"Just let me speak to her. She needs to understand," Zuri said.

I heard footsteps coming closer, but they stopped abruptly.

"You need to give her space. I will let her know where you can be found when she is ready. As for now, you need to stay out of her sight. Don't try to find her or use any of your resources to track her down, or there will be repercussions."

"Don't think I didn't see how you were looking at her during the meeting in Sanjry," she responded.

"I'm losing my patience," Axel said through tight teeth.

"I'm sorry, Ax. Just...just tell her that I'm sorry. I didn't mean for any of it to go this way."

"I will, I promise. Now go away. We will be late to dinner because of this little outburst of yours."

I ran back into my closet to pretend I didn't hear the argument just as Axel's knuckles banged on the door.

"It's me," he exclaimed from the hall.

"Come in, I'm almost done!" I yelled.

I slipped off my shoe to pretend I was just putting it on when he opened the door and he turned to find me in the doorway of my closet.

"You look..." he trailed off, his gaze running up and down my body, hunger flashing in his eyes for a moment before he pulled it back in. "Gorgeous, you look gorgeous."

"Thanks for the dress and, well, all eight hundred of the others in my closet," I laughed.

"There's honestly quite a few more where that came from, but this one was actually one of my favorites," he finished as he motioned with his finger for me to spin around.

Normally, the smug machismo would have had me wanting to punch him in his face, but I had a feeling he wanted to see the scars more than my ass.

"Divine perfection," he said, but it came out as more of a growl than I think he intended.

"Thanks, you don't look too bad yourself," I retorted.

We matched, but I could have guessed that as his favorite color seemed to be black. His dimples were on display as I walked toward him, sweeping all of my hair to one side of my head.

"Is there anything, in particular, I should know about the people at dinner?"

Axel gestured for me to loop my arm in his, and I did as he asked, walking out of the room and down the hall.

"You met everyone who will be at this dinner, and they were all their true selves at the meeting mostly, so you shouldn't be worried about anything."

I nodded, but the odd sensation I was being watched hit me, and I looked over my shoulder to find Zuri still in the hall she was before, talking to a tall male. She was staring at me with pain in her eyes, and for a fraction of a second, I wanted to turn and run to her. But it was quickly swallowed by rage, and I snapped my neck back in the direction I was heading.

"She shouldn't have been there," Axel growled. "I told her to give you space. When you're ready, I'll make sure you can find her."

"Thank you," I whispered.

"She did say she was sorry and that she didn't mean for things to end up like this."

"She already said that," I muttered.

Axel nodded, dropping the subject as he squeezed my arm in his slightly. We walked the rest of the way in silence. I'd been to plenty of rooms with powerful people, so I wasn't nervous, but I wasn't sure how much these people knew about me. We made it to the door I assumed went into a dining hall, and I stopped Axel before he pushed them open.

"What do they know about me?" I asked.

"Only what you've told them before. Well, Ishani does know about our prior...meeting. I told her about it before I knew it was you. She figured it out when she met you. As for the new information, I told them that your mother died and there is a new situation with Kaizer. I will leave the rest to you."

"Okay." I nodded.

Axel looked at me for a moment longer, giving me a second to fix my face into its usual unbothered state. He pushed open the doors, and laughter filled the air. Ishani, Axel's sister, was practically rolling on the floor while Akari, their highest-ranking general, was clutching her shoulder in laughter. Paxx, their head of intelligence, stared at them with a flat face while Xavier snickered from where he sat at the table.

"They ganging up on you already?" Axel asked Paxx.

"I don't know why they enjoy it so much," Paxx responded flatly.

All eyes turned to Axel and then me, the laughter dying down as they all sat straight and continued looking in my direction.

"Don't let me stop the fun," I taunted.

Ishani got up from the table and ran over to me, wrapping her arms around my body like we were old friends.

"I'm sorry for what has happened to your mother," she said into my shoulder.

"You may want to hear the whole story before you go offering apologies," I mumbled.

Axel chuckled. "She's not wrong."

Ishani pulled back and looked into me with her dark green eyes as she rubbed my arms and grabbed a bottle of wine on the way back to her seat. "We can probably all start with this," she said, taking the contents of the wine from the bottle with her magic and dropping a portion into each of our cups.

I hadn't seen much of Dusran magic, and Axel and Ishani seemed to be more powerful than most, but I mostly looked forward to seeing how they used it in battle.

"Thank you," I said before taking a sip.

Staff filtered in and dropped a plate of food before each of us, and they all picked up their forks and started eating. I felt Paxx's stare on me and tried to ignore it, but after a few minutes I snapped my neck to him.

"Do you have something to say?" I bit out.

Paxx shook his head and started eating again, and I looked over at Axel who laughed and set his fork down. "Paxx, use your manners, please. It's his job to know everything about everyone. I think he's curious about you."

Paxx nodded. "I didn't mean to be rude. I'm sorry."

"It's okay. I am...a little on edge."

Akari was surveying me this time, but her gaze wasn't bearing down to my soul like Paxx's was. I looked back at her, her tawny skin, her light brown hair, the fullness of her lips.

"Are you related to Zuri?" I blurted.

"She is my cousin," Akari admitted.

"Well, I hope you're less of a liar than your cousin," I said before I could stop myself.

Akari's brows raised, and she went to open her mouth, but she looked over at Axel and closed it. *You're really winning over the crowd here, dumbass.*

"Would you like to share what has happened to you now, Dayanara?" Axel asked.

Staff came in to take our empty dishes, and dropped off dessert, a plate filled of small brown squares with nuts peppered over the top of them.

I cleared my throat. "When I met you all in Sanjry, I was engaged to Kaizer. Since then, I found out that he and my mother were working together to try to kill me. My mother thought it would bring back the Goddess of Air and Essence, and Kaizer hoped to return some sort of false deity, but they both hoped they'd be all-powerful. I killed her before she killed me, and I left Kaizer in Sanjry. He...believes himself in love with me and says that he wants me back. I beat his ass, but I don't think it will be enough to deter him. Because of the treaty between Dusra and us, the land is technically already joined. He can come to Caldera and find me if I stayed there, so I came here. Hoping that you all would be able to help me."

"It's now confirmed that he is still looking for access to old magic so that he can take over all of Malva. Killing Dayanara was the beginning of that plan. I'm not sure what the next steps are, so we may need more eyes out there now that Zuri is no longer in the palace."

I rolled my eyes at the mention of her name, but Paxx nodded once.

"Well, I'm still sorry," Ishani started with her gaze on me. "Just for different reasons, I suppose."

"Will your armies side with him?" Akari asked.

"They didn't see what happened, so I'm not sure what lies they are telling my clan. My mother had witches helping Kaizer, so I couldn't stay long enough to warn them. It will be split, the ones who were loyal to my mother and the ones who are loyal to me."

"What's the next move?" Xavier asked Axel.

"We need intelligence out there, and then we need to ready the armies. I'm not sure of the next move is until we know what his is, but we need to be prepared for anything."

Xavier nodded, looking out in the distance like he was working through what he needed to do after leaving the meeting.

"I will fight. I will do anything I need to do to get back my kingdom," I stated.

"She will start training with me. She has some newfound powers that will be helpful in whatever is to come," Axel added.

"Do you need anything right now, Dayanara?" Ishani asked.

"No, not right now. I just need to...adjust," I responded.

Ishani nodded eagerly and stood from the table. "Okay, I think we all have things we need to take care of now."

"Let me know if there is anything you need my assistance with. I'm going to show Dayanara around," Axel exclaimed.

Everyone nodded and left the room in a hurry, off to take care of whatever duties they had. Axel watched me, and I closed my eyes and sat back in the chair with a sigh.

Chapter Forty-Five

"I can give you the tour later if you're not up to it," Ax suggested.

"No, it's fine," I said, standing to my feet.

"It'll be quick, promise," Axel said with a wink.

I rolled my eyes and smirked as I followed him out and down the hall, my dress swishing with every step.

"That room is where we take our more intimate dinners. For more formal ones, there's another hall down here," Axel said as he pointed to an open door.

I peeked my head in, the room far bigger than the one in my palace or Sanjry's. Axel continued moving, and I followed him down another hall making a few turns before we came to another room with vast doors like his office. He pushed the doors open, and a beautiful throne room came into view. A dais sat on the far end of the room, tall silver pillars on each side connected by an intricate arch with two black thrones sitting between them.

"Who sits in that one?" I asked, pointing to the smaller one.

"Nobody since my mother," Axel responded with a small smile.

I took a step closer to it. "Looks inviting."

"Don't sit on it unless you plan to remain there." Axel smirked.

I shrugged, walking up the stairs and running my fingers over the stone thrones. I walked in front of it and let my skirt brush the stone as Axel watched me with raised brows. Laughing, I walked past it and down the stairs to join him.

"So close," he whispered.

It felt good to be joking with him, flirting even. I just wanted to feel any inkling of joy after my last few days. I didn't really care how it happened, I didn't want to stir in all the pain that would overtake me if I let it. He showed me a few other rooms, the library, the other's offices, and the hall where Zuri lived, before bringing me back outside to a courtyard connected to his room. The stars lit up the sky, and the moon shone down onto an intricate fountain nestled in the middle of the space.

Axel stopped and looked into the fountain. "I'm all for being the one to distract you from your problems, Daya. But I know you're going through things far more serious."

I sighed and sat on the edge of the fountain before looking back into the sky. "I don't really know what to say. I've never had a normal life. This is just more of that, I suppose."

"Daya, your mother tried to kill you—did kill you. The man you were engaged to assisted and took your kingdom. You haven't had a normal life, but I'd say that's a bit worse than your day-to-day abnormality."

"What do you want me to say?" I snapped.

Axel's jaw ticked. "Tell me why you were crying so loud that your air shield didn't hold it in. Tell me why you're so mad at Zuri. Tell me why you look as if you're going to explode into a million pieces at any given moment. Tell me anything, Daya. Tell me how to help."

Ax sat beside me on the fountain, forcing me to meet his gaze, and I took a deep breath before looking over at him. His eyes were pleading for me to give him anything, and for someone who I really had only met twice, I really wanted to do it.

"Zuri." I sighed. "Zuri was one of the few people I let in, probably ever. Not just as a...lover but truly let in. I didn't hide anything from her, even the things most people might have said I should have hidden. For me to be that open and for her to not tell me something so big, it's a betrayal I don't know if I can get over."

"She was doing a job I put her there to do, be mad at me instead," Axel replied.

My lip pulled back. "You may have put her there, but you didn't tell her to get so close to me and lie about it, did you?"

"I certainly didn't tell her to get that close to you, no."

I huffed and ran my fingers through the crystal-clear water in the fountain for a moment, watching as the ripples moved across the surface and the bubbles from the streaming water moved. I didn't want to talk about this, I hadn't even had a real chance to digest what happened. "As for the other stuff, I don't think anything can help right now."

"I'll bring you Kaizer's dead body," Axel growled.

Kaizer was another story, my mother killed me, yes, but Kaizer went along with this plan without any true evidence. My mother was misguided as Naom said, but he was driven by his need for more power. I'd never seen him so unhinged as I did when we fought, like he'd been acting the entire time I was there. He threatened Zuri, threatened to force me into love with him by taking everything from me. Stole my kingdom, and didn't seem to realize how I wouldn't want to be with him. I never wanted to marry him, and I'm glad that I never developed any genuine feelings for him, because I had no internal concerns with ending his fucking life to get my kingdom back.

"I don't need you to bring me his body. I need you behind me, watching my back while I kill him myself," I said through tight teeth.

"There she is," Axel said with a smirk. "You are more powerful than 99 percent of the people in this world. You could be even more powerful than me and Ishani. I won't know until we train together. But, Daya, you need to remember who you are. You don't have to be who your mother made you, who Kaizer wanted you to be, or even who you thought Zuri saw when she looked at you. You get to decide who you are; from this moment, you don't do shit that you don't want to do. You don't act like anyone other than your authentic self. I know you don't need me to do your heavy work, but I'll assist in any way I can. If you want that kill, it's yours. I'll help deliver it to you."

I leaned my head onto his shoulder, not wanting him to see the effects that his words had on me. I was Dayanara fucking Amapola, one of the most powerful beings in all of Malva. I wasn't some bargaining chip for my mother to use, some pretty thing for Kaizer to flaunt around. I was a force to be reckoned with, and starting at this moment, I wouldn't forget it. We sat in silence for a while listening to the sound of the water rushing in the fountain until exhaustion hit me.

"I'm ready to go inside," I said around a yawn.

"This way," Ax said, pointing back to the way we came as we stood.

"Isn't this your room right here?" I asked.

He shrugged one shoulder. "Well, yes."

"My room is across from yours, so why don't we just go through there?"

"I suppose you're right," Axel said with a laugh.

Ax laid his hand on the door, and it opened under his touch before he pushed it open and held it for me to enter.

"So this is where the magic happens?" I asked, wiggling my eyebrows.

The room was a mirror of mine, but his was slightly bigger, with a bed that looked like five or six people could sleep in it.

"Something like that," Axel said as he continued walking toward the door.

I ran my hand over his bed, and he glanced over his shoulder to see where I was. He stopped and smirked, crossing his arms over his chest.

"What are you doing?" he asked.

"It just looked soft. I wanted to touch it," I shrugged.

"I share a similar sentiment to certain parts of your body," he joked.

I ran my hands over my ass and shrugged. "I see what you mean."

He shook his head and held out his hand for me to follow him; I pretended to pout and followed along out of his room and to the door of mine.

"You can put your own magical lock on if you like, but the castle is pretty much impenetrable."

I nodded as he reached across my body and opened the door, his arm grazing my stomach as he pulled back. I stepped backward into my room and looked up at him.

"I won't wake you at any particular time, but breakfast is served around eight if you're awake," Ax said, leaning against the door frame.

I took a deep breath and nodded. "Sounds good."

Neither of us moved. We just continued staring at each other. My eyes bounced from his eyes to his lips as he did the same to me. I felt things for Ax, that was for sure, but I hadn't really had time to really go deep into my feelings about Zuri. Part of me wanted to let him explore every part of my body, make me scream his name and forget about everything that had happened. But I didn't think it would help in the grand scheme of things. Yet.

"I'll see you in the morning," I said as I slowly closed the door.

"Sleep well, Daya," he responded, and took a step back to watch me close the door.

I held my hand on the door for a few moments before taking his advice and letting my magic add a second lock so no one could get in. Especially a particular curly-haired girl who knew where to find me. *Fuck.* I didn't have it in me to dissect that quite yet. I'd have to see her eventually, I was living in her home, but I really didn't want to. This situation, being in Dusra, was literally the last resort, and I never would have guessed it was one I had to turn to. Some people had referred to me as a know-it-all in my time, and even I thought I had a good grasp on my surroundings. Now I knew that was complete bullshit; everyone around me had been lying.

That's what made the situation with Zuri so difficult. I didn't expect *her* to lie to me, especially after she found out about all the other lies from Kaizer and my mother. *How could I trust her? Did Paxx know about Ximena? About the situation with Ax from before? She was in Caldera with me; did she gather intel on my people too?* I snapped out of my spiraling thoughts when I noticed the bright glow of purple in my hands, the magic practically dripping to the ground. It wasn't the power of Naom since it was just purple and not the mixture like before, so I could use my original power. I hadn't used it since I got the Acna power.

I took a deep breath and extinguished the magic before pulling off the velvet dress and placing it back on the hanger. There were plenty of silk pajamas available and I pulled one of the lacey nightgown options on before I sat on the window sill. I leaned my head back and looked out into the kingdom, my room faced a huge expanse of untouched land. Large fluffy clouds covered most of the moon, and without any homes to cast out light on the terrain it was extremely dark. Dusra had closed their borders definitively for hundreds of years, and I wondered what it must have been like to be living in peace for so long.

I wondered if peace was ever something I could achieve, if I would even be able to exist in a world without chaos. That wasn't a life I'd ever known, I was born into war and death, molded to be its bringer. I lived without any sort of light, without any sort of happiness to come home to. Naom mentioned that I needed to be ready for what was to come, but didn't give me any more information about what it could be.

I doubted that it was just the threat of Kaizer, it sounded much more significant than that, and I almost wished she hadn't said anything. Vague ideas were what put me in the position I was in. I could take it only one step at a time, and that first step would be covering Sanjry in so much blood the only vampires left would be the Dusrans. I'd let Kaizer watch, let him witness me take his kingdom from him, and then I'd give him a death that my mother would approve of. *Ha, guess I'll make her proud after all.*

It was dark, so dark that I didn't know where I was. A breeze blew through wherever I was, and the rustling of leaves made me believe I was outside somewhere. Small orange orbs popped up around me in the distance, and they got closer, I saw the hooded figures holding them.

"You thought you got rid of me that easily?"

I whirled around to find my mother, her green magic seeping from every part of her. She had a dark bruise around her neck from where I'd crushed her windpipe and snapped her spine with my bare hands.

"I'm part of you. You are part of me. I live in you for as long as you do. You'll never escape me."

She laughed something so dark and cruel it had my stomach churning.

"You know I'll find you, right, Daya?" Kaizer's voice came from behind me.

I moved to the side, not turning my back to my mother but shifting enough to face Kaizer. He looked like he hadn't slept in days, he had dark smudges under his eyes, stubble on his cheeks, and his hair was more unruly than I'd ever seen it. I blasted his feet with my magic, and he looked down at them, slowly lifting his gaze and smiling wide.

"Wherever you are, I'll bring you back. You will be my queen whether you want to or not. We will rule, Daya. We will rule it all. You'll bear me children, and our line will live long. You'll be mine, and I'll be yours. In time."

"Looks like you may have done what I was aiming to do," my mother said through tight teeth. "I can feel her magic on you; it's stronger than me, than my mother, and hers before her. You can do what I started out to do, Daya. You can save the witches. Nobody can stop you. Not even him," she sneered, pointing her lips toward Kaizer.

"Tell her that I wanted to go back on the deal, Lupe. Tell her that I love her, that we should be together."

"Oh shut up, you are so insignificant in this plan," my mother retorted.

I hadn't said anything to either of them, like my voice was stuck in my throat, locked up, and unable to be used. Kaizer and my mother started bickering, their shouts muffling together as I put my hands to my ears.

"The Embers are close," Kaizer growled. "We will find what we're looking for."

I still couldn't speak so I crouched down on the ground with my hands still on my ears and screamed at the top of my lungs, no sound escaping me. They both turned to me, my mother scowling and Kaizer smiling far too wide. They each took a step closer to me, my mother had her talons out, and Kaizer had a dagger in his hand I hadn't seen before. I looked down to find my body now in chains, my wrists locked up and anchored to the trees nearby. My clothes were gone, and I was completely naked.

"It's time for you to learn your lesson," my mother growled.

My arms were pulled tight, and I looked over my shoulder to see Kaizer gaining on me, no whip in his hands, just the dagger, while my mother had a knife of her own.

"Lashes clearly did nothing. It's time we try something new," my mother said with a smirk.

I pulled at my chains, my entire body becoming lit with my magic, but I couldn't move, I couldn't scream, I couldn't do anything. The first drag of the knife across my back had my entire body going tight in such pure pain I wasn't sure I was dreaming anymore; but something exploded nearby. Or maybe I exploded. I couldn't tell. All I could see was the bright light of magic surrounding me as the trees bent away and the stars retreated far from my sight.

"Daya!" someone screamed, but I couldn't find them. I couldn't see anything.

"Fuck. Come on, Daya!" the person screamed again.

I felt my shoulders being shaken, but my eyes were rolling behind my head, and I couldn't get myself out of whatever it was my body was doing to itself. The hands pulled from my shoulders, but I was still convulsing like I was being shaken. Icy water so cold that it brought me back to consciousness poured over me, and I jumped from wherever I was and got into an attacking position. Somebody was in front of me, and my hand darted around their neck, squeezing until I felt their windpipe waiver under my hold.

"Daya," the voice barely got out.

I blinked a couple times as my surroundings came back into focus. Blood was starting to drip down my fingers, and I looked back over to my hand to find it wrapped around Axel's throat. "Fuck," I yelped, pulling my hand from his neck.

Axel leaned one arm onto the bed as he caught his breath, his chest heaving and his eyes watering slightly.

"Ax, I'm sorry," I said as I tried to get close to him.

He held up one finger, took one more deep breath, and stood as the coloring on his face already started to return. "It's fine, I promise."

He smiled gently, but I was so close to killing him without even knowing it. My hands were dripping with his blood, the marks my nails created on his neck still leaking.

I opened my mouth, but he shook his head. "What happened? The entire wing started to shake. Everything in your room was levitating when I finally broke through your lock."

Everything was scattered on the floor, my drawers were half open, and one of the mirrors previously hanging on the wall was in pieces.

"I...had a nightmare—I think."

"What do you mean, you think?"

"I don't know. It felt real. I felt pain, I couldn't speak or fight back. It was worse than anything I ever experienced in a nightmare before."

Axel bit the inside of his cheek. "I wonder if it's your new magic. It can take some time to adjust."

My heart slowed to a normal pace and my breathing came in more evenly by the second. I reached over my shoulder to feel if there were any wounds, but my skin remained unmarked. I blasted myself with a quick burst of air to dry me and the bed off from where Axel used his water magic.

I swallowed. "Well, I don't think I'm going to sleep ever again. That fucking sucked."

By the time I looked back at Axel he had already healed his wounds and was walking away from me to pull a chair over from my fireplace.

"Lay down," he demanded.

I arched a brow at the tone he used, and he chuckled, taking a seat beside my bed and patting the pillow.

"You could always make me," I retorted with a smirk.

I didn't want to go back to bed. I didn't want to relive whatever the fuck that was, and if I had to choose a way to keep myself awake...Axel wasn't a terrible choice.

Axel shook his head at my advancement and kept his gaze in mine. "Just trust me."

I bit the inside of my cheek and laid back down reluctantly, I didn't know what he planned on doing and I could always tell him to fuck off if needed.

"On your stomach," he muttered.

I listened, rolling to my stomach and looking at him through my lashes, wiggling my ass. "On my stomach."

He rolled his eyes, his dimples popping up for just a second before he stretched his hand over my body. I thought he was going to grab a handful of my ass. Wanted him to, really, but an odd sensation started to roll up my spine. I lifted to my elbows, and he smacked one from under me, making me fall back down onto the pillow.

"Close your eyes," he said.

I didn't listen and strained my neck to see what he was doing to me. Water rolled up and down my back, but it didn't get my clothes wet at all. The sensation was so relaxing, like some sort of magical massage. He raised his brows as I looked back over at him before he tilted his head to the side and I did as he asked. The water rolled up and down my back, up to my neck, and back down to the base of my spine.

"My mother used to do this for me when I had trouble sleeping, just keep your eyes closed, and you'll fall asleep before you know it."

I nodded, taking deep breaths; I opened my eyes slightly one more time, seeing him wave his hand back and forth with a small smile on his face. I closed my eyes again, and like he said, before I knew it, sleep had taken me.

Chapter Forty-Six

Dim light was filtering in through the window in my room, and I sighed, happy that I was fully rested. A small snore had me turning in the other direction, and I laughed quietly at the sight before me. Axel still sat in the chair, his head on his shoulder with his mouth slightly open, and he had the corner of my blanket on his lap. I wasn't sure if it was the darkness or the situation at hand last night, but I didn't realize he was shirtless. He had small silk shorts on; the blanket covering most of them. His chest and arms were covered in tattoos, swirling symbols running up and down his body. I lifted my head slightly to see they traveled down to his legs too, at least to his knees, which was as much as I could see with the blanket hanging off his lap. *Fuck,* he was beautiful.

The kind of beautiful that surely had a plethora of women, probably men too, falling to their knees to get any kind of attention from him. His body looked like it was made for battle. With so many muscles, I wasn't sure how he moved so nimbly. He was riddled with scars, too, some small and some that looked like he might have been close to losing his life at the time they were etched into his skin. He shifted slightly, his loose curls moving across his forehead as he sat up straight and rubbed his eyes with the back of his hand. The movement had the blanket slipping from his body, and my eyebrows shot up as his silk shorts didn't leave much to the imagination.

Axel smiled, disregarding the raging fucking morning wood that was between us. "Good morning," he muttered sleepily.

I clamped my lip between my teeth with wide eyes as I tried to pull them away from his cock and up to his eyes, but it was like it was staring at me, and I couldn't look away. He cleared his throat, and I broke out of the trance and sat up as I pulled the covers with me and brought them to my chest.

"Good morning," I said, my voice cracking.

Axel crossed his ankle over his knee, hiding his boner a bit, and stretched his arms out wide, groaning slightly as he kept his hands behind his head, flexing those muscles I was just admiring.

"You stayed," I stated flatly.

"When I tried to leave, you shifted, and I was worried you'd have nightmares again. I kept running the magic up and down your back until I eventually fell asleep myself."

I nodded before looking around at the disaster I created. My hair was a ragged mess, and the thin strap of my nightgown fell off my shoulder and hung over my bicep, exposing a good bit of my breast. When I looked back at Axel, he quickly looked away like he had noticed, too, and I laughed as I fixed the strap and scooted to the end of the bed in front of him. He watched me as I moved, his gaze running down to my bare legs as I leaned my weight into my hands at the edge of the bed.

"Well, thank you," I whispered.

"You're welcome," he whispered back before removing his hands from behind his head and leaning on the armrest.

"I'm sorry I woke you last night."

"I wasn't asleep. I'm glad I got to you before you took down this wing of the castle," he laughed out.

I scowled. "I hope no one else noticed."

"Unlikely. You are..." he trailed off as his brow pinched.

"Dangerous? Untamed? Out of control?" I scoffed.

"Glorious."

My mouth went flat at the compliment, and he laughed as he adjusted himself in his shorts and stood up. He lifted the chair, placed it back by the fireplace, and rested one hand on it as he looked over at me. "It looks like we missed breakfast.

I don't usually sleep this late. I'll see if the kitchen can bring us something to the training wing."

"You have a whole wing for training?" I gasped.

He nodded. "We do. I'm going to put some more clothes on, and we can head down there. You should do the same, although I don't object to you wearing that."

I threw a ball of air at him, and he laughed, running out of my room and across the hall to his. I had almost forgotten the nightmare since I woke up so well-rested. Joking and flirting with Axel had helped for sure, which I could bet my money on was the reason he'd made any of the comments he did. Part of me hated that I felt so comfortable with him; I should have had my guard up and reinforced double time after the bullshit I'd been through.

But, for some reason, I knew deep down that Axel wouldn't hurt me. He'd had plenty of chances, and he'd done nothing but help me every time our paths crossed. Maybe it was the part witch in him that made me feel at home when he was around, although plenty of witches had hurt me at this point in my life. I gave up on figuring it out and went into my closet. Some of my clothes were on the floor from the commotion I caused, and I stepped over them to get to my leathers. I pulled some on and exited the closet, finding Axel waiting for me in my doorway, leaning against the frame like he had last night.

"Ready?" he asked.

I slipped my feet into some boots and pulled my hair to the side as I weaved it into a braid and walked toward him. "Yup, how'd you do on breakfast?"

He laughed. "It'll be waiting for us when we get there."

"Perfect, I'm starving. Can't beat your ass on an empty belly."

"At this point, I'm not sure that's an accurate assessment."

I shrugged and followed him, trying to memorize the halls, their twists and turns, so I could portal if I wanted to at a later date. We entered the training wing, and fuck, it really was a whole wing in the castle. It was impressive, with indoor rooms lining a colossal courtyard where different battle training items were peppered throughout.

The space was already riddled with people training, but Axel led us over to a table in one room where our breakfast awaited us. Scrambled eggs with sautéed vegetables and some sort of round white dish sat in the middle of the table with a plate for us each to use. Blood and orange juice sat in pitchers, and Axel poured us both a glass of the blood.

"You drink goat blood?" I asked.

"I do. Any blood, really."

I tilted my head. "Do you drink from people, too?"

"I do," he said with a smile.

"Hm," I replied, keeping that in the back of my mind for a later time.

I scooped out some of the eggs and vegetables and took a bite. I moaned, the spices so rich and different from what I was used to. Where our flavors were rich and spicy, these had a sweet earthy taste I couldn't quite pinpoint. I grabbed the white thing, inspecting it closer to find it was some sort of rice dish. I pushed it between my lips and moaned again. Dusran cuisine was fucking delicious. I finished the blood and washed it down with some orange juice before smacking my lips and looking over at Axel, who was finishing up as well.

"Let's do this shit," I exclaimed with a clap of my hands.

"Let's," Axel replied suggestively.

I stepped out of the room, but a light brown lobo ran across the courtyard, their large wolf form stopping me in my tracks. "Holy shit, they're beautiful," I muttered.

"Haven't met very many lobos?" Axel asked.

"No, they all live here, and you know how tight your borders are," I whispered, watching it move gracefully.

Their hairs shifted on their back as they jumped onto Akari and pushed her to the ground. In the blink of an eye, the wolf shifted into their other form, and I growled. It was fucking Zuri.

"Zuri is a fucking lobo?" I yelled.

Everyone around us stopped and looked over at me, including Zuri and her cousin, Akari.

"That explains her weird scent," I mumbled.

Ax raised a brow. "I hid it. I'm surprised you could still smell it."

Zuri ran across the room toward us, and Axel took a step forward, but I waved him off.

"Daya," she started, her eyes roaming my body.

She looked like she was looking for any sign that I wasn't okay, but that couldn't be found physically.

"You're a lobo."

She cleared her throat. "I am."

"Add it to the list of fucking lies," I said, before walking away from her.

She quickly shifted and moved in front of me. "Daya, can we please talk now? I know you're upset, but I promise I never meant to hurt you."

"I don't want to talk; I can't trust you. I won't ever be able to trust you again. You should move on."

"Please, Daya. Please, I can't do life without you."

"You should have thought about that before," I said, moving her out of my way and grabbing a sparring sword.

"You missed breakfast," Zuri growled at Axel. "You both did."

Power rolled off Axel, making me catch my breath for a second. It was all-consuming, so potent and formidable that it had my magic rising to the surface. I wasn't sure what he and Ishani were exactly, but they were fucking powerful. He stepped toward her with his lips pulled back, and to my surprise, Zuri held her chin high, looking up at him with a dare in her eyes. I picked up a dagger and threw it between them and watched as the blade embedded itself in the wall beside them.

"I won't talk, but I'll fight," I exclaimed.

Zuri yanked her gaze from Axel and walked over to me. "I'm not going to fight you. I just want you to listen to me."

I swung the sparring sword at her, and she sidestepped it. "Not an option."

She didn't pick up a weapon, and I huffed. "Fine, no weapons," I said, before tossing my sword to the ground.

"I didn't report anything back to them that you wouldn't have wanted me to. Only the things that put Dusra at risk."

I swung my fist, and she dodged, looking over at me with wide eyes. I lifted my leg and shifted my weight as I aimed for her side, and she blocked my kick with her forearm.

"Fine," she growled.

Zuri spun around my body, her fist connecting with my side.

"I'm assuming our little training sessions were fake too? Ms. Undercover Spy?"

She was behind me, and I swung my elbow out toward her as I twisted to face her.

"You actually did teach me quite a few things, but no, I wasn't a complete novice."

She swung her fist out at me, and I swiped it out of the way with my left arm, my right arm swinging out in a fist. It connected with her jaw, and she stumbled back a step. *Fuck, that felt good.*

Axel stepped forward as Zuri rubbed her jaw and shook her head. "I deserve that," she mumbled.

"You deserve more than that," I bit out.

Akari had made her way over to us, standing a few feet to the side. She looked at Axel, and he shrugged before looking back at us.

"Okay, if you don't want to talk, that's fine. I'll give you your space. Just...promise you'll at least hear me out before you move on."

I snapped my gaze up and down her and turned around, not giving her an answer. I heard four paws hit the ground behind me, and Akari looked down at me as she brushed past and shifted into her wolf form to chase after her.

"Feel better?" Axel asked.

"Not really," I mumbled.

"Didn't think so." He laughed and handed me my sword I threw to the ground.

"I'm not advocating for you to forgive her or take her back. But you should hear her story. She didn't go into this because she wanted to lie to people."

"I don't want a sob story. I have my own, and I don't go around ruining people's lives," I murmured.

I swung my sword out, and he blocked it with his own. "I'm just saying, listening won't hurt anyone. Don't forgive her or rekindle anything if you don't want to, but hearing her out might make you feel a little better."

I spun around him, ducking under his arm as he slashed for me and swung my sword out at his side. He was fast and brought his sword back close to him to block. "I'll think about it," I said.

"Hey!" Ishani's voice came from behind me.

I turned, and Axel swiped my legs from under me. "Never get distracted. You should know better." He smirked.

"Oops, that was my bad," Ishani said with a scowl.

I looked over my shoulder at Axel and rolled my eyes; he lifted me up by my waist and placed me back on my feet. "Were you calling for him or me?" I asked Ishani.

"Either of you, I guess. Did you feel the quake in the middle of the night?"

Axel looked at me, letting me be the one to answer.

"Uh, yes. That was me. I lost control of my power in my sleep."

"Fuck, you really are strong. I felt it from the other side of the castle. Shit was falling off the walls in some parts."

"Yeah, I had a rather vivid nightmare. I couldn't tell if I was asleep or awake," I mumbled.

"Don't be embarrassed. We've both done it," she said, pointing to Axel.

He nodded, his eyes telling me he was debating whether he should tell his sister where he was at the time of the nightmare, but I butted in before he could make the decision. "How old are you two?"

"That's rude." Ishani chuckled.

I lifted my hands in the air. "I'm just curious because of how powerful you two are; it seems like you should be thousands of years old."

"I told you our mother was half witch. Her mother was a witch, and her father was a lobo. While the witches and the vampires have mingled and survived, the children between lobos and witches didn't always make it. My mother was one of the ones that survived, and she got the full power from both of her parents, but her mother died in childbirth. Our mother was able to conceive after hundreds of years, but just once with us; after that, her womb was barren. We got her powers, and our father's just like she did, he was of the royal bloodline and one of the strongest of our kingdom. Just the right chance in genetics, I guess. Because she herself was so old, the power didn't wane with the generations like most people who conceive younger. Anyway, we're seven hundred seventeen years old."

"Holy shit," I spat, my mouth gaped.

"She lived to be almost two thousand, so we're still young by those standards," Ishani joked.

"Damn, I don't even know what to say," I said.

"Everyone here is so used to it. It's kind of funny that you are so shocked." Ishani laughed.

"That is why I think we'd be capable of helping you with your magic," Axel explained.

"Uh, yeah, I think you might be the only ones qualified," I replied.

Ishani clapped loud, catching the attention of people around her, but she didn't seem to notice. "Show me what you got."

Chapter Forty-Seven

"You know, for you two to be so old, you sure are ruthless," I said, my chest heaving as I tried to get the glass of water to my lips. Ishani and Axel stood beside me, barely even fazed by the training. I did most of the work, so it didn't surprise me, but damn.

"Oh great, we're going to get tons of old people jokes from you, aren't we?" Ishani rolled her eyes, but she smiled.

"Probably," I answered honestly.

"I was right in my original assumption. Your magic is just as strong as I thought. I don't know if you're necessarily Naom reborn, but she gifted you far more than your predecessors."

"Wish I knew why," I said under my breath.

Naom told me I wasn't a singular thing, and I wanted to believe that, but it still didn't answer the question of why I was so much stronger, or what I would have to do with this power.

"Maybe she saw what you had to deal with for a mother and decided to help you out," Ishani suggested.

"Possibly." I shrugged.

I downed the rest of the water and shook out my muscles. "So, what now?"

"We need to wait to hear what Paxx can find out; the treaty stops us from crossing Kaizer's borders as much as it stops him from ours. There are ways around with the spies we have, but it takes time."

"I don't know how much time my people have," I stated.

Axel's face softened. "I know, we will do our best to make it as quick as possible. Is there anyone you can fully trust in Caldera?"

I looked into the open sky, watching the clouds roll by as I thought about who might have been in on my mother's scheme. "Maybe one or two. Cat, one of my generals for sure, a few others possibly."

Axel looked over at Ishani. "Do we still have any contacts in Caldera?"

"I'm not sure. I'll check with Paxx now," Ishani responded before she ran out of the training courtyard.

"Unfortunately, this part of war is dreadfully slow, but I promise we will take back your land," Axel reassured.

I nodded. "The war between Caldera and Sanjry had already started when I was born, and I've fought in plenty of battles since then. I hate the waiting."

"We've heard even here about you on the battlefield. I can't wait to see you in action, slicing off heads and turning vampires to ash," Axel said with a smile.

"Morbid, but I like it," I said, bumping into his side with my shoulder. "I need to bathe."

The sweat on my body began to rattle, and I looked down to see it lifting from my skin, the droplets combining into one blob of liquid. Axel flicked his wrist and sent the sweat to the base of a nearby tree and smiled back at me.

"All clean. Now you can come with me," he said before walking away. I didn't move and stood my ground with my hands on my hips.

He looked back over his shoulder. "You coming?"

"I'm not sure what kind of women you usually hang around. I'm sure they all run after you like you're some kind of man god with a giant magical cock, but I can assure you that I don't like demands being made of me."

"Oh?" he said, turning back toward me.

"Mhm, so go ahead and ask nicely. Maybe I'll decide I have better things to do."

I raised my chin to him as he stalked in my direction slowly. He came to stand just inches from me as his large form towered over me, his body casting mine in shadows. "I'm a king," he muttered.

"I'm a queen," I responded.

A growl reverberated from his chest, but he smirked, raising his hand to push a strand of hair behind my ear. "Don't ever forget that." He took a step back and offered me his hand. "Will you please join me?"

I raised my pointer finger to my chin and tapped. "Well, my kingdom is miles away, and under the power of a stupid ass vampire, I think most of my prior engagements have been canceled. And...you asked so nicely."

I grabbed his hand as he laughed and dragged me along with him. He released my hand once we got to the hall and pointed toward one of the last rooms before we exited the wing. "War council room. I'm sure we'll be there before your stay comes to an end."

I peeked my head in; the room was huge, with enough space for everyone involved. The glass was one-way, nobody could see in, but the people in the room could watch the troops train.

"You met my inner council, but I'll be presenting you to the larger council on Friday. We'll advise them of what is happening."

"That's when I'll meet the head of the witch clan?"

"Yes," he replied as we made our way down the hall, and my thoughts turned back to Zuri.

"Who is the head of the lobos?"

"Well, it should be Zuri. Her parents were their version of royals before they died, but she gave the position to someone else. Akari was already my general, so it went to the next in line."

I jerked my head in his direction. "Zuri's a princess?"

"Not really in that sense of the word. The lobos had their own system of authority. They sat at the head of it, similar to the witches. They didn't really consider themselves royals."

"You two aren't...related, are you?"

Axel scoffed. "No, not at all. Completely different families."

I sighed in relief. "They aren't many of them left, are there?"

"No, there aren't. You probably heard that they were nearly eradicated before the Piedra was raised. It's been thousands of years, but they never regained their numbers. There's only a few thousand left, from only a few families, so it makes reproduction less common."

"It's why I didn't recognize her scent; I had never met one before. I knew it was something different, but I was just starting to think it was because of what I felt for her," I admitted.

Something about her scent changed when we had sex. I was too tired to really realize but when I thought back on it, I did wonder if it meant something more.

Axel looked down at me, his face tight. "You thought you might have been Verdaji?"

Verdaji, your one true mate. It was only something I'd heard of, never something I saw for myself. Witches didn't really lean into much in the way of love, but I'd heard stories. The closest thing I'd seen was the ceremonies where witches tied their souls to each other, but even that was a choice. Some said the moment your eyes met with your Verdaji, you both knew. Others said their scent called to them, and some said they didn't know until much later. Verdajis were chosen by the Creators, the person who matched you, who complimented you.

I shrugged. "I don't know. I'm not really sure I even know what regular run-of-the-mill love feels like, much less what a soulmate feels like."

Axel's mouth softened, but he didn't push, only continued directing us to wherever it was we were going. The castle was huge; there was no way I'd be able to memorize it all in a few days. It would take at least a week or two until I could portal.

"So, do you have witch magic?" I asked.

"Something like it. It's raw and powerful. Mine is much darker than Ishani's," he said, letting some black magic slide between his fingers. "But it operates the same as yours. I can't portal, though. Only Ishani got that."

"What a shame. She has one up on you," I retorted.

"I wouldn't say that, but she probably would," he laughed.

"What about the lobo magic?" I questioned.

He licked his lips and smirked. "You'll just have to find that out for yourself."

I glared at him through slitted eyes as we walked out of the castle and looked out into the distance. There wasn't a wall that protected the castle like in Sanjry or in Caldera, but we were on a hill, and I couldn't make out too much below. The landscape was jaw dropping, though. There was green as far as the eye could see, and I could make out a body of water far in the distance before we continued walking and another building blocked my view.

"Where are we going?" I questioned.

"Here, actually," he said as he pointed toward the tall building in front of us.

We walked up the marble stairs, and Axel pushed open the door. The ceiling was made of glass, just as high as the ceilings in the castle. The outside light illuminated the building, spotlighting the art hung within the space. So much artwork lined the walls that I didn't really know where to start.

"I wanted you to see how much better my art is," Axel said as he lifted his arms to the side wide.

He wasn't wrong; the painting ahead of me alone rivaled anything I'd seen in my time in Sanjry. It was an intricate piece, the lines and colors all working together to create something so beautiful it invoked some emotion in me I couldn't quite put my finger on. It was like I felt what the painter felt at the time it was made; it was so...sad. The colors were dark, but there were spots of bright colors, purples and yellows, peeking through, like there was some goodness to be found, and it was fighting tooth and claw to get out. I felt Axel's presence behind me, and his eyes turned sad as his gaze made it to the painting. My eyes trailed to the corner where it was signed '*Ax.*'

I whirled around to face him, and his gaze was still on the painting.

"People praise me for this, but I have no idea what they see in it," he muttered.

"You're an artist?"

"This is my only piece of art, so I don't think I can call myself an artist, no."

"It's beautiful, in an entirely depressing and emotional kind of way."

He nodded once and turned around, his face pulling back into the nonchalant easy-going smile he usually wore. "Take a look around. There's much better art than mine here."

I wondered what he'd gone through to evoke such a painting, but he didn't look like he wanted to talk about it, so I moved along to the next piece of artwork.

"You said the sculpture of that woman in Sanjry was actually the first queen here, right?"

"Yes, my grandmother, a few generations back."

"Do you know how it would have ended up there?"

"No, I looked into it when I got back here, too. I find it interesting they are so sure that she was theirs, but they've been known to lie and steal."

"Have your kingdoms been rivals forever?"

"Close to it. How much vampire history do they teach you in Caldera?"

"Just the basics. The fact you've been enemies for as far back as people can remember, the war between you two, the original treaty."

Axel nodded, walking toward another painting. "The vampires were one nation at first, before the Piedra. They fell under the rule of my family, but the now Sanjryans were what the other side feared. They were cruel, killing and drinking the blood of the creatures that now reside in Bonda. They are the reason we are now separated, not that I mind that part."

Axel chuckled slightly and placed his hand on my back to guide me over to a large sculpture. "There was a civil war that lasted nearly a millennium as we both tried to take the other's kingdom. There is some rather...nastier history, but I won't bore you with that for now. The main thing is I don't trust them, and I know what his kind will do to get what they desire, no matter what they have to go through to get it."

"Do you have any ideas about what he's after?"

"This is the land we shared before the Piedra. There are tons of old relics and magical items in Dusra. I have some people pulling some old books to go through, but I'm hoping Paxx can figure it out quickly."

I nodded and ran my finger over a dark sculpture of a mother breastfeeding their baby; the mother watched her baby eat with so much joy and contentment it made me think of how different my mother was. She looked at me like this once, but I could barely remember it. I only had a decade of memories from when she was loving, and it was so long ago I honestly couldn't recall what her smile looked like. Axel came into view on the other side of the sculpture, watching me intently. "Do you want to talk about the nightmare?"

"Not especially," I mumbled and walked away from him.

"Someone in your lineage was a necromancer, yes?"

I looked over my shoulder. "You really do know about everything, don't you?"

"I make it my business to know everything about everyone."

"So why ask the question?" I asked with my head tilted.

He laughed. "Seems rude if you don't already know that I know."

I rolled my eyes. "Yes, there was. There's been a few witches with the gift over the centuries, but my grandmother was the strongest. What about it?"

"I think that it might have been a factor in your nightmare."

"You think I'm a necromancer?"

"You may not have the gift to speak willingly with the dead. But I wonder if you have the ability to let their spirits contact you. You said you could feel pain?"

"Yeah, she cut me."

I couldn't be hurt in the actual spirit realm, but seemed whatever plane we went to when we slept was open for it. His fists tightened, and his jaw ticked as he came to stand beside me.

"Actually," I started, looking up at him. "We have this place where we bury our dead; I've always felt like I could feel their spirits, hear their whispers."

Axel nodded. "Some people are more in tune with the spirit world than others. You may not be a necromancer, but it seems like you might have a slight connection of some sort."

I wasn't sure if that was necessarily true, but I was more concerned with the necromancy. "So that can happen any time I sleep? It's never happened before."

"You've never had such a strong connection to a dead spirit. At least, that's my assumption."

I shook my head. "Not really. I'd say the woman I came from would be the biggest connection."

"Then yes, I think that it could happen at any given time if you don't learn to control it."

"But Kaizer was there. He's not dead," I retorted.

"No, that part was just the dream."

My gaze fell to the ground as I thought about having to confront her even after she was gone. Give it to my mother to find a way to torment me, even in her afterlife.

Axel placed a finger under my chin and lifted it. "We'll figure it out."

"You talk a whole lot of 'we.' How do you know I even want to be around you?" I asked with a small smile.

"I told you not to do shit you don't want to do, so I'm assuming if you didn't want to be around me, you wouldn't."

I shrugged. "You're not terrible, I guess."

"You have no idea just how terrible I can be," he joked as we walked out of the museum and back toward the castle.

"So, do you have any tips for what I should do in the meeting on Friday when I meet the rest of your people?"

"What do you mean?"

"Like certain things I shouldn't say, anyone I should avoid, et cetera."

Axel shook his head. "I won't ask you to be anything but yourself. You should know that by now."

I'd gotten so used to being handled and directed—by mother and then by Kaizer—I half expected a list of dos and don'ts. But that's not how things were handled in Dusra.

"Fair enough," I responded, trying to hide the smile pulling at my lips.

The question of who I was without the influence of outside parties—that was still up in the air.

Chapter Forty-Eight

Axel showed me the rest of the castle; it took a few hours, which really spoke for the size of the compound. It was stunning, the intricacy of their architecture. So many arches and designs etched into the walls. Even some of the floors had motifs that I could stare at for days and never fully be able to appreciate. It was lunchtime, and Axel had a meeting he had to attend, so I sat in the courtyard alone, eating a sandwich and watching the flowers bend in the breeze.

"You look like you're enjoying solitude," Ishani's voice came from behind me.

"Well, I was," I teased before taking another bite of my food.

Ishani stopped in her tracks. "I can leave you alone if you want?"

"No, it's fine. I can't be alone with my thoughts for too long," I responded, not realizing how honest it was until she looked at me with apologetic eyes.

"I can relate," she said as her lips turned down slightly. "What have you been up to today?"

"Ax showed me a museum and some of the castle. He had a meeting, so he left me in the courtyard to eat."

"*Ax*, huh?" she responded with her eyebrows raised.

"Shut up," I said, pushing her on her shoulder. "That's what he was introduced to me as. I honestly keep forgetting he's king here."

"I think that's part of why my brother likes you," Ishani said before plucking a grape from my plate and popping it into her mouth.

I looked from her hand to her mouth, and she laughed as she sat back and tilted her head to the sky with her eyes closed. It was midday, so it was the brightest the orange sky of our world would get. It sent a warm glow over her light brown skin, making her look as otherworldly as she felt.

"What did you do today?" I asked.

She opened one eye and looked over at me with a small smile. "I spent a good part of my day listening to Zuri complain about you, actually."

"Ugh," I replied, crossing my arms and sitting back. "You all are far too close."

"We're practically family. That is common among families." She shrugged.

"I wouldn't know," I muttered.

I didn't mean to let my attitude be affected by the mere mention of Zuri's name, and I immediately regretted it. I wasn't sure how Ishani would take my comment, as our friendship was still so new.

"That's a fair point. You've got a pretty fucked up upbringing," she laughed.

I liked Ishani.

"Anyway, yeah, we've pretty much grown up together; well, she grew up more so since I'm *so old*." She laughed. "Our families have been close. She's been gone for a few years, but our bond remains."

"Well, I hope she's not telling you this was my fault."

"She's not at all, actually. It's one of the first things you learn in her line of job. You never get close to anyone. She knows she failed in that sense and in the sense of whatever was happening between you two. She just wants the opportunity to make sure you understand before you completely move on. She's...worried about Ax."

"She made that clear this morning. She practically fought him after insinuating something was happening between us."

Ishani's eyebrows rose. "Is it?"

"I don't know. I've felt a connection to him since the moment I laid my eyes on him; I just can't tell if it's a sexual thing between us or more than that. I also don't know which I'd prefer."

"Gross." She scoffed. "My brother is picky, and he's had his days of fucking whatever spreads their legs for him. I'm sure there's a sexual aspect to it because, well, look at you. But if he has an interest in you, it's most likely more than that as well."

"I can't tell if you want me to get with your brother or Zuri," I joked.

Ishani shrugged. "That part isn't my business. I just want everyone to be happy. However that comes. They've both been through far too much to deserve anything less."

"Ax mentioned Zuri had a story I should hear, too," I groaned.

"I get it. Lying is an exceptionally touchy subject with you; which is entirely understandable."

"I just don't see the point. There's no world where I'd be able to trust her again."

She sat forward and brushed her hair behind her shoulder. "Who does it hurt to at least give her closure? Both of you closure?"

"Old and wise, it seems. Where is she?"

Ishani walked me over to Zuri's room, advising me that Zuri had said she was going to clean herself up after she trained with her.

I knocked on the door and heard shuffling in the room and Zuri's voice exclaiming, "One second!"

Placing my hands in front of me and clasping them together, I waited, wondering if this was a mistake. The doorknob turned, and I suddenly felt the need to back away, but Zuri's face was in front of mine before I could run away.

"Daya," she muttered as she knotted the tie around her waist that held her silk robe together.

"Do you still want to talk?" I asked.

"Yes." She nodded. "Come in."

She sidestepped and held the door, and I walked into her room, the space as warm and cozy as I would have expected from the duplicitous little wench. I stood in the center of the room, not speaking, just staring at her in anticipation of an explanation.

Zuri bit her lip and looked away. "We can sit if you like."

She walked over to a chair and sat before I could respond, and I followed her over, sitting straight and crossing my legs.

"I never meant for it to go this way," she stated.

"Yes, you've said that. New information would be appreciated," I huffed.

"They sent me there a few years ago, the first time that we found Sanjryans trying to cross our border, right after Kaizer took over. I was there to get information, Kaizer treats the staff in his palace like they don't exist, so it didn't seem like a difficult task. I got as much information as I could. He was occupied with the war between you two often, but I got enough to know that he was looking for something. I was close to figuring out what, but then the union between you two put a stop to it. We decided to try to see if you were in on it, but I found out pretty quickly you weren't. I swear I didn't tell them anything personal, just the moves that were being made between the kingdoms."

I nodded, not offering any words of forgiveness.

"At the point that Axel came to visit, we weren't...well...you know. Paxx had me stay and said that I could come back after the wedding if there weren't any new findings. He figured with the treaty and your union, we'd be fine until they tried again. I agreed, but then we got closer. On top of the fact I had some...feelings I knew I shouldn't have had in this profession. I wanted to tell you so many times; every time you opened up to me or asked me about my past, I wanted to tell you. But...I didn't know how you'd react after we got that far. Dusra's security was my biggest concern. If, for some reason, you turned on me and told Kaizer, it would not have been good for my people."

"I would have appreciated that chance," I snapped.

"Yes, I know. I told myself that I'd tell you before the wedding, after The Ritual, which I'm sure sounds like a lie now, but I swear it, on everything, I was going to tell you. Once you said we were coming here, I didn't know what to do. I knew you'd find out, and by the time we were at the border, I was out of time."

"Mhm," I said, biting the inside of my cheek. "Ax said there was a reason you were even there in the first place, above your mission."

Zuri looked away from me for the first time since we'd started the conversation, down at her hands in her lap.

"As you know now, I'm a lobo. There are few of us. We were almost wiped out completely thousands of years ago. My parents were...the best kind of people. Axel is king, but our people have always had a say, we've always been on his council, and he's never done us wrong. We had our own section of land, but the wolves didn't think it was enough. My parents were killed by their own kin because they wouldn't fight for us to be separated from Axel's family and revolted. I had to kill my own people, wolves I'd grown up with, wolves I thought were my family. I killed so many of them, tore through them all with my teeth, Akari and me together, nearly cutting our already low numbers in half. I could have tried to listen to them or tried to stop them, but I didn't. The moment I saw my parents lying in pools of their own blood, I snapped. Anyone in my path fell that day, I could have killed innocents, I have no idea. I was given the gift of healing. Maybe I could have saved more of them if I stopped for a second." She squeezed her hands together like she could will the past to change.

"I laid between my parent's dead bodies for hours. Ishani found me later that day, still in my wolf form and covered in the blood of so many. After that, I vowed I'd never do it voluntarily. I'd defend myself or those I loved, but I didn't want to ever be covered in that much blood again. I started training with Paxx soon after, doing intelligence work instead of training to be a warrior like I should have been, as my parents expected of me. I gave up my position to someone I trusted, but only Akari and I remain of our direct bloodline." She cleared her throat. "I never wanted to lie to you. I wanted you to see who I really was. I wanted to know if you'd still want me. I just...I know we had something special, Daya. Everything else was real. My feelings were real. I just want you to give me another chance. I'll show you how much you mean to me."

Zuri got up from the chair and fell to her knees before me, grabbing my hands in hers as tears started to well in her eyes. I didn't know what to do. On one hand, I could empathize with her situation, but I didn't think I could get over it. I'd always wonder what parts of her were real and what parts weren't. What parts of our relationship were fabricated for her to get close to me, and what parts were genuine.

Even now, looking down at her, I wondered if the story was true. I was mostly sure it was, but that inkling of doubt was still in the back of my mind. Zuri was everything to me for a few weeks; I was willing to bring the world down around me to be with her. She'd evoked such a deep emotion from me, something I didn't think I was even capable of. I...might have loved her with more time. Truly loved her.

"Daya, please say something."

I felt tears threatening to make an appearance, and I looked away from her, not able to watch her in such pain. "I forgive you," I whispered.

Zuri jumped up to hug me, a smile so wide it hurt me to put my hand between us and stop her. "But I can't be with you. I won't be able to trust you. I'm sorry."

Zuri's smile faded as fast as it had appeared, and my chest tightened as tears spilled down her cheeks, and she nodded her head rapidly. "I...I wish it wasn't this way, Zuri. I mean that genuinely. You were possibly the only light in my life in over a century. It hurts me to say that, but I'll always wonder if you're lying, and I can't be in a relationship with someone I don't trust fully."

"I understand. I'm really sorry," she whispered, her voice cracking with each word.

Zuri took a step back, and I stood, offering her a weak smile and rubbing her arm as I walked out of her room. I looked back over my shoulder, and she held the part of her arm I touched, her shoulders shaking as she tried to control her tears. It took all of my effort not to run to her and try to comfort her. Almost everything inside me screamed that it would be okay, that she was still the person I'd nearly fallen in love with. But...I turned around and left her room.

I tried not to hear the sob that came as the door closed behind me, but my witch hearing didn't seem to want to turn itself off. I listened to Zuri sob for the entire way down the hall, the sound only fading as I walked out into the courtyard, where some sort of loud construction was happening. I walked around the gardeners behind a tall hedge and fell into the grass, snapping an air shield around me and screaming at the top of my lungs until my throat burned.

It fucking *hurt* to confront the fact it was over. It was so much easier being angry with her, so much easier leaning into all the fury and bitterness. I didn't have to think about my feelings when I was so angry that I couldn't even hear them. But now, they were exposed. The wound was somehow even more open and brutal.

I fell onto my back and stared into the sky, letting my emotions drown me, hidden in the courtyard until night fell.

Chapter Forty-Nine

My eyes were still closed, and it was dark, but it suddenly felt even darker than before. I opened my eyes to find Axel's face above mine as he leaned over slightly with his hands behind his back.

"Are you enjoying the fresh air?" he asked with a smirk.

I didn't laugh, his smirk faded, and he extended his hand to help me up. "What's wrong?"

"I talked to Zuri." I sighed as I looked away from him.

"I'm assuming it didn't go well?"

"She told me her story, but I just can't get past the lying. We're done, for good."

His gaze ran up and down my body with the corners of his mouth pulled down. "I'm sorry, Daya."

I arched a brow, and he shook his head. "I mean it; I really am sorry. I just want the both of you to be happy."

"You sound like Ishani," I muttered.

"She talked to you?" Ax questioned as he took a step closer.

"Yeah, she had spent the day with Zuri before I talked to her. She's the one who convinced me to at least hear her out. She asked about you too, but just said she wants all of us to be happy."

He nodded and looked out into the courtyard. "It's late, we should get you to bed."

I snapped open a portal and put one foot in, looking over my shoulder at him. "You coming?"

He followed me through the portal, and I snapped it closed behind him, the purple smoke clearing and my room coming into view.

"How was the rest of your day?" I asked.

I didn't want to talk about Zuri anymore tonight, so I really needed to change the topic before he tried to double down on the concern.

"Good," he said as he took a seat by my fire. "Just had some regular kingly duties to attend to."

"Sounds exciting," I replied, stepping into my bathroom to change into something more comfortable.

Axel's back was turned to me, so I didn't bother closing the door to make sure he could still hear me.

"Not particularly. There's a possible issue out on the island. I have my men taking care of it, but if it escalates, I'll bring you along with me so you can see it."

"Now that actually sounds exciting." I walked back out of the bathroom to join him in silk shorts and a short sleeve button-down shirt. Walking beside Axel's chair and across from him, I plopped down into a chair and pulled my hair in front of my shoulders.

"Are you not going to sleep?" he asked.

"I'm not tired yet. You going to keep me company?"

Axel smiled, his dimples showing as he sat back and nodded. "I can do that."

"So, how are you going to entertain me?"

Axel ran his hand through his short curls, his bicep bulging with the movement, drawing my attention to his muscled arms. "How would you like to be entertained?"

I tapped my finger to my chin. "Surely you can figure something out."

I grabbed a leather band on the table beside me and pulled my hair into a high ponytail, knowing my exposed neck was practically a taunt to the vampires. I wanted to feel *something*, the pain and pleasure that came with a bite was more than inviting. Ax placed one of his hands under his chin as he watched me with his elbow rested on the armrest of his chair, smirking. He didn't say anything, just watched me as I swished the ponytail behind me and let my nails extend into sharp talons. I tapped it against my neck gently, tapping increasingly harder until I almost broke the skin.

"You're playing a dangerous game, Daya. Your blood has been provoking me since you arrived."

"Oh, Ax, don't you know I *am* danger?" I said as I ran my tongue over my bottom lip.

I tapped my nail again, finally hard enough to draw blood. His fang dug into his bottom lip as he went still, the amusement slipping as his nostrils flared slightly. His gaze fell to the small wound as tiny droplets of blood trickled out of it. I got out of my seat and slowly walked over to the chair beside him, rubbing his arm slightly with the hand I drew the blood. He was still leaning his elbow on the arm of his chair, and I leaned in closer, just a few inches from him. I smiled as I ran my tongue along my fangs and he remained still.

"Daya," he growled as he looked at me from his peripheral vision.

The sound sent a shiver through my body, making my mouth drop open slightly. "Come on, play with me," I taunted.

He slowly turned his head toward me, and my Ax wasn't there anymore. His normally amused gaze and smile were gone, and a predator stared back at me. I wasn't sure what it was about my blood that drove vampires crazy, but I'd use it to my advantage if I could. I blinked, and Ax was before me, caging me in between his arms in the chair.

"You still have his mark on you," he snarled.

I hadn't even thought about Kaizer's mark on my body, it was faded enough that I couldn't see it unless I really tried, but it was still there. "Do something about it," I responded.

He wrapped his large hand around my neck, forcing a gasp from my body as he squeezed it slightly. His eyes didn't leave mine as a warm tingle bloomed beneath my skin, his healing magic removing the wound Kaizer's fangs had left behind. We stared at each other, his gaze alone setting my core on fire. I couldn't imagine what he could do to my body, with my body. I really wanted a release; I honestly didn't care how I got it, but I would let him do whatever he wanted to me right now. As long as he wrung out every bit of pleasure he could. My breathing was getting heavier under his gaze, and I grabbed him by his shirt and pulled him closer to me. He fell to his knees between my legs, and I thought he was going to go for my neck, but he ripped open my shirt and sunk his fangs into the top of my breast instead.

"Fuck," I got out, swallowing hard.

Kaizer's bite had hurt initially and then turned into pleasure, but Axel's was *pure* pleasure. The pain somehow felt good as his venom started coursing through my veins, heightening the sensation to something I never experienced with Kaizer. He scooped me up by my ass and turned us around, dropping into the seat with his mouth still on me. I straddled him and hovered on my knees slightly so he didn't have to crane his neck, the movement having my center lining up with his stomach.

His hands were squeezing my sides, but I wanted them everywhere. The warm sensation his bite caused had spread to every inch of my body, and I couldn't stop myself from grabbing his wrists and placing one of his hands on my ass and the other on my pussy. Axel growled at the contact and looked up at me as best as he could with his fangs still in my breast. The question of if I really wanted this in his eyes, but I ground my hips against his hand in answer, telling him that I wanted this. Needed this.

He held my gaze for a moment longer, and I watched as his throat bobbed and he drank my blood with vigor. I dragged my hips again, and his eyes rolled back as the pull from his mouth got even more intense. He rubbed my pussy outside of my shorts, the contact alone having me ready for him to get inside of them. Axel's fingers played with the ties of my shorts, and I pulled the knot loose in impatience. He chuckled darkly with his fangs still in me as he dipped his fingers under the band of my shorts. I was wet the instant he wrapped his hands around my neck, and I hadn't gotten anything but more wet since. Axel's mouth stopped pulling in blood as his fingers slid through it, every muscle in his body seeming to go tight. His mouth picked up again, forcing a moan from me as he pushed his fingers inside and his thumb rubbed my clit.

"Oh, fuck," I muttered.

I dragged my nails across his shirt, ripping it open and pushing it off his body. My hands trailed over his tattooed shoulders and biceps while he continued his pumping even faster. He pulled his fangs from my flesh and looked up at me, my blood dripping down his chin. I moved to press my mouth to his, but he grabbed my chin with his other hand and shook his head.

"I want to see you fall apart for me," he growled.

I realized he had been toying with me before because his hands picked up to a speed I didn't think was possible with just his fingers. My hips undulated on their own accord, and he sat back to watch his hand move against me.

"That's it. Fuck my hand, Daya. Chase it."

I did as he asked, and he met my every movement, letting go of my chin in favor of using his other hand to rub circles around my clit. He brought his hand to his mouth, sucking me off his thumb, and groaned at the taste. Ax brought some of his water magic to his finger, letting it ice over the tip, and ran it down my stomach and right to the top of my pubic bone. The chill of it did something to me as he applied pressure and pushed his other fingers inside with force and held. I exploded.

My muscles tightened around his fingers as I came so hard that I screamed, my head falling back again as I fell into his lap, feeling the hard length of him ready. I pushed against it, and his jaw ticked at the contact. I reached down for his cock, needing to know what he could do with it if his fingers alone could make me come that hard. He caught my wrist and squeezed it hard; his throat bobbing as he shook his head.

"Tonight isn't about me. I'm happy to give you a release, but when I fuck you, Daya." He paused, running his thumb over the bite wound and healing it. "I want to be the only thing on your mind."

I suddenly realized that he hadn't touched me anywhere I hadn't instructed him to; he didn't kiss me or try to take my breasts out. Outside of drinking my blood, which was something I baited him into doing, he didn't try to take any pleasure for himself. I nodded my head as my chest still fell and rose in heavy pants.

"Okay," I whispered.

He sighed as his gaze ran up and down my body straddled across his like he wanted to do anything but stick by his word, but he lifted me by my hips and placed me on the ground before him.

"You are going to ruin me," he muttered as he pulled off his tattered shirt, the light of the fire reflecting on his bare skin.

"Probably," I smiled, shrugging as I turned away from him.

I felt his eyes on my back, and I looked at him over my shoulder to find him in the same spot. "Changing your mind?"

I slowly sat down on the edge of my bed and rubbed the spot beside me, beckoning him, trying to get him to stop being a gentleman and fucking rail me.

He closed his eyes and shook his head. "As much as my cock hates me for it, no, I'm not changing my mind tonight."

"Boo," I pouted.

"Goodnight, Daya," he mumbled.

He turned to walk away, and I watched every muscle in his back shift as he moved across the room and to the door.

"Goodnight, Ax," I exclaimed before he walked out of the room, and the door slammed behind him.

I extinguished the fire and decided to take off the shirt since Ax had popped half the buttons off it. Laying down, I pulled the covers over my body and closed my eyes. I wished for a night of peace like I'd had before, with Ax helping me sleep, wanting the bliss I'd experienced to continue. But as the darkness crept in and a flicker of green smoke started behind my eyes, I knew my wish wouldn't be answered.

Chapter Fifty

Ax had been busy the last few days, so I spent a lot of time with Ishani. She and Paxx had reached out to their contact in Caldera, which both pissed me off and made me feel a shit ton better. The fact they'd had spies in my kingdom this whole time made me want to punch Paxx in his face, but it would pay off now that I needed the connection. Ishani told me that it was one of the witches that lived in Dusra, so they were able to fit in undetected. I asked Paxx to ask them to get in contact with Cat—there wasn't really anyone else that I trusted enough, I just hoped she was still alive. They were incredibly cautious, so like everything else, it would take time to hear back, but I had hopes that it wouldn't take as long as gathering the information on Kaizer.

Today was the day I'd meet the rest of Ax's people, and I'd have to see Zuri. I'd avoided her the best I could since we talked, but she'd be at the meeting. While she had given up her spot as the lobo's leader, Ax still let her attend and speak if she wanted, even though she wouldn't have the last say among her people.

I stood in my closet, running my hands over the dresses Ax had made for me, trying to figure out which I should wear. My hands stopped on a shimmering green fabric, a color I'd mostly avoided over the years, but I pulled the dress down and held it out in front of me. It didn't sparkle with glitter, but the fabric itself had a sheen to it that changed the hue slightly depending on the angle I turned it. I slipped out of my robe and pulled the dress on. The neckline came to two sharp points, the center of it plunging deep, not as deep as the other dress that nearly ran to my navel but deep enough to show off my well-endowed chest. The straps fell off the shoulders, made of thin gold chains that joined together as one where they met the dress. The ruching accentuated my waist and my wide hips, with a slit that ran up to the top of my thigh.

Axel had someone drop off a box I had yet to open up but said that I should wear whatever was in it. It was small, so I assumed it was jewelry; I just hoped it matched this dress because there was no way I'd be changing. I slipped into some gold heels and walked over to my vanity where I'd left the box, my heels clicking against the hard stone with every step.

I lifted the top off it, and my breath caught at what was inside. There were three items within the box, but the one that I wanted the most was a bracelet, much like the one I'd worn before. A bracelet with all the witch stones in it, a safeguard to make sure I could fulfill any spell I might need. I slid the bracelet on and lifted the next item, a beautifully crafted golden necklace with a raw black diamond pendant. The last item was wrapped in an additional cloth, and I unwrapped it to find a note within it.

"Regardless of the current situation, remember who you are. This still belongs to you, and I will help you reclaim it."

I set the note down and found a golden signet ring with something etched onto the surface. I brought it closer to my face so I could inspect it, and the wings of Caldera sat on the surface with a bloodstone on each tip. I didn't know why he'd given me such a gift after barely talking to me for days, but I couldn't help but want to run and find him to thank him. To be able to defend myself and fight with the help of the bracelet and to be able to look down at my finger and be reminded of what I was fighting for. It meant more than I could put into words. A knock at the door pulled me out of my thoughts, and I walked to the door with a smile stretched across my face. I turned the handle and opened the door, finding Ax looking down at me.

"Hi," I muttered.

His dimples deepened as the corner of his mouth ticked up. "Hello, forceful."

He wore his typical all-black, all of it tailored to perfection as it always was. His hair was slightly more manicured than usual, the curls swept back from his face and held in place with the help of some product. He took me in, and I spun for him, letting him see all angles of the dress.

"I've been waiting for you to wear this one," he stated as his gaze finally came back to mine.

"You're quite the designer," I responded.

"I didn't necessarily design them, just asked for some things I felt were you." He shrugged.

He reached his hand out, and I noticed the golden ring on his pinky that matched mine in his own signet. I grabbed his hand and looked at the water dragon on his ring, but the memory of what these hands did to me suddenly had me clenching my thighs.

"It looks good on you," he said as he turned my hand in his to see the ring he'd gifted me.

"Thank you for all of it. I..." I trailed off, looking away. "I really appreciate it."

I wouldn't tell him that no one had ever done anything this nice for me. At least not without wanting something in return. He nodded and smiled, bringing our hands down and closing the door before he looped my hand in his arm and pulled me along with him toward the meeting.

"Where have you been?" I asked.

"I had a few meetings, and I had to go out to the coast to monitor the progress of some of our troops."

I nodded, it seemed like something was bothering him, and I was starting to feel like maybe it was me.

"Did I do something wrong," I whispered.

He stopped us and turned to me. "You did nothing wrong," he stated firmly.

"Oh, okay, I thought maybe you were trying to avoid me or something."

"I wasn't—"

Ishani cut him off as she glided over to us in an all-white sleeveless dress that brushed the ground in a way that made her look like she was floating. Her dark curls were pulled back with two silver combs, and the black diamonds set into them sparkled as she moved.

"Hey, you two ready?" she asked.

Axel and I nodded, and I turned back to see if he would finish his thought, but he had already continued walking.

"What's up his ass?" Ishani asked.

"I have no idea," I whispered back.

Ishani shrugged, and we followed behind him to the war council room in the training wing.

"Why are we meeting there?" I questioned.

"This will inevitably turn to war; everyone who's joining would join the war council as well," she said with a small smile.

"It was stupid of me to think I'd get a break from war," I sighed.

"Every day is war," Ishani retorted.

I looked at her, turning my head slightly at the words I'd used before. While Ishani was undeniably more optimistic and brighter than me, we were honestly a lot alike. I'd seen her shift into warrior mode in training the last few days, she was just as ruthless as me, and I honestly couldn't wait to fight beside her. We made it to the room, and Axel waited for me at the door, letting Ishani into the room and looking over at me.

"Are you sure we're okay?" I asked.

"*We?*" he taunted with a smile.

"Hush," I responded, knocking him on my shoulder.

His smile faded as his face transitioned to a serious glare. "I told you I didn't want you to be anyone but who you are. That's especially important in this meeting. They will follow my command as their king, but make them want to follow you, too."

I nodded, and he straightened, the look of a centuries-old king gracing his face. I'd been around him with his family, where he was king, yes, but he was also just a brother and friend. This Axel, though, I hadn't seen since the meeting with Sanjry, and fuck was it attractive. He let some of his power roll off him as he stepped into the room and stood at the end of the table, looking over at me as I walked in behind him. Everyone in the room stood, even Ishani, and bowed at the waist, holding and waiting for him to release them.

"Rise," he boomed.

They all rose as one, and Axel sat, the rest of them following close behind as I took my seat beside him.

"Thank you all for attending," he started, running his gaze down the table. "Some of you have met our guest, but some of you are meeting for the first time now. This is Dayanara Amapola, the Acna of the brujas, goddess blessed, rightful heir to Caldera."

My throat tightened slightly at the titles, some I'd heard and some he added on. All eyes turned to me, and mine immediately fell on a woman who sat a few seats down across the table from me. She was a witch; I could feel her energy, and I knew she was the leader of the clan that resided here.

"Hello, thank you for allowing me to join." I stated, making eye contact with them all the way Ax had. I could see Zuri's hair at the far end of the table but wasn't able to look at her as she was sitting back in her chair.

Ishani sat forward across from me. "This is Maeve, the leader of the witch clan in Dusra," she said as she pointed to the woman I'd pegged as a witch a few moments ago.

Maeve dipped her chin. "It's a pleasure to meet you, Acna."

"I didn't know there were any other witches outside of Caldera," I said with a tilt of my head.

"We've been here for a long time, far before you were born," she responded.

I nodded, not sure what the proper response was. If she'd fled, it could be assumed they didn't leave on good terms.

"This is Nia," Ishani said, directing her hand toward the woman sitting beside Zuri. "Leader of the lobos."

Nia nodded at me once, and Zuri shifted slightly beside her. Akari sat beside Zuri, and Ishani pointed to the men between Akari and Xavier. "Maverick and Damon, captains in my army."

They both nodded and gave their best smile, but they didn't seem like the smiling type, so the movement fell short.

"Everyone else you've met, Xavier, Akari, Paxx, Zuri," she trailed off, looking away from me.

"Thank you, Ishani. Dayanara," Axel exclaimed before he waved his hand to advise the floor was mine.

"Tell them your story, all of it," Axel spoke into my mind.

I took a deep centering breath. "I was raised as a weapon for my mother, the prior Acna of the brujas. From a young age, she planned to kill me in hopes to bring back our creator, Naom. She devised a plan with Kaizer, the King of Sanjry, and they attempted to kill me a few days ago." I paused as I felt Axel's magic let loose again. Zuri's head popped out and looked over at him as I did the same.

"She failed." I stated, looking away from Axel. "They both did. Unfortunately for my kingdom at the time we signed the treaty with yours, the land became under the rule of Kaizer. Caldera is his right now. He's on the search for a dark relic that will help him take over all of Malva; we are convinced he thinks it's here. He has a group of fanatics called the Embers that are helping him, and it is only time until he makes a move. My mother had people working for her before I killed her, so I'm not sure who I can trust there."

Nobody spoke, but they looked to Axel for his reaction.

"Kaizer is planning on taking Dusra, on taking all of Malva. That will not happen. We are looking into what he might be looking for; Paxx hasn't let us down yet, so we can assume we'll have that information soon. I don't foresee a way out of this that avoids war," Axel added.

"Will the witches fight with Sanjry?" Nia asked.

"Not all of them, but the ones who followed my mother will."

"I have our contact in Caldera validating the numbers. They will report back on how many they believe will follow her," Paxx expressed.

Paxx didn't speak often, he seemed to prefer to watch people instead. A lot of what I've had to say to him had gone through Ishani. I wasn't sure if he didn't trust me, but he always watched me more than the others.

"The armies haven't had a true war in centuries. They're ready for blood. The ones who have chosen to leave the site on the coast have been summoned back to start training again," Ishani said.

"What is your Acna gift?" Maeve asked.

I took a deep breath and stood, and I noticed Paxx place his hand atop the weapon at his side at the sudden movement. I called to the power that felt like it always wanted to escape me, granting its wish and letting it encompass me. My skin glowed with the swirl of galaxy-like colors that came with this power, the wings settling on my back and spreading to their full wingspan. My hair shifted around my shoulders as I felt my eyes start to glow. I let some of my power roll off me like Axel had, and the room shook, papers shifting on the table. I lifted my hand and allowed some of the magic to pool in my hand, letting it grow and float from my fingers before closing my fist and looking back at the people around me.

"Goddess blessed," Maeve started, looking over at Axel. "That is...That's incredible. I don't even have words."

I smirked at her and nodded my appreciation. Ishani and I had been working on trying to get the wings to stay without my skin turning into a beacon of light. I did what we practiced, willing the magic in my skin to pull back in and the wings to remain. The magic listened to me faster than it had when I tried before. I pulled the wings in tight, the muscles still not used to the movement, and sat in the chair. I looked down at the table to find Zuri watching me, like everyone else had, but her eyes still looked so sad. I cleared my throat and looked back at Maeve. "I don't know if I have any other capabilities, but so far, that is what I've found."

"I'd say that you've gotten more than most," she responded.

"That she has indeed," Axel agreed.

I found his gaze heavy on me like it had been a few days ago, and I had to look away before it had the same effect on me.

"Of course, we will advise of anything we find out," Ishani started, and I watched Axel shake from his daze and look at her from my peripheral vision. "As for now, assume war is coming and plan accordingly among your people."

Nia and Maeve nodded, and Axel stood, forcing everyone else to stand as well. I wasn't notified that was something I should do, so I was the last to stand.

"You all are welcome to stay for dinner; I believe a feast has been prepared in the main dining hall."

"Yes, that is correct," Xavier added.

They referred to Xavier as Axel's second, but I'd come to realize that was actually Ishani in reality. She commanded the armies, but everyone respected her as the royalty she was. Xavier seemed to handle the more day-to-day things; he went out to the island to deal with whatever issue Axel had talked about before. Today was his first day back since the day I'd gotten here, and he watched me in a similar way to Paxx, but not nearly as mysteriously. I could see in his eyes he was worried about Axel, surely wondering what the dark witch in the castle could do to his king.

"You are all dismissed. I'll see you shortly," Axel exclaimed.

Everyone started shuffling out of the room; I stood, forgetting I still had the wings out and accidentally brushed Axel's side with my right wing.

"Oops," I muttered as the last person left the room.

"You should put those away." Axel laughed.

The first real smile since he'd picked me up at my room, but the crinkle in his eyes that came with the smile made me notice slight smudges under them. I hadn't heard him come or go from his room at all, and I wondered if he'd slept since.

"You going to tell me what's wrong with you?" I asked.

His jaw ticked. "Your blood...it did something to me. I don't know how to explain it, but it's like my own special brand of drug. I had to stop myself from going back to your room and demanding more. I didn't feel in control, so I had to leave. I didn't want to hurt you."

"I think you're underestimating how much I can take," I teased.

"I'm serious, Daya. It felt like bloodlust, and I hadn't even gone an hour since feeding from you."

I pulled my wings back in, feeling the weight vanish, and stood up straighter. I took a step toward him, and he looked away from me as his body went rigid.

"I'm not scared of you, Ax."

He still hadn't moved, and I took another two steps until I was only an inch away from him and tilted my chin up to look into his eyes. "I'll give you more blood if you need it."

"I've had three cups of goat blood today just to make sure I didn't attack you the moment I laid eyes on you. I can smell it now." He sniffed.

I put my hand on his arm and smiled. "You get one taste of me, and you're obsessed, huh?"

He smirked, and I knew I had him.

"Just wait until you get the full meal," I whispered.

"I'll have to leave for a week." He chuckled.

"I'd rather you not." I hit his chest and backed up a step. "Did that go well?" I gestured to the table where his council sat previously.

He nodded. "It did. I don't like that I don't have all the information to tell them, but it seemed like everyone was on the same page."

"I don't think Paxx likes me." I laughed.

"I told you, you're a mystery to him. He doesn't like mysteries."

"Don't think Xavier likes me either, actually...I think the only person in your council who likes me is Ishani."

"And me," he added with a smile. "Xavier is chronically worried about me; I think he believes it's his job. Akari, well, I think you know why she doesn't like you."

I grimaced. "Yeah, I don't have much hope for that one."

"Well, it's time to go have dinner with all of your best friends."

I rolled my eyes and laughed as Axel walked past me to the door. *Here goes nothing.*

Chapter Fifty-One

Dinner went better than expected, with only a few questions directed at me. They weren't invasive questions, and mostly from Nia and Maeve. Zuri had sat as far away from me again, which was appreciated. I forgave her, more for myself than for her, but I still didn't want to make small talk with her. Axel had changed the subject when he felt me not wanting to answer more, and I also appreciated that.

They'd brought the wine out now, and I was already one glass in as we moved away from the long table and over to a space with high tables and couches throughout. I waited for my glass to be refilled, so I was the last one in the room. Maeve flagged me down before I could choose where to go, and I walked over to where she was leaning against one of the tables.

"So, Acna, I'm sure you have questions."

"I do, a shit ton, actually," I responded.

Maeve laughed and took a sip of her wine, licking her lips before looking back at me. "We came here a few thousand years ago. Your grandmother a few generations back and my kin did not see eye to eye. You know the brujas. We're ruthless, but we didn't think that had to be the only way to live. My family had a friendship with Ax's mother's family, and they offered them refuge so they didn't have to stay in the Inbetween."

"Was my grandmother like my mother?"

She pursed her lips. "Your mother seemed to be her own brand of cruel," she said, her eyes seeming to look through my body to the scars on my back. "From what I know, your ancestor was power hungry, but she did not make anywhere near the type of decisions your mother did."

I studied her face; her brown skin had some slight wrinkles, the only sign of her age. She had very short black hair, almost as cropped as Paxx, but with slightly more length allowing a single curl. Her dark eyes studied me back, and I could feel that she had more questions for me, but wasn't sure if she should ask.

"If we are to work together, you may ask me whatever you wish," I said, breaking our stare.

"My people don't want to fall under the rule of a tyrant. I worry about what is to come."

"You believe me to be a tyrant?" I asked.

"I believe you haven't discovered the true depth of your power yet. I know you can feel it; I can feel it just standing near you. Axel was not lying when he said you were goddess blessed. But that much power can bring a certain level of ill-directed confidence. You are not indestructible, but sometimes it can feel that way when you wield the magic you do."

"I just want my kingdom back. I will do what it takes to make that happen," I retorted, the power she spoke of pressing against my skin.

"That is what I worry about. At what expense? At *who's* expense?"

"At Sanjry's."

She nodded, her gaze warming slightly. "I hope that is all."

Ishani came over and leaned her elbows on the table we were standing at. "Why do you two look so serious? It's the after party. Drink, be happy. While we still can."

Maeve laughed and took another sip of her wine. "I'm afraid it is time for me to retire; I can't hang with you young folk anymore."

She rubbed my arm as she walked by, a gesture that felt maternal, and bid her goodbyes to everyone. Paxx and Xavier left shortly after, followed by the captains I met. Leaving me, Akari, Zuri, Ishani, and Axel. Axel was sitting on a couch by himself, watching the others across the room laugh together at something I didn't hear, and I sat beside him.

"Why are you just watching?" I asked.

"I like to see them like this. Akari missed her cousin, Ishani missed her friend," he responded as he took a sip of his wine and put his arm on the back of the couch behind me.

I followed his gaze and watched as Zuri flailed her arms in the air, appearing to be reenacting something they'd all been through. Akari's light brown braids shifted in front of her face as she bent over and put her hand on Zuri's knee. Ishani pushed Zuri over into Akari, and their laughter picked up.

"Zuri and I were never as close as them. We're both Alphas in our own right and we butt heads pretty often," he added before bringing his glass back up to his lips.

"Well, I currently like you better, so I'm fine with staying over here," I joked.

He looked at me and smiled, a smile that nearly had me melting. But beyond the magnetic pull I had with him, we really hadn't talked that much about ourselves.

"Tell me something about yourself that I don't know. Something real," I said.

"What do you want to know?"

I shrugged, and he laughed, tapping his finger to his chin in a mocking gesture. "I like the water. I have a house on the island I like to visit when I'm feeling overwhelmed."

"Your kingdom's power is water. That seems like a given," I taunted.

"It remains true."

Trying to build a genuine connection with someone was sort of odd. I hadn't really done much of it outside of Zuri. I felt like I should be asking deeper questions to get to know him better, and I thought back to his face when we were in the museum looking at his painting.

"Tell me about the painting," I said.

Axel's smile faded, and he looked over at Ishani, still locked in conversation with her friends. He turned his gaze back to me; one of his curls had broken free from his style and shifted in front of his forehead in the movement.

"That is not a happy story," he said flatly.

I tilted my head. "I didn't say it had to be happy, just real."

He scratched his chin and nodded, turning his body slightly more toward mine. "During a battle in the war against Sanjry hundreds of years ago, I was separated from my battalion. I was just another soldier in the army at this point, not yet king. I chased a soldier away from the battle, and I lost them in the thick of a forest. Some substance fell over me in the woods, and it immobilized my magic."

"A magic suppressant?" I asked. That was witch magic, a magic my mother was quite fond of.

He nodded. "I fought hard, but there were at least twenty soldiers waiting for me. They captured me and took me back to Sanjry, keeping me in a cell in the dungeons for months. They tortured me and brought me to bloodlust over and over. At some point I lost track of time. There are days I don't even remember. I'd wake up in the cell with new scars, new bruises but no recollection of what I did to get them...I try not to think about that too much. What I might have done during the hours and days I couldn't remember." Shadows ran over his eyes as he looked away from me and swallowed. "They wanted to use me to get information on our next move, but I didn't give them anything. Using me against my parents as a bargaining chip was their plan, but it didn't work as they intended. There was one day the guard didn't dose me with the suppressant in time. I had just enough magic to kill him, but I hadn't had proper blood in months and didn't escape. I was punished for that."

He paused and lifted his shirt, exposing his tattooed chest. I hadn't realized before that one of the tattoos was covering a scar. It was brutal and ragged and had to be given to him with a poisoned blade to reject healing magic.

"My parents were trying to play their cards right to win the battle and get me back. I wouldn't have wanted my kingdom sacrificed to save me, and they knew that. Ishani didn't agree, and it forced a rift between them until the day they died. She is the one who saved me, her and Xavier. They brought the war outside Sanjry's capital, and she obliterated their army. She cut her way straight to the palace, killing everyone in her path. I still don't know how she did it. I was barely conscious when she found me, and I nearly killed her because I was so far gone. She portaled us home, and Xavier forced me to feed from him. It took me months to get back to my former self. After trying a few other things and visiting some old friends, someone suggested I try art to get the rage out of me. I painted the painting, and from that day, I decided it was my past. I haven't missed a day of training since then, making sure I never fully rely on my magic. No matter how powerful."

It finally dawned on me that the others had stopped laughing, and I realized it had stopped after Axel showed me his scar. Ishani's bright magic was rolling down her shoulders, and Zuri and Akari watched us with sad eyes.

"I'm...sorry," I said, a weak response, but I wasn't sure what words I could offer him.

"It's behind me. I'm just happy to be here."

Zuri and Akari left the room, and Ishani walked over to us, placing her hand on her hip. "You two are real downers, you know that?"

The tight air in the room dissipated, and we both laughed.

"She asked a question. I merely answered," Ax responded.

"Well, I'm going into the city to find some fun. You guys want to join?"

I shrugged. "I'm in."

We both looked over at Ax, and he smiled, standing to his feet. "Fun sounds great."

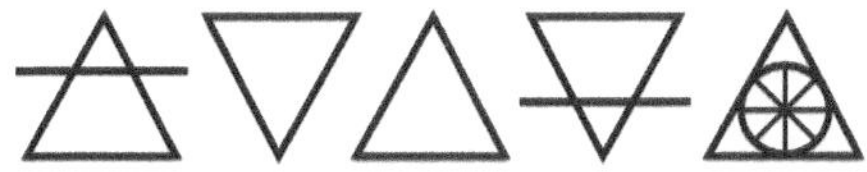

Ishani had us change before we left, which I was thankful for because we would have been ridiculously overdressed for the pub we ended up at. It was a shitty establishment, but I'd come to love this type of place over the years. Ishani was on the dance floor with some large man, a vampire from the looks of it; she whispered something into his ear and then sank her fangs into his neck. The man laughed and pulled her close as she fed from him. I looked over at Axel, who rolled his eyes but laughed at his sister.

"She's wilder than I would have expected." I laughed.

"Ishani does as she pleases, that's for sure," he replied.

The combination of wine and ale in me had my face warm, and the beat of the music had me dancing where I sat.

"Come dance with me," I said, grabbing Ax's hand.

He didn't move and looked up at me. "I've never been very good. You go," he said.

I shrugged and danced over to where Ishani had just yanked her fangs from the man's neck. He pulled her by her hand, but she pulled back when she saw me. "Later," she muttered to the man, and he nodded before taking her empty cup with him to the bar.

"Found your fun, did you?" I asked.

I started dancing, swaying my hips to the beat as Ishani laughed. "He might be. We'll see."

I could barely hear anything but the music, and I let it transport me to a place where I wasn't in a strange land and I hadn't lost my kingdom. I kept moving until Ishani mysteriously backed away toward the large man she had been dancing with earlier, and I waved my hand, shooing her away.

"Go," I mouthed, and she ran toward him.

I turned around and felt a hand around my waist, a handsome man with dark skin and darker eyes coming up behind me. I ground my hips against him, and he ran his hand through my hair. I could feel Axel's gaze on me, swore I could hear him growling in my head, but I hadn't looked at him yet. I bent over before flipping my hair and looking him dead in his eyes. Axel stared back, his jaw ticking and his fist clenched. I wasn't sure why I enjoyed provoking him, but it was probably because I liked the monster that lived within him.

After spending my life as the predator, hunting whatever prey my mother set me on, being the hunted sent a thrill through my body I couldn't explain. I had Kaizer to thank for that realization, regretfully. I turned around and pushed my chest against the man, swaying my hips in tune with his as he stared down at me like he'd just won the prize of the night.

He hadn't, but I'd let him think it so I could continue my little game. I felt his hands run up my back, and I turned around to push my ass against him instead. The man dipped his nose into the crook of my neck, and I looked back over to the table Ax was sitting at, but he wasn't there anymore. The man behind me stopped moving, and I heard a gurgle, finding Axel with his hand around the man's throat, tossing him to the side.

He grabbed me and tossed me over his shoulder before carrying me up a set of stairs I hadn't noticed before. The hall wasn't well-lit, and I heard noises coming from one of the far rooms that sounded like someone was having a *wonderful* time. Axel dropped me on the ground and pushed me up against the wall, caging me in between his arms. His magic was pulsing around us, the dark feel of it getting my heart beating even faster.

"Jealous, Ax?" I taunted.

He growled in my ear and ran his nose up the side of my neck instead of answering.

"You could have danced with me. You're the one who decided to be boring and stay at the table."

The wood on the wall creaked beneath Axel's arm as he pushed harder against it, the faint glow of his black magic rolling down his arms.

"I'll show you boring," he muttered.

I didn't see him move because of how dark it was, but I felt his hands lift me up as he wrapped my legs around him and pushed me against the wall so hard my head banged against it. My eyes glowed purple from the force of it, and it sent a soft radiance across his face. His eyes were pinning me down, his gaze not moving from my mouth.

"Hurry up and do someth—"

His mouth was on mine before I could get the words out, and a gasp escaped me as he immediately pushed his tongue into my mouth. I could feel how hard he was already as he ground his hips into mine. The slice of his fang across my bottom lip shocked me as blood spilled from it. He sucked my whole lip into his mouth, and I felt the blood pull from the cut as he moaned at the taste. His hands ran up my sides and into my hair as he wrapped his hand around it and yanked my head to the side. He kissed down my neck, running his fangs across the sensitive flesh before he licked back up and propped me up on his hips.

Ax pulled at my shirt. "Take it off," he demanded.

I did as he asked and pulled it over my head, exposing the bra I wore beneath the shirt that pushed my breasts up. He ran his gaze over them before he pulled it to the side and lifted me high enough to take one of my nipples in his mouth. He toyed with my other nipple, rolling it between his fingers and squeezing it before moving to suck on it as well. I ran my fingers through his hair as I bit my lip, my core on fire with need. He brought me back down and pressed his mouth to mine again as his hand reached between us, and he pressed his palm over my pussy.

"Is this where you want me?" he asked.

I nodded rapidly as I pulled at the band of his pants.

"Use your words," he growled.

My chest was heaving, and I swallowed hard. "Yes."

"Yes, what?"

He pushed his hand harder against me, and I tightened my legs around him. "Yes, that's where I want you," I got out between gasps.

"Good girl," he growled.

He turned me around and pulled my pants down so they hung around my knees, and then I heard the rustling of his pants coming down as well. I looked over my shoulder just as he drove himself right into me. I screamed, and he grabbed me by my chin and turned it toward him, swallowing the sound. We were only at the top of the stairs, and there were people in the rooms around us as well as downstairs, but I couldn't help it.

He pulled back out slowly and thrust back in with force. I didn't have to see his cock to know how big it was. I felt it in places I'd never been touched within me. He let my face go and gripped my hips as he picked up his pace and drove in and out of me. His hand wrapped around my throat from behind, muffling my moans, as I could barely breathe enough to form the sound.

Ax squeezed harder, and I bit my lip as he thrust again, holding it there so deep inside me I wasn't sure where he ended and I began. My vision started to blur at the edges, and he released the hold, turning me around and lifting me in the air as he pulled my pants off the rest of the way. I wrapped my arms around his neck, and he pushed back inside of me, gripping me by my ass and using his hold on me to move me along his cock. I closed my eyes, and my head fell back; he pulled out to his tip and put one hand behind my head, pushing it to tilt it back down.

"Eyes on me, Daya."

I did as he asked, and I bit my lip as he rammed back inside me, the new position setting every piece of me on fire.

"That's it, watch me move in you," he rasped.

I met every push of his hips with mine, and the sound of flesh on flesh bounced around the hallway just as a doorknob rattled down the hall.

"Fuck," I whispered.

I flicked out a tendril of air magic and wrapped it around the doorknob on the door behind us, hoping that no one was in the room. I yanked, and the door swung open; I blasted another bit of my magic to float us into the thankfully empty room and slammed the door behind us. Axel pressed my body into his as he kissed my neck, and I pushed his head harder into me. Moaning, I flicked my wrist again to light an orb of magic so we could see. He backed up until his legs hit the bed, and he sat down, pulling out and bringing me down with him. I pushed him by his chest to try to get him to lie on his back, and he didn't move. *Someone doesn't like being told what to do.* I pushed harder, and he bobbed but didn't lie back all the way still.

"It's my turn to fuck you," I declared.

I formed ropes of air with my magic around his wrists, wrapping them around the bed frame and pulling hard enough to force him back. His arms were pulled out to the sides, and I straddled him again, wrapping my hands around his gleaming cock. Axel leaned his head up and watched as I put it back inside me, sitting back to take all of him in. I placed my hands on his chest and leaned against it for leverage as I lifted my hips tortuously slow and brought them back down even slower. Axel's arms bulged, but my magic remained intact; I was sure he could break it if he really wanted to, but he was playing along for now.

"You want to touch me?" I asked, leaning in and rubbing my chest against his. I brought my mouth to his ear and nipped at his ear lobe. "All you have to do is ask," I whispered.

I lifted my hips, picking up speed and bouncing my ass up and down along his cock. He leaned to the side to watch, and I smirked as his mouth fell open slightly. His dark magic rolled out from his hands, wrapping around my air and strangling them until they dissipated. He quickly flipped us and pulled me up to my knees before he grabbed both of my wrists and held them behind my back.

His magic caressed my mind, the feel of it somehow heightening the sensation of him inside me. *"You want control?"* he growled inside my head. *"All you have to do is ask."*

His grip around my wrists was bruising as he inserted himself again, but this time, he picked up speed immediately. He drove himself into me so hard and fast that my cheek pressed into the mattress. I had no way to stop the sounds coming from me as I screamed so loud that I felt my throat start to burn. I pushed some of my witch magic from my hands into my wrists, burning his hands, but he didn't let go. I pushed my magic harder. He finally let go, and I pushed him down to the ground.

I straddled him, and he put himself back inside me, both of us over the game and ready to fucking come. He gripped the back of my neck and pulled my head toward him, sinking his fangs into my flesh. He drank from me deeply as I rode him like my life depended on it. He thrust up with every drag of my hips, and we moved together until ecstasy blasted into me. I felt his cock twitch inside of me as he moaned my name around my neck. His venom was still coursing through me, elongating the orgasm to a blissful extent of time. It was almost too much, and my legs went weak as I put my full weight on him, and he continued drinking. He pulled his fangs from me, and I rolled over onto the floor beside him with my legs across his body.

"Fuck," I got out between pants.

"I take it back. I'll need a month away from you to get back control," he rasped.

"We can do that a hundred more times. No need for control," I said, rolling onto my side.

He laughed and closed his eyes as he caught his breath, and I watched his chest heave, the tattoos moving along with every pant. It wasn't love, it wasn't quite what I had with Zuri, but fuck was it mind-blowing.

Chapter Fifty-Two

Paxx notified Ax that he had an update from his contact in Caldera, and Ax knocked on my door far earlier than I would have woken up after a night of drinking. I didn't remember getting back to my room; after me and Ax's mind-shattering sex, we went back down to join Ishani and drank way too much. Well, I did, at least. From what I remember, Ax mostly monitored me and his sister, who at one point got on a table and danced like she was being paid for it, but no one really batted an eye at her. I was surprised at the acceptance of such behavior from vampires. Most of my experience had been with the Sanjryans, and they were prude as fuck. There was something heartwarming about Ishani being exactly who she wanted to be no matter where she was or who she was with. Something I always *said* I was, but I didn't always live up to it. Axel eventually got her down when she almost fell off the table, but he didn't seem bothered by the act itself.

"You almost ready?" Axel shouted.

"Yeah," I responded, coming out of my closet with a boot in hand. "Just need to put my shoes on, and I'm ready."

Another thing I loved about Dusra was that no one seemed to feel the need to be dressed up all the time. Wearing my leathers wasn't frowned upon, and I took advantage of that today.

"Did he say what information he had?"

"No, I just checked in with him when I woke up, and he said that he received intel."

I tilted my head. "Do you mind-to-mind check on all of your council every morning?"

"Yes, actually."

"Will I be getting that treatment, too, at some point?" I questioned with a smirk.

"Well, I'd like to roll over and check on you, but if I'm not here, sure. I can add you to my morning check-in list," he said with a smile that had my heart doing flips.

I laughed and pulled my hair back. "Ready."

I was trying to keep my expectations in check, as I had no real idea what Paxx was going to say. But...a small part of me was hoping that it would be good news. I could count on one hand how many times the tiny optimistic voice in my head had been right, which was why I considered myself more of a pessimist. A realist, really, life wasn't all rainbows and sparkly shit, and I had more than enough experience to back that up. Ax had glanced at me a few times, and I was starting to worry if he thought yesterday was a mistake.

"Why do you keep looking at me like that?" I finally asked, the words coming out harsher than I meant.

"I just have a bad feeling about what he's going to say," he sighed.

I was relieved when he came to my room so early today; the last time we had an intimate moment, he was gone for days. I didn't regret it at all, but I honestly couldn't think of a time I regretted having sex with anyone. Not everyone looked at it as recreationally as I did, and I hadn't had too much experience being rejected, so I was thankful that wasn't what was happening now.

"Me too," I agreed.

We turned the corner toward Paxx's office, and I balled my hands into fists, suddenly more anxious than I was when I left my room. Axel pushed the door open, and Paxx sat behind his desk, writing on a piece of paper.

"Good morning," Axel exclaimed.

"Hey, thanks for coming by so fast," Paxx started, looking over at me. "Good morning, Dayanara," he finished.

I hated that I couldn't read his face. He never showed an ounce of what was going on in his head. He was actually rather attractive, something I hadn't really noticed before, as I never looked at him very long. His dark skin was so smooth it didn't seem real, only rivaled by those piercing black eyes. He had a strong beard-covered jawline with high cheekbones to match, and his lashes were exceptionally long and curly, much like Axel's.

"What have you heard?" I asked.

Paxx motioned for us to sit, and I sat across from him, beside Axel, and leaned forward, waiting for him to hurry up and say something.

"My contact had advised of the status of your kingdom. Some of it is good, and some of it is less than ideal," Paxx said before pausing.

"Fucking spit it out," I retorted, and Ax bit his lip to stop from laughing.

Paxx chuckled, the most regular noise I'd heard from him since meeting him. "It appears that your mother had more people in on her plan than you originally thought. It seems like it's most of the older generation who have followed her. Some of them have moved over to Sanjry, and some of them have stayed to get the others in line. My contact was able to get in touch with Catalina, and she has gone into hiding with a number of witches who have vowed to follow you and not Kaizer. She said that you would know where she was, but that you wouldn't like it. They also said that they believe the Embers to be close to whatever it is Kaizer has them looking for. They weren't able to get into your vaults, but whatever they are looking for now isn't in Caldera. The only information she had about it was that the Embers had moved away from Caldera and back to Sanjry. But there is talk from my other contacts in Sanjry that it's some sort of artifact that will give him the power of all the elements."

"Do you know of anything like that?" I asked Ax.

He rubbed the stubble on his jaw. "No, I don't know what that could be."

"Do you know where Catalina is?" Paxx asked.

"If she said I wouldn't like it, she's in the desert. I fucking hate the desert."

"From what I'm told, they are in hiding because your mother's followers have sworn to kill anyone who follows you. I'm not sure if it is because your mother had a contingency plan, or if he's actually lured them to his side. Either way, your loyal witches are being hunted. It may be worth trying to get them out. You could bring them here," Paxx added.

"Isn't the one sworn rule of being a witch that you must follow the Acna?" Axel asked.

I nodded. "It is because the Acna was the most powerful thing in our land. It seems they think whatever Kaizer is going to find will create someone even more powerful. Between that and the fact he has our kingdom, they're betting on him for their survival."

"They don't know the power you were given, do they?" Paxx asked.

"No, I didn't receive it until I fought my mother. They were all gone at that point."

"You could probably sway some of them to follow you if you show them," Paxx suggested.

I shrugged one shoulder. "Did they say anything about Kaizer?"

He tapped his knuckle on the desk a few times, his only tell that he wasn't sure how to word what he wanted to say. "Kaizer has declared that you two were married the night of your ascension. He is claiming that after the marriage, you killed your mother in cold blood and fled the scene. He is offering a reward for information about where you might be and has said that he will do anything to return you to where you belong. He's looking for you and Zuri, actually. He knows you left together, and that she'd probably have information about where you are. The only stipulation he has is that if you are to be found that you are returned to him alive."

A sound emitted from Axel's chest, somewhere between a snarl and a growl, as my mouth turned up in disgust.

"For what? There's no way he still wants me as queen if that's what he's telling people. The people didn't accept me before. They won't accept me now if they believe I'm an unhinged murderer who fled my *husband*."

Paxx looked at Axel and back over to me. "He said that you would…bear him the most powerful children, that they would be what's best for the kingdom. He also said that you would be kept under watch to ensure you behaved when you're returned."

I barked a laugh; the fucker was delusional. There was no other explanation. "I'd sooner bite his fucking dick off," I sneered.

"There's no world where you're ever returned to him," Axel snapped.

I bit the inside of my cheek, unsure of what I should do next. "I thought he was looking for the element stones at first, but even with them, he can't use anything other than the firestone. It can't be possible, right? To wield all four elements? Surely that much magic would kill the wielder."

"I think we would be smart not to rule anything out. The question is that he believes whatever he's looking for is in my land. We may need to visit the island soon. If it's something my ancestors knew of, it would be there."

Paxx nodded. "I already have any information regarding the topic being pulled from the Great Library; I'm just not sure how much there will be."

"How in control of your new powers do you feel?" Ax asked.

"Pretty in control, but I haven't been in a real battle yet. I'm not sure what heightened emotions would do to that control."

"It's up to you what we do next. We can go and collect Catalina and those who are in hiding, or we can hope they remain safe long enough for us to figure out what Kaizer is looking for."

"I need to get them out. They are what I'm fighting for right now. Plus, they can help in battle," I answered.

"We can leave immediately if you're sure you know where they are," Axel responded.

"I'm sure. The desert is the only place in all of Caldera I don't like." I paused. "Wait…can you cross the border into Caldera, Ax?"

"As far as the magic is concerned, I can't send you there. That is why I let you make the choice. I was very specific with the agreement. Regarding the treaty itself, no I'm technically not allowed. But I will go," Axel advised.

"You should take a few more people with you. I'm not sure what you're going to face when you get there," Paxx added.

"Ishani and Xavier are out on the coast. We'll have to take Akari, maybe one other soldier," Axel suggested.

Great, I'd love to spend time with Akari.

"I'll take care of things here while you're gone," Paxx exclaimed.

We both got up and swiftly left the room to find Akari. At this time, she should be in the training wing...most likely with Zuri. Paxx didn't say how many people were with Cat, but I was sure it would be at least a few thousand. There was only one place that would hold that many people, so I was pretty certain of where they were. Axel's steps were hurried as we made it over to the training wing, finding Akari and the castle guard in the middle of their morning training. They all stopped as Axel and I walked in, and he waved his hand to tell them to continue what they were doing. The noise picked back up as we headed toward where Akari stood on the side of the courtyard near one of the rooms.

"What's wrong?" she asked, her hand dipping to her sword on her side.

"We got information about some of the witches in Caldera being hunted for following Dayanara. The ones who have sworn alliance with Kaizer are trying to track them down; we have an idea of where they are and are going to retrieve them. We need you to come with us since we aren't sure what we're running into."

Akari nodded once. "Just me, or should we bring more?"

"Bring one more soldier, one of your best," Axel responded.

"I'm going to grab some more weapons," I said as I turned toward the armory room.

I never went on a mission without at least four weapons, and I only had one dagger on me right now since I wasn't expecting to be leaving the castle when I woke up. The armory was in the far corner of the wing, and a few of the soldiers training watched me as I walked by. Everyone seemed curious about me, and I wasn't sure if I should be feeling threatened or not under their gaze.

I pushed the door open and flicked on the light, hundreds of sparkling blades coming into view. The walls were lined with bigger weapons, swords, spears, short swords, and larger daggers, and shelves held smaller daggers and knives. I grabbed one of the knives and tucked it into the holster on my leathers, and eyed the rest of the weapons. I felt a presence coming up from behind me, and I whirled around with a knife from one of the shelves in my hand to find Zuri standing in the doorway.

"Hey," she muttered.

I released a breath and set the knife back down. "Hi," I responded.

She didn't say anything else, so I went back to looking for weapons before she went into one of the closets in the room. I did my best to try to ignore her and grabbed another dagger, bigger than the one I already had strapped to my left thigh, and strapped that one to my right thigh. I ran my fingers over the swords when Zuri came back into the room with a bundle of fabric.

"I," she started, her voice cracking slightly. "I had this made for you when we got here. I was hoping it would be a way to win you back, but...I realize that isn't going to happen. Anyway, it's yours."

She unraveled the fabric and pulled out a great steel sword from within it. The dark blade curved slightly, something etched into its surface. The hilt was black as well, with a purple amethyst stone set into the pommel. Zuri twisted it in her hand and handed it to me, her skin brushing against mine as I took it from her. I ran my finger down the blade to find the etchings to be flowers and vines, like the ones from the courtyard of my home and my tattoos.

"It's...beautiful," I said, flicking my gaze up to hers. "Thank you, Zuri."

"I just want you to know that no matter what, I'll support you. I imagine this war is going to make it hard for any type of bad blood on our side, so I just wanted to make sure you knew that I don't blame you for any of what happened."

I nodded, my chest tightening slightly at the gift. The second gift I received this week that meant more than her or Axel would know. I wasn't as mad at Zuri as I was initially. There was a *slight* chance I over reacted, but I was still rightfully pissed. I didn't think I would necessarily take her back, but I definitely missed her. Axel's large form filled the doorway behind Zuri, and she stepped to the side slightly, but as he walked by, her nose scrunched as she took a whiff of his scent.

Her eyes went wide, and her lips pursed before she threw him a look that could kill, and left the room.

Axel scratched his chin. "Lobos have an exceptional sense of scent. I think she smelled you on me."

He looked at me like he was worried that I regretted what we did, and I looked down at the sword in my hand. "She made her choices. I'm allowed to make mine."

"She had that made for you?" Ax asked as he reached his hand out for the weapon. I handed it over to him, and he inspected the craftsmanship.

I nodded. "Yeah."

"It's quite the weapon," he muttered, like he didn't want to admit it. "She must have had the royal blacksmith make it; nobody else could have achieved this."

I didn't know what to say, so I pulled another knife from the shelf and tucked it into my other ankle. I stood up, and Ax moved my hair over and wrapped the sword scabbard around my back, latching it in place before he slid the sword into the sheath.

"No time to decipher such a gift from a woman who loved you?" he said with a laugh.

"I think love is a stretch," I breathed.

Axel shrugged like he knew better and grabbed a dagger from off the wall.

"Akari is ready, and Damon is coming with us. You met him at the dinner," Axel said as we walked out of the armory.

They met us at the door and followed behind as we walked out into the courtyard. It was early enough in the day that the desert shouldn't be too deadly, but there wasn't any guarantee of that. One of the castle staff was waiting outside with a chalice, and they came to hand it to me. I looked down in the cup to find goat's blood and turned to Axel.

"I figured you'd need the magic boost," Axel said with a lazy smile.

I smirked and downed the blood, handing the cup back to the staff and clapping my hands.

"Wait!" Zuri yelled as she ran toward us.

I turned my head and lifted my chin in expectation of why she was stopping us.

"I want to come with you," she said as she finished strapping a blade to her waist.

Axel looked over at me, allowing me to decide, and I shook my head. "No."

"I just want to help, after everything, please," she begged.

I bit my lip and looked away. "Akari, you're responsible for her."

"She doesn't need a babysitter," Akari quipped as her nose twitched.

"My focus is going to be on getting my brujas back. I can't worry about her," I said before I could stop the last half of the statement.

Zuri looked away quickly with the slightest smile, and I internally cursed myself but stepped forward.

"You all are going to hate this," I said before snapping open a portal big enough for the five of us.

I stepped through to ensure nothing was waiting for us on the other side and stepped back to advise them it was safe to follow. After Akari stepped through, I snapped the portal closed and cleared the violet smoke from around us. We stood on the top of a sand dune in my least favorite place in all of Malva. The Fallen City.

Chapter Fifty-Three

The desert was terrible, but the Fallen City took the cake for the worst place in Caldera. It was referred to as the Fallen City, but it was really more like the decimated city. Mariana, the first Acna and the one depicted in the mural I'd shown Kaizer and Zuri before, had completely demolished the city. The witches that lived here at the time revolted against her, not wanting to fall in line with the rest of the kingdom and follow her as our 'queen.' She had recently gotten her new magic, and the texts said that she released her full power on them, killing everyone who stepped to her and practically flattening every building. Which was no easy task, the sandstone was made to be nearly indestructible against the sandstorms that raged this terrain, but it was no match for her.

Only one small sanction lived in the desert, but none of them lived here. People said this land was cursed by Mariana, but I was pretty sure no one wanted to be reminded of just how powerful my line was. It was rather ironic that the desert was where she died; one of the first places she killed after becoming the Acna was where she met her own end.

"You think they're here?" Akari asked.

"When Cat and I were young, we used to like getting into stupid shit. Before we realized just how dangerous the desert was, we used to come here," I said as I walked over to one of the dilapidated buildings.

I pushed my shoulder into the door and took a step back, waiting to see if the building would come down on itself before opening it the rest of the way and peeking my head in.

"This is one of the oldest places in Caldera, and the people who lived here got used to battling the harsh conditions. They eventually made the sandstone to protect them from the elements and the monsters that roamed the terrain, but before that, they had a different form of protection."

They followed behind me, and I looked around as I tried to find what Cat and I had seen before. It had been well over a century since we'd been here, and so much sand and debris covered the floor that I wasn't sure I had even picked the right house.

"Stand back," I muttered.

They listened and stood against the wall while I created a small tornado in the room and picked up all the loose sand, sending it shooting out of the door.

"Ah," I exclaimed as I crouched down to the floor and lifted the floorboards. A steel door was exposed, and I looked over my shoulder at my companions and smirked. "They built bunkers, some of them span for miles of interconnecting tunnels."

Axel raised his eyebrows, impressed at me or my fellow brujas, I wasn't sure. I yanked the door, but it didn't budge; Axel came to try to help, but I held up my hand for him to stop.

"I think it's sealed," I muttered.

I laid my hand on the warm steel, sending my magic into the substance to feel for a spell. It ran up and down the door before the whole thing lit purple and my magic dissolved. I yanked again, and the door opened, a small rope ladder unraveling and falling to the ground.

"You guys go first. I'm going to set the room back to how it looked before we got here," I commanded.

Axel went first, followed by Damon, Zuri, and then Akari. I created a tornado again outside of the door, picking up sand and letting it spin in the room for a second. I stepped into the bunker and held the door in one hand, flicking my wrist and filling the room with even more sand than before right as I closed the door and resealed it. Unfortunately for the people with me, none of them had any sort of magic that could illuminate the space, so it was pitch black until I lit a purple orb and floated it above our heads. I found myself an inch from Zuri, and her arm brushed mine as I stepped forward to lead the way.

"Now, we're all just as lost because I don't know where they are down here," I admitted.

Akari side-eyed me, and Axel looked around. "Can you make another orb so we can see ahead instead of just around us?"

"Sure," I said, creating two more, sending one down into the hall and the other to float behind us.

"Either of you smell anything?" Axel asked Akari and Zuri.

Akari took a couple sniffs of the air and took a few steps down the path. "No, there were definitely people here before, but I can't tell where they went."

I closed my eyes. "She probably covered her tracks." I listened for anything, but I didn't hear any heartbeats, no rustling of feet, no chatter.

"I'd bet they have a hell of an air shield blocking wherever they are. We're just going to have to search," I said.

"Anything down here we should know about?" Akari asked, drawing her weapon.

"Um, that's an excellent question. There wasn't the last time I was here, but that was over a century ago, so I'd say be on watch."

"Great," Akari muttered.

We moved forward slowly as a unit, thankful that the bunker seemed to be the end of one of the tunnels, so there was nothing behind us for now. If I knew Cat, she would have left me some sort of clues for me to find them, but I just had to figure out what they were. The whole ordeal brought me back to how shitty of a friend I'd been to Cat over the years. I'd be better now, or at least I'd try to be. I didn't really know how to be a good friend just yet, but she was going to extreme lengths to support me, and I knew I could try to return the favor. It was my turn to be loyal and get her out of this shit hole. I felt someone moving to the front of the line with me and I kept my gaze forward, I could tell it was Zuri immediately.

"I hate to take the opportunity of you not being able to run away from me." She sighed. "But I feel like I have to."

I looked over at her and watched as the light from my purple orb floating above us poured over her hair and sparkled in her eyes.

"I just want you to know I meant what I said earlier, I'm on your side. I don't want the fact you hate me to hurt us," she said.

"I don't *hate* you," I whispered. "Maybe I did at first. It hurt, the fact you lied. Everything with my mother and Kaizer was so fresh, it all piled on. I'm not saying what you did was okay. I'm still fucking pissed, but...hate isn't the right word."

"I really am sorry," her voice cracked.

"I know," I responded, turning my gaze back to the hall.

Hate was reserved for people like my mother, like Kaizer. *Hurt* was more of what I'd describe as the situation between Zuri and me. Pain that was still too fresh to move on from, even if I'd forgiven her to a certain extent. A kind of wound that would take time to repair if I ever wanted to make that attempt. Zuri and I felt inevitable before, and while I had said I didn't believe in fate, I had to wonder if that was still true as Zuri grazed my arm. The contact sent tingles under my skin, but she pulled away quickly and went back to walk with Akari.

We'd been walking for an hour, and suddenly my chest got tight, and the air was knocked from my lungs.

"Do you guys feel that?" I asked, looking over my shoulder.

They all shook their heads, and I stopped to run my hands over the walls as I caught my breath. I turned a corner, and the feeling came again. I put my hand on my chest and looked up to find something on the ceiling. Bringing the orb closer, I pushed some air to the ground to help me levitate for a second so I could see the markings. I laughed and released my magic to stand on my feet again. "We used to play this game when we were kids. We'd shoot things with our magic, and we marked how many we got on each side of a barrier, horizontal lines for the left, vertical lines for the right."

Axel came to stand next to me and squinted at the ceiling. "Left, left, right, left, right, right."

"Yeah, they'll be after that last right if she marked it correctly." I smiled.

"Impressive friend," Akari stated.

I nodded and followed her directions, practically running and leaving everyone a few yards behind me. My feet were knocked from under me as I turned the corner and fell on my ass.

"What the fuck," I muttered as I blasted some air on either side of me and got back to my feet.

A rattle sounded, and I immediately grabbed the sword from my back. Axel appeared at my side immediately with his sword drawn, Akari, Zuri, and Damon behind him.

"What is—" Axel started.

A horned viper came charging toward us with its fangs on display, poison dripping from them. These snakes got big; it had to be at least twenty feet long, two or three in circumference.

"Don't let the poison touch you!" I yelled.

I dodged the first snap of its jaws, but in the tight space, it was hard to move, and one of its horns sliced my arm. It whirled its head around for me, its body slithering to follow, now taking up the entire hallway as it chased after me. Akari came charging, her sword slicing into its back, but its scales were thick enough for it only to leave a nick behind.

"How do we kill it?" Axel yelled.

He dodged the snap of its jaws, pulling his sword from its neck with force where he tried to behead the beast.

"Its underside doesn't have armor!" I screamed.

I jumped, putting my foot on the wall and pushing off with a blast of air magic as the snake lifted from the ground to try to trap me in its jaws. Suddenly the floor was frozen, and the snake lost its purchase on the slippery surface. Axel slid underneath it with his sword raised, and the snake's eyes rolled back as its mouth snapped shut an inch from my leg and fell to the ground. I fell on top of it, trying to catch my footing so none of the horns pierced me, and the snake froze over into a block of ice, covering the sharp points. I looked over to see frost on Zuri's fingers as she stood a few feet away from Axel.

"You all were really in sync there," Akari said as her gaze bounced around us.

I looked to Axel, he looked to Zuri, and they both looked to me for a moment, but I quickly turned around to get from under the weight of the stare. We all moved on instinct to protect each other, and I didn't want to look too deeply into that when I needed to get to Cat and my clan.

"One more right, and we should be there," I exclaimed and moved forward.

We turned and met a dead end, and we all stopped, their heads snapping in my direction.

"Did you read the markings correctly?" Akari asked.

"Yeah," I muttered, "one second, stand back."

I took a deep breath and turned my palms to the ceiling, letting my magic escape them and fill the end of the hall. My magic licked up against the walls, searching for a spell or another clue from Cat. It locked onto something, the magic pooling at the corner of the space. I brought my hands down and ran my finger over the corner, feeling a cloaking spell in the stone.

"Got ya," I whispered.

My magic worked to disable the spell, and the stone of the wall disintegrated, another steel door sitting behind it. The handle turned, and the door opened, a thick air shield sitting a few feet from the entry, as I suspected. The others followed behind me, and I closed the door and set the cloaking spell back in place. A hole formed in the shield, and the commotion from within blared through in the silence.

"Daya!" Cat's voice shouted from within.

We stepped through the hole, and Cat barreled into me, knocking me into Axel's hard body. She squeezed me so hard I thought I might pop; my arms were hanging at my sides. I hadn't been hugged like this in…I couldn't tell you how long.

"I was worried they got to you," she whispered into my chest.

I lifted my arms up and returned the embrace, a small yelp escaping Cat as I squeezed her, probably a little too hard. She pulled back and looked up at me with tears in her eyes, and my chest started to tingle.

"I'm alive. I'm here to get you guys out," I exclaimed.

Cat looked over my shoulder at my companions, and her face pulled tight. "Zuri, what are you doing here?"

"I'll explain later," I said quickly, not wanting to dive into that quite yet.

Cat nodded. "And who are they?"

"Um," I started, turning to Axel. "I've been in Dusra. They're helping our cause."

"You trust that?" Cat said, her gaze running up and down Axel.

"I do." I nodded.

"Good enough for me." She shrugged.

Cat turned around and waved her arms out at her sides as she took a step into the space and closed the air shield hole. "We've been here since the day after your ascension. Kaizer told us that you two were married and that you killed your mother, but we didn't believe him. He said you fled him, which apparently is against the law in Sanjry. Who knew?"

"We weren't married. And, well, I did kill my mother," I started, scratching my head. "She tried to kill me first, so it was warranted."

"Why did she attack you?" Cat asked.

"She thought it would return Naom, and she wanted to gain more power. Kaizer was on his own search for old magic, so they joined causes. I'm sure she planned on killing him once she was successful, but she met her end."

"Well shit, she was always a bitch, but I didn't expect that," Cat responded.

I shrugged. "Is what it is. How many are here?"

"There's about 10,000 of us down here; there are some people who haven't chosen a side yet, but there are more people siding with Kaizer than I would have thought."

"Daya said she thinks it's because they believe Kaizer will become more powerful than her. Do you agree?" Ax asked.

Cat's brows raised. "Daya?" she questioned me, and I rolled my eyes. "I can agree with that; the reason the Acna was followed in the first place was because she wielded powers above what we already have."

I looked around the space, and there were tons of witches in this main area, with some of them going up and down halls connected to it.

"How bad has it been down here?" I asked.

Cat sighed, tilting her head to the side. "We've been fine so far. We've had small groups going out for resources every couple of days, but they're definitely getting a bit restless. We don't belong underground."

I nodded my agreement. "You have space for 10,000?" I asked Axel.

"We do. We can take them to the palace for now. Akari can show them to the coast. There should be plenty of space there."

I looked around again, finding a large rock to stand on so everyone could hear me. Small rocks fell with each step until I was high enough to see everyone around me. "May the Acna rule long," I boomed.

"May the witches remain loyal," every witch in the space said in unison.

I smiled. "Each one of you is here because you chose to follow me. My mother is dead—that part is true. By my hand, that part is also true." Witches shifted in the space, and I raised my hand, demanding silence. "She planned on sacrificing me. That is all I will say for now. I have taken refuge in Dusra, Kaizer plans on moving against them, and we have a common enemy. Dusra has offered to house all of us, and we will join their army against Sanjry. Anyone here who has not chosen a side will remain until they have chosen. Anyone siding with Kaizer will be dealt death without question."

All eyes shifted over to Axel, Akari, Zuri, and Damon, and they all stood straight, staring back at them.

"This is King Axel, Akari, a general, Damon, a captain, and Zuri, my..." I hesitated. "Friend. I give you my word that we will be safe with them, but you all can't stay here much longer. There are only so many places to hide in Caldera, and while the witches believe this place is cursed, the vampires don't. They will end up here, eventually. If you want to return home, that is up to you, but I can't offer you any protection from Kaizer's people."

Cat clapped her hands twice. "Pack up your shit. It's time to go."

Every person in the space listened, none of them choosing to return home, every single one of them choosing to follow me.

I jumped down, and Axel watched me; he kept his distance, which I appreciated. I didn't want my clan to think I was hopping over to the next powerful cock in Malva.

"We're going to have to combine power. There's too many of us for me to open one portal," I told Cat.

"I'll get our strongest magic wielders," Cat responded before running off.

"10,000 isn't bad," Ax exclaimed.

"It's not enough. That leaves far too many undecided or on Kaizer's side," I responded.

"Like Paxx said, they can be swayed if they see your power."

"We'll see," I responded.

The movement in the underground space was so loud I could barely hear anything as all 10,000 of my loyal followers grabbed their things, and we made it back out into the desert.

Chapter Fifty-Four

It took nearly an hour for everyone to get out of the bunker, but we were finally all out in the desert. Now we just needed to get everyone back to Dusra before the creatures of the desert smelled so many people in one area. It was still pretty early for them, but the possibility was always there.

"If I asked you to help with the portal, get on the front line!" Cat yelled.

A hundred or so witches shifted to the front and joined hands to power share. It wasn't something that witches did often, and I hadn't even done it myself. It could be an intimate experience, and witches tended not to volunteer for that kind of vulnerability.

"Remember what we're doing this for," Cat exclaimed before she joined hands with two witches beside her, closing the line.

Here goes nothing. I created a portal to the castle and stepped back, placing my hand on Cat's shoulder with my other hand stretched out in front of me.

"Now!" I yelled.

All of their power rushed into me at once, and my eyes went wide at the amount of energy flowing through me. The portal grew a hundred times bigger and stabilized, a combination of every color of our magic.

"Go!" I commanded.

Axel, Zuri, and Akari directed everyone around us as they all ran through the portal and vanished into Dusra. My knees were starting to buckle under the amount of magic. I was powerful, but being the single conduit for the portal with a hundred witches pouring their magic into me was starting to drain me. I was the only one who knew the location, so I had to remain until everyone got through. Axel watched me from behind Cat, his eyes starting to grow more and more worried as I bit my lip and closed my eyes tight. There were a few hundred left. I just needed to hold on for a few more minutes. I felt a hand on my shoulder and looked over to find Axel standing over me.

"Let me help," he muttered.

I nodded my head. It wasn't the time to be stubborn, as much as I wanted to do this myself. His power rushed into me where his hand laid on my shoulder, and my body immediately perked up. It was a strange feeling, I had a hundred other people's magic rushing through me, but he was distinct. It was...rich, I didn't really know how else to describe it. Whatever combination of witch, lobo, and vampire genes he had made something wholly unique. I could see the black of his magic swirling in the portal as the last few people made it through.

"The rest of you go," I commanded.

The witches started to peel off, one by one, at each end of the line until they all made it through, leaving Cat, Axel, Akari, Zuri, and Damon.

"Damon, Akari, Zuri, Cat, you guys go now. I need to do something before I get back," I exclaimed, allowing the portal to shrink to a more manageable size.

"I'm staying for whatever it is you need to do," Cat exclaimed.

"Me too," Zuri added.

Cat held her chin high, and Zuri's eyes were adamant about staying. I really didn't want to fight while holding open this portal so I nodded for Damon and Akari to head back to Dusra.

"Take them to the coast. We'll meet you there when we get back," Axel yelled.

Akari tossed one more look over to Zuri, and she nodded for her to go. Damon followed behind her and I snapped the portal closed, swaying on my feet and throwing a hand onto Cat and Axel both to stabilize myself.

"Do you have blood?" Axel asked Cat.

She nodded and dipped her hand into the satchel on her shoulder, pulling out a container and screwing off the top.

"I didn't know we were going to have a detour, or I would have brought more," she explained as she handed it over.

I drank half of it and felt my power replenishing, the Acna power now at the forefront.

"Here, let's keep it just in case." I licked my lips and stretched my neck out. "I need to go back to the palace. Do you know what's waiting there?"

Cat nodded. "When we left, there were only a few witches there to guard it. Most of the others went to Sanjry or are stationed in each sanction. Some creepy ass people in orange robes have been around too, but not a ton of them."

"The Embers," I growled.

"Yeah, that's right. They creeped us all out when they showed up."

"Do you remember how they were stationed around the palace?" Axel asked.

Cat nodded and drew a picture in the sand, marking the spots she remembered guards being present with small Xs.

"Let's portal here," I said, pointing toward the wing near the vault I was trying to get to. "There are only two guards on either side. If they're still there, we can take them. They have no idea the vault is there. It's part of the reason my mother placed it where it is. There's nothing around it that would need to be monitored. It was our family secret, so I just have to hope she kept her word and didn't tell anyone about it."

"Okay, why are we going there?" Cat asked.

"The elemental stone is there, I don't know if it's needed for whatever Kaizer has planned, but I'd feel better if it was with me."

"Can we portal directly inside?" Axel asked.

"No, there's a block. Even for us."

"Alright, let's do it," Cat said with a clap.

"As soon as I open this portal, we need to step in. There's a chance we'll portal directly in front of someone," I said.

I looked over at Zuri, realizing that Akari wasn't keeping an eye on her anymore so I'd have to make sure nothing happened to her. My magic reserves were lower than I would have liked, but I had to work with what I had.

"Ready?" I asked as I rubbed my hands together.

They nodded as they stood directly next to me so they could jump through. I snapped open the portal, and we all jumped through simultaneously. I crossed my wrists and pushed out a gush of air to clear the purple smoke, and of course, there was an Ember at the end of the hall. I brought my ankle up, grabbing the knife in the holster, and flung it down the hall. The blade spun hilt over tip until it embedded in the man's neck. I softened his landing with a blanket of air to avoid any extra sound, and he was gone before he even realized we were there.

"Get rid of his body," I whispered to Cat.

She nodded and ran over to him, putting her hand on his shoulder and reducing him to ash. I placed my hand on the wall and made to break the spell while Catalina lifted the ashes of the man in a gust of air and sent them out a window. Axel and Zuri stood at my back as the lock clicked and the steel door appeared. Cat backed up toward me, facing away to see any danger as we stepped into the vault. She made it past the door frame, and I quickly closed the door and replaced the spell. I ran over to the glass case and released a sigh of relief when the stone still sat within it. Axel leaned over my shoulder and looked at the stone, his breath on my neck.

"Yours is beautiful," he muttered.

"Do you hold the water stone?" I asked.

He nodded. "We do. I'm not sure how my people were the ones to take it over the sirens after the Piedra, but it's in my vault on the island. I haven't looked at it in decades."

"Alright," I said, tucking it into my pocket. "Let's get the fuck out of here. As soon as we step out, we portal back to Dusra, okay?"

They both nodded, and I broke the spell as I stepped out in the hall to make sure nobody was there. I motioned for them to come out and resealed the spell before turning to open another portal back to Dusra. I rubbed my hands together but a sudden cloud of blue appeared before us and two witches stepped through a portal.

I shot a stream of bruja magic at the one closest to me, but she had an air shield up. My magic broke the shield but the barrier dampened the force and didn't kill her. I reached back and pulled the sword Zuri had made for me and admired how the light gleamed against the black blade for a moment before charging the witch.

She pulled two daggers from her side and crossed them to block my first hit, and I pushed with more force until she broke the block and stumbled back. I swiped at her leg as she lost her footing and sent her to the ground so hard her head cracked against the marble, and she dropped her weapons. She reached for her daggers, but I wrapped two tendrils of air around them and skewered both of her wrists to keep her down.

"How did you know I was here?" I asked.

"Detection spell," she gasped out.

These witches had to be waiting around for me to show up if they got here this fast, and the thought had me ready to rip her throat out with my teeth.

"What does Kaizer want?" I growled.

She closed her mouth, and I stabbed my sword into her leg, earning a blood curdling scream from the bitch. "He wants you back, he's looking for you and your handmaiden, we're just doing what we're told," she sobbed.

"And betraying your people in the fucking process," I snapped.

"You don't know what you're up against, *Acna. He*'s going to be even more powerful than you, than anyone in our existence. We'd be stupid not to side with that."

"You have no idea how powerful I am," I said through tight teeth as my body glowed and her eyes went wide. "You're a traitor to our clan and will not go to rest among us."

She opened her mouth, but before she could respond, I brought my blade down and severed her head from her neck. Blood splattered on the walls and on my face, and I watched it leak from the wound as my chest heaved with fucking fury. I reached both hands toward her and screamed as I let my new power encompass her and burn her until nothing was left behind but scorched marble.

I turned around to find Zuri, Axel, and Cat all covered in blood but very much alive, thankfully. "There's a detection spell, we need to get out of here before more come," I huffed.

Wiping some of the blood from my face with the back of my hand, I turned around and opened a portal back into Dusra. I looked back over my shoulder to find Axel and Cat directly behind me, and Zuri turned to grab her weapon from off the floor. Suddenly a puff of light green smoke filled the hallway, hands reached for Zuri, and she was tossed into a portal in the blink of an eye.

"No!" I yelled as I pushed Axel and Cat out of the way.

They turned to see where I was going and both gasped as they saw what was unfolding behind them. I tried to see where the portal was transporting to, but I didn't recognize the background behind the witch. I threw a stream of bruja magic toward her, but she smirked at me and snapped it shut before it made it to her.

I screamed as my whole body lit in my power, and my hands balled into fists at my side. My magic truly let loose for the first time. I blasted the ceiling off the hall we stood in as my wings burst from my leathers and I lifted off the ground. The world went dark as my body lit, the only source of light remaining. I felt my hair lift into the air, and Axel and Cat watched me with wide eyes as another burst of my power escaped me. Everything around us shifted away, and Axel and Cat held on to pillars to keep from being tossed across the space. The world went deathly quiet, the only thing I could hear was my heartbeat until I heard faint whispers running past my ears. I closed my eyes, listening to their words.

"Vengeance, retribution, power, death."

I didn't care what it took, who I had to kill, what I had to lose. Kaizer would pay for this with his life. He had no idea the monster he'd awoken in me, but he'd come to meet her very soon.

Chapter Fifty-Five

Kaizer

My journal was lying flat in front of me, the page on the right utterly blank. Joseph had found this journal a few decades ago and advised that it was a way to speak to the Flame. I was skeptical at first, but he was right. I had no idea how it worked, but he wrote on one page, and an answer appeared on the next in just a few moments. It played a significant role in overthrowing the previous royals. The last king never recovered from the loss to Dusra, and trying to reignite that war would have been detrimental. The fact I had royal blood pushed the Embers to get me to take over. The journal told Joseph and me what to say and do to get the people of Sanjry to follow me. The Embers didn't want any more war. It was one of the reasons they believed the Flame found us unjust. I wasn't always too sure about Joseph. He seemed fairly radical at times, and his desire to return the Flame as high priest rivaled even my own. He would go down in our history as close to a god if that happened while he sat at the head of the church. Regardless, I needed guidance even more than before, and the Flame was completely silent.

My foot was tapping against the hard marble floor at a speed that shouldn't have been possible as I stared at the pages. Daya hated when I did this, but she wasn't here to tell me to cut it out right now. I had no idea where she was, but I knew I needed to find her. She didn't understand. I had to *make* her understand. This was all for the greater good. Nothing would ever be able to threaten us again if I wielded the power that I sought. We could rule everything, and I couldn't fathom why she wouldn't want that. I knew she didn't love me the way I did her, but I really thought she was getting there lately. We'd spent so much time together before The Ritual. She'd casted glances my way, rubbed my arm, and I felt her body's response every time I drank from her. She'd love me one day; who wouldn't love the most powerful man in the world?

I needed blood, but the thought of drinking from anyone but her made my stomach turn. I'd drank from Quinn, knowing that it wouldn't make her feel anything for me as she wasn't attracted to men, but her blood was nothing like Daya's. Daya was more powerful than anyone here; whether I'd admit it to her or not, she was even more powerful than me. That kind of blood was addictive, and I'd found myself pining for it with every passing minute.

A knock on the door sounded, and I sat up straight and ran my hand through my unstyled hair quickly. "Come in," I bellowed.

The door to my bedchamber was opened, and Abel walked in, his hand firmly wrapped around Athena's arm. Her red hair shifted around her shoulders as she sauntered into the space with her head held high. Like she wasn't rotting in her own shit a few hours ago.

"You've had your bath, and you've got new clothes. Are you ready to tell us what Daya was doing in your cell?" I asked.

Athena had somehow heard that Daya was missing and let her guards know that she had been in the dungeon not too long ago visiting her. I didn't know what information she would have, but I was taking anything I could get at this point.

"I believe there were one or two more things I asked for," she said, running her finger over the neckline of her dress.

I waved my hand to Abel, and he grabbed the wine and plate of food she requested as well. I'd spent a lot of time with Athena, more than any of my other conquests. She somehow got me to trust her, and I'd told her more about my plans than anyone else outside of my council. She sat across from me as Abel set her requested items down beside her, and she grabbed the glass of wine. Athena looked at Abel with her nose scrunched.

"I just want to talk to you, Kaizer," she muttered, turning her gaze to me.

Abel's body tightened, and he looked over at me, his face conveying he didn't think it was a good idea.

"Oh, please. I'm hardly a match against the King of Sanjry. Surely you aren't worried I'd hurt him?" Athena taunted Abel.

"I'm more worried about what you'll try to get out of this," Abel growled.

She shrugged and sipped her wine, playing with her long red locks with her other hand.

"It's fine, Abel. I'll come and get you if you're needed," I said.

Abel leaned in close to Athena and whispered something in her ear that had her eyebrows raising and eyes going wide for just a second before he pulled back, and she smirked at him sarcastically. The door slammed behind Abel, and I leaned forward on my elbows, waiting for her to finally tell us if she had any information about Daya. She took her time, drinking her wine and cutting into the steak on the plate.

"Athena," I stated.

"Oh, baby. I've missed you," she said before reaching across the desk and brushing my face.

I stood still, not giving her a reaction, and she pulled back to continue eating. "We really should talk about the fact that I've been in a cell for weeks. I know you needed to save face for your *betrothed*." She drew the word out in disgust. "But I would have thought I'd at least received some conjugal visits."

"You can't be serious," I growled. "You tried to revolt against me. You started an entire riot trying to overthrow me."

She tsked. "You know that is not what happened. I was revolting against that bitch of a fiancée."

My nails dug into my legs as I tried to keep my composure, but she was testing me, and I was too close to the edge to be tested. "What did she say when you saw her?"

"Did you know there's no sewage system down in the dungeons? I had to relieve myself into a bucket; it's disgusting."

"Athena, I'm losing my patience," I said as I ground my jaw.

"She didn't say much. She really just came down there to gloat. I told her that it could have been her in that cell if you would have taken my advice and wiped them all clean in the battle."

"You told her about the ashes?"

The magic I'd used in the battle. The Flame advised us of an urn buried in my land with the old language inscribed on it. It was filled with ashes from the time the forest of Incen burned, I tested them out where nobody lived, and the explosion they created was incredible. I used half of the urn in the battle, worried that if I used the whole thing, I'd do too much damage to my own army.

"No, I didn't get into specifics," she answered.

"Why did you say you had information on her then? That's not helpful in the slightest bit," I said through tight teeth.

"I think it's good she's gone. I can come out of the cell. If you're still worried about me, you can just lock me up in your room. Keep an eye on me." She winked.

My sight went dark, and I blinked to find my hand around Athena's delicate neck. She grabbed my hand for a second before she relaxed slightly and looked up at me through hooded eyes.

"Oh baby, you know this isn't a threat to me. If you wanted your cock sucked, all you had to do was ask," she purred.

She dug her fang into her lip, and blood spilled from the small cut, causing my nostrils to flare at the proximity of it. Her blood wasn't Daya's, but I'd had enough of it over the years that my body immediately reacted. I'd rarely ever drunk from her without either her lips or pussy wrapping around my cock by the end of it.

Athena ran her hand up my hardened cock as she squeezed more blood from her cut. I'd been on edge for weeks, and I needed a release. And I needed blood. It didn't have to mean anything. I still wanted Daya to return; but I had no idea when that would be. She watched me as I ran through this all in my head, and she pushed her palm up against me.

"Come on, baby. Let me help you like I always have. I can tell you need blood. Take it. I'll give you a little more when we're done."

She brushed her hair over one shoulder and leaned closer to me. I was too far gone; before I knew what I was doing, my fangs were in her neck. Athena moaned as my venom rushed through her, and she continued rubbing her hand up and down my cock. I was so hard I felt like I was going to burst already, and as she slipped her hand into my pants, I knew there wasn't any going back. I drank deep and quick, taking mouthfuls of her blood at a time until I was satisfied enough to pull my fangs from her neck. Athena wasted no time as she fell to her knees and pulled my pants down, my cock springing free and nearly smacking her in the face.

"I forgot how big you are," she muttered.

I sat back on my bed, and as she took me into her mouth and her hands started pumping, the only thing on my mind was Daya.

It had been two days since the meeting with Athena, and I rolled out of my bed, leaving her naked body nestled in the covers. I knew Daya would hate this, but I could have Athena thrown back into the dungeon when she returned. Or maybe I could even let Daya kill Athena. I didn't want to risk starting something new with someone solely to get the releases my body demanded of me. I pulled on a pair of pants and a shirt, not bothering to tuck it in before slipping my feet into my boots.

Making my way to my office, I ran over the same list of things I'd gone over every morning for the last few weeks. Daya's favorite places in Caldera, the places she liked in Sanjry, the look in Zuri's eye as she scurried to Daya's side after I held the neck to her throat. They were close; I had asked the head of staff what information she had about her, but there wasn't much. If there was someone who knew something, it would be Zuri. They'd practically been joined at the hip since Daya got here. If I found her, I'd probably find Daya.

I pushed open the door to my office, and Abel and Otto were waiting for me. They both shot from their seats near the window and ran to meet me at my desk.

"We have the handmaiden," Otto exclaimed.

It took some convincing to get them to care about my search for Dayanara. They didn't understand why I needed her. They thought I should have been occupied with my search for the relic that would grant me the ability to wield all four elements. The relic the Flame told me about in the journal. But I needed her. I wasn't going to rest until I had her back, and they gave up on trying to stop me. They worked with the witches to figure out the fastest way to get her back, so that we could get back to the 'more important' objective.

"Where is she?" I asked.

"In the dungeons," Abel answered.

My heart skipped a beat with the memory of Dayanara being whipped in those dungeons. Her mother said it was necessary, but when I saw her open and bleeding like that, something inside of me changed. We were only a few days into the agreement, but it sowed the initial seed of doubt.

"Excellent," I answered. "Let's get the information out of her."